The Black Tower

P. D. James was born in Oxford in 1920 and educated at Cambridge High School for Girls. From 1949 to 1968 she worked in the National Health Service and subsequently in the Home Office, first in the Police Department and later in the Criminal Policy Department. All that experience has been used in her novels. She is a Fellow of the Royal Society of Literature and of the Royal Society of Arts and has served as a Governor of the BBC, a member of the Arts Council, where she was Chairman of the Literary Advisory Panel, on the Board of the British Council and as a magistrate in Middlesex and London. She has won awards for crime writing in Britain, America, Italy and Scandinavia, including the Mystery Writers of America Grandmaster Award and The National Arts Club Medal of Honor for Literature (US). She has received honorary degrees from seven British universities, was awarded an OBE in 1983 and was created a life peer in 1991. In 1997 she was elected President of the Society of Authors.

She lives in London and Oxford and has two daughters, five grandchildren and seven great-grandchildren.

P. D. JAMES

The Black Tower

faber and faber

First published in 1975
by Faber and Faber Limited
Bloomsbury House, 74–77 Great Russel Street, London WC1B 3DA

Published by Sphere Books in 1977
Published in paperback by Penguin Books
in association with Faber and Faber in 1990
Reprinted twenty-four times

This Faber and Faber paperback edition published in 2010
Photoset by RefineCatch Limited, Bungay, Suffolk
Printed in England by CPI Bookmarque, Croydon

The right of P. D. James to be identified as author of this work has been
asserted in accordance with Section 77 of the Copyright,
Designs and Patents Act 1988

A CIP record for this book
is available from the British Library

ISBN 978-0-571-24886-5

2 4 6 8 10 9 7 5 3

Contents

Author's note

Lovers of Dorset will, I hope, forgive me for the liberties I have taken with the topography of their beautiful county and in particular for my temerity in erecting my twin follies of Toynton Grange and the black tower on the Purbeck coast. They will learn with relief that, although the scenery is borrowed, the characters are completely my own and bear no resemblance to any person living or dead.

ONE

Sentence of Life

It was to be the consultant physician's last visit and Dalgliesh suspected that neither of them regretted it, arrogance and patronage on one side and weakness, gratitude and dependence on the other being no foundation for a satisfactory adult relationship however transitory. He came into Dalgliesh's small hospital room preceded by Sister, attended by his acolytes, already dressed for the fashionable wedding which he was to grace as a guest later that morning. He could have been the bridegroom except that he sported a red rose instead of the customary carnation. Both he and the flower looked as if they had been brought and burnished to a peak of artificial perfection, gift-wrapped in invisible foil, and immune to the chance winds, frosts and ungentle fingers which could mar more vulnerable perfections. As a final touch, he and the flower had both been lightly sprayed with an expensive scent, presumably an aftershave lotion. Dalgliesh could detect it above the hospital smell of cabbage and ether to which his nose had become so inured during the past weeks that it now hardly registered on the senses. The attendant medical students grouped themselves round the bed. With their long hair and short white coats they looked like a gaggle of slightly disreputable bridesmaids.

Dalgliesh was stripped by Sister's skilled impersonal hands for yet another examination. The stethoscope moved, a cold disc, over his chest and back. This last examination was a formality but the physician was, as always, thorough; nothing he did was perfunctory. If, on this occasion, his original diagnosis had been wrong his self-esteem was too secure for him to feel the need for more than a token excuse. He straightened up and said:

'We've had the most recent path. report and I think we can be certain now that we've got it right. The cytology was always obscure, of course, and the diagnosis was complicated by the pneumonia. But it isn't acute leukaemia, it isn't any type of leukaemia. What you're recovering from – happily – is an atypical mononucleosis. I congratulate you, Commander. You had us worried.'

'I had you interested; you had me worried. When can I leave here?'

The great man laughed and smiled at his retinue, inviting them to share his indulgence at yet one more example of the ingratitude of convalescence. Dalgliesh said quickly:

'I expect you'll be wanting the bed.'

'We always want more beds than we can get. But there's no great hurry. You've a long way to go yet. Still, we'll see. We'll see.'

When they had left him he lay flat on his back and let his eyes range round the two cubic feet of anaesthetized space, as if seeing the room for the first time. The wash basin with its elbow-operated taps; the neat functional bedside table with its covered water jug; the two vinyl-covered visitors' chairs; the earphones curled above his head; the window curtains with their offensive flowered pattern, the lowest denominator of taste. They were the last objects he had expected to see in life. It had seemed a meagre, impersonal place in which to die. Like a hotel room, it was designed for transients. Whether its occupants left on their own feet or sheeted on a mortuary trolley, they left nothing behind them, not even the memory of their fear, suffering and hope.

The sentence of death had been communicated, as he suspected such sentences usually were, by grave looks, a certain false heartiness, whispered consultations, a superfluity of clinical tests, and, until he had insisted, a reluctance to pronounce a diagnosis or prognosis. The sentence of life, pronounced with less sophistry when the worst days of his illness were over, had certainly produced a greater outrage. It was, he had thought, uncommonly inconsiderate if not negligent of his doctors to reconcile him so thoroughly to death and then change their minds. It was embarrassing now to recall with what little regret he had let slip his pleasures and preoccupations, the imminence of loss revealing them for what they were, at best only a solace, at worst a trivial squandering of time and energy. Now he had to lay hold of them again and believe that they were important, at least to himself. He doubted whether he would ever again believe them important to other people. No doubt, with returning strength, all that would look after itself. The physical life would re-assert itself given time. He would reconcile himself to living since there was no alternative and, this perverse fit of resentment and accidie conveniently put down to weakness, would come to believe that he had had a lucky escape. His colleagues, relieved of embarrassment, would congratulate him.

3

Now that death had replaced sex as the great unmentionable it had acquired its own pudency; to die when you had not yet become a nuisance and before your friends could reasonably raise the ritual chant of 'happy release' was in the worst of taste.

But, at present, he wasn't sure that he could reconcile himself to his job. Resigned as he had become to the role of spectator – and soon not even to be that – he felt ill-equipped to return to the noisy playground of the world and, if it had to be, was minded to find for himself a less violent corner of it. It wasn't something he had thought about deeply during his periods of consciousness; there hadn't been time. It was more a conviction than a decision. The time had come to change direction. Judges' Rules, rigor mortis, interrogation, the contemplation of decomposing flesh and smashed bone, the whole body business of manhunting, he was finished with it. There were other things to do with his time. He wasn't yet sure which things but he would find them. He had over two weeks of convalescence ahead, time to formulate a decision, rationalize it, justify it to himself and, more difficult, find the words with which he would attempt to justify it to the Commissioner. It was a bad time to leave the Yard. They would see it as desertion. But then, it would always be a bad time.

He wasn't sure whether this disenchantment with his job was caused solely by his illness, the salutary reminder of inevitable death, or whether it was the symptom of a more fundamental malaise, that latitude in middle-life of alternate doldrums and uncertain winds when one realizes that hopes deferred are no longer realizable, that ports not visited will now never be seen, that this journey and others before it may have been a mistake, that one has no longer even confidence in charts and compass. More than his job now seemed to him trivial and unsatisfactory. Lying sleepless as so many patients must have done before him in that bleak impersonal room, watching the headlamps of passing cars sweep across the ceiling, listening to the secretive and muted noises of the hospital's nocturnal life, he took the dispiriting inventory of his life. His grief for his dead wife, so genuine, so heartbreaking at the time – how conveniently personal tragedy had excused him from further emotional involvement. His love affairs, like the one which at present spasmodically occupied a little of his time and somewhat more of his energy, had been detached, civilized, agreeable, undemanding. It was understood that his time was never completely his own but that his heart most certainly was. The women were liberated. They had interesting jobs, agreeable flats, they were adept at settling for what they could get. Certainly they were liberated from the messy, clogging, disruptive emotions which embroiled other female lives. What, he wondered, had those carefully spaced encoun-ters, both participants groomed for pleasure like a couple of sleek cats, to do with love, with untidy bed-rooms, unwashed dishes, babies' nappies, the warm, close, claustrophobic life of marriage and commitment. His bereavement, his job, his poetry, all had been used to justify self-sufficiency. His women had been more amenable to the claims of his poetry than of his dead wife. They had small regard for sentiment, but an exag-gerated respect for art. And the worst of it – or perhaps the best – was that he couldn't now change even if he wanted and that none of it mattered. It was absolutely of no importance. In the last fifteen years he hadn't deliberately hurt a single human being. It struck him now that nothing more damning could be said about anyone.

Well, if none of that could be changed, his job could. But first there was one personal commitment to fulfil, one from which perversely he had been relieved that death would so conveniently excuse him. It wasn't going to excuse him now. Propping himself on his elbow he reached out and took Father Baddeley's letter from his locker drawer and read it carefully for the first time. The old man must be nearly eighty now; he hadn't been young when, thirty years ago, he had first come to the Norfolk village as curate to Dalgliesh's father, timid, ineffective, maddeningly inefficient, muddling in everything but the essentials, but never less than his uncompromising self. This was only the third letter which Dalgliesh had received from him. It was dated 11th September and read:

My dear Adam,
I know that you must be very busy but I would
very much welcome a visit from you as there
is a matter on which I would be glad of your
professional advice. It isn't really urgent, except
that my heart seems to be wearing out before
the rest of me so that I ought not to rest too
confidently on the thought of tomorrow. I am here
every day, but perhaps a weekend would suit you
best. I ought to tell you, so that you will know
what to expect, that I am Chaplain to Toynton

Grange, a private home for the young disabled,
and that I live here in Hope Cottage on the estate
through the kindness of the Warden, Wilfred
Anstey. Usually I eat my midday and evening
meal at the Grange but this may not be agreeable
to you and it would, of course, lessen our time
together. So I shall take the opportunity of
my next visit to Wareham to lay in a store of
provisions. I have a small spare room into which
I can move so that there will be a room for
you here.

Could you send me a card to let me know when
you will arrive? I have no car but if you come
by train William Deakin, who has a car hire
service about five minutes from the station (the
station staff will direct you), is very reliable and
not expensive. The buses from Wareham are
infrequent and don't come beyond Toynton
Village. There is then a mile and a half to walk
which is quite pleasant if the weather is good but
which you may wish to avoid at the end of a long
journey. If not, I have drawn a map on the back
of this letter.

The map could be guaranteed to confuse anyone
accustomed to depend on the orthodox publications of
the National Survey rather than on early seventeenth-
century charts. The wavy lines presumably represented
the sea. Dalgliesh felt the omission of a spouting whale.
The Toynton bus station was clearly marked, but the
tremulous line thereafter meandered uncertainly past a
diversity of fields, gates, pubs and copses of triangular,

serrated firs, sometimes retreating upon itself as Father Baddeley realized that metaphorically he had lost his way. One tiny phallic symbol on the coast, and seemingly included as a landmark, since it was nowhere near the marked path, bore the legend 'the black tower'.

The map affected Dalgliesh much as a child's first drawing might affect an indulgent father. He wondered to what depth of weakness and apathy he must have sunk to reject its appeal. He fumbled in the drawer for a postcard and wrote briefly that he would arrive by car early in the afternoon of Monday, 1st October. That should give him plenty of time to get out of hospital and return to his Queenhythe flat for the first few days of convalescence. He signed the card with his initials only, stamped it for first-class delivery and propped it against his water jug so that he shouldn't forget to ask one of the nurses to post it.

There was one other small obligation and one he felt less competent to handle. But it could wait. He must see or write to Cordelia Gray and thank her for her flowers. He didn't know how she discovered that he was ill except perhaps through police friends. Running Bernie Pryde's Detective Agency – if it hadn't by now collapsed, as it should have done by all the laws of justice and economics – probably meant that she was in touch with one or two policemen. He believed, too, that there had been a casual mention of his inconvenient illness in the London evening papers when they had commented on recent losses in the higher echelons of the Yard.

It had been a small, carefully arranged, personally picked bouquet, as individual as Cordelia herself, a charming contrast to his other offerings of hothouse roses, over-large chrysanthemums shaggy as dust mops, forced spring flowers and artificial-looking gladioli, pink plastic flowers smelling of anaesthetic rigid on their fibrous stems. She must have been recently in a country garden; he wondered where. He wondered too, illogically, whether she was getting enough to eat, but immediately put this ridiculous thought from him. There had, he remembered clearly, been silver discs of honesty, three sprigs of winter heather, four rosebuds, not the starved tight buds of winter but furls of orange and yellow, gentle as the first buds of summer, delicate sprigs of outdoor chrysanthemums, orange-red berries, one bright dahlia like a jewel in the centre, the whole bouquet surrounded by the grey furry leaves he remembered from his childhood as rabbits' ears. It had been a touching, very young gesture one knew that an older or more sophisticated woman would never have made. It had arrived with only a brief note to say that she had heard of his illness and had sent the flowers to wish him well again. He must see or write to her and thank her personally. The telephone call which one of the nurses had made on his behalf to the Agency was not enough.

But that, and other more fundamental decisions, could wait. First he must see Father Baddeley. The obligation was not merely pious or even filial. He discovered that, despite certain foreseen difficulties and embarrassments, he was looking forward to seeing the old priest again. He had no intention of letting Father Baddeley, however unwittingly, entice him back to his job. If this were really police work, which he doubted, then the Dorset Constabulary could take it over. And, if this pleasant early autumn sunshine continued unbroken, Dorset would be as agreeable a place as any in which to convalesce.

But the stark oblong of white, propped against his water jug, was oddly intrusive. He felt his eyes constantly drawn towards it as if it were a potent symbol, a written sentence of life. He was glad when the staff nurse came in to say that she was now going off duty, and took it away to post.

TWO

Death of a Priest

I

Eleven days later, still weak and with his hospital pallor but euphoric with the deceptive well-being of convalescence, Dalgliesh left his flat high above the Thames at Queenhythe just before the first light and drove southwest out of London. He had finally and reluctantly parted with his ancient Cooper Bristol two months before the onset of his illness and was now driving a Jensen Healey. He was glad that the car had been run in and that he was already almost reconciled to the change. To embark symbolically on a new life with a totally new car would have been irritatingly banal. He put his one case and a few picnic essentials including a corkscrew in the boot and, in the pocket, a copy of Hardy's poems, *The Return of the Native* and Newman and Pevsner's guide to the buildings of Dorset. This was to be a convalescent's holiday: familiar books; a brief visit to an old friend to provide an object for the journey; a route left to each day's whim and including country both familiar and new; even the salutary irritant of a personal problem to justify solitude and self-indulgent idleness. He was disconcerted when, taking his final look round the flat, he found his hand reaching for his scene-of-crime kit. He couldn't remember when last he had travelled without it, even on holiday. But now to leave it behind was the first confirmation of a decision which he would dutifully ponder from time to time during the next fortnight but which he knew in his heart was already made.

He reached Winchester in time for late breakfast at a hotel in the shadow of the Cathedral, then spent the next two hours rediscovering the city before finally driving into Dorset via Wimborne Minster. Now he sensed in himself a reluctance to reach journey's end. He meandered gently, almost aimlessly, north-west to Blandford Forum, bought there a bottle of wine, buttered rolls, cheese and fruit for his lunch and a couple of bottles of Amontillado for Father Baddeley, then wandered southeast through the Winterbourne villages through Wareham to Corfe Castle.

The magnificent stones, symbols of courage, cruelty and betrayal, stood sentinel at the one cleft of the ridge of the Purbeck Hills as they had for a thousand years. As he ate his solitary picnic, Dalgliesh found his eyes constantly drawn to those stark embattled slabs of mutilated ashlar silhouetted high against the gentle sky. As though reluctant to drive under their shadow and unwilling to end the solitude of this peaceful undemanding day he spent some time searching unsuccessfully for marsh gentians in the swampy scrubland before setting off on the last five miles of his journey.

Toynton village; a thread of terraced cottages, their undulating grey stone roofs glittering in the afternoon sun; a not too picturesque pub at the village end; the glimpse of an uninteresting church tower. Now the road, bordered with a low stone wall, rose gently between sparse plantations of fir and he began to recognize the landmarks on Father Baddeley's map. Soon the road would branch, one narrow route turning westward to skirt the headland, the other leading through a barrier gate to Toynton Grange and the sea. And here, predictably, it was, a heavy iron gate set into a wall of flat, uncemented stones. The wall was up to three feet thick, the stones intricately and skilfully fitted together, bound with lichen and moss and crowned with waving grasses, and it formed a barrier as permanent as the headland from which it seemed to have grown. On each side of the gate was a notice painted on board. The one on the left read:

OF YOUR CHARITY PLEASE RESPECT
OUR PRIVACY

The one on the right was more didactic, the lettering faded but more professional.

KEEP OUT
THIS LAND IS STRICTLY PRIVATE
DANGEROUS CLIFFS NO ACCESS TO BEACH
CARS AND CARAVANS PARKED HERE
WILL BE MOVED

Under the notice was fixed a large postbox.

Dalgliesh thought that any motorist unmoved by this nicely judged mixture of appeal, warning and threats would hesitate before risking his car springs. The track deteriorated sharply beyond the gate and the contrast between the comparative smoothness of the approach

13

road and the boulder-edged and stony way ahead was an almost symbolic deterrent. The gate, too, although unlocked, had a heavy latch of intricate design, the manipulation of which gave an intruder ample time in which to repent of his rashness. In his still weakened state, Dalgliesh swung back the gate with some difficulty. When he had driven through and finally closed it behind him it was with a sense of having committed himself to an enterprise as yet imperfectly understood and probably unwise. The problem would probably be embarrassingly unrelated to any of his skills, something that only an unworldly old man – and he perhaps getting senile – could have imagined that a police officer could solve. But at least he had an immediate objective. He was moving, even if reluctantly, back into a world in which human beings had problems, worked, loved, hated, schemed for happiness, and since the job he had determined to relinquish would go on despite his defection, killed and were killed.

Before he turned again to the car his eye was caught by a small clump of unknown flowers. The pale pinkish white heads rose from a mossy pad on top of the wall and trembled delicately in the light breeze. Dalgliesh walked over and stood stock still, regarding in silence their unpretentious beauty. He smelt for the first time the clean half-illusory salt tang of the sea. The air moved warm and gentle against his skin. He was suddenly suffused with happiness and, as always in these rare transitory moments, intrigued by the purely physical nature of his joy. It moved along his veins, a gentle effervescence. Even to analyse its nature was to lose hold of it. But he recognized it for what it was, the first clear intimation since his illness that life could be good.

The car bumped gently over the rising track. When some two hundred yards further on he came to the summit of the rise he expected to see the English Channel spread blue and wrinkled before him to the far horizon and experienced all the remembered disappointment of childhood holidays when after so many false hopes, the eagerly awaited sea still wasn't in sight. Before him was a shallow rock-strewn valley, criss-crossed with rough paths, and to his right what was obviously Toynton Grange.

It was a powerfully built square stone house dating, he guessed, from the first half of the eighteenth century. But the owner had been unlucky in his architect. The house was an aberration, unworthy of the name of Georgian. It faced inland, north-east he estimated, thus offending against some personal and obscure canon of architectural taste which, to Dalgliesh, decreed that a house on the coast should face the sea. There were two rows of windows above the porch, the main ones with gigantic keystones, the row above unadorned and mean in size as if there had been difficulty in fitting them beneath the most remarkable feature of the house, a huge Ionic pediment topped by a statue, a clumsy and, at this distance, unidentifiable lump of stone. In the centre was one round window, a sinister cyclops eye glinting in the sun. The pediment debased the insignificant porch and gave a lowering and cumbersome appearance to the whole façade. Dalgliesh thought that the design would have been more successful if the façade had been balanced by extended bays, but either inspiration or money had run out and the house looked curiously unfinished. There was no sign of life behind the intimidating frontage. Perhaps the

15

inmates – if that was the right word for them – lived at the back. And it was only just three-thirty, the dead part of the day as he remembered from hospital. Probably they were all resting.

He could see three cottages, a pair about a hundred yards from the Grange and a third standing alone higher on the foreland. He thought there was a fourth roof just visible to seaward, but couldn't be sure. It might be only an excrescence of rock. Not knowing which was Hope Cottage it seemed sensible to make first for the nearer pair. He had briefly turned off his car engine while deciding what next to do and now, for the first time, he heard the sea, that gentle continuous rhythmic grunt which is one of the most nostalgic and evocative of sounds. There was still no sign that his approach was observed; the headland was silent, birdless. He sensed something strange and almost sinister in its emptiness and loneliness which even the mellow afternoon sunlight couldn't dispel.

His arrival at the cottages produced no face at the window, no cassock-clad figure framed in the front porch. They were a pair of old, limestone single-storeyed buildings, whose heavy stone roofs, typical of Dorset, were patterned with bright cushions of emerald moss. Hope Cottage was on the right, Faith Cottage on the left; the names comparatively recently painted. The third more distant cottage was presumably Charity, but he doubted whether Father Baddeley had had any hand in this eponymous naming. He didn't need to read the name on the gate to know which cottage housed Father Baddeley. It was impossible to associate his remembered almost total uninterest in his surroundings with those chintzy curtains, that hanging basket of trailing ivy and fuchsia over the door of Faith Cottage or the two brightly painted yellow tubs still garish with summer flowers which had been artfully placed one each side of the porch. Two mushrooms, looking mass-produced in concrete, stood each side of the gate, seeming so cosily suburban that Dalgliesh was surprised that they weren't crowned with squatting gnomes. Hope Cottage, in contrast, was starkly austere. There was a solid oak bench in front of the window serving as a seat in the sun, and a conglomeration of sticks and an old umbrella littered the front porch. The curtains, apparently of some heavy material in a dull red, were drawn across the windows.

No one answered to his knock. He had expected no one. Both cottages were obviously empty. There was a simple latch on the door and no lock. After a second's pause he lifted it and stepped into the gloom inside to be met with a smell, warm, bookish, a little musty, which immediately took him back thirty years. He drew back the curtains and light streamed into the cottage. And now his eyes recognized familiar objects: the round single-pedestal rosewood table, dull with dust, set in the middle of the room; the roll-top desk against one wall; the high-backed and winged armchair, so old now that the stuffing was pushing through the frayed cover and the dented seat was worn down to the wood. Surely it couldn't be the same chair? This stab of memory must be a nostalgic delusion. But there was another object, equally familiar, equally old. Behind the door hung Father Baddeley's black cloak with, above it, the battered and limp beret.

It was the sight of the cloak that first alerted Dalgliesh to the possibility that something was wrong. It was odd that his host wasn't here to greet him, but he could think of a number of explanations. His postcard might have gone astray, there might have been an urgent call to the Grange, Father Baddeley might have gone into Wareham to shop and missed the return bus. It was even possible that he had completely forgotten the expected arrival of his guest. But if he were out, why wasn't he wearing his cloak? It was impossible to think of him in summer or winter wearing any other garment.

It was then that Dalgliesh noticed what his eye must have already seen but disregarded, the little stack of service sheets on top of the bureau printed with a black cross. He took the top one over to the window as if hoping that a clearer light would show him mistaken. But there was, of course, no mistake. He read:

Michael Francis Baddeley, Priest
Born 29th October 1896
Died 21st September 1974 RIP.
Buried at St Michael & All Angels,
Toynton, Dorset
26th September 1974

He had been dead eleven days and buried five. But he would have known that Father Baddeley had died recently. How else could one account for that sense of his personality still lingering in the cottage, the feeling that he was so close that one strong call could bring his hand to the latch? Looking at the familiar faded cloak with its heavy clasp – had the old man really not changed it in thirty years? – he felt a pang of regret, of grief even, which surprised him by its intensity. An old man was dead. It must have been a natural death; they had buried him quickly enough. His death and burial had been unpublicized. But there had been something on his mind and he had died without confiding it. It was suddenly very important that he should be reassured that Father Baddeley had received his postcard, that he hadn't died believing that his call for help had gone unregarded.

The obvious place to look was in the early Victorian bureau which had belonged to Father Baddeley's mother. Father Baddeley, he remembered, had kept this locked. He had been the least secretive of men, but any priest had to have at least one drawer or desk private from the prying eyes of cleaning women or over-curious parishioners. Dalgliesh could remember Father Baddeley fumbling in the deep pockets of his cloak for the small antique key, secured by string to an old-fashioned clothes peg for easier handling and identification, which opened the lock. It was probably in one of the cloak pockets still.

He dug his hand into both pockets with a guilty feeling of raiding the dead. The key wasn't there. He went over to the bureau and tried the lid. It opened easily. Bending down he examined the lock, then fetched his torch from the car and looked again. The signs were unmistakable: the lock had been forced. It had been quite a neat job and one requiring little strength. The lock was decorative but unsubstantial, intended as a defence against the idly curious but not against determined assault. A chisel or knife, probably the blade of a penknife, had been forced between the desk and the lid and used to pry the lock apart. It had done surprisingly little damage, but the scratch marks and the broken lock itself told their story.

But not who had been responsible. It could have been Father Baddeley himself. If he had lost the key there would have been no chance of replacing it, and how in this remote spot would he have found a locksmith? A physical assault on the desk lid was an unlikely expedient for the man, Dalgliesh remembered; but it wasn't impossible. Or it might have been done after Father Baddeley's death. If the key couldn't be found, someone at Toynton Grange would have had to break open the lock. There might have been documents or papers which they needed; a health insurance card; names of friends to be notified; a will. He shook himself free from conjecture, irritated to find that he had actually considered putting on his gloves before looking further, and made a rapid examination of the contents of the desk drawers.

There was nothing of interest there. Father Baddeley's concern with the world had apparently been minimal. But one thing immediately recognizable caught his eye. It was a neatly stacked row of quarto-size child's exercise books bound in pale green. These, he knew, contained Father Baddeley's diary. So the same books were still being sold, the ubiquitous pale-green exercise books, the back cover printed with arithmetical tables, as evocative of primary school as an ink-stained ruler or india rubber. Father Baddeley had always used these books for his diary, one book for each quarter of the year. Now, with the old black cloak hanging limply on the door, its musty ecclesiastical smell in his nose, Dalgliesh recalled the conversation as clearly as if he were still that ten-year-old boy and Father Baddeley, middle-aged then but already seeming ageless, sitting at his desk.

'It's just an ordinary diary then, Father? It isn't about your spiritual life?'

'This is the spiritual life; the ordinary things one does from hour to hour.'

Adam had asked with the egotism of the young:

'Only what you do? Aren't I in it?'

'No. Just what I do. Do you remember what time the Mothers' Union met this afternoon? It was your mother's drawing-room this week. The time was different, I think.'

'It was two forty-five p.m. instead of three p.m., Father. The Archdeacon wanted to get away early. But do you have to be accurate?'

Father Baddeley had seemed to ponder this question, briefly but seriously as if it were new to him and unexpectedly interesting.

'Oh, yes, I think so. I think so. Otherwise it would lose its point.'

The young Dalgliesh, to whom the point was already lost beyond ken, had wandered away to pursue his own more interesting and immediate concerns. The spiritual life. It was a phrase he had often heard on the lips of his father's more ultra-mundane parishioners although never on the Canon's own. He had occasionally tried to visualize this mysterious other existence. Was it lived at the same time as the ordinary regulated life of getting up, meal times, school, holidays; or was it an existence on some other plane to which he and the uninitiated had no access but into which Father Baddeley could retreat at will? Either way it had surely little to do with this careful recording of daily trivia.

He picked up the last book and looked through it. Father Baddeley's system had not been changed. It was all here, two days to the page, neatly ruled off. The times at which he had daily said morning prayer and evensong; where he had walked and how long it had taken; the monthly trip by bus into Dorchester; the weekly trip to Wareham; his hours spent helping at Toynton Grange; odd treats baldly recorded; the methodical account of how he had disposed of every hour of his working day year after unremarkable year, documented with the meticulousness of a book-keeper. 'But this is the spiritual life; the ordinary things that one does from day to day.' Surely it couldn't be as simple as that?

But where was the current diary, the book for the third quarter of 1974? It had been Father Baddeley's habit to keep old copies of his diary covering the last three years. There should have been fifteen books here; there were only fourteen. The diary stopped at the end of June 1974. Dalgliesh found himself searching almost feverishly through the desk drawers. The diary wasn't there. But he did find something. Pushed beneath three receipted bills for coal, paraffin and electricity was a sheet of cheap rather thin paper with Toynton Grange printed inexpertly and lopsidedly at the top. Underneath someone had typed:

'Why don't you get out of the cottage you silly old hypocrite and let someone have it who would really be some use here? Don't think we don't know what you and Grace Willison get up to when you're supposed to be hearing her confession. Don't you wish you could really do it? And what about that choir boy? Don't think we don't know.'

Dalgliesh's first reaction was to be more irritated by the note's silliness than angered by its malice. It was a childish piece of gratuitous spite but without even the dubious merit of verisimilitude. Poor old seventy-seven-year-old Father Baddeley, accused simultaneously of fornication, sodomy and impotence! Could any reasonable man have taken this puerile nonsense seriously enough even to be hurt by it? Dalgliesh had seen plenty of poison pen letters in his professional life. This was a comparatively mild effort; he could almost suppose that the writer's heart hadn't been in it. 'Don't you wish you could really do it?' Most poison pen writers could find a more graphic description of that implied activity. And the belated reference to the choir boy, no name, no date. That hadn't been dredged from any real knowledge. Could Father Baddeley really have been concerned enough to have sent for a professional detective and one he hadn't seen for nearly thirty years just to advise on or investigate this petty nastiness? Perhaps. This might not be the only letter. If the trouble were endemic at Toynton Grange, then it was more serious. A poison pen at work in a closed community could cause real trouble and distress, occasionally he or she could literally be a killer. If Father Baddeley suspected that others had received similar letters he might well have looked around for professional help. Or, and this was more interesting, had someone intended Dalgliesh to believe precisely that? Had the note been deliberately planted for him to find? It was odd, surely, that no one had discovered and destroyed it after Father Baddeley's death. Someone from Toynton Grange must have looked through his papers. This was hardly a note one would leave for others to read.

He folded it away in his wallet and began to wander around the cottage. Father Baddeley's bedroom was much as he had expected. A mean window with a dingy cretonne curtain, a single bed still made-up with sheets and blankets but with the counterpane pulled taut over the single lumpy pillow; books lining two walls; a small bedside table with a shoddy lamp; a Bible; a cumbersome and gaudily decorated china ashtray bearing an advertisement for beer. Father Baddeley's pipe still rested in its bowl and beside it Dalgliesh saw a half-used booklet of cardboard matches, the kind given away in restaurants and bars. This bore an advertisement for Ye Olde Tudor Barn near Wareham. One single used match was in the ashtray; it had been shredded down to the burnt-out tip. Dalgliesh smiled. So this small personal habit, too, had survived over thirty years. He could recall Father Baddeley's small squirrel-like fingers delicately shredding the sliver of thin cardboard as if attempting to beat some previous personal record. Dalgliesh picked up the match and smiled; six segments. Father Baddeley had excelled himself.

He wandered into the kitchen. It was small, ill-equipped, neat but not very clean. The small gas stove of old-fashioned design looked as if it would soon qualify for a folk museum. The sink under the window was of stone fitted on one side with a scarred and discoloured wooden draining board smelling of stale fat and sour soap. The faded cretonne curtains faintly patterned with overblown roses and daffodils unseasonably intertwined were pulled back to show an inland view of the far Purbeck hills. Clouds tenuous as smoke puffs were drifting and dissolving in the limitless blue sky and the sheep lay like white slugs on their distant pasture.

He explored the pantry. Here at least was evidence that he was expected. Father Baddeley had indeed bought extra food and the tins were a dispiriting reminder of what for him had constituted an adequate diet. Pathetically, he had obviously provided for two, one of whom he confidently expected to have a larger appetite. There was one large tin and one small of many of the staple provisions: baked beans, tuna fish, Irish stew, spaghetti, rice pudding.

Dalgliesh went back to the sitting-room. He was aware of weariness, that the journey had tired him more than he had expected. He saw by the heavy oak clock over the fireplace, still ticking solidly on, that it was still not four o'clock, but his body protested that this had already been a long hard day. He craved tea. There had been a caddy of tea in the pantry but no milk. He wondered whether the gas was still on.

It was then that he heard the footfall at the door, the clank of the latch. There was a woman's figure framed against the afternoon light. He heard a gravelly deep but very feminine voice with a trace, no more, of an Irish accent.

'For God's sake! A human being and a male at that. What are you doing here?'

She came into the room leaving the door open behind her and he saw her clearly. She was about thirty-five, he guessed, sturdy, long-legged, her mane of yellow hair, visibly darker at the roots, worn in a long sweep to her shoulders. Her eyes were full-lidded and narrow in the square face, her mouth wide. She was wearing brown ill-fitting slacks with a strap under the foot, dirty, grass-stained white plimsoles and a sleeveless white cotton top, low-necked, which showed a brown and mottled triangle of sunburn. She wore no brassière and the full, heavy breasts swung loose under the thin cotton. Three wooden bangles clanked on her left forearm. The total impression was of a raffish but not unattractive sexuality, so strong that, although she wore no scent, she brought into the room her own female and individual smell.

He said: 'My name's Adam Dalgliesh. I came here intending to visit Father Baddeley. It seems that it won't now be possible.'

'Well, that's one way of putting it. You're exactly eleven days late. Eleven days too late to see him and five days too late to bury him. Who are you, a chum? We didn't know that he had any. But then, there were quite a number of things we didn't know about our Reverend Michael. He was a secretive little man. He certainly kept you hidden.'

'We hadn't met except briefly since I was a boy and I only wrote to tell him I was coming the day before he died.'

'Adam. I like that. They call a lot of kids that nowadays. It's getting trendy again. But you must have found it a bit of a drag when you were at school. Still, it suits you. I can't think why. You aren't exactly of the earth, earthy are you? I know about you now. You've come to collect the books.'

'Have I?'

'The ones Michael left you in his will. To Adam Dalgliesh, only son of the late Canon Alexander Dalgliesh, all my books to keep or dispose of as he sees fit. I remember it exactly because I thought the names were so

26

unusual. You haven't lost much time, have you? I'm surprised that the solicitors have even got round to writing to
you. Bob Loder isn't usually that efficient. But I shouldn't
get too excited if I were you. They never looked particularly valuable to me. A lot of dry old theological tomes.
By the way, you weren't expecting to be left any of his
money, were you? If so, I've got news for you.'

'I didn't know that Father Baddeley had any money.'

'Nor did we. That was another of his little secrets. He
left £19,000. Not a great fortune, but useful. He left it
all to Wilfred for the benefit of Toynton Grange, and it
came just in time from all I hear. Grace Willison is the
only other legatee. She got that old bureau. At least she
will get it when Wilfred bothers to have it moved.'

She had settled down in the fireside chair, her hair
thrown back against the headrest, both legs splayed
wide. Dalgliesh pulled out one of the wheel-backed
chairs and sat facing her.

'Did you know Father Baddeley well?'

'We all know each other well here, that's half our
trouble. Are you thinking of staying here?'

'In the district perhaps for a day or two. But it doesn't
seem possible now to stay here . . .'

'I don't see why not if you want to. The place is
empty, at least until Wilfred finds another victim –
tenant, I should say. I shouldn't think that he'd object.
Besides you'll have to sort out the books, won't you?
Wilfred will want them out of the way before the next
incumbent moves in.'

'Wilfred Anstey owns the cottage then?'

'He owns Toynton Grange and all the cottages except
Julius Court's. He's further out on the headland, the

only one with a sea view. Wilfred owns all the rest of the property and he owns us.'

She looked at him appraisingly.

'You haven't any useful skills, have you? I mean you're not a physiotherapist or a male nurse or doctor, or even an accountant? Not that you look like one. Anyway, if you are I'd advise you to keep away before Wilfred decides that you're too useful to let go.'

'I don't think that he'd find my particular skills of much use.'

'Then I should stay on if it suits you. But I'd better put you in the picture. You might then change your mind.'

Dalgliesh said:

'Start with yourself. You haven't told me who you are.'

'Good God, nor have I! Sorry. I'm Maggie Hewson. My husband is resident medical officer at the Grange. At least, he lives with me in a cottage provided by Wilfred and appropriately named Charity Cottage, but he spends most of his time at Toynton Grange. With only five patients left you'd wonder what he finds to amuse him. Or would you? What do you suppose he finds to amuse him, Adam Dalgliesh?'

'Did your husband attend Father Baddeley?'

'Call him Michael, we all did except Grace Willison. Yes, Eric looked after him when he was alive and signed the death certificate when he died. He couldn't have done that six months ago, but now that they've graciously restored him to the Medical Register he can actually put his name to a piece of paper to say that you're properly and legally dead. God, what a bloody privilege.'

She laughed, and fumbling in the pockets of her slacks produced a packet of cigarettes and lit one. She handed the packet to Dalgliesh. He shook his head. She shrugged her shoulders and blew a puff of smoke towards him.

Dalgliesh asked:

'What did Father Baddeley die of?'

'His heart stopped beating. No, I'm not being facetious. He was old, his heart was tired and on 21st September it stopped. Acute myocardiac infarction complicated by mild diabetes, if you want the medical jargon.'

'Was he alone?'

'I imagine so. He died at night, at least he was last seen alive by Grace Willison at seven forty-five p.m. when he heard her confession. I suppose he died of boredom. No, I can see I shouldn't have said that. Bad taste, Maggie. She says he seemed as usual, a bit tired of course, but then he'd only been discharged from hospital that morning. I came in at nine o'clock the next day to see if he wanted anything from Wareham – I was taking the eleven o'clock bus; Wilfred doesn't allow private cars – and there he lay, dead.'

'In bed?'

'No, in that chair where you're sitting now, slumped back with his mouth open and his eyes closed. He was wearing his cassock and a purple ribbon thing round his neck. All quite seemly. But very, very dead.'

'So it was you who first found the body?'

'Unless Millicent from next door came pussy-footing in earlier, didn't like the look of him and tiptoed home again. She's Wilfred's widowed sister in case you're

29

interested. Actually, it's rather odd that she didn't come in, knowing that he was ill and alone.'

'It must have been a shock for you.'

'Not really. I was a nurse before I married. I've seen more dead bodies than I can remember. And he was very old. It's the young ones – the kids particularly – who get you down. God, am I glad to be finished with all that messy business.'

'Are you? You don't work at Toynton Grange then?'

She got up and moved over to the fireplace before replying. She blew a cloud of smoke against the looking glass over the mantelpiece then moved her face close to the glass as if studying her reflection.

'No, not when I can avoid it. And by God, do I try to avoid it. You may as well know. I am the delinquent member of the community, the non-co-operator, the drop-out, the heretic. I sow not, neither do I reap. I am impervious to the charms of dear Wilfred. I close my ears to the cries of the afflicted. I do not bend the knee at the shrine.'

She turned towards him with a look half challenging, half speculative. Dalgliesh thought that the outburst had been less than spontaneous, the protest had been made before. It sounded like a ritual justification and he suspected that someone had helped her with the script. He said:

'Tell me about Wilfred Anstey.'

'Didn't Michael warn you? No, I suppose he wouldn't. Well, it's an odd story but I'll try to make it short. Wilfred's great-grandfather built Toynton Grange. His grandfather left it in trust jointly to Wilfred and his sister Millicent. Wilfred bought her out when he started the Home. Eight years ago Wilfred developed multiple sclerosis. It progressed very swiftly; within three months he was chairbound. Then he went on a pilgrimage to Lourdes and got himself cured. Apparently he made a bargain with God. You cure me and I'll devote Toynton Grange and all my money to serving the disabled. God obliged, and now Wilfred's busy fulfilling his part of the bargain. I suppose he's afraid to back out of the agreement in case the disease returns. I don't know that I blame him. I'd probably feel the same myself. We're all superstitious at heart, particularly about disease.'

'And is he tempted to back out?'

'Oh, I don't think so. This place gives him a sensation of power. Surrounded by grateful patients, regarded as a half-superstitious object of veneration by the women, Dot Moxon – the matron so-called – fussing round him like an old hen. Wilfred's happy enough.'

Dalgliesh asked:

'When exactly did the miracle happen?'

'He claims, when they dipped him in the well. As he tells it, he experienced an initial shock of intense cold followed immediately by a tingling warmth which suffused his whole body, and a feeling of great happiness and peace. That's exactly what I get after my third whisky. If Wilfred can produce it in himself by bathing in ice-cold germ-laden water, then all I can say is, he's lucky. When he got back to the hospice he stood on his legs for the first time in six months. Three weeks later he was skipping around like a young ram. He never bothered to return to St Saviour's Hospital in London where he was treated, so that they could record the miraculous cure on his medical record. It would have been rather a joke if he had.'

She paused as if about to say something further and then merely added:

'Touching, isn't it?'

'It's interesting. How does he find the money to fulfil his part of the bargain?'

'The patients pay according to means and some of them are sent here under contractual arrangements by local authorities. And then, of course, he's used his own capital. But things are getting pretty desperate, or so he claims. Father Baddeley's legacy came just in time. And, of course, Wilfred gets the staff on the cheap. He doesn't exactly pay Eric the rate for the job. Philby, the odd job man, is an ex-convict and probably otherwise unemployable; and the matron, Dot Moxon, wouldn't exactly find it easy to get another job after that cruelty investigation at her last hospital. She must be grateful to Wilfred for taking her on. But then, we're all terribly, terribly grateful to dear Wilfred.'

Dalgliesh said:

'I suppose I'd better go up to the Grange and introduce myself. You say there are only five patients left?'

'You're not supposed to refer to them as patients, although I don't know what else Wilfred thinks you can call them. Inmates sounds too much like a prison although, God knows, it's appropriate enough. But there are only five left. He's not admitting from the waiting list until he's made up his mind about the Home's future. The Ridgewell Trust's angling for it and Wilfred's considering handing the whole place over to them, lock, stock and gratis. Actually, there were six patients a fortnight or so ago, but that was before Victor Holroyd threw himself over Toynton Head and smashed himself on the rocks.'

'You mean he killed himself?'

'Well, he was in his wheelchair ten feet from the cliff-edge and either he slipped the brakes and let himself be carried over or Dennis Lerner, the male nurse with him, pushed him. As Dennis hasn't the guts to kill a chicken let alone a man, the general feeling is that Victor did it himself. But as that notion is distressing to dear Wilfred's feelings we're all busy pretending that it was an accident. I miss Victor, I liked him. He was about the only person here I could talk to. But the rest hated him. And now, of course, they've all got bad consciences wondering if they may have misjudged him. There's nothing like dying for putting people at a disadvantage. I mean, when a chap keeps on saying that life isn't worth living you take it that he's just stating the obvious. When he backs it up with action you begin to wonder if there wasn't more to him than you thought.'

Dalgliesh was spared the need to reply by the sound of a car on the headland. Maggie, whose ears were apparently as keen as his own, sprang from her chair and ran outside. A large black saloon was approaching the junction of the paths.

'Julius,' Maggie called back to him in brief explanation and began a boisterous semaphoring.

The car stopped and then turned towards Hope Cottage. Dalgliesh saw that it was a black Mercedes. As soon as it slowed down Maggie ran like an importunate schoolgirl beside it, pouring her explanation through the open window. The car stopped and Julius Court swung himself lightly out.

He was a tall, loose-limbed young man dressed in slacks and a green sweater patched army fashion on the shoulders and elbows. His light brown hair, cut short, was shaped to his head like a pale glinting helmet. It was an authoritative, confident face but with a trace of self-indulgence in the perceptible pouches under the wary eyes and the slight petulance of the small mouth set in a heavy chin. In middle age he would be heavy, even gross. But now he gave an immediate impression of slightly arrogant good looks, enhanced rather than spoilt by the white triangular scar like a colophon above his right eyebrow.

He held out his hand and said:

'Sorry you missed the funeral.'

He made it sound as if Dalgliesh had missed a train. Maggie wailed:

'But darling, you don't understand! He hasn't come for the funeral. Mr Dalgliesh didn't even know that the old man had snuffed out.'

Court looked at Dalgliesh with slightly more interest.

'Oh, I'm sorry. Perhaps you'd better come up to the Grange. Wilfred Anstey will be able to tell you more about Father Baddeley than I. I was at my London flat when the old man died so I can't even provide interesting death-bed revelations. Hop in, both of you. I've got some books in the back for Henry Carwardine from the London Library. I may as well deliver them now.'

Maggie Hewson seemed to feel that she had been remiss in not affecting a proper introduction; she said belatedly:

'Julius Court. Adam Dalgliesh. I don't suppose you've come across each other in London. Julius used to be a diplomat, or is it diplomatist?'

As they got into the car Court said easily:

'Neither is appropriate at the comparatively lowly level I reached in the service. And London is a large place. But don't worry, Maggie. Like the clever lady in the TV panel game, I think I can guess what Mr Dalgliesh does for a living.'

He held open the car door with elaborate courtesy. The Mercedes moved slowly towards Toynton Grange.

II

Georgie Allan looked up from the narrow bed in the sick bay. His mouth began to work grotesquely. The muscles of his throat stood out hard and taut. He tried to raise his head from the pillow.

'I'll be all right for the Lourdes pilgrimage, won't I? You don't think I'll be left behind?'

The words came out in a hoarse, discordant wail. Helen Rainer lifted up the edge of the mattress, tucked the sheet neatly back into place in the orthodox hospital-approved style and said briskly:

'Of course you won't be left behind. You'll be the most important patient on the pilgrimage. Now stop fretting, that's a good boy, and try to rest before your tea.'

She smiled at him, the impersonal, professionally reassuring smile of the trained nurse. Then lifted her eyebrow at Eric Hewson. Together they went over to the window. She said quietly:

'How long can we go on coping with him?'

Hewson replied:

'Another month or two. It would upset him terribly to have to leave now. Wilfred too. In a few months' time both of them will be readier to accept the inevitable. Besides, he's set his heart on this Lourdes trip. Next time we go I doubt whether he will be alive. He certainly won't be here.'

'But he's really a hospital case now. We aren't registered as a nursing home. We're only a home for the young chronic sick and disabled. Our contract is with the local authorities not the National Health Service. We don't pretend to offer a full medical nursing service. We aren't even supposed to. It's time Wilfred gave up or made up his mind what he's trying to do here.'

'I know.' He did know, they both did. This wasn't a new problem. Why, he wondered, had so much of their conversation become a boring repetition of the obvious, dominated by Helen's high didactic voice?

Together they looked down at the small paved patio, bordered by the two new single-storey wings which contained the bedrooms and dayrooms, where the little group of remaining patients had gathered for the last sit in the sun before tea. The four wheelchairs were carefully placed a little apart and faced away from the house. The two watchers could see only the back of the patients' heads. Unmoving they sat looking fixedly toward the headland. Grace Willison, her grey untidy hair ruffled by the light breeze; Jennie Pegram, her neck sunk into her shoulders, her aureole of yellow hair streaming over the back of her wheelchair as if bleaching in the sun; Ursula Hollis's small round poll on its thin neck, high and motionless as a decapitated head on a pole; Henry Carwardine's dark head on its twisted neck, slumped sideways like a broken puppet. But then, they were all puppets. Dr Hewson had a momentary and insane picture of himself rushing on to the patio and setting the four heads nodding and wagging, pulling invisible strings at the back of the necks so that the air was filled with their loud, discordant cries.

'What's the matter with them?' he asked suddenly. 'Something's wrong about this place.'

'More than usual?'

'Yes. Haven't you noticed?'

'Perhaps they're missing Michael. God knows why. He did little enough. If Wilfred's determined to carry on here he can find a better use for Hope Cottage now. As a matter of fact, I thought about suggesting that he let me live there. It would be easier for us.'

The thought appalled him. So that was what she had been planning. The familiar depression fell on him, physical as a lead weight. Two positive, discontented women, both wanting something that he couldn't give. He tried to keep the panic from his voice.

'It wouldn't do. You're needed here. And I couldn't come to you at Hope Cottage, not with Millicent next door.'

'She hears nothing once she's switched on the TV. We know that. And there's a back door if you do have to make a quick get-away. It's better than nothing.'

'But Maggie would suspect.'

'She suspects now. And she's got to know some time.'

'We'll talk about it later. It's a bad time to worry Wilfred just now. We've all been on edge since Victor died.'

Victor's death. He wondered what perverse masochism had made him mention Victor. It reminded him of those early days as a medical student when he would uncover a suppurating wound with relief because the sight of blood,

37

inflamed tissue and pus was so less frightening than the imagination of what lay beneath the smooth gauze. Well, he had got used to blood. He had got used to death. In time he might even get used to being a doctor.

They moved together into the small clinical room at the front of the building. He went to the basin and began methodically sluicing his hands and forearms as if his brief examination of young Georgie had been a messy surgical procedure requiring a thorough cleansing. Behind his back he could hear the clink of instruments. Helen was unnecessarily tidying the surgical cupboard yet once more. With a sinking heart he realized that they were going to have to talk. But not yet. Not yet. And he knew what she would say. He had heard it all before, the old insistent arguments spoken in that confident school prefect's voice. 'You're wasted here. You're a doctor, not a dispensing chemist. You've got to break free, free of Maggie and Wilfred. You can't put loyalty to Wilfred before your vocation.' His vocation! That was the word his mother had always used. It made him want to break into hysterical laughter.

He switched on the tap to full and the water came gushing out, swirling round the basin, filling his ears like the sound of the incoming tide. What had it been like for Victor, that hurtle into oblivion? Had the clumsy wheelchair, heavy with its own momentum, sailed into space like one of those ridiculous flying contraptions in a James Bond film, the little manikin secure among his gadgets, ready to pull the lever and sport wings? Or had it twisted and tumbled through the air, bouncing off the rock face, with Victor confined in canvas and metal, flailing impotent arms, adding his screams to the cry of the gulls? Had his heavy body broken free of the strap in mid-air, or had the canvas held until that final annihilating crash against the flat-iron rocks, the first sucking wave of the relentless unthinking sea? And what had been in his mind? Exaltation or despair, terror or a blessed nothingness? Had the clean air and the sea wiped it all away, the pain, the bitterness, the malice?

It was only after his death that the full extent of Victor's malice had been known, in the codicil to his will. He had taken trouble to let the other patients know that he had money, that he paid the full fee at Toynton Grange, modest though that was, and wasn't, as were all the others except Henry Carwardine, dependent upon the benevolence of a local authority. He had never told them the source of his wealth – he had, after all, been a schoolmaster and they were hardly well paid – and they still didn't know. He might have told Maggie of course. There were a number of things he might have told Maggie. But on this she had been unaccountably silent.

Eric Hewson didn't believe that Maggie had taken an interest in Victor simply because of the money. They had, after all, had something in common. They had both made no secret that they hated Toynton Grange, that they were there of necessity not of choice, that they despised their companions. Probably Maggie found Victor's rebarbative malice to her liking. They had certainly spent a great deal of time together. Wilfred had seemed almost to welcome it, almost as if he thought Maggie was at last finding her proper place at Toynton. She had taken her turn at wheeling Victor in his heavy chair to his favourite spot. He had found some kind of peace in sight of the sea. Maggie and he had spent hours together, out of sight of the house, high on the edge of the cliff. But it hadn't worried him. He knew, none better, that Maggie could never love a man who couldn't satisfy her physically. He welcomed her friendship. At least it gave her something to occupy her time, kept her quiet.

He couldn't remember exactly when she had begun to become excited about the money. Victor must have said something. Maggie had changed almost overnight. She had become animated, almost gay. There had been a kind of feverish and suppressed excitement about her. And then Victor had suddenly demanded that he be driven to London for an examination at St Saviour's Hospital and to consult his solicitor. It was then that Maggie had hinted to him about the will. He had caught something of her excitement. He wondered now what either of them had hoped for. Had she seen the money as a release merely from Toynton Grange, or also from him? Either way, surely, it would have brought salvation for them both. And the idea wasn't absurd. It was known that Victor had no relatives except a sister in New Zealand to whom he never wrote. No, he thought, reaching for the towel and beginning to dry his hands, it hadn't been an absurd dream; less absurd than the reality.

He thought of that drive back from London; the warm, enclosed world of the Mercedes; Julius silent, his hands resting lightly on the wheel; the road a silver reel punctuated with stars slipping endlessly under the bonnet; road signs leaping out of darkness to pattern the blue-black sky; small petrified animals, fur erect, briefly glorified in the headlamps; the road verges drained pale gold in their glare. Victor had sat with Maggie in the back, wrapped in his plaid cloak and smiling, always smiling. And the air had been heavy with secrets, shared and unshared.

Victor had indeed altered his will. He had added a codicil to the bequest which left the whole of his fortune to his sister, a final testimony of petty malice. To Grace Willison, a bar of toilet soap; to Henry Carwardine, a mouthwash; to Ursula Hollis, body deodorant; to Jennie Pegram, a toothpick.

Eric reflected that Maggie had taken it very well. Really very well indeed; if you could call that wild, ringing, uncontrolled laughter taking it well. He recalled her now, reeling about their small stone sitting-room, helpless with hysteria, throwing back her head and baying out her laughter so that it echoed harshly back from the walls, like a menagerie, and rang out over the headland so that he was afraid they would hear it as far as Toynton Grange.

Helen was standing by the window. She said, her voice sharp:

'There's a car outside Hope Cottage.'

He walked over to her. Together they looked out. Slowly their eyes met. She took his hand, and her voice was gentle, the voice he had heard when they had first made love.

'You've got nothing to worry about, darling. You know that, don't you? Nothing to worry about at all.'

III

Ursula Hollis closed her library book, shut her eyes against the afternoon sun and entered into her private

41

daydream. To do so now in the brief fifteen minutes before teatime was an indulgence, and quick as always to feel guilty at so ill-disciplined a pleasure, she was at first afraid that the magic wouldn't work. Usually, she made herself wait until she was in bed at night, wait even until Grace Willison's rasping breath, heard through the unsubstantial partition, had gentled into sleep before she allowed herself to think of Steve and the flat in Bell Street. The ritual had become an effort of will. She would lie there hardly daring to breathe because the images, however clearly conjured up, were so sensitive, so easily dispelled. But now it was happening beautifully. She concentrated, seeing the amorphous shapes and the changing patterns of colour focus into a picture, clearly as a developing negative, tuning in her ears to the sounds of home.

She saw the brick wall of the nineteenth-century house opposite with the morning sun lighting its dull façade so that each brick was individually distinct, multi-coloured, a pattern of light. The pokey two-roomed flat above Mr Polanski's delicatessen, the street outside, the crowded heterogeneous life of that square mile of London between Edgware Road and Marylebone Station had absorbed and enchanted her. She was back there now, walking again with Steve through Church Street market on Saturday morning, the happiest day of the week. She saw the local women in their flowered overalls and carpet slippers, heavy wedding rings sunk into their bulbous toil-scarred fingers, their eyes bright in amorphous faces, as they sat gossiping beside their prams of second-hand clothes; the young people, joy-fully garbed, squatting on the kerbstone behind their stalls of bric-à-brac; the tourists cheerfully impulsive or cautious and discerning by turns, conferring over their dollars or displaying their bizarre treasures. The street smelt of fruit, flowers and spice, of sweating bodies, cheap wine and old books. She saw the black women with their jutting buttocks and high barbaric staccato chatter, heard their sudden deep-throated laughter, as they crowded round the stall of huge unripe bananas and mangoes as large as footballs. In her dreams she moved on, her fingers gently entwined with Steve's like a ghost passing unseen down familiar paths.

The eighteen months of her marriage had been a time of intense but precarious happiness, precarious because she could never feel that it was rooted in reality. It was like becoming another person. Before, she had taught herself contentment and had called it happiness. After, she realized that there was a world of experience, of sensation, of thought even, for which nothing in those first twenty years of life in the Middlesbrough suburb, or the two and a half years in the YWCA hostel in London, had prepared her. Only one thing marred it, the fear which she could never quite suppress that it was all happening to the wrong person, that she was an imposture of joy.

She couldn't imagine what it was about her that had so capriciously caught Steve's fancy that first time when he had called at the inquiry desk in the Council offices to ask about his rates. Was it the one feature which she had always thought of as close to a deformity; the fact that she had one blue and one brown eye? Certainly it was an oddity which had intrigued and amused him, had given her, she realized, an added value in his eyes.

43

He had changed her appearance, making her grow her hair shoulder length, bringing home for her long gaudy skirts in Indian cotton found in the street markets or the shops in the back streets of Edgware Road. Sometimes, catching a glimpse of herself in a shop window, so marvellously altered, she would wonder again which strange predilection had led him to choose her, what possibilities undetected by others, unknown to herself, he had seen in her. Some quality in her had caught his eccentric fancy as did the odd items of bric-à-brac on the Bell Street stalls. Some object, unregarded by the passers-by, would catch his eye and he would turn it to the light this way and that in the palm of his hand, suddenly enchanted. She would make a tentative protest.

'But darling, isn't it rather hideous?'

'Oh, no, it's amusing. I like it. And Mogg will love it. Let's buy it for Mogg.'

Mogg, his greatest and, she sometimes thought, his only friend, had been christened Morgan Evans but preferred to use his nickname, regarding it as more appropriate to a poet of the people's struggle. It was not that Mogg struggled greatly himself; indeed Ursula had never met anyone who drank and ate so resolutely at other people's expense. He chanted his confused battle cries to anarchy and hatred in local pubs where his hairy and sad-eyed followers listened in silence or spasmodically banged the table with their beer mugs amid grunts of approval. But Mogg's prose style had been more comprehensible. She had read his letter only once before returning it to the pocket in Steve's jeans, but she could recall every word. Sometimes she wondered whether he had intended her to find it, whether it was

44

fortuitous that he had forgotten to clear out the pockets of his jeans on the one evening when she always took their dirty clothes to the washeteria. It was three weeks after the hospital had given her a firm diagnosis.

'I would say I told you so except that this is my week for abjuring platitudes. I prophesied disaster, but not total disaster. My poor bloody Steve! But isn't it possible for you to get a divorce? She must have had some symptoms before you married. You can – or could – get a divorce for V.D. existing at the time of marriage and what's a dose of clap compared with this? It astounds me, the irresponsibility of the so-called establishment about marriage. They bleat about its sanctity, about protecting it as a staple foundation of society, and then let people acquire a wife with less physical check-up than they would give to a second-hand car. Anyway, you do realize that you must break free, don't you? It will be the end of you if you don't. And don't take refuge in the cowardice of compassion. Can you really see yourself wheeling her invalid chair and wiping her bottom? Yes, I know some men do it. But you never did get much of a kick out of masochism, did you? Besides, the husbands who can do that know something about loving, and even you, my darling Steve, wouldn't presume to claim that. By the way, isn't she an R.C.? As you married in a Registry Office I doubt whether she considers herself properly married at all. That could be a way out for you. Anyway, see you in the Paviours Arms, Wednesday eight p.m. I will celebrate your misfortune with a new poem and a pint of bitter.'

She hadn't really expected him to wheel her chair. She hadn't wanted him to perform the simplest, least

45

intimate physical service for her. She had learnt very early in their marriage that any illness, even transitory colds and sickness, disgusted and frightened him. But she had hoped that the disease would spread very slowly, that she could continue to manage on her own at least for a few precious years. She had schemed how it might be possible. She would get up early so that he needn't be offended by her slowness and ungainliness. She could move the furniture just a few inches, he probably wouldn't even notice, to provide unobtrusive supports so that she needn't take too quickly to sticks and callipers. Perhaps they could find an easier flat, one on the ground floor. If she could have a front door ramp she could get out in the daytime to do her shopping. And there would still be the nights together. Surely nothing could change those?

But it had quickly become evident that the disease, moving inexorably along her nerves like a predator, was spreading at its own pace, not hers. The plans she had made, lying stiffly beside him, distanced in the large double bed, willing that no spasm of muscle should disturb him, had become increasingly unrealistic. Watching her pathetic efforts, he had tried to be considerate and kind. He hadn't reproached her except by his withdrawal, hadn't condemned her growing weakness except by demonstrating his lack of strength. In her nightmares she drowned; thrashing and choking in a limitless sea, she clutched at a floating bough and felt it sink, sponge soft and rotten, beneath her hands. She sensed morbidly that she was acquiring the propitiatory simperingly pathetic air of the disabled. It was hard to be natural with him, harder still to talk. She remembered how he used to lie full length on the sofa watching her while she read or sewed, the creature of his selection and creation, draped and celebrated with the eccentric clothes which he had chosen for her. Now he was afraid for their eyes to meet.

She remembered how he had broken the news to her that he had spoken to the medical social worker at the hospital and that there might be a vacancy soon at Toynton Grange.

'It's by the sea, darling. You've always liked the sea. Quite a small community too, not one of those huge impersonal institutions. The chap who runs it is very highly regarded and it's basically a religious foundation. Anstey isn't a Catholic himself but they do go regularly to Lourdes. That will please you; I mean that you've always been interested in religion. It's one of the subjects that we haven't really seen eye to eye about. I probably wasn't as understanding about your needs as I ought to have been.'

He could afford now to be indulgent of that particular foible. He had forgotten that he had taught her to do without God. Her religion had been one of those possessions that, casually, neither understanding them nor valuing them, he had taken from her. They hadn't really been important to her, those consoling substitutes for sex, for love. She couldn't pretend that she had relinquished them with much of a struggle, those comforting illusions taught in St Matthew's Primary School, assimilated behind the draped terylene curtains of her aunt's front sitting-room in Alma Terrace, Middlesbrough, with its holy pictures, its photograph of Pope John, its framed papal blessing of her aunt and uncle's wedding.

47

All were part of that orphaned, uneventful, not unhappy childhood which was as remote now as a distant once-visited alien shore. She couldn't return because she no longer knew the way.

In the end she had welcomed the thought of Toynton Grange as a refuge. She had pictured herself with a group of patients sitting in their chairs in the sun and looking at the sea; the sea, constantly changing but eternal, comforting and yet frightening, speaking to her in its ceaseless rhythm that nothing really mattered, that human misery was of small account, that everything passed in time. And it wasn't, after all, to be a permanent arrangement. Steve, with the help of the local authority social services department, planned to move into a new and more suitable flat; this was only to be a temporary separation.

But it had lasted now for eight months; eight months in which she had become increasingly unhappy. She had tried to conceal it since unhappiness at Toynton Grange was a sin against the Holy Ghost, a sin against Wilfred. And for most of the time she thought that she had succeeded. She had little in common with the other patients. Grace Willison, dull, middle-aged, pious. Eighteen-year-old Georgie Allan with his boisterous vulgarity; it had been a relief when he became too ill to leave his bed. Henry Carwardine, remote, sarcastic, treating her as if she were a junior clerk. Jennie Pegram, for ever fussing with her hair and smiling her stupid secret smile. And Victor Holroyd, the terrifying Victor, who had hated her as much as he hated everyone at Toynton Grange. Victor who saw no virtue in concealing unhappiness, who frequently proclaimed that if people were dedicated to the practice of charity they might as well have someone to be charitable about.

She had always taken it for granted that it was Victor who had typed the poison pen letter. It was a letter as traumatic in its way as the one she had found from Mogg. She felt for it now, deep in a side pocket in her skirt. It was still there, the cheap paper limp with much handling. But she didn't need to read it. She knew it now by heart, even the first paragraph. She had read that once, and then had turned the paper over at the top so that the words were hidden. Even to think about them burnt her cheek. How could he – it must be a man surely? – know how she and Steve had made love together, that they had done those particular acts and in that way? How could anyone know? Had she, perhaps, cried out in her sleep, moaning her need and her longing? But, if so, only Grace Willison could possibly have heard from the adjoining bedroom, and how could she have understood?

She remembered reading somewhere that obscene letters were usually written by women, particularly by spinsters. Perhaps it hadn't been Victor Holroyd after all. Grace Willison, dull, repressed, religious Grace. But how could she have guessed what Ursula had never admitted to herself?

'You must have known you were ill when you married him. What about those tremors, the weakness in your legs, the clumsiness in the mornings? You knew you were ill, didn't you? You cheated him. No wonder he seldom writes, that he never visits. He's not living alone, you know. You didn't really expect him to stay faithful, did you?'

49

And there the letter broke off. Somehow she felt that the writer hadn't really come to the end, that some more dramatic and revelationary finish was intended. But perhaps he or she had been interrupted; someone might have come into the office unexpectedly. The note had been typed on Toynton Gránge paper, cheap and absorbent and with the old Remington typewriter. Nearly all the patients and staff occasionally typed. She thought she could remember seeing most of them use the Remington at one time or another. Of course, it was really Grace's machine; it was recognized as primarily hers; she used it to type the stencils for the quarterly newsletter. Often she worked alone in the office when the rest of the patients considered that they had finished the working day. And there would be no difficulty in ensuring that it reached the right recipient.

Slipping it into a library book was the surest way of all. They all knew what the others were reading, how could they help it? Books were laid down on tables, on chairs, were easily accessible to anyone. All the staff and patients must have known that she was reading the latest Iris Murdoch. And, oddly enough, the poison letter had been placed at exactly the page she had reached.

At first she had taken it for granted that this was just a new example of Victor's power to hurt and humiliate. It was only since his death that she had felt these doubts, had glanced surreptitiously at the faces of her fellow inmates, had wondered and feared. But surely this was nonsense? She was tormenting herself unnecessarily. It must have been Victor and, if it were Victor, then there would be no more letters. But how could even he have known about her and Steve; except that Victor did mysteriously know things. She remembered the scene when she and Grace Willison had been sitting with him here in the patients' patio. Grace lifting her face to the sun and wearing that silly, gentle smile had begun to talk of her happiness, about the next Lourdes pilgrimage. Victor had broken in roughly:

'You're cheerful because you're euphoric. It's a feature of your disease, D.S. patients always have this unreasonable happiness and hope. Read the textbooks. It's a recognized symptom. It's certainly no virtue on your part and it's bloody irritating for the rest of us.'

She recalled Grace's voice already tremulous with hurt.

'I wasn't claiming happiness as a virtue. But even if it's only a symptom, I can still give thanks for it; it's a kind of grace.'

'As long as you don't expect the rest of us to join in, give thanks by all means. Thank God for the privilege of being no bloody use to yourself or anyone else. And while you're about it, thank Him for some of the other blessings of His creation; the millions toiling to get a living out of barren soil swept by flood, burnt by drought; for pot-bellied children; for tortured prisoners; for the whole doomed, bloody, pointless mess.'

Grace Willison had protested quietly through the first smart of her tears:

'But Victor, how can you talk like that? Suffering isn't the whole of life; you can't really believe that God doesn't care. You come with us to Lourdes.'

'Of course I do. It's the one chance to get out of this boring crack-brained penitentiary. I like movement, I

51

like travel, I like the sight of the sun shining on the Pyrenees, I enjoy the colour. I even get some kind of satisfaction from the blatant commercialism of it all, from the sight of thousands of my fellow beings who are more deluded than I.'

'But that's blasphemy!'

'Is it? Well, I enjoy that too.'

Grace persisted: 'If only you would talk to Father Baddeley, Victor. I'm sure that he would help you. Or perhaps to Wilfred. Why not talk to Wilfred?'

He had burst into raucous laughter, jeering but strangely and frighteningly shot through with genuine amusement.

'Talk to Wilfred! My God, I could tell you something about our saintly Wilfred that would give you a laugh, and one day, if he irritates me enough, I probably shall. Talk to Wilfred!'

She thought she could still hear the distant echo of that laughter. 'I could tell you something about Wilfred.' Only he hadn't told them, and now he never would. She thought about Victor's death. What impulse had led him on that particular afternoon to make his final gesture against fate? It must have been an impulse: Wednesday wasn't his normal day for an outing and Dennis hadn't wanted to take him. She remembered clearly the scene on the patio. Victor, importunate, insistent, exerting every effort of will to get what he wanted. Dennis flushed, sulky, a recalcitrant child, finally giving way but with a poor grace. And so, they had left together for that final walk, and she had never seen Victor again. What was he thinking of when he released those brakes and hurled himself and the chair

52

towards annihilation? Surely it must have been the impulse of a moment. No one could choose to die with such spectacular horror while there were gentler means available. And surely there were gentler means; sometimes she found herself thinking about them, about those two most recent deaths, Victor's and Father Baddeley's. Father Baddeley, gentle, ineffectual, had passed away as if he had never been; his name now was hardly mentioned. It was Victor who seemed to be still among them. It was Victor's bitter uneasy spirit which hung over Toynton Grange. Sometimes, particularly at dusk, she dared not turn her face towards an adjacent wheelchair in case she should see, not the expected occupant, but Victor's heavy figure shrouded in his heavy plaid cloak, his dark sardonic face with its fixed smile like a rictus. Suddenly, despite the warmth of the afternoon sun, Ursula shivered. Releasing the brakes on her chair she turned and wheeled herself towards the house.

IV

The front door of Toynton Grange was open and Julius Court led the way into a high square hall, oak panelled and with a chequered black and white marble floor. The house struck very warm. It was like passing through an invisible curtain of hot air. The hall smelt oddly; not with the usual institutional smell of bodies, food and furniture polish overlaid with antiseptic, but sweeter and strangely exotic as if someone had been burning incense. The hall was as dimly lit as a church. An impression reinforced by the two front windows of Pre-Raphaelite stained glass one on each side of the main door. To the left was the expulsion from Eden, to the right the sacrifice of Isaac. Dalgliesh wondered what aberrant fancy had conceived that effeminate angel with his curdle of yellow hair under the plumed helmet or the sword embellished with glutinous lozenges in ruby, bright blue and orange with which he was ineffectively barring the two delinquents from an apple-orchard Eden. Adam and Eve, their pink limbs tactfully if improbably entwined with laurel, wore expressions respectively of spurious spirituality and petulant remorse. On the right the same angel swooped like a metamorphosized batman over Isaac's bound body, watched from the thicket by an excessively woolly ram whose face, understandably, bore an expression of the liveliest apprehension.

There were three chairs in the hall, bastard contraptions in painted wood covered with vinyl, themselves deformities, one with an unusually high seat, two very low. A folded wheelchair rested against the far wall and a wooden rail was screwed waist high into the panelling. To the right an open door gave a glimpse of what could be a business room or cloakroom. Dalgliesh could see the fold of a plaid cloak hanging on the wall, a pegboard of keys and the edge of a heavy desk. A carved hall table bearing a brass tray of letters and surmounted by a huge fire bell stood to the left of the door.

Julius led the way through a rear door and into a central vestibule from which rose a heavily carved staircase, its banister half cut away to accommodate the metal cage of a large modern lift. They came to a third door. Julius threw it dramatically open and announced:

'A visitor for the dead. Adam Dalgliesh.'

The three of them passed into the room together. Dalgliesh, flanked by his two sponsors, had the unfamiliar sensation of being under escort. After the dimness of the front hall and the central vestibule the dining-room was so bright that he blinked. The tall mullioned windows gave little natural light but the room was harshly lit by two tubes of fluorescent lighting incongruously suspended from the moulded ceiling. Images seemed to fuse together and then parted and he saw clearly the inhabitants of Toynton Grange grouped like a tableau round the oak refectory table at tea.

His arrival seemed to have struck them momentarily into silent surprise. Four of them were in wheelchairs, one a man. The two remaining women were obviously staff; one was dressed as a matron except for the customary status symbol of a cap. Without it, she looked curiously incomplete. The other, a fair-haired younger woman, was wearing black slacks and a white smock but succeeded, despite this unorthodox uniform, in giving an immediate impression of slightly intimidating competence. The three able-bodied men all wore dark-brown monk's habits. After a second's pause, a figure at the head of the table rose and came with ceremonial slowness towards them with hands held out.

'Welcome to Toynton Grange, Adam Dalgliesh. My name is Wilfred Anstey.'

Dalgliesh's first thought was that he looked like a bit-player acting with practised conviction the part of an ascetic bishop. The brown monk's habit suited him so well that it was impossible to imagine him in any other garb. He was tall and very thin, the wrists from which the full woollen sleeves fell away were brown and brittle as autumn sticks. His hair was grey but strong and shaved very short revealing the boyish curve of the skull. Beneath it the thin long face was mottled brown as if the summer tan were fading unevenly; two shining white patches on the left temple had the appearance of diseased skin. It was difficult to guess his age; fifty perhaps. The gentle questioning eyes with their suggestion of other people's suffering meekly borne were young eyes, the blue irises very clear, the whites opaque as milk. He smiled, a singularly sweet lopsided smile spoilt by the display of uneven and discoloured teeth. Dalgliesh wondered why it was that philanthropists so often had a reluctance to visit their dentist.

Dalgliesh held out his hand and felt it imprisoned between Anstey's two palms. It took an effort of will not to flinch from this clammy encounter of moist flesh. He said:

'I had hoped to pay a few days' visit to Father Baddeley. I'm an old friend. I didn't know until I arrived that he was dead.'

'Dead and cremated. His ashes were buried last Wednesday in the churchyard of St Michael's, Toynton. We knew that he would wish them to lie in consecrated ground. We didn't announce his death in the papers because we didn't know that he had friends.'

'Except us here.' It was one of the women patients who added the gentle but firm correction. She was older than the other patients, grey-haired and angular as a Dutch doll propped in her chair. She looked at Dalgliesh steadily with kind and interested eyes.

Wilfred Anstey said:

'Of course. Except us here. Grace was, I think, closer to Michael than anyone else and was with him on the night he died.'

Dalgliesh said:

'He died alone, Mrs Hewson tells me.'

'Unhappily yes. But so at the last do we all. You'll join us for tea, I hope. Julius, you too, and Maggie of course. And did you say that you hoped to stay with Michael? Then you must, of course, spend the night here.'

He turned to the matron.

'Victor's room, I think, Dot. Perhaps, after tea, you would prepare it for our guest.'

Dalgliesh said:

'That's very kind of you, but I don't want to be a nuisance. Would there be any objection if, after tonight, I spent a few days in the cottage? Mrs Hewson tells me that Father Baddeley left me his library. It would be helpful if I could sort and pack the books while I'm here.'

Was it his imagination that the suggestion wasn't entirely welcome? But Anstey hesitated only for a second before saying:

'Of course, if that is what you prefer. But first let me introduce you to the family.'

Dalgliesh followed Anstey in a formal charade of greetings. A succession of hands, dry, cold, moist, reluctant or firm clasped his. Grace Willison, the middle-aged spinster; a study in grey; skin, hair, dress, stockings, all of them slightly dingy so that she looked like an old-fashioned, stiffly jointed doll neglected too long in a dusty cupboard. Ursula Hollis; a tall, spotty-faced girl dressed in a long skirt of Indian cotton who gave him a tentative smile and brief, reluctant handshake. Her left hand lay limply in her lap as if wearied by the weight of the thick wedding ring. He was aware of something odd about her face but had moved on before he realized that she had one blue eye, one brown. Jennie Pegram; the youngest patient but probably older than she looked with a pale, sharp face and mild lemur-like eyes. She was so short-necked that she seemed hunched into her wheelchair. Corn-gold hair, parted in the middle, hung like a crimped curtain around the dwarfish body. She cringed deprecatingly at his touch, gave him a sickly smile and whispered 'hullo' on a gasp of intaken breath. Henry Carwardine; a handsome, authoritative face but cut with deep lines of strain; a high beaky nose and long mouth. The disease had wrenched his head to one side so that he looked like a supercilious bird of prey. He took no notice of Dalgliesh's proffered hand but said a brief 'how do you do' with an uninterest amounting almost to discourtesy. Dorothy Moxon, the matron; sombre, stout and gloomy-eyed under the dark fringe. Helen Rainer; large, slightly protruding green eyes under lids as thin as grape skins and a shapely figure which even the loose-fitting smock couldn't wholly disguise. She would, he thought, be attractive were it not for the disconnected droop of the slightly marsupial cheeks. She shook hands firmly with Dalgliesh and gave him a minatory glance as if welcoming a new patient from whom she expected trouble. Dr Eric Hewson; a fair, good-looking man with a boyish vulnerable face, mud-brown eyes fringed with remarkably long lashes. Dennis Lerner; a lean, rather weak face, eyes blinking nervously behind the steel-rimmed spectacles, a moist handshake.

Anstey added, almost as if he thought Lerner needed a word of explanation, that Dennis was the male nurse.

'The two remaining members of our family, Albert Philby, our handyman, and my sister Millicent Hammitt you will meet later, I hope. But I mustn't, of course, forget Jeoffrey.' As if catching his name, a cat, who had been slumbering on a window seat, uncurled himself, dropped ponderously to the floor and stalked towards them, tail erect. Anstey explained:

'He is named after Christopher Smart's cat. I expect you remember the poem.

> For I will consider my cat Jeoffrey.
> For he is the servant of the living God, duly
> and daily serving him,
> For he counteracts the powers of darkness by his
> electric skin and glaring eyes,
> For he counteracts the Devil, who is death, by
> brisking about the life.'

Dalgliesh said that he knew the poem. He could have added that if Anstey had destined his cat for this hieratic role, then he had been unlucky in his choice of the litter. Jeoffrey was a barrel-shaped tabby with a tail like a fox's brush who looked as if his life were dedicated less to the service of his creator than to the gratification of feline lusts. He gave Anstey a disagreeable look compounded of long suffering and disgust and leapt with lightness and precision on to Carwardine's lap, where he was ill-received. Gratified at Carwardine's obvious reluctance to acquire him, he settled down with much purring and foot padding and permitted his eyes to close.

Julius Court and Maggie Hewson had settled them-selves at the far end of the long table. Suddenly Julius called out:

'Be careful what you say to Mr Dalgliesh, it may be taken down and given in evidence. He chooses to travel incognito but actually he's Commander Adam Dalgliesh of New Scotland Yard. His job is catching murderers.'

Henry Carwardine's cup began an agitated rattle in its saucer. He tried ineffectively to steady it with his left hand. No one looked at him. Jennie Pegram gave an apprehensive gasp, then looked complacently round the table as if she had done something clever. Helen Rainer said sharply:

'How do you know?'

'I live in the world, my darlings, and occasionally read the newspapers. There was a notorious case last year which gained the Commander some public notice.'

He turned to Dalgliesh:

'Henry will be drinking wine with me after dinner tonight and listening to some music. You may care to join us. You could perhaps wheel him over. Wilfred will excuse you, I know.'

The invitation hardly seemed courteous, excluding as it did all but two of the company and peremptorily claiming the new arrival with no more than a token acknowledgement to his host. But no one seemed to mind. Perhaps it was usual for the two men to drink together when Court was at his cottage. After all, there was no reason why the patients should be compelled to share each other's friends, or those friends obliged to issue a general invitation. Besides, Dalgliesh was obviously invited to provide an escort. He said a brief thank-you and sat down at the table between Ursula Hollis and Henry Carwardine.

It was a plain, boarding-school tea. There was no cloth. The scarred oak table, reamed with scorch marks, held two large brown teapots wielded by Dorothy Moxon, two plates of thickly cut brown bread, thinly spread with what Dalgliesh suspected was margarine, a jar of honey and one of Marmite, a dish of rock buns, home-made and pebbled with an excrescence of bullet black currants. There was also a bowl of apples. They looked like windfalls. Everyone was drinking from brown earthenware mugs. Helen Rainer went over to a cupboard set under the window and brought over three similar mugs and matching plates for the visitors.

It was an odd tea party, Carwardine ignored the guest except to push the plate of bread and butter towards him, and Dalgliesh at first made little headway with Ursula Hollis. Her pale intense face was turned perpetually towards him, the two discordant eyes searched his. He felt uncomfortably that she was making some demand on him, desperately hoping to evoke a response of interest, of affection even, which he could neither recognize nor was competent to give. But, by happy chance, he mentioned London. Her face brightened, she asked him if he knew Marylebone, the Bell Street market? He found himself involved in a lively, almost obsessive discussion about London's street markets. She became animated, almost pretty and, strangely, it seemed to give her some comfort.

Suddenly Jennie Pegram leaned forward across the table and said with a moue of simulated distaste:

'A funny job catching murderers and getting them hanged. I don't see how you fancy it.'

'We don't fancy it, and nowadays they don't get hanged.'

'Well, shut up for life then. I think that's worse. And I bet some of those you caught when you were younger got hanged.'

He detected the anticipatory, almost lascivious gleam in her eyes. It wasn't new to him. He said quietly:

'Five of them. It's interesting that those are the ones people always want to hear about.'

Anstey smiled his gentle smile and spoke as one determined to be fair.

'It isn't only a question of punishment though, Jennie, is it? There is the theory of deterrence; the need to mark public abhorrence of violent crime; the hope of reforming and rehabilitating the criminal; and, of course, the importance of trying to ensure that he doesn't do it again.'

He reminded Dalgliesh of a schoolmaster he had much disliked who was given to initiating frank discussion as a matter of duty but always with the patronizing air of permitting a limited expression of unorthodox opinion provided the class came back within the allotted time to a proper conviction of the rightness of his own views. But now Dalgliesh was neither compelled nor disposed to co-operate. He broke into Jennie's simple, 'Well, they can't do it again if they're hanged, can they?' by saying:

'It's an interesting and important subject, I know. But forgive me if I don't personally find it fascinating. I'm on holiday – actually I'm convalescing – and I'm trying to forget about work.'

'You've been ill?' Carwardine, with the deliberate care of a child uncertain of its powers, reached across and helped himself to honey.

'I hope your call here isn't, even subconsciously, on your own behalf. You aren't looking for a future vacancy? You haven't a progressive incurable disease?'

Anstey said:

'We all suffer from a progressive incurable disease. We call it life.'

Carwardine gave a tight self-congratulatory smile, as if he had scored a point in some private game. Dalgliesh, who was beginning to feel himself part of a mad hatter's tea party, wasn't sure whether the remark was spuriously profound or merely silly. What he was sure was that Anstey had made it before. There was a short, embarrassed silence, then Anstey said:

'Michael didn't let us know he was expecting you.' He made it sound like a gentle reproof.

'He may not have received my postcard. It should have arrived on the morning of his death. I couldn't find it in his bureau.'

Anstey was peeling an apple, the yellow rind curved over his thin fingers. His eyes were intent on his task. He said:

'He was brought home by the ambulance service. It wasn't convenient that morning for me to fetch him. I understand that the ambulance stopped at the postbox to collect any letters, probably at Michael's request. He later handed a letter to me and one to my sister, so he should have received your card. I certainly found no postcard when I looked in the bureau for his will and for any other written instructions he may have left. That was early on the morning after his death. I may, of course, have missed it.'

Dalgliesh said easily:

'In which case it would still be there. I expect Father Baddeley threw it away. It's a pity you had to break into the bureau.'

'Break into?' Anstey's voice expressed nothing but a polite, unworried query.

'The lock has been forced.'

'Indeed. I imagine that Michael must have lost the key and was forced to that extremity. Forgive the pun. I found the bureau open when I looked for his papers. I'm afraid I didn't think to examine the lock. Is it important?'

'Miss Willison may think so. I understand that the bureau is now hers.'

'A broken lock does, of course, reduce its value. But you will find that we place little store on material possessions at Toynton Grange.'

He smiled again, dismissing a frivolity, and turned to Dorothy Moxon. Miss Willison was concentrating on her plate. She didn't look up. Dalgliesh said:

'It's probably foolish of me, but I wish I could be sure that Father Baddeley knew that I hoped to visit him. I thought he might have slipped my postcard into his diary. But the last volume isn't in his desk.'

This time Anstey looked up. The blue eyes met the dark brown, innocent, polite, unworried.

'Yes, I noticed that. He gave up keeping a diary at the end of June apparently. The surprise is that he kept one, not that he gave up the habit. In the end one grows impatient of the egotism which records trivia as if it had a permanent value.'

'It's unusual surely after so many years to stop in mid-year.'

64

'He had just returned from hospital after a grave illness and can't have been in much doubt about the prognosis. Knowing that death could not be far off, he may have decided to destroy the diaries.'

'Beginning with the last volume?'

'To destroy a diary must be like destroying a memory. One would begin with the years one could best endure to lose. Old memories are tenacious. He made a start by burning the last volume.'

Grace Willison again spoke her gentle but firm correction:

'Not by burning, Wilfred. Father Baddeley used his electric fire when he got home from hospital. The grate is filled with a jam pot of dried grasses.'

Dalgliesh pictured the sitting-room of Hope Cottage. She was, of course, right. He recalled the old-fashioned grey stone jar, the crumpled bunch of dried leaves and grasses filling the narrow fireplace and thrusting their dusty and soot-laden stalks between the bars. They probably hadn't been disturbed for the best part of a year.

The animated chatter at the other end of the table died into speculative silence as it does when people suddenly suspect that something interesting is being said which they ought to hear.

Maggie Hewson had seated herself so close to Julius Court that Dalgliesh was surprised that he had room to drink his tea and had been overtly flirting with him during the meal, whether for her husband's discomfiture or Court's gratification it was difficult to say. Eric Hewson, when he glanced towards them, had the shame-faced look of an embarrassed schoolboy. Court, perfectly at

65

his ease, had distributed his attention among all the women present, with the exception of Grace. Now Maggie looked from face to face and said sharply:

'What's the matter? What did she say?'

No one replied. It was Julius who broke the moment of sudden and inexplicable tension:

'I forgot to tell you. You're doubly privileged in your visitor. The Commander doesn't confine his talents to catching murderers, he publishes verse. He's Adam Dalgliesh, the poet.'

This announcement was met with a confused con-gratulatory murmur during which Dalgliesh fastened on Jennie's comment of 'how nice' as the most irritat-ingly inept. Wilfred smiled encouragingly and said:

'Of course. We are certainly privileged. And Adam Dalgliesh comes at an opportune time. We are due to hold our monthly family social evening on Thursday. May we hope that our guest will recite some of his poems for our pleasure?'

There were a number of answers to that question but, in the present disadvantaged company, none of them seemed either kind or possible.

Dalgliesh said:

'I'm sorry but I don't travel with copies of my own books.'

Anstey smiled.

'That will present no problem. Henry has your last two volumes. I am sure he will lend them.'

Without looking up from his plate, Carwardine said quietly:

'Given the lack of privacy in this place, I've no doubt you could provide a verbal catalogue of my whole library. But, since you've shown a complete lack of interest in Dalgliesh's work until now, I have no intention of lending my books so that you can blackmail a guest into performing for you like a captive monkey!'

Wilfred flushed slightly and bent his head over his plate.

There was nothing further to be said. After a second's silence, the talk flowed on, innocuous, commonplace. Neither Father Baddeley nor his diary was mentioned again.

V

Anstey was obviously unworried by Dalgliesh's expressed wish after tea to talk to Miss Willison in private. Probably the request struck him as no more than the pious protocol of courtesy and respect. He said that Grace had the task of feeding the hens and collecting the eggs before dusk. Perhaps Adam could help her?

The two larger wheels of the chair were fitted with a second interior wheel in chrome which could be used by the occupant to drive the chair forward. Miss Willison grasped it and began to make slow progress down the asphalt path jerking her frail body like a marionette. Dalgliesh saw that her left hand was deformed and had little power so that the chair tended to swivel, and progress was erratic. He moved to her left and, while walking beside her, he laid his hand unobtrusively on the back of the chair and gently helped it forward. He hoped he was doing the acceptable thing. Miss Willison might resent his tact as much as she did the implied pity. He thought that she sensed his embarrassment and had resolved not to add to it even by smiling her thanks.

As they walked together he was intensely aware of her, noting the details of her physical presence as keenly as if she were a young and desirable woman and he on the verge of love. He watched the sharp bones of her shoulders jerking rhythmically under the thin grey cotton of her dress; the purple tributaries of the veins standing like cords on her almost transparent left hand, so small and fragile in contrast to its fellow. This, too, looked deformed in its compensating strength and hugeness as she gripped the wheel as powerfully as a man. Her legs, clad in wrinkled woollen stockings, were thin as sticks; her sandalled feet, too large surely for such inadequate supports, were clamped to the footrest of her chair as if glued to the metal. Her grey hair flecked with dandruff had been combed upward in a single heavy plait fixed to the crown of her head with a plastic white comb, not particularly clean. The back of her neck looked dingy either with fading suntan or inadequate washing. Looking down he could see the lines on her forehead contracting into deeper furrows with the effort of moving the chair, the eyes blinking spasmodically behind the thin-framed spectacles.

The hen house was a large ramshackle cage bounded by sagging wire and creosoted posts. It had obviously been designed for the disabled. There was a double entry so that Miss Willison could let herself in and fasten the door behind her before opening the second door into the main cage, and the smooth asphalt path, just wide enough for a wheelchair, ran along each side and in front of the nesting boxes. Inside the first door a rough wooden shelf had been nailed waist high to one of the supports. This held a bowl of prepared meal, a plastic can of water and a wooden spoon riveted to a long handle, obviously for the collection of eggs. Miss Willison took them in her lap with some difficulty and reached forward to open the inner door. The hens, who had unaccountably bunched themselves in the far corner of the cage like the nervous virgins, lifted their beady spiteful faces and instantly came squawking and swooping towards her as if determined on a feathered hecatomb. Miss Willison recoiled slightly and began casting handfuls of meal before them with the air of a neophyte propitiating the Furies. The hens began an agitated pecking and gulping. Scraping her hand against the rim of the bowl Miss Willison said:

'I wish I could get more fond of them, or they of me. Both sides might get more out of this activity. I thought that animals developed a fondness for the hand that feeds them but it doesn't seem to apply to hens. I don't see why it should really. We exploit them so thoroughly, first take their eggs and when they're past laying wring their necks and consign them to the pot.'

'I hope you don't have to do the wringing.'

'Oh, no, Albert Philby has that unpleasant job; not that I think he finds it altogether unpleasant. But I eat my share of the boiled fowl.'

Dalgliesh said:

'I feel rather the same. I was brought up in a Norfolk vicarage and my mother always had hens. She was fond of them and they seemed fond of her but my father and I thought they were a nuisance. But we liked the fresh eggs.'

'Do you know, I'm ashamed to tell you that I can't really tell the difference between these eggs and the ones from the supermarket. Wilfred prefers us not to eat any food which hasn't been naturally produced. He abhors factory farming and, of course, he's right. He would really prefer Toynton Grange to be vegetarian, but that would make the catering even more difficult than it is now. Julius did some sums and proved to him that these eggs cost us two and a half times more than the shop ones, not counting of course for my labour. It was rather discouraging.'

Dalgliesh asked:

'Does Julius Court do the book-keeping here then?'

'Oh, no! Not the real accounts, the ones included in the annual report. Wilfred has a professional accountant for those. But Julius is clever with finance and I know Wilfred looks to him for advice. It's usually rather disheartening advice, I'm afraid; we run on a shoe-string really. Father Baddeley's legacy was a real blessing. And Julius has been very kind. Last year the van which we hired to drive us back from the port after our return from Lourdes had an accident. We were all very shaken. The wheelchairs were in the back and two of them got broken. The telephone message that reached here was rather alarmist; it wasn't as bad as Wilfred thought. But Julius drove straight to the hospital where we had been taken for a check-up, hired another van, and took care of everything. And then he bought the specially adapted bus which we have now so that we're completely independent. Dennis and Wilfred between them can drive us all the way to Lourdes. Julius never comes with us, of course, but he's always here to arrange a welcome home party for us when we return after the pilgrimage.'

This disinterested kindness was unlike the impression that, even after a short acquaintanceship, Dalgliesh had formed of Court. Intrigued he asked carefully:

'Forgive me if I sound crude but what does Julius Court get out of it, this interest in Toynton?'

'Do you know, I've sometimes asked myself that. But it seems an ungracious question when it's so apparent what Toynton Grange gets out of him. He comes back from London like a breath of the outside world. He cheers us all. But I know that you want to talk about your friend. Shall we just collect the eggs and then find somewhere quiet?'

Your friend. The quiet phrase, quietly spoken, rebuked him. They filled up the water containers and collected the eggs together, Miss Willison scooping them up in her wooden spoon with the expertise born of long practice. They found only eight. The whole procedure, which an able-bodied person could have completed in ten minutes, had been tedious, time-consuming and not particularly productive. Dalgliesh saw no merit in work for the sake of work, wondered what his companion really thought about a job which had obviously been designed in defiance of economics to give her the illusion of being useful.

They made their way back to the little courtyard behind the house. Only Henry Carwardine was sitting there, a book on his lap but his eyes staring towards the invisible sea. Miss Willison gave him a quick worried glance and seemed about to speak. But she said nothing until they had settled themselves some thirty yards from the silent figure; Dalgliesh at the end of one of the wooden benches and she at his side. Then she said:

'I can never get used to being so close to the sea and yet not being able to look at it. One can hear it so plainly sometimes as we can now. We're almost surrounded by it, we can sometimes smell it and listen to it, but we might be a hundred miles away.'

She spoke wistfully but without resentment. They sat for a moment in silence. Dalgliesh could indeed hear the sea clearly now, the long withdrawing rasp of the shingled tide borne to him on the onshore breeze. To the inmates of Toynton Grange that ceaseless murmur must evoke the tantalizingly close but unobtainable freedom of wide blue horizons, scudding clouds, white wings falling and swooping through the moving air. He could understand how the need to see it might grow into an obsession. He said deliberately:

'Mr Holroyd managed to get himself wheeled to where he could watch the sea.'

It had been important to see her reaction and he realized at once that to her the remark had been worse than tactless. She was deeply shaken and distressed. Her right hand tightened on the arm of the chair. Her face crimsoned in an unlovely wave, and then became very pale. For a moment he almost wished that he hadn't spoken. But the regret was transitory. It was returning despite himself, he thought with sardonic humour, this professional itch to seek out the facts. They were seldom discovered without some cost, however irrelevant or important they finally proved to be, and it wasn't usually he who paid. He heard her speaking so quietly that he had to bend his head to catch the words.

'Victor had a special need to get away by himself. We understood that.'

'But it must have been very difficult to push a light wheelchair like this over the rough turf and up to the edge of the cliff.'

'He had a chair which belonged to him, like this type but larger and stronger. And it wasn't necessary to push him up the steep part of the headland. There's an inland path which leads, I understand, to a narrow sunken lane. You can get to the cliff edge that way. Even so it was hard on Dennis Lerner. It took him half an hour hard pushing each way. But you wanted to talk about Father Baddeley.'

'If it won't distress you too much. It seems that you were the last person to see him alive. He must have died very soon after you left the cottage since he was still wearing his stole when Mrs Hewson found his body next morning. Normally he would surely have taken it off very soon after hearing a confession.'

There was a silence as if she were making up her mind to something. Then she said:

'He did take it off, as usual, immediately after he'd given me absolution. Folded it up and placed it over the arm of his chair.'

This, too, was a sensation which in the long dog days in hospital he had thought never to experience again, the frisson of excitement along the blood at the first realization that something important had been said, that although the quarry wasn't yet in sight nor his spore detectable, yet he was there. He tried to reject this unwelcome surge of tension but it was as elemental and involuntary as the touch of fear. He said:

'But that means that Father Baddeley put on his stole again after you had left. Why should he do that?'

73

Or someone else had put it on for him. But that thought was best unspoken and its implications must wait.

She said quietly:

'I assume that he had another penitent; that is the obvious explanation.'

'He wouldn't wear it to say his evening Office?'

Dalgliesh tried to remember his father's practice in these matters on the very rare occasions when the rector did not say his Office in church; but memory provided only the unhelpful boyhood picture of them both holed up in a hut in the Cairngorms during a blizzard, himself watching, half bored, half fascinated, the patterns of the swirling snow against the windows, his father in leggings, anorak and woollen cap quietly reading from his small black prayer book. He certainly hadn't worn a stole then.

Miss Willson said:

'Oh no! He would wear it only when administering a sacrament. Besides, he had said Evensong. He was just finishing when I arrived and I joined him in a last Collect.'

'But if someone followed you, then you weren't the last person to see him alive. Did you point that out to anyone when you were told of his death?'

'Should I have done? I don't think so. If the person himself – or herself – didn't choose to speak it wasn't for me to invite conjecture. Of course, if anyone but you had realized the significance of the stole it wouldn't have been possible to avoid speculation. But no one did, or if they did, they said nothing. We gossip too much at Toynton, Mr Dalgliesh. It's inevitable perhaps, but it isn't – well – healthy morally. If someone other than I went to confession that night, it's nobody's business but theirs and Father Baddeley's.'

Dalgliesh said:

'But Father Baddeley was still wearing his stole next morning. That suggests that he might have died while his visitor was actually with him. If that happened surely the first reaction, however private the occasion, would be to summon medical help?'

'The visitor might have had no doubts that Father Baddeley had died and was beyond that kind of help. If so there might be a temptation to leave him there sitting peaceably in his chair and slip away. I don't think Father Baddeley would call that a sin, and I don't think you could call it a crime. It might seem callous but would it necessarily be so? It could argue an indifference to form and decorum perhaps, but that isn't quite the same thing, is it?'

It would argue, too, thought Dalgliesh, that the visitor had been a doctor or a nurse. Was that what Miss Willison was hinting? The first reaction of a lay person would surely be to seek help, or at least confirmation that death had actually occurred. Unless, of course, he knew for the best or worst of reasons that Baddeley was dead. But that sinister possibility seemed not to have occurred to Miss Willison. Why, indeed, should it? Father Baddeley was old, he was sick, he was expected to die and he had died. Why should anyone suspect the natural and the inevitable? He said something about determining the time of death and heard her gentle, inexorable reply.

'I expect that in your job the actual time of death is always important and so you get used to concentrating

75

on that fact. But in real life does it matter? What matters is whether one dies in a state of grace.'

Dalgliesh had a momentary and impious picture of his detective sergeant punctiliously attempting to determine and record this essential information about a victim in an official crime report and reflected that Miss Willison's nice distinction between police work and real life was a salutary reminder of how other people saw his job. He looked forward to telling the Commissioner about it. And then he remembered that this wasn't the kind of casual professional gossip which they would exchange in that final slightly formal and inevitably disappointing interview which would mark the end of his police career.

Ruefully, he recognized in Miss Willison the type of unusually honest witness whom he had always found difficult. Paradoxically, this old-fashioned rectitude, this sensitivity of conscience, were more difficult to cope with than the prevarications, evasions, or flamboyant lying which were part of a normal interrogation. He would have liked to have asked her who at Toynton Grange was likely to have visited Father Baddeley for the purpose of confession, but recognized that the question would only prejudice confidence between them and that, in any case, he wouldn't get a reply. But it must have been one of the able-bodied. No one else could have come and gone in secret, unless, of course, he or she had an accomplice. He was inclined to dismiss the accomplice. A wheelchair and its occupant, whether pushed from Toynton Grange or brought by car, must surely have been seen at some stage of the journey.

Hoping that he wasn't sounding too much like a detective in the middle of an interrogation he asked:

'So when you left him he was – what?'

'Just sitting there quietly in the fireside chair. I wouldn't let him get up. Wilfred had driven me down to the cottage in the small van. He said that he would visit his sister at Faith Cottage while I was with Father Baddeley and be outside again in half an hour unless I knocked on the wall first.'

'So you can hear sounds between the two cottages? I ask because it struck me that if Father Baddeley had felt ill after you'd left, he might have knocked on the wall for Mrs Hammitt.'

'She says that he didn't knock, but she might not have heard if she had the television on very loudly. The cottages are very well built, but you can hear sounds through that interior wall, particularly if voices are raised.'

'You mean that you could hear Mr Anstey talking to his sister?'

Miss Willison seemed to regret that she had gone so far, and she said quickly:

'Well, just now and then. I remember that I had to make an effort of will to prevent it disturbing me. I wished that they would keep their voices lower, and then felt ashamed of myself for being so easily distracted. It was good of Wilfred to drive me to the cottage. Normally, of course, Father Baddeley would come up to the house to see me and we would use what is called the quiet room next to the business room just inside the front door. But Father Baddeley had only been discharged from hospital that morning and it wasn't right that he should leave the cottage. I could have postponed my visit until he was stronger but he wrote to me from hospital to say that he hoped I would come and precisely at what time. He knew how much it meant to me.'

'Was he fit to be alone? It seems not.'

'Eric and Dot – that's Sister Moxon – wanted him to come here and be looked after at least for the first night, but he insisted on going straight back home. Then Wilfred suggested that someone should sleep in his spare room in case he wanted help in the night. He wouldn't agree to that either. He really was adamant that he should be left alone that night; he had great authority in his quiet way. Afterwards I think Wilfred blamed himself for not having been more firm. But what could he do? He couldn't bring Father Baddeley here by force.'

But it would have been simpler for all concerned if Father Baddeley had agreed to spend at least his first night out of hospital at Toynton Grange. It was surely untypically inconsiderate of him to resist the suggestion so strenuously. Was he expecting another visitor? Was there someone he wanted to see, urgently and in private, someone to whom, like Miss Willison, he had written to give a precisely timed appointment? If so, whatever the reason for the visit, that person must have come on his own feet. He asked Miss Willison if Wilfred and Father Baddeley had spoken together before she had left the cottage.

'No. After I'd been with Father Baddeley about thirty minutes he knocked on the wall with the poker and, soon afterwards, Wilfred honked on the horn. I manoeuvred my chair to the front door just as Wilfred arrived to open it. Father Baddeley was still in his chair. Wilfred called out goodnight to him, but I don't think he answered. Wilfred seemed in rather a hurry to get home. Millicent came out to help push my chair into the back of the van.'

So neither Wilfred nor his sister had spoken to Michael before driving away that evening, neither had seen him closely. Glancing down at Miss Willison's strong right hand Dalgliesh toyed momentarily with the possibility that Michael was already dead. But that notion, apart from its psychological unlikelihood, was of course, nonsense. She couldn't have relied on Wilfred not coming into the cottage. Come to think of it, it was odd that he hadn't done so. Michael had only returned from hospital that morning. Surely it would have been natural to come in and inquire how he was feeling, to spend at least a few minutes in his company. It was interesting that Wilfred Anstey had made so quick a getaway, that no one had admitted visiting Father Baddeley after seven forty-five.

He asked:

'What lighting was there in the cottage when you were with Father Baddeley?' If the question surprised her, she didn't show it.

'Only the small table lamp on the bureau top behind his chair. I was surprised that he could see to say Evensong, but the prayers, of course, would be familiar to him.'

'And the lamp was off next morning?'

'Oh yes, Maggie said that she found the cottage in darkness.'

Dalgliesh said:

'I find it rather strange that no one looked in later that night to inquire how Father Baddeley was or help him get to bed.'

She said quickly:

'Eric Hewson thought that Millicent was going to look in last thing and she had somehow got the impression that Eric and Helen – Nurse Rainer, you know – had agreed to do so. They all blamed themselves very much the next day. But, as Eric told us, medically it could have made no difference. Father Baddeley died quite peaceably soon after I left.'

They sat in silence for a minute. Dalgliesh wondered whether this was the right time to ask her about the poison pen letter. Remembering her distress over Victor Holroyd, he was reluctant to embarrass her further. But it was important to know. Looking sideways at the thin face with its look of resolute tranquillity, he said:

'I looked in Father Baddeley's writing bureau very soon after I arrived, just in case there was a note or unposted letter for me. I found a rather unpleasant poison pen letter under some old receipts. I wondered whether he had spoken to anyone about it, whether anyone else at Toynton Grange had received one.'

She was even more distressed by the question than he had feared. For a moment she could not speak. He stared straight ahead until he heard her voice. But, when at last she answered, she had herself well in hand.

'I had one, about four days before Victor died. It was . . . it was obscene. I tore it into small fragments and flushed it down the lavatory.'

Dalgliesh said with robust cheerfulness:

'Much the best thing to do with it. But, as a policeman, I'm always sorry when the evidence is destroyed.'

'Evidence?'

'Well, sending poison pen letters can be an offence; more important, it can cause a great deal of unhappiness. It's probably best always to tell the police and let them find out who's responsible.'

'The police! Oh, no! We couldn't do that. It isn't the kind of problem the police can help us with.'

'We aren't as insensitive as people sometimes imagine. It isn't inevitable that the culprit would be prosecuted. But it is important to put a stop to this kind of nuisance, and the police have the best facilities. They can send the letter to the forensic science laboratory for examination by a skilled document examiner.'

'But they would need to have the document. I couldn't have shown the letter to anyone.'

So it had been as bad as that. Dalgliesh asked:

'Would you mind telling me what kind of letter it was? Was it handwritten, typed, on what kind of paper?'

'The letter was typed on Toynton Grange paper, in double spacing, on our old Imperial. Most of us here have learned typewriting. It's one of the ways in which we try to be self-supporting. There was nothing wrong with the punctuation or spelling. There were no other clues that I could see. I don't know who typed it, but I think the writer must have been sexually experienced.'

So, even in the middle of her distress, she had applied her mind to the problem. He said:

'There are only a limited number of people with access to that machine. The problem wouldn't have been too difficult for the police.'

Her gentle voice was stubborn.

'We had the police here over Victor's death. They were very kind, very considerate. But it was terribly upsetting.

81

It was horrible for Wilfred – for all of us. I don't think we could have stood it again. I'm sure that Wilfred couldn't. However tactful the police are, they have to keep on asking questions until they've solved the case, surely? It's no use calling them in and expecting them to put people's sensitivities before their job.'

This was undeniably true and Dalgliesh had little to argue against it. He asked her what, if anything, she had done apart from flushing away the offending letter.

'I told Dorothy Moxon about it. That seemed the most sensible thing to do. I couldn't have spoken about it to a man. Dorothy told me that I shouldn't have destroyed it, that no one could do anything without the evidence. But she agreed that we ought to say nothing at present. Wilfred was particularly worried about money at the time and she didn't want him to have anything else on his mind. She knew how much it would distress him. Besides, I think she had an idea who might have been responsible. If she was right, then we shan't be getting any more letters.'

So Dorothy Moxon had believed, or had pretended to believe, that Victor Holroyd was responsible. And if the writer now had the sense and self-control to stop, it was a comfortable theory which, in the absence of the evidence, no one could disprove.

He asked whether anyone else had received a letter. As far as she knew, no one had. Dorothy Moxon hadn't been consulted by anyone else. The suggestion seemed to distress her. Dalgliesh realized that she had seen the note as a single piece of gratuitous spite directed against herself. The thought that Father Baddeley had also received one, was distressing her almost as much as the original letter. Knowing only too well from his experience the kind of letter it must have been, he said gently:

'I shouldn't worry too much about Father Baddeley's letter. I don't think it would have distressed him. It was very mild really, just a spiteful little note suggesting that he wasn't of much help to Toynton Grange and that the cottage could be more usefully occupied by someone else. He had too much humility and sense to be bothered by that kind of nonsense. I imagine that he only kept the letter because he wanted to consult me in case he wasn't the only victim. Sensible people put these things down the WC. But we can't always be sensible. Anyway, if you do receive another letter, will you promise to show it to me?'

She shook her head gently but didn't speak. But Dalgliesh saw that she was happier. She put out her withered left hand and placed it momentarily over his, giving it a slight press. The sensation was unpleasant, her hand was dry and cold, the bones felt loose in the skin. But the gesture was both humbling and dignified.

It was getting cold and dark in the courtyard; Henry Carwardine had already gone in. It was time for her to move inside. He thought quickly and then said:

'It isn't important, and please don't think that I take my job with me wherever I go. But if during the next few days you can recall how Father Baddeley spent the last week or so before he went into hospital, it would be helpful to me. Don't ask anyone else about this. Just let me know what he did from your own memory of him, the times he came to Toynton Grange, where else he may have spent his hours. I should like to have a picture in my mind of his last ten days.'

83

She said:

'I know that he went into Wareham on the Wednesday before he was taken ill, he said to do some shopping and to see someone on business. I remember that because he explained on the Tuesday that he wouldn't be visiting the Grange as usual next morning.'

So that, thought Dalgliesh, was when he had bought his store of provisions, confident that his letter wouldn't go unanswered. But then he had been right to be confident.

They sat for a minute not speaking. He wondered what she had thought of so odd a request. She hadn't seemed surprised. Perhaps she saw it as perfectly natural, this wish to build up a picture of a friend's last ten days on earth. But suddenly he had a spasm of apprehension and caution. Ought he perhaps to stress that his request was absolutely private? Surely not. He had told her not to ask anyone else. To make more of it would only arouse suspicion. And what danger could there be? What had he to go on? A broken bureau lock, a missing diary, a stole replaced as if for confession. There was no real evidence here. With an effort of will he reasoned away this inexplicable spasm of apprehension, strong as a premonition. It was too disagreeable a reminder of those long nights in hospital when he had struggled in restless half-consciousness against irrational terrors and half-understood fears. And this was equally irrational, equally to be resisted by sense and reason, the ridiculous conviction that a simple, almost casual and not very hopeful request had sounded so clearly a sentence of death.

THREE

A Stranger for the Night

I

Before dinner Anstey suggested that Dennis Lerner should show Dalgliesh round the house. He apologized for not escorting the guest himself, but he had an urgent letter to write. The post was delivered and collected shortly before nine o'clock each morning from the box on the boundary gate. If Adam had letters to send he had only to leave them on the hall table, and Albert Philby would take them to the box with the Toynton Grange letters. Dalgliesh thanked him. There was one urgent letter he needed to write, to Bill Moriarty at the Yard, but he proposed to post that himself later in the day at Wareham. He had certainly no intention of leaving it exposed to the curiosity or speculation of Anstey and his staff.

The suggestion for a tour of the Grange had the force of a command. Helen Rainer was helping the patients wash before dinner and Dot Moxon had disappeared with Anstey, so that he was taken round only by Lerner accompanied by Julius Court. Dalgliesh wished the tour were over, or better still, that it could have been avoided without giving hurt. He recalled with discomfort a visit he had paid as a boy with his father to a geriatric hospital on Christmas Day; the courtesy with which the patients accepted yet one more invasion of their privacy, the public display of pain and deformity, the pathetic eagerness with which the staff demonstrated their small triumphs. Now, as then, he found himself morbidly sensitive to the least trace of revulsion in his voice and thought that he detected what was more offensive, a note of patronizing heartiness. Dennis Lerner didn't appear to notice it and Julius walked jauntily with them looking round with lively curiosity as if the place were new to him. Dalgliesh wondered whether he had come to keep an eye on Lerner or on Dalgliesh himself.

As they passed from room to room, Lerner lost his first diffidence and became confident, almost voluble. There was something endearing about his naïve pride in what Anstey was trying to do. Anstey had certainly laid out his money with some imagination. The Grange itself, with its large, high rooms and cold marble floors, its oppressively panelled dark oak walls and mullioned windows, was a depressingly unsuitable house for disabled patients. Apart from the dining-room and the rear drawing-room, which had become a TV and communal sitting-room, Anstey had used the house mainly to accommodate himself and his staff and had built on to the rear a one-storey stone extension to provide ten individual patients' bedrooms on the ground floor and a clinical room and additional bedrooms on the floor above. This extension had been joined to the old stables which ran at right angles to it, providing a sheltered patio for the patients' wheelchairs. The stables themselves had been adapted to provide garages, a workshop and a patients' activity room for woodwork and modelling. Here, too, the handcream and bath powder which the Home sold to help with finances were made and packed at a workbench behind a transparent plastic screen, erected, presumably, to indicate respect for the principle of scientific cleanliness. Dalgliesh could see, hanging on the screen, the white shadows of protective overalls.

Lerner said:

'Victor Holroyd was a chemistry teacher and he gave us the prescription for the handcream and powder. The cream is really only lanolin, almond oil and glycerine but it's very effective and people seem to like it. We do very well with it. And this corner of the workroom is given over to modelling.'

Dalgliesh had almost exhausted his repertoire of appreciative comments. But now he was genuinely impressed. In the middle of the workbench and mounted on a low wooden base was a clay head of Wilfred Anstey. The neck, elongated and sinewy, rose tortoise-like from the folds of the hood. The head was thrust forward and held a little to the right. It was almost a parody, and yet it had an extraordinary power. How, Dalgliesh wondered, had the sculptor managed to convey the sweetness and the obstinacy of that individual smile, to model compassion and yet reduce it to self-delusion, to show humility garbed in a monk's habit and yet convey an overriding impression of the puissance of evil. The plastic-wrapped lumps and rolls of clay which lay, disorderly, on the workbench only emphasized the force and technical achievement of this one finished work.

Lerner said:

'Henry did the head. Something's gone a little wrong with the mouth, I think. Wilfred doesn't seem to mind it but no one else thinks that it does him justice.'

Julius put his head on one side and pursed his lips in a parody of critical assessment.

'Oh, I wouldn't say that. I wouldn't say that. What do you think of it, Dalgliesh?'

'I think it's remarkable. Did Carwardine do much modelling before he came here?'

It was Dennis Lerner who answered:

'I don't think he did any. He was a senior civil servant before his illness. He modelled this about a couple of months ago without Wilfred giving him a sitting. It's quite good for a first effort, isn't it?'

Julius said:

'The question which interests me is did he do it intentionally, in which case he's a great deal too talented to waste himself here, or were his fingers merely obeying his subconscious? If so, it raises interesting speculations about the origin of creativity and even more interesting ones about Henry's subconscious.'

'I think it just came out like that,' said Dennis Lerner simply. He looked at it with puzzled respect, clearly seeing nothing in it either for wonder or explanation.

Lastly, they went into one of the small rooms at the end of the extension. It had been arranged as an office and was furnished with two wooden ink-stained desks which looked as if they were rejects from a government office. At one Grace Willison was typing names and addresses on a perforated sheet of sticky labels. Dalgliesh saw with some surprise that Carwardine was typing what looked like a private letter at the other desk. Both the typewriters were very old. Henry was using an Imperial; Grace a Remington. Dalgliesh stood over her and glanced at the list of names and addresses. He saw that the newsletter was widely distributed. Apart from local rectories, and other homes for the chronic sick, it went to addresses in London and even to two in the United States and one near Marseilles. Flustered at his interest, Grace jerked her elbow clumsily and the bound list of names and addresses from which she was working fell to the floor. But Dalgliesh had seen enough; the una-ligned small e, the smudged o, the faint almost indeci-pherable capital w. There was no doubt that this was the machine on which Father Baddeley's note had been typed. He picked up the book and handed it to Miss Willison. Without looking at him, she shook her head and said:

'Thank you, but I don't really need to look at it. I can type all the sixty-eight names by heart. I've done it for so long you see. I can imagine what the people are like just from their names and the names they give their houses. But I've always been good at remembering names and addresses. It was very useful to me when I worked for a charity to help discharged prisoners and there were so many lists to type. This is quite short, of course. May I add your name so that you get our quarterly magazine? It's only ten pence. I'm afraid with postage so expensive we have to charge more than we'd like.'

Henry Carwardine looked up and spoke:

'I believe this quarter we have a poem by Jennie Pegram which begins:

Autumn is my favourite time,
I love its glowing tints.

89

It's worth ten pence to you Dalgliesh, I should have thought, to discover how she tackles that little problem of rhyming.'

Grace Willison smiled happily.

'It's only an amateur production I know, but it does keep the League of Friends in touch with what is going on here; our personal friends too, of course.'

Henry said:

'Not mine. They know I've lost the use of my limbs but I've no wish to suggest that I've lost the use of my mind. At best the newsletter reaches the literary level of a parish magazine; at worst, which is three issues out of four, it's embarrassingly puerile.'

Grace Willison flushed and her lip trembled. Dalgliesh said quickly:

'Please add my name. Would it be easier if I paid for a year now?'

'How kind! Perhaps six months would be safer. If Wilfred does decide to transfer the Grange to the Ridgewell Trust they may have different plans for the newsletter. I'm afraid the future is very uncertain for all of us at present. Would you write your address here? Queenhythe. That's by the river, isn't it? How pleasant for you. You won't be wanting any of the handcream or bath powder, I suppose, although we do send the powder to one or two gentlemen customers. But this is really Dennis's department. He sees to the distribution and does most of the packing himself. I'm afraid our hands are too shaky to be much use. But I'm sure he could spare you some of the bath powder.'

Dalgliesh was saved from the need to reply to this wistful inquiry by the booming of the gong. Julius said:

'The warning gong. One more boom and dinner will be on the table. I shall return home and see what my indispensable Mrs Reynolds has left for me. By the way, have you warned the Commander that dinner at Toynton Grange is eaten Trappist fashion in silence? We don't want him to break the rule with inconvenient questions about Michael's will or what possible reason a patient in this abode of love could have for hurling himself over the cliff.'

He disappeared at some speed as if afraid that any tendency to linger would expose him to the risk of an invitation to dine.

Grace Willison was obviously relieved to see him go but she smiled bravely at Dalgliesh.

'We do have a rule that no one talks during the evening meal. I hope that it won't inconvenience you. We take it in turns to read from any work we choose. Tonight it's Wilfred's turn so we shall have one of Donne's sermons. They're very fine of course – Father Baddeley enjoyed them, I know – but I do find them rather difficult. And I don't really think that they go well with boiled mutton.'

II

Henry Carwardine wheeled his chair to the lift, drew back the steel grille with difficulty, clanged the gate closed and pressed the button to the floor above. He had insisted on having a room in the main building, firmly rejecting the unsubstantial, meanly proportioned cells in the annexe, and Wilfred, despite what Henry thought were obsessive, almost paranoid fears that he might be trapped in a fire, had reluctantly agreed. Henry had confirmed his committal to Toynton Grange by moving one or two chosen pieces of furniture from his Westminster flat and virtually all his books. The room was large, high ceilinged and pleasantly proportioned, its two windows giving a wide view south-west across the headland. Next door was a lavatory and shower which he shared only with any patient being nursed in the sickroom. He knew, without the least qualm of guilt, that he had the most comfortable quarters in the house. Increasingly he was retreating into this tidy and private world, closing the heavy carved door against involvement, bribing Philby to bring up occasional meals on a tray, to buy for him in Dorchester special cheeses, wines, pâté and fruit to augment the institutional meals which the staff of the Grange took it in turns to cook. Wilfred had apparently thought it prudent not to comment on this minor insubordination, this trespass against the law of togetherness.

He wondered what had provoked him to that spatter of malice against harmless, pathetic Grace Willison. It wasn't the first time since Holroyd's death that he had caught himself speaking with Holroyd's voice. The phenomenon interested him. It set him thinking again about that other life, the other one he had so prematurely and resolutely renounced. He had noticed it when chairing committees, how the members played their individual roles, almost as if these had been allocated in advance. The hawk; the dove; the compromiser; the magisterial elder statesman; the unpredictable maverick. How swiftly, if one were absent, a colleague modified his views, subtly adapted even his voice and manner to fill the gap. And so, apparently, he had assumed the mantle of Holroyd. The thought was ironic and not unsatisfying. Why not? Who else at Toynton Grange better fitted that rebarbative, non-conforming role?

He had been one of the youngest Under Secretaries of State ever appointed. He was confidently spoken of as the future head of a Department. That was how he saw himself. And then the disease, touching nerves and muscles at first with tentative fingers, had struck at the roots of confidence, at all the carefully laid plans. Dictating sessions with his personal assistant had become mutual embarrassments to be dreaded and deferred. Every telephone conversation was an ordeal; that first insistent, anxiety-pitched ring was enough to set his hand trembling. Meetings which he had always enjoyed and chaired with a quiet if abrasive competence had become unpredictable contests between mind and unruly body. He had become unsure where he had been most confident.

He wasn't alone in misfortune. He had seen others, some of them in his own Department, being helped from their grotesquely graceless invalid cars into their wheelchairs, accepting a lower grade and easier work, moving to a division which could afford to carry a passenger. The Department would have balanced expediency and the public interest with proper consideration and compassion. They would have kept him on long after his usefulness justified it. He could have died, as he had watched others die, in official harness, harness lightened and adjusted to his frail shoulders, but nevertheless harness. He accepted that there was a kind of courage in that. But it wasn't his kind.

It had been a joint meeting with another Department, chaired by himself, that had finally decided him. He still couldn't think of the shambles without shame and horror. He saw himself again, feet impotently padding, his stick beating a tattoo on the floor as he strove to take one step towards his chair, the mucus spluttering out with his welcoming words to shower over his neighbour's papers. The ring of eyes around the table, animals' eyes, watchful, predatory, embarrassed, not daring to meet his. Except for one boy, a young good-looking Principal from the Treasury. He had looked fixedly at the Chairman, not with pity but with an almost clinical interest, noting for future reference one more manifestation of human behaviour under stress. The words had come out at last, of course. Somehow he had got through the meeting. But for him, it had been the end.

He had heard of Toynton Grange as one did hear of such places, through a colleague whose wife received the Home's quarterly newsletter and contributed to the funds. It had seemed to offer an answer. He was a bachelor without family. He couldn't hope indefinitely to look after himself, nor on a disability pension could he buy a permanent nurse. And he had to get out of London. If he couldn't succeed, then he would opt out completely, retire to oblivion, away from the embarrassed pity of colleagues, from noise and foul air, from the hazards and inconveniences of a world aggressively organized for the healthy and able bodied. He would write the book on decision-making in Government planned for his retirement, catch up on his Greek, re-read the whole of Hardy. If he couldn't cultivate his own garden, at least he could avert fastidious eyes from the lack of cultivation in everyone else's.

And for the first six months it had seemed to work. There were disadvantages which, strangely, he hadn't expected or considered; the unenterprising, predictable meals; the pressures of discordant personalities; the delay in getting books and wine delivered; the lack of good talk; the self-absorption of the sick, their preoccupation with symptoms and bodily functions; the awful childishness and spurious joviality of institutional life. But it had been just supportable and he had been reluctant to admit failure since all alternatives seemed worse. And then Peter had arrived.

He had come to Toynton Grange just over a year ago. He was a polio victim, the seventeen-year-old only child of a haulage contractor's widow from the industrial Midlands who had made three preparatory visits of officious and ill-informed inspection before calculating whether she could afford to accept the vacancy. Henry suspected that, panicked by the loneliness and debased status of the early months of widowhood, she was already looking for a second husband and was beginning to realize that a seventeen-year-old chair-bound son was an obstacle to be carefully weighed by likely candidates against her late husband's money, her own ageing and desperate sexuality. Listening to her spate of obstetric and marital intimacies, Henry had realized once again that the disabled were treated as a different breed. They posed no threat, sexual or otherwise, offered no competition. As companions they had the advantage of animals; literally anything could be spoken in front of them without embarrassment.

So Dolores Bonnington had expressed herself satisfied and Peter had arrived. The boy had made little impression on him at first. It was only gradually that he had come to appreciate his qualities of mind. Peter had been nursed at home with the help of district nurses and had been driven, when his health permitted, to the local comprehensive school. There he had been unlucky. No one, least of all his mother, had discovered his intelligence. Henry Carwardine doubted whether she was capable of recognizing it. He was less ready to acquit the school. Even with the problem of understaffing and over-large classes, the inevitable logistic difficulties of a huge city comprehensive, someone on the staff of that over-equipped and ill-disciplined menagerie, he thought with anger, ought to have been able to recognize a scholar. It was Henry who conceived the idea that they might provide for Peter the education he had lost; that he might in time enter a university and become self-supporting.

To Henry's surprise, preparing Peter for his 'O' levels had provided the common concern, the sense of unity and community at Toynton Grange which none of Wilfred's experiments had achieved. Even Victor Holroyd helped.

'It seems that the boy isn't a fool. He's almost totally uneducated, of course. The staff, poor sods, were probably too busy teaching race relations, sexual technique and other contemporary additions to the syllabus and preventing the barbarians from pulling the school down around their ears to have time for someone with a mind.'

'He ought to have maths and one science, Victor, at least at "O" level. If you could help . . .'

'Without a lab?'

96

'There's the clinical room, you could fix something up there. He wouldn't be taking a science as a main subject at "A" level?'

'Of course not. I realize my disciplines are included merely to provide an illusion of academic balance. But the boy ought to be taught to think scientifically. I know the suppliers of course. I could probably fix something up.'

'I shall pay, of course.'

'Certainly. I could afford it myself but I'm a great believer in people paying for their own gratifications.'

'And Jennie and Ursula might be interested.'

Henry had been amazed to find himself making the suggestion. Affection – he had not yet come to use the word love – had made him kind.

'God forbid! I'm not setting up a kindergarten. But I'll take on the boy for maths and general science.'

Holroyd had given three sessions a week each of a carefully measured hour. But there had been no doubt about the quality of his teaching.

Father Baddeley had been pressed into service to teach Latin. Henry himself took English literature and history and undertook the general direction of the course. He discovered that Grace Willison spoke French better than anyone else at Toynton Grange and after some initial reluctance, she agreed to take French conversation twice a week. Wilfred had watched the preparations indulgently, taking no active part but raising no objections. Everyone was suddenly busy and happy.

Peter himself was accepting rather than dedicated. But he proved incredibly hard-working, gently amused perhaps by their common enthusiasm but capable of the sustained concentration which is the mark of a scholar. They found it almost impossible to overwork him. He was grateful, biddable, but detached. Sometimes Henry, looking at the calm girlish face, had the frightening feeling that the teachers were all seventeen-year-old children and the boy alone burdened with the sad cynicism of maturity.

Henry knew that he would never forget that moment when, at last, and joyfully, he had acknowledged love. It had been a warm day in early spring; was it really only six months ago? They had been sitting together where he sat now in the early afternoon sunshine, books on their laps ready to begin the two-thirty history lesson. Peter had been wearing a short-sleeved shirt, and he had rolled up his own sleeves to feel the first warmth of the sun pricking the hairs of his forearm. They had been sitting in silence as he was sitting now. And then, without turning to look at him, Peter had lain the length of his soft inner forearm against ·Henry's and deliberately, as if every movement were part of a ritual, an affirmation, had twined their fingers together so that their palms too were joined flesh against flesh. Henry's nerves and blood remembered that moment and would do until he died. The shock of ecstasy, the sudden realization of joy, a spring of sheer unalloyed happiness which for all its surging excitement was yet paradoxically rooted in fulfilment and peace. It seemed in that moment as if everything which had happened in life, his job, his illness, coming to Toynton Grange, had led inevitably to this place, this love. Everything – success, failure, pain, frustration – had led to it and was justified by it. Never had he been so aware of another's body:

the beat of the pulse in the thin wrist; the labyrinth of blue veins lying against his, blood flowing in concert with his blood; the delicate unbelievably soft flesh of the forearm; the bones of the childish fingers confidently resting between his own. Besides the intimacy of this first touch all previous adventures of the flesh had been counterfeit. And so they had sat silently, for unmeasured unfathomable time, before turning to look, at first gravely and then smilingly, into each other's eyes.

He wondered now how he could have so underestimated Wilfred. Happily secure in the confidence of love acknowledged and returned, he had treated Wilfred's innuendoes and expostulations – when they pierced his consciousness – with pitying contempt, seeing them as no more real or threatening than the bleatings of a timid, ineffectual schoolmaster obsessively warning his boys against unnatural vice.

'It's good of you to give so much time to Peter, but we ought to remember that we are one family at Toynton Grange. Other people would like a share of your interest. It isn't perhaps kind or wise to show too marked a preference for one person. I think that Ursula and Jennie and even poor Georgie sometimes feel neglected.'

Henry had hardly heard; had certainly not bothered to reply.

'Henry, Dot tells me that you've taken to locking your door when giving Peter his lessons. I would prefer that you didn't. It is one of our rules that doors are never locked. If either of you needed medical help suddenly, it could be very dangerous.'

Henry had continued to lock his door keeping the key always with him. He and Peter might have been the only two people at Toynton Grange. Lying in bed at night he began to plan and to dream, at first tentatively and then with the euphoria of hope. He had given up too early and too easily. There was still some future before him. The boy's mother hardly visited him, seldom wrote. Why shouldn't the two of them leave Toynton Grange and live together? He had his pension and some capital. He could buy a small house, at Oxford or Cambridge perhaps, and get it adapted for their two wheelchairs. When Peter was at university he would need a home. He made calculations, wrote to his bank manager, schemed how it might be organized so that the plan in its ultimate reasonableness and beauty could be presented to Peter. He knew that there were dangers. He would get worse; with luck Peter might even slightly improve. He must never let himself be a burden to the boy. Father Baddeley had only once spoken to him directly of Peter. He had brought over to Toynton Grange a book from which Henry had planned to set a passage of précis. On leaving he had said gently, as always not baulking the truth:

'Your disease is progressive, Peter's isn't. One day he's going to have to manage without you. Remember that, my son.' Well, he would remember.

In early August Mrs Bonnington arranged for Peter to spend a fortnight with her at home. She called it taking him for a holiday. Henry had said:

'Don't write. I never expect anything good from a letter. I shall see you again in two weeks.'

But Peter hadn't come back. The evening before he was due to return Wilfred had announced the news at dinner, eyes carefully avoiding Henry's.

'You'll be glad for Peter's sake to hear that Mrs Bonnington has found a place for him nearer his home and that he won't be returning to us. She hopes to marry again fairly soon and she and her husband want to visit Peter more frequently and have him home for occasional weekends. The new home will make arrangements for Peter's education to continue. You have all worked so hard with him. I know you'll be glad to hear that it won't be wasted.'

It had been very cleverly planned; he had to give Wilfred that credit. There must have been discreet telephone calls and letters to the mother, negotiations with the new home. Peter must have been on the waiting list for weeks, possibly months. Henry could imagine the phrases.

'Unhealthy interests; unnatural affection; driving the boy too hard; mental and psychological pressure.'

Hardly anyone at Toynton Grange had spoken to him about the transfer. They had avoided the contamination of his misery. Grace Willison had said, shrinking from his angry eyes:

'We shall all miss him, but his own mother . . . It's natural that she should want him close to her.'

'Of course. By all means let us defer to the sacred rights of motherhood.'

Within a week they had apparently forgotten Peter and returned to their old pursuits as easily as children discarding new and unwanted Christmas toys. Holroyd had disconnected his apparatus and packed it away.

'Let it be a lesson to you, my dear Henry. Put not your trust in pretty boys. We can hardly expect that he was dragged to the new home by force.'

'He may have been.'

'Oh, come now! The boy is practically of age. He has the use of brain and speech. He can hold a pen. We have to face it that our company here was less fascinating than we had deluded ourselves. Peter is amenable. He made no objections when he was dumped here and I've no doubt he made none when he was dragged away.'

Henry, on impulse, had grasped Father Baddeley's arm as he passed and asked him:

'Did you collude in this triumph for morality and mother-love?'

Father Baddeley had briefly shaken his head, a gesture so slight that it was hardly discernible. He had seemed about to speak and then, with one pressure on Henry's shoulder, had moved on, for once at a loss, offering no comfort. But Henry had felt a spurt of anger and resentment against Michael as he hadn't against anyone else at Toynton Grange. Michael, who had the use of his legs and voice, who wasn't reduced by anger into a jibbering, slobbering buffoon. Michael, who could surely have prevented this monstrous thing if he hadn't been inhibited by timidity, by his fear and disgust of the flesh. Michael, who had no place at Toynton Grange if not to affirm love.

There had been no letter. Henry had been reduced to bribing Philby to collect the post. His paranoia had reached the stage when he believed that Wilfred might be intercepting letters. He didn't write himself. Whether or not to do so was a preoccupation which took most of his waking hours. But, less than six weeks later, Mrs Bonnington had written to Wilfred to say that Peter was dead of pneumonia. It could, Henry knew, have happened anywhere at any time. It didn't necessarily mean that the medical and nursing care at the new home had been less than at Toynton Grange. Peter had always been peculiarly at risk. But in his heart Henry knew that he could have kept Peter safe. In scheming his transfer from Toynton Grange Wilfred had killed him.

And Peter's murderer went about his business, smiled his indulgent lop-sided smile, ceremoniously drew the folds of his cloak around him to preserve him from the contamination of human emotion, surveyed complacently the flawed objects of his beneficence. Was it his imagination, Henry wondered, that Wilfred had become afraid of him? Now they seldom spoke. Naturally solitary, Henry had become morose since Peter's death. Except for meal times he spent most of his days in his room, looking out over the desolate headland, neither reading nor working, possessed by a profound ennui. He knew that he hated rather than felt hatred. Love, joy, anger, grief even, were emotions too powerful for his diminished personality. He could entertain only their pale shadows. But hatred was like a latent fever dormant in the blood; sometimes it could flare into terrifying delirium. It was during one such mood that Holroyd had whispered to him, had wheeled his chair across the patio and manoeuvred it close to Henry. Holroyd's mouth, pink and precise as a girl's, a neat, suppurating wound in the heavy blue jaw, puckered to discharge its venom. Holroyd's breath sour in his nostrils.

'I have learnt something of interest about our dear Wilfred. I shall share it with you in time but you must forgive me if I savour it alone for a little longer. There will be a right moment for disclosure. One strives always for the maximum dramatic effect.' Hatred and boredom had reduced them to secrets together, planning their petty stratagems of vengeance and betrayal.

He looked out of the tall, curved window westward over the rising headland. The darkness was falling. Somewhere out there the restless tide was scouring the rocks, rocks washed clean for ever of Holroyd's blood. Not even a twist of torn cloth remained for the barnacles to fasten on. Holroyd's dead hands like floating weeds moving sluggishly in the tide, sand-filled eyes turned upwards to the swooping gulls. What was that poem of Walt Whitman which Holroyd had read at dinner on the night before he died:

> Approach strong deliveress,
> When it is so, when thou hast taken them I
>   joyously sing the dead,
> Lost in the loving floating ocean of thee,
> Laved in the flood of thy bliss O death.
>
> The night in silence under many a star,
> The ocean shore and the husky whispering wave
>   whose voices I know,
> And the soul turning to thee O vast and well-
>   veiled death,
> And the body gratefully nestling close to thee.

Why that poem, in its sentimental resignation, at once so alien to Holroyd's embattled spirit, and yet so prophetically apposite? Was he telling them, even subconsciously, that he knew what must happen, that he embraced and welcomed it? Peter and Holroyd.

Holroyd and Baddeley. And now this policeman friend of Baddeley's had arrived out of his past. Why, and for what? He might learn something when they drank together after dinner with Julius. And so, of course, might Dalgliesh. 'There is no art to find the mind's construction in the face.' But Duncan was wrong. There was a great deal of art and one in which a Commander of the Metropolitan Police would be better practised than most. Well, if that was what he had come for, he could make a beginning after dinner. Tonight he, Henry, would dine in his room. Philby when summoned would bring up his tray and plonk it unceremoniously and grudgingly in front of him. It wasn't possible to buy civility, from Philby but it was possible, he thought with grim exultation, to buy almost anything else.

III

'My body is my prison; and I would be so obedient to the Law, as not to break prison; I would not hasten my death by starving or macerating this body. But if this prison be burnt down by continual fevers, or blown down with continual vapours, would any man be so in love with the ground upon which that prison stood, as to desire rather to stay there than to go home?'

It wasn't so much, thought Dalgliesh, that the Donne didn't go with the stewed mutton, as that the mutton didn't go with the home-brewed wine. Neither was in itself unpalatable. The mutton, cooked with onions, potatoes and carrots, and flavoured with herbs, was unexpectedly good if a little greasy. The elderberry wine was a nostalgic reminder of duty visits paid with his father to house-bound and hospitable parishioners. Together they tasted lethal. He reached for the water carafe.

Opposite him sat Millicent Hammitt, her square slab of a face softened by the candlelight, her absence during the afternoon explained by the pungent scent of lacquer which was wafted to him from the stiff, corrugated waves of greying hair. Everyone was present except the Hewsons, dining presumably in their own cottage, and Henry Carwardine. At the far end of the table, Albert Philby sat a little apart, a monkish Caliban in a brown habit, half crouching over his food. He ate noisily, tearing his bread into crusts and wiping them vigorously around his plate. All the patients were being helped to eat. Dalgliesh, despising his squeamishness, tried to shut his ears to the muted slobbering, the staccato rattle of spoon against plate, the sudden retching, unobtrusively controlled.

'If thou didst depart from that Table in peace, thou canst depart from this world in peace. And the peace of that Table is to come to it in peace desiderii, with a contented minde . . .'

Wilfred stood at a reading desk at the head of the table, flanked by two candles in metal holders. Jeoffrey, distended with food, lay ceremoniously curved at his feet. Wilfred had a good voice and knew how to use it. An actor manqué? Or an actor who had found his stage and played on, happily oblivious of the dwindling audience, of the creeping paralysis of his dream? A neurotic driven by obsession? Or a man at peace with himself, secure at the still centre of his being?

Suddenly the four table candles flared and hissed. Dalgliesh's ears caught the faint squeak of wheels, the gentle thud of metal against wood. The door was slowly swinging open. Wilfred's voice faltered, and then broke off. A spoon rasped violently against a plate. Out of the shadows came a wheelchair, its occupant, head bent, swaddled in a thick plaid cloak. Miss Willison gave a sad moan and scratched the sign of the cross on her grey dress. There was a gasp from Ursula Hollis. No one spoke. Suddenly Jennie Pegram screamed, thin and insistent as a tin whistle. The sound was so unreal that Dot Moxon jerked her head round as if uncertain where the sound was coming from. The scream subsided into a giggle. The girl clamped her hand against her mouth. Then she said:

'I thought it was Victor! That's Victor's cloak.'

No one else moved or spoke. Glancing along the table, Dalgliesh let his eyes rest speculatively on Dennis Lerner. His face was a mask of terror which slowly disintegrated into relief, the features seeming to droop and crumble, amorphous as a smudged painting. Carwardine wheeled his chair to the table. He had some difficulty in getting out his words. A globule of mucus gleamed like a yellow jewel in the candlelight and dribbled from his chin. At last he said in his high distorted voice:

'I thought I might join you for coffee. It seemed discourteous to absent myself on our guest's first night.'

Dot Moxon's voice was sharp:

'Did you have to wear that cloak?'

He turned to her:

'It was hanging in the business room and I felt cold. And we hold so much in common. Need we exclude the dead?'

Wilfred said:

'Shall we remember the Rule?'

They turned their faces to him like obedient children. He waited until they had again begun to eat. The hands which gripped the sides of the reading desk were steady, the beautiful voice perfectly controlled.

'That so riding at Anchor, and in that calme, whether God enlarge thy voyage, by enlarging thy life, or put thee into the harbour by the breath, by the breathlesnesse of Death, either way, East or West, thou maist depart in peace . . .'

IV

It was after eight-thirty before Dalgliesh set out to wheel Henry Carwardine to Julius Court's cottage. The task wasn't easy for a man in the first stages of convalescence. Carwardine, despite his leanness, was surprisingly heavy and the stony path wound uphill. Dalgliesh hadn't liked to suggest using his car since to be hoisted through the narrow door might be more painful and humiliating for his companion than the customary wheelchair. Anstey had been passing through the hall as they left. He had held open the door and helped guide the wheelchair down the ramp, but had made no attempt to assist, nor did he offer the use of the patients' bus. Dalgliesh wondered whether it was his imagination that detected a note of disapproval of the enterprise in Anstey's final goodnight.

Neither man spoke for the first part of the journey. Carwardine rested a heavy torch between his knees and tried to steady its beam on the path. The circle of light, reeling and spinning before them with every lurch of the chair, illumined with dazzling clarity a secret night world of greenness, movement and scurrying life. Dalgliesh, a little light-headed with tiredness, felt disassociated from his physical surroundings. The two thick rubber handgrips, slippery to the touch, were loose and twisted irritatingly beneath his hands, seeming to have no relation to the rest of the chair. The path ahead was real only because its stones and crevices jarred the wheels. The night was still and very warm for autumn, the air heavy with the smell of grass and the memory of summer flowers. Low clouds had obscured the stars and they moved forwards in almost total darkness towards the strengthening murmur of the sea and the four oblongs of light which marked Toynton Cottage. When they were close enough for the largest oblong to reveal itself as the rear door of the cottage, Dalgliesh said on impulse:

'I found a rather disagreeable poison pen letter in Father Baddeley's bureau. Obviously someone at Toynton Grange didn't like him. I wondered whether this was personal spite or whether anyone else had received one.'

Carwardine bent his head upwards. Dalgliesh saw his face intriguingly foreshortened, his sharp nose a spur of bone, the jaw hanging loose as a marionette's below the shapeless void of mouth. He said:

'I had one about ten months ago, placed inside my library book, I haven't had one since, and I don't know of anyone else who has. It's not the kind of thing people talk about, but I think the news would have got around if the trouble had been endemic. Mine was, I suppose, the usual muck. It suggested what methods of somewhat acrobatic sexual self-gratification might be open to me supposing I still had the physical agility to perform them. It took the desire to do so for granted.'

'It was obscene, then, rather than merely offensive?'

'Obscene in the sense of calculated to disgust rather than to deprave or corrupt, yes.'

'Have you any idea who was responsible?'

'It was typed on Toynton Grange paper and on an old Remington machine used chiefly by Grace Willison to send out the quarterly newsletter. She seemed the most likely candidate. It wasn't Ursula Hollis; she didn't arrive until two months later. And aren't these things usually sent by respectable middle-aged spinsters?'

'In this case I doubt it.'

'Oh, well – I defer to your greater experience of obscenity.'

'Did you tell anyone?'

'Only Julius. He counselled against telling anyone else and suggested I tear the note up and flush it down the WC. As that advice coincided with my own inclination, I took it. As I said, I haven't had another. I imagine that the sport loses its thrill if the victim shows absolutely no sign of concern.'

'Could it have been Holroyd?'

'It didn't really seem his style. Victor was offensive but not, I should have thought, in that particular way. His weapon was the voice, not the pen. Personally I didn't mind him as much as some of the others did. He hit out rather like an unhappy child. There was more personal bitterness than active malice. Admittedly, he added a somewhat childish codicil to his will the week before he died; Philby and Julius's housekeeper, Mrs Reynolds, witnessed it. But that was probably because he'd made up his mind to die and wanted to relieve us all of any obligation to remember him with kindness.'

'So you think he killed himself?'

'Of course. And so does everyone else. How else could it have happened? It seems the most likely hypothesis. It was either suicide or murder.'

It was the first time anyone at Toynton Grange had used that portentous word. Spoken in Carwardine's pedantic, rather high voice it sounded as incongruous as blasphemy on the lips of a nun.

Dalgliesh said:

'Or the chair brakes could have been defective.'

'Given the circumstances, I count that as murder.'

There was silence for a moment. The chair lurched over a small boulder and the torch light swung upwards in a wide arc, a miniature and frail searchlight. Carwardine steadied it and then said:

'Philby oiled and checked the chair brakes at eight-fifty on the night before Holroyd died. I was in the workroom messing about with my modelling clay at the time. I saw him. He left the workroom shortly afterwards and I stayed on until about ten o'clock.'

'Did you tell the police that?'

'Since they asked me, yes. They inquired with heavy tact where exactly I had spent the evening and whether I had touched Holroyd's chair after Philby had left. Since I would hardly have admitted the fact if I had, the question was naïve. They questioned Philby, although not in my presence, and I've no doubt that he confirmed my story. I have an ambivalent attitude towards the police; I confine myself strictly to answering their questions, but on the premise that they are, in general, entitled to the truth.'

They had arrived. Light streamed from the rear door of the cottage and Julius Court, a dark silhouette, emerged to meet them. He took the wheelchair from Dalgliesh and pushed it along the short stone passage leading into the sitting-room. On the way Dalgliesh just had time to glimpse through an open door the pine-covered walls, red-tiled floor and gleaming chrome of Julius's kitchen, a kitchen too like his own where a woman, overpaid and underworked to assuage her employer's guilt for hiring her at all, cooked the occasional meal to gratify one person's over-fastidious taste.

The sitting-room occupied the whole of the front ground floor of what had obviously been two cottages. A fire of driftwood crackled on the open hearth but both the long windows were open to the night. The stone walls vibrated with the thudding of the sea. It was disconcerting to feel so close to the cliff edge and yet not know precisely how close. As if reading his thoughts, Julius said:

'We're just six yards from the forty-foot drop to the rocks. There's a stone patio and low wall outside; we might sit there later if it's warm enough. What will you drink, spirits or wine? I know Henry's preference is for claret.'

Dalgliesh didn't repent of his choice when he saw the labels on the three bottles which were standing, two already uncorked, on the low table near the hearth. He was surprised that wine of such quality should be produced for two casual guests. While Julius busied himself with the glasses, Dalgliesh wandered about the room. It contained enviable objects, if one were in a mood to prize personal possessions. His eyes lit on a splendid Sunderland lustreware jug commemorating Trafalgar, three early Staffordshire figures on the stone mantelpiece, a couple of agreeable seascapes on the longest wall. Above the door leading to the cliff edge was a ship's figure-head finely and ornately carved in oak; two cherubs supported a galleon topped with a shield and swathed with heavy seaman's knots. Seeing his interest, Julius called out:

'It was made about 1660 by Grinling Gibbons, reputedly for Jacob Court, a smuggler in these parts. As far as I can discover, he was absolutely no ancestor of mine, worse luck. It's probably the oldest merchant ship figure-head known to exist. Greenwich think they have one earlier, but I'd give mine the benefit of a couple of years.'

Set on a pedestal at the far end of the room and faintly gleaming as if luminous was the marble bust of a winged child holding in his chubby hand a posy of rosebuds and lilies of the valley. The marble was the colour of pale coffee except over the lids of the closed eyes, which were tinged with a faint pink. The unveined hands held the flowers with the upright, unselfconscious grip of a child; the boy's lips were slightly parted in a half-smile, tranquil and secretive. Dalgliesh stretched out a finger and gently stroked the cheek; he could imagine it warm to his touch. Julius came over to him carrying two glasses.

'You like my marble? It's a memorial piece, of course, seventeenth or very early eighteenth century and derived from Bernini. Henry, I suspect, would like it better if it were Bernini.'

Henry called out:

'I wouldn't like it better. I did say I'd be prepared to pay more for it.'

Dalgliesh and Court moved back to the fireplace and settled down for what was obviously intended to be a night of serious drinking. Dalgliesh found his eyes straying around the room. There was no bravura, no conscious striving after originality or effect. And yet, trouble had been taken; every object was in the right place. They had, he thought, been bought because Julius liked them; they weren't part of a careful scheme of capital appreciation, nor acquired out of an obsessive need to add to his collection. Yet Dalgliesh doubted whether any had been casually discovered or cheaply bought. The furniture, too, betrayed wealth. The leather sofa and the two winged and back-buttoned leather chairs were perhaps too opulent for the proportions and basic simplicity of the room, but Julius had obviously chosen them for comfort. Dalgliesh reproached himself for the streak of puritanism which compared the room unfavourably with the snug, unindulgent shabbiness of Father Baddeley's sitting-room.

Carwardine, sitting in his wheelchair and staring into the fire above the rim of his glass, asked suddenly:

'Did Baddeley warn you about the more bizarre manifestations of Wilfred's philanthropy, or was your visit here unpremeditated?'

It was a question Dalgliesh had been expecting. He sensed that both men were more than casually interested in his reply.

'Father Baddeley wrote to say that he would be glad to see me. I decided to come on impulse. I've had a spell in hospital and it seemed a good idea to spend a few days of my convalescence with him.'

Carwardine said:

'I can think of more suitable places than Hope Cottage for convalescence, if the inside is anything like the exterior. Had you known Baddeley long?'

'Since boyhood; he was my father's curate. But we last met, and only briefly, when I was at university.'

'And having been content to know nothing of each other for a decade or so, you're naturally distressed to find him so inconveniently dead.'

Unprovoked, Dalgliesh replied equably:

'More than I would have expected. We seldom wrote except to exchange cards at Christmas but he was a man more often in my thoughts, I suppose, than some people I saw almost daily. I don't know why I never bothered to get in touch. One makes the excuse of busyness. But, from what I remember of him, I can't quite see how he fitted in here.'

Julius laughed:

'He didn't. He was recruited when Wilfred was going through a more orthodox phase, I suppose to give Toynton Grange a certain religious respectability. But in recent months I sensed a coolness between them, didn't you, Henry? Father Baddeley was probably no longer sure whether Wilfred wanted a priest or a guru. Wilfred picks up any scraps of philosophy, metaphysics and orthodox religion which take his fancy to make his Technicolor dreamcoat. As a result, as you'll probably discover if you stay long enough, this place suffers from the lack of a coherent ethos. There's nothing more fatal to success. Take my London club, dedicated simply to the enjoyment of good food and wine and the exclusion of bores and pederasts. It's unstated of course, but we all know where we stand. The aims are simple and comprehensible and, therefore, realizable. Here the poor dears don't know whether they're in a nursing home, a commune, a hotel, a monastery or a particularly dotty lunatic asylum. They even have meditation sessions from time to time. I'm afraid Wilfred may be getting a touch of the Zens.'

Carwardine broke in:

'He's muddled, but which of us isn't? Basically he's kind and well meaning, and at least he's spent his own personal fortune at Toynton Grange. In this age of noisy and self-indulgent commitment when the first principle of private or public protest is that it mustn't relate to anything for which the protestor can be held in the least responsible or involve him in the slightest personal sacrifice that, at least, is in his favour.'

'You like him?' asked Dalgliesh.

Henry Carwardine answered with surprising roughness.

'As he's saved me from the ultimate fate of incarceration in a long-stay hospital and gives me a private room at a price I can afford, I'm naturally bound to find him delightful.'

There was a short, embarrassed silence. Sensing it, Carwardine added:

'The food is the worst thing about Toynton, but that can be remedied, even if I do occasionally feel like a greedy schoolboy feasting alone in my room. And listening to my fellow inmates read their favourite bleeding chunks from popular theology and the less enterprising anthologies of English verse is a small price to pay for silence at dinner.'

Dalgliesh said:

'Staffing must be a difficulty. According to Mrs Hewson, Anstey chiefly relies on an ex-convict and an otherwise unemployable matron.'

Julius Court reached out for the claret and refilled the three glasses. He said:

'Dear Maggie, discreet as always. It's true that Philby, the handyman, has some kind of record. He's not exactly an advertisement for the place, but someone has to sluice the foul linen, slaughter the chickens, clean the lavatories and do the other jobs which Wilfred's sensitive soul cringes at. Besides, he's passionately devoted to Dot Moxon, and I've no doubt that helps to keep her happy. Since Maggie has let slip so much, you may as well know the truth about Dot. Perhaps you remember something of the case – she was that notorious staff nurse at Netting-field Geriatric Hospital. Four years ago she struck a patient. It was only a light blow but the old woman fell, knocking her head against a bedside locker and nearly died. Reading between the lines of the subsequent inquiry report, she was a selfish, demanding, foul-mouthed virago who would have tempted a saint. Her family would have nothing to do with her – didn't even visit – until they discovered that there was a great deal of agree-able publicity to be made out of righteous indignation. Perfectly proper too, no doubt. Patients, however disa-greeable, are sacrosanct and it's in all our ultimate inter-ests to uphold that admirable precept. The incident sparked off a spate of complaints about the hospital. There was a full-dress inquiry covering the administration, medical services, food, nursing care, the lot. Not surprisingly, they found plenty to inquire into. Two male nurses were subsequently dismissed and Dot left of her own accord. The inquiry, while deploring her loss of control, exonerated her from any suspicion of deliberate cruelty. But the damage was done; no other hospital wanted her. Apart from the suspicion that she wasn't exactly reliable under stress, they blamed her for provoking an inquiry which did no one any good and lost two men their jobs. Afterwards, Wilfred tried to get in touch with her; he thought from the accounts of the inquiry that she'd been hard done by. He took some time to trace her, but succeeded in the end and invited her here as a kind of matron. Actually, like the rest of the staff, she does anything that's needed from nursing to cooking. His motives weren't entirely beneficent. It's never easy to find nursing staff for a remote specialized place like this, apart from the unorthodoxy of Wilfred's methods. If he lost Dorothy Moxon he wouldn't easily find a replacement.'

Dalgliesh said:

'I remember the case but not her face. It's the young blonde girl – Jennie Pegram, isn't it? – who looks familiar.'

Carwardine smiled; indulgent, a little contemptuous.

'I thought you might ask about her. Wilfred ought to find a way of using her for fund-raising, she'd love it. I don't know anyone who's better at assuming that expression of wistful, uncomprehending, long-suffering fortitude. She'd make a fortune for the place properly exploited.'

Julius laughed:

'Henry, as you have gathered, doesn't like her. If she looks familiar, you may have seen her on television about eighteen months ago. It was the month for the media to lacerate the British conscience on behalf of the young chronic sick, and the producer sent out his underlings to scavenge for a suitable victim. They came up with Jennie. She had been nursed for twelve years, and very well nursed, in a geriatric unit, partly, I gather, because they couldn't find a more suitable place for her, partly because she rather liked being the petted favourite of the patients and visitors, and partly because the hospital had group physiotherapy and occupational therapy facilities of which our Jennie took advantage. But the programme, as you can imagine, made the most of her situation – "Unfortunate twenty-five-year-old girl incarcerated among the old and dying; shut away from the community; helpless; hopeless." All the most senile patients were carefully grouped round her for the benefit of the camera with Jennie in the middle doing her stuff magnificently. Shrill accusations against the inhumanity of the Department of Health, the regional hospital board, the hospital managers. Next day, predictably, there was a public outburst of indignation which lasted, I imagine, until the next protest programme. The compassionate British public demanded that a more suitable place be found for Jennie. Wilfred wrote offering a vacancy here, Jennie accepted, and fourteen months ago, she arrived. No one quite knows what she makes of us. I should give a lot to look into what passes for Jennie's mind.'

Dalgliesh was surprised that Julius had such an intimate knowledge of the patients at Toynton Grange, but he asked no more questions. He dropped unobtrusively out of the chatter and sat drinking his wine, half listening to the desultory voices of his companions. It was the quiet, undemanding talk of men who had acquaintances and interests in common, who knew just enough about each other and cared just sufficiently to create an illusion of companionship. He had no particular wish to share it. The wine deserved silence. He realized that this was the first fine wine he had drunk since his illness. It was reassuring that yet another of life's pleasures still held its power to solace. It took him a minute to realize that Julius was talking to him directly.

'I'm sorry about the proposed poetry reading. But I'm not altogether displeased. It illustrates one thing that you'll realize about Toynton. They exploit. They don't mean to, but they can't help it. They say that they want to be treated as ordinary people, and then make demands no ordinary person would dream of making, and naturally one can't refuse. Now, perhaps, you won't think too harshly of those of us who seem less than enthusiastic about Toynton.'

'Us?'

'The little group of normals anyway, in thrall to the place.'

'Are you?'

'Oh, yes! I get away to London or abroad so that the spell never really has a chance to take hold. But think of Millicent, stuck in that cottage because Wilfred lets her have it rent-free. All she wants is to get back to the bridge tables and cream cakes of Cheltenham Spa. So why doesn't she? And Maggie. Maggie would say that all she wanted was a bit of life. Well, that's what we all want, a bit of life. Wilfred tried to get her interested in birdwatching. I remember her reply. "If I have to watch another bloody seagull shitting on Toynton Head I'll run screaming into the sea." Dear Maggie. I rather take to Maggie when she's sober. And Eric? Well, he could break away if he had the courage. Looking after five patients and medically supervising the production of hand lotion and bath powder is hardly an honourable job for a registered medical practitioner, even one with an unfortunate predilection for little girls. And then there's Helen Rainer. But I rather fancy that our enigmatic Helen's reason for staying is more elemental and understandable. But they're all a prey of boredom. And now I'm boring you. Would you like to hear some music? We usually listen to records when Henry's here.'

The claret, unaccompanied by speech or music, would have contented Dalgliesh. But he could see that Henry was as anxious to hear a record as Julius probably was to demonstrate the superiority of his stereo equipment. Invited to choose Dalgliesh asked for Vivaldi. While the record was playing he strolled out into the night. Julius followed him and they stood in silence at the low barricade of stone at the cliff edge. The sea lay before them, faintly luminous, ghostly under a scatter of high, unemphatic stars. He thought that the tide was on the ebb but it still sounded very close, thudding against the rocky beach in great chords of sound, a base accompaniment to the high, sweet counterpoint of the distant violins. Dalgliesh thought that he could feel the spume light on his forehead, but when he put up his hand he found it was only a trick of the freshening breeze.

So there must have been two poison pen writers, only one genuinely committed to his or her obscene trade. It was obvious from Grace Willison's distress and Carwardine's laconic disgust that they had received a very different type of letter from the one found at Hope Cottage. It was too great a coincidence that two poison pens should be operating at the same time in so small a community. The assumption was that Father Baddeley's note had been planted in the bureau after his death, with small attempt at concealment, for Dalgliesh to find. If this were so, then it must have been put there by someone who knew about at least one of the other letters; had been told that it was typed on a Toynton Grange machine and on Toynton Grange paper, but who hadn't actually seen it. Grace Willison's letter had been typed on the Imperial machine and she had confided only in Dot Moxon. Carwardine's, like Father Baddeley's, had been typed on the Remington, and he had told Julius Court. The inference was obvious. But how could a man as intelligent as Court expect such a childish ruse to deceive a professional detective, or even an enthusiastic amateur? But then, had it been intended to? Dalgliesh had signed his postcard to Father Baddeley only with his initials. If it had been found by someone with a guilty secret as he searched feverishly through the bureau it would have told him nothing except that Father Baddeley was expecting a visitor on the afternoon of 1st October, a visitor who was probably as innocuous as a fellow clergyman or an old parishioner. But, just in case Father Baddeley had confided that something was on his mind, it might have seemed worthwhile to concoct and plant a false clue. Almost certainly, it had been placed in the bureau shortly before his arrival. If Anstey were telling the truth about looking through Father Baddeley's papers on the morning after his death, it was impossible that he should have missed the poison pen note or failed to remove it.

But even if all this were an elaborate and over-sophisticated edifice of conjecture, and Father Baddeley had indeed received the poison pen note, Dalgliesh now felt certain that it wasn't the reason for his summons. Father Baddeley would have felt perfectly competent both to discover the sender and to deal with him. He was unworldly but not naïve. Unlike Dalgliesh, he had probably seldom become involved professionally with the more spectacular sins but that didn't mean they were outside his comprehension or, for that matter, his compassion. It was arguable, anyway, that those were the sins which did least damage. Of the more corrosive, petty, mean-minded delinquencies in all their sad but limited variety he, like any other parish priest, would have had his fill. He had his answer ready, compassionate but inexorable, offered, Dalgliesh remembered wryly, with all the gentle arrogance of absolute certainty. No, when Father Baddeley wrote he wanted professional advice he meant just that; advice which he could only get from a police officer on a matter which he felt unable to deal with himself. And that was unlikely to include the detection of a spiteful but not particularly vicious poison pen writer operating in a small community of which every member must have been known intimately to him.

The prospect of trying to discover the truth filled Dalgliesh with a profound depression. He was at

Toynton Grange merely as a private visitor. He had no standing, no facilities, no equipment even. The task of sorting Father Baddeley's books could be stretched to cover a week, perhaps longer. After that, what excuse would he have to remain? And he had discovered nothing which would justify bringing in the local police. What did these vague suspicions, this sense of foreboding amount to? An old man, dying of heart disease, suffering his final and expected attack peacefully in his fireside chair, reaching perhaps in his last conscious moment for the familiar feel of his stole, lifting it over his head for the last time for reasons, probably only half understood, of comfort, of reassurance, of symbolism, of the simple affirmation of his priesthood or his faith. One could think of a dozen explanations, all simple, all more plausible than the secret visit of a murderous mock penitent. The missing diary; who could ever prove that Father Baddeley hadn't himself destroyed it before his admission to hospital? The forced bureau lock; nothing but the diary was missing and, as far as he knew, nothing valuable had been stolen. In the absence of other evidence, how could he possibly justify an official inquiry into a mislaid key and a broken lock?

But Father Baddeley had sent for him. There had been something on his mind. If Dalgliesh, without too great involvement, inconvenience or embarrassment, could discover in the next week or ten days what it had been, then he would do so. He owed that at least to the old man. But there it would end. Tomorrow he would pay a duty visit to the police and to Father Baddeley's solicitor. If anything came to light, then the police could deal with it. He was finished with police work, professional or amateur, and it would take more than the death of one old priest to change that decision.

V

When they got back to Toynton Grange shortly after midnight Henry Carwardine said roughly:

'They'll be relying on you to help me to bed, I'm afraid. Dennis Lerner usually wheels me to Toynton Cottage and calls for me at midnight, but since you're here . . . As Julius said, we're great exploiters at Toynton Grange. And I'd better shower. Dennis is off duty tomorrow morning and I can't stomach Philby. My room is on the first floor. We take the lift.'

Henry knew that he sounded ungracious but that, he guessed, would be more acceptable to his silent companion than humility or self-pity. It struck him that Dalgliesh looked as if he could have done with help himself. Perhaps the man had been more sick than they realized. Dalgliesh said calmly:

'Another half-bottle and I suspect we would both have needed help. But I'll do my best. Put down my clumsiness to inexperience and the claret.'

But he was surprisingly gentle and competent, getting Henry out of his clothes, supporting him to the lavatory, and finally wheeling him under the shower. He spent a little time examining the hoist and equipment and then used them intelligently. When he didn't know what was needed, he asked. Apart from these brief and necessary exchanges, neither spoke. Henry thought that he had seldom been put to bed with such imaginative gentleness. But, catching a glimpse in the bathroom mirror of his companion's drawn preoccupied face, of the dark secretive eyes cavernous with fatigue, he wished suddenly that he hadn't asked for help, that he had tumbled unshowered and fully dressed on to his bed, free from the humiliating touch of these competent hands. He sensed that, behind the disciplined calm, every contact with his naked body was a disagreeable duty. And for Henry himself, illogically and surprisingly, the touch of Dalgliesh's cool hands was like the touch of fear. He wanted to cry out:

'What are you doing here? Go away; don't interfere; leave us in peace.' The urge was so strong that he could almost believe that he had spoken the words aloud. And when, at last, he was comfortably bedded by his temporary nurse and Dalgliesh said an abrupt goodbye and immediately left him without another word, he knew that it was because he couldn't bear to hear even the most perfunctory and least gracious word of thanks.

FOUR

The Dreadful Shore

I

He awoke sluggishly soon before seven to disagreeably familiar noises; intrusive plumbing, the clang of apparatus, the squeal of chair wheels, sudden hurrying footsteps, determinedly cheerful exhortatory voices. Telling himself that the bathrooms would be needed for the patients, he shut his eyes resolutely on the bleak, impersonal room and willed himself to sleep again. When he woke an hour later after a fitful doze the annexe was silent. Someone – he dimly remembered a brown cloaked figure – had placed a mug of tea on his bedside table. It was cold, the greyish surface mottled with milk. He dragged on his dressing gown and went in search of the bathroom.

Breakfast at Toynton Grange was, as he had expected, laid out in the communal dining-room. But, at eight-thirty, he was either too early or too late for the majority of the inmates. Only Ursula Hollis was breakfasting when he arrived. She gave him a shy good-morning, then returned her eyes to the library book precariously propped against a jar of honey. Dalgliesh saw that the breakfast was simple, but adequate. There was a bowl of stewed apples; home-made muesli consisting mostly of porridge oats, bran and shredded apple; brown bread and margarine, and a row of boiled eggs each in its eggcup and individually named. The two remaining were cold. Presumably they were all cooked together earlier in the morning, and those who wanted their egg warm took the trouble to be on time. Dalgliesh helped himself to the egg pencilled with his name. It was glutinous at the top and very hard at the bottom, a result which he felt must have taken some perverse culinary skill to achieve.

After breakfast he went in search of Anstey to thank him for his overnight hospitality and to ask if there was anything he wanted from Wareham. He had decided that some of the afternoon had better be given over to shopping if he were to make himself comfortable in Michael's cottage. A short search of the seemingly deserted house found Anstey with Dorothy Moxon in the business room. They were seated together at the table with an open ledger before them. As he knocked and entered they looked up simultaneously with something of the air of guilty conspirators. It seemed to take a couple of seconds before they realized who he was. Anstey's smile, when it came, was as sweet as ever but his eyes were perfunctory. Dalgliesh sensed that he wouldn't be sorry to see him go. Anstey might see himself in the role of a welcoming medieval abbot, always ready with the bread and ale, but what he really craved were the gratifications of hospitality without the inconvenience of a guest. He said there was nothing he wanted in Wareham and then asked Dalgliesh how long he expected to be in the cottage. There was absolutely no hurry, of course. Their guest wasn't to feel himself at all in the way. When Dalgliesh replied that he would stay only until Father Baddeley's books were sorted and packed, it was difficult for him to conceal his relief. He offered to send Philby to Hope Cottage with some packing cases. Dorothy Moxon said nothing. She continued to stare fixedly at Dalgliesh as if determined not to betray her irritation at his presence and her desire to get back to the ledger by so much as a flicker of her sombre eyes.

It was comforting to be back in Hope Cottage, to smell again the familiar faintly ecclesiastical smell and to look forward to a long exploratory walk along the cliff before setting out for Wareham. But he had scarcely had time to unpack his case and change into stout walking shoes when he heard the patients' bus stopping outside and, going to the window, saw Philby unloading the first of the promised packing cases. Swinging it on his shoulder, he marched up the short path, kicked open the door, bringing with him into the room a powerful smell of stale sweat, and dropped the case at Dalgliesh's feet with a brusque:

'There's a couple more in the back.'

It was an obvious invitation to help unload them, and Dalgliesh took the hint. It was the first time he had seen the handyman in the full light, and the sight wasn't agreeable. He had, in fact, seldom encountered a man whose physical appearance so repelled him. Philby was only a little over five feet and stockily built with short plump arms and legs as pale and shapeless as peeled tree trunks. His head was round and his skin, despite his outdoor life, was pink and glossy and very smooth as if blown up with air. His eyes would have been remarkable in a more attractive face. They were slightly slanted and the irises were large and blue-black in colour. His black hair was scanty and combed straight back over the domed skull to end in an untidy and greasy fringe. He was wearing sandals, the right one fastened with string; a pair of dirty white shorts, so brief that they were almost indecent; and a grey vest, stained with sweat. Over this he wore, loosely open and held together only by a cord at the waist, his brown monk's habit. Without this incongruous garb he would have looked merely dirty and disreputable. With it he looked positively sinister.

As he made no attempt to go once the cases were unloaded, Dalgliesh deduced that he expected a tip. The proffered coins were slipped into the pocket of the habit with sly expertise but with no thanks. Dalgliesh was interested to learn that, despite the expensive experiment with home-produced eggs, not all the economic laws were defunct in this unworldly abode of brotherly love. Philby gave the three boxes a vicious valedictory kick as if to earn his tip by demonstrating that they were sound. As they disappointingly remained intact, he gave them a final look of sour displeasure and then departed. Dalgliesh wondered where Anstey had recruited this particular member of the staff. To his prejudiced eye the man looked like a category 'A' rapist on licence, but perhaps that was going a little too far even for Wilfred Anstey.

His second attempt to set out was frustrated by a second visitor, this time Helen Rainer, who had cycled the short distance from Toynton Grange with her bicycle basket piled high with linen from his bed. She explained that Wilfred was concerned in case the sheets at Hope

Cottage were inadequately aired. It surprised Dalgliesh that she hadn't taken the opportunity to come with Philby in the bus. But perhaps, understandably, she found his proximity distasteful. She came in quietly but briskly and without too obviously making Dalgliesh feel he was a nuisance, unmistakably conveyed the impression that this wasn't a social visit, that she hadn't come to chat, and that there were more important duties awaiting her. They made the bed together, Nurse Rainer flicking the sheets into place and neatly mitring each corner with such brisk expertise that Dalgliesh, a second or two behind her, felt himself slow and incompetent. At first they worked in silence. He doubted whether this was the time to ask, however tactfully, how the misunderstanding had arisen over the neglected visit to Father Baddeley on the last night of his life. His stay in hospital must have intimidated him. It took an effort of will to say:

'I'm probably being over-sensitive, but I wish that someone had been with Father Baddeley when he died, or at least had looked in on him later that night to see that all was well.'

She could with justice, he thought, reply to this implied criticism by pointing out that it came inappropriately from someone who had shown no concern for the old man for nearly thirty years. But she said without rancour, almost eagerly:

'Yes, that was bad. It couldn't have made any difference medically, but the misunderstanding shouldn't have happened, one of us ought to have looked in. Do you want this third blanket? If not, I'll take it back to Toynton Grange, it's one of ours.'

'Two will be enough. What exactly happened?'

'To Father Baddeley? He died of acute myocarditis.'

'I mean, how did the misunderstanding arise?'

'I served him a cold lunch of chicken and salad when he arrived back from hospital and then settled him for his afternoon rest. He was ready for it. Dot took him his afternoon tea and helped him to wash. She got him into his pyjamas and he insisted on wearing his cassock on top. I cooked scrambled eggs for him in the kitchen here shortly after six-thirty. He was absolutely insistent that he wanted to spend the evening undisturbed, except, of course, for Grace Willison's visit, but I told him that someone would come in about ten and he seemed perfectly happy with that. He said that he'd rap on the wall with the poker if he were in any distress. Then I went next door to ask Millicent to listen for him and she offered to look in on him last thing. At least, that's what I understood. Apparently she thought that Eric or I would come. As I said, it shouldn't have happened. I blame myself. It wasn't Eric's fault. As his nurse, I should have ensured that he was seen again professionally before he went to bed.'

Dalgliesh said:

'This insistence on being alone; did you get the impression that he was expecting a visitor?'

'What visitor could he be expecting, other than poor Grace? I think he'd had enough of people while he was in hospital and just wanted some peace.'

'And you were all here at Toynton Grange that night?'

'All except Henry, who hadn't got back from London. Where else could we be?'

'Who unpacked his case for him?'

'I did. He was admitted to hospital as an emergency and had very few things with him, only those which we found by his bed and packed.'

'His Bible, prayer book and his diary?'

She looked up at him briefly, her face expressionless, before bending again to tuck in a blanket.

'Yes.'

'What did you do with them?'

'I left them on the small table beside his chair. He may have moved them later.'

So the diary had been with Father Baddeley in hospital. That meant that the record would have been up to date. And if Anstey were not lying about its being missing next morning, then it had been removed some time within those twelve hours.

He wondered how he could phrase his next question without arousing her suspicions. Keeping his voice light, he said:

'You may have neglected him in life but you looked after him very thoroughly after he died. First cremation and then burial. Wasn't that a little over-conscientious?'

To his surprise she burst out as if he had invited her to share a justified indignation:

'Of course it was! It was ridiculous! But that was Millicent's fault. She told Wilfred that Michael had frequently expressed his strong wish to be cremated. I can't think when or why. Although they were neighbours, she and Michael didn't exactly live in each other's pockets. But that's what she said. Wilfred was equally sure that Michael would want an orthodox Christian burial, so the poor man got both. It meant a lot of extra trouble and expense and Dr McKeith from

Wareham had to sign a medical certificate as well as Eric. All that fuss just because Wilfred had a bad conscience.'

'Did he? About what?'

'Oh, nothing. I just got the impression that he felt that Michael had been a bit neglected one way and another, the usual self-indulgent compunction of the bereaved. Is this pillow going to be adequate? It feels very lumpy to me, and you look as if you could do with a good night's rest. Don't forget to come up to the Grange if there's anything you need. The milk is delivered to the boundary gate. I've ordered a pint for you each day. If that's too much, we can always use it. Now, have you everything you need?'

With the sensation of being under firm discipline Dalgliesh said meekly that he had. Nurse Rainer's briskness, her confidence, her concentration on the job in hand, even her reassuring smile of farewell, all relegated him to the status of a patient. As she wheeled her bicycle down the path and remounted, he felt that he had been visited by the district nurse. But he felt an increased respect for her. She hadn't appeared to resent his questions, and she had certainly been remarkably forthcoming. He wondered why.

II

It was a warm misty morning under a sky of low cloud. As he left the valley and began to trudge up the cliff path a reluctant rain began to fall in slow heavy drops. The sea was a milky blue, sluggish and opaque, its sloping waves pitted with rain and awash with shifting patterns of floating foam. There was a smell of autumn as if someone far off, undetected even by a wisp of smoke, was burning leaves. The narrow path rose higher skirting the cliff edge, now close enough to give him a brief vertiginous illusion of danger, now twisting inland between a tatter of bronzed bracken crumpled with the wind, and low tangles of bramble bushes, their red and black berries tight and meagre compared with the luscious fruit of inland hedgerows. The headland was dissected by low broken walls of stone and studded with small limestone rocks. Some, half buried, protruded tipsily from the soil like the relics of a disorderly graveyard.

Dalgliesh walked warily. It was his first country walk since his illness. The demands of the job meant that walking had always been a rare and special pleasure. Now he moved with something of the uncertainty of those first tentative steps of convalescence, muscles and senses rediscovering remembered pleasures, not with keen delight but with the gentle acceptance of familiarity. The brief metallic warble and churling note of stonechats, busy among the brambles; a solitary black-headed gull motionless as a ship's figure-head on a promontory of rock; clumps of rock samphire, their umbels stained with purple; yellow dandelions, pinpoints of brightness on the faded autumnal grass.

After nearly ten minutes of walking the cliff path began to slope gently downhill and was eventually dissected by a narrow lane running inland from the cliff edge. About six yards from the sea it broadened into a gently sloping plateau of bright-green turf and moss. Dalgliesh stopped suddenly as if stung by memory. This, then, must be the place where Victor Holroyd had chosen to sit, the spot from which he had plunged to his death. For a moment he wished that it hadn't lain so inconveniently in his path. The thought of violent death broke disagreeably into his euphoria. But he could understand the attraction of the spot. The lane was secluded and sheltered from the wind, there was a sense of privacy and peace; a precarious peace for a man captive in a wheelchair and with only the power of his brakes holding the balance between life and death. But that may have been part of the attraction. Perhaps only here, poised above the sea on this secluded patch of bright moss, could Holroyd, frustrated and chairbound, gain an illusion of freedom, of being in control of his destiny. He might always have intended to make here his final bid for release, insisting month after month on being wheeled to the same spot, biding his time so that no one at Toynton Grange suspected his real purpose. Instinctively, Dalgliesh studied the ground. Over three weeks had passed since Holroyd's death but he thought he could still detect the faint indentation of the soft turf where the wheels had rested and, less plainly, marks where the short grass had been matted with the scuffle of policemen's feet.

He walked to the cliff edge and looked down. The view, spectacular and frightening, made him catch his breath. The cliffs had changed and here the limestone had given place to an almost vertical wall of blackish clay larded with calcareous stone. Almost a hundred and fifty feet below, the cliff tumbled into a broad fissured causeway of boulders, slabs and amorphous chunks of blue-black rock which littered the foreshore as if hurled in wild disorder by a giant hand. The tide was out and the oblique line of foam moved sluggishly among the furthest rocks. As he looked down on this chaotic and awe-inspiring waste of rock and sea and tried to picture what the fall must have done to Holroyd, the sun moved fitfully from behind the clouds and a band of sunlight moved across the headland lying warm as a hand on the back of his neck, gliding the bracken, marbling the strewn rocks at the cliff edge. But it left the foreshore in shadow, sinister and unfriendly. For a moment Dalgliesh believed that he was looking down on a cursed and dreadful shore on which the sun could never shine.

Dalgliesh had been making for the black tower marked on Father Baddeley's map, less from a curiosity to see it than from the need to set an object for his walk. Still musing on Victor Holroyd's death, he came upon the tower almost unexpectedly. It was a squat intimidating folly, circular for about two-thirds of its height but topped with an octagonal cupola like a pepperpot pierced with eight glazed slit windows, compass points of reflected light which gave it something of the look of a lighthouse. The tower intrigued him and he moved round it touching the black walls. He saw that it had been built of limestone blocks but faced with the black shale as if capriciously decorated with pellets of polished jet. In places the shale had flaked away giving the tower a mottled appearance; black nacreous scales littered the base of the walls and gleamed among the grasses. To the north, and sheltered from the sea, was a tangle of plants as if someone had once tried to plant a garden. Now nothing remained but a dishevelled clump of Michaelmas daisies, patches of self-seeded antirrhinums, marigolds and nasturtiums, and a single etiolated rose with two white, starved buds, its stem bent double against the stone as if resigned to the first frost.

To the east was an ornate stone porch above an iron-bound oak door. Dalgliesh lifted the heavy handle and twisted it with difficulty. But the door was locked. Looking up he saw that there was a rough stone plaque set in the wall of the porch with a carved inscription:

IN THIS TOWER DIED
WILFRED MANCROFT ANSTEY
27TH OCTOBER 1887 AGED 69 YEARS
CONCEPTIO CULPA NASCI PENA
LABOR VITA NECESSI MORI
ADAM OF ST. VICTOR AD 1129

A strange epitaph for a Victorian landed gentleman and a bizarre place in which to die. The present owner of Toynton Grange had perhaps inherited a degree of eccentricity. CONCEPTIO CULPA: the theology of original sin had been discarded by modern man with other inconvenient dogma; even in 1887 it must have been on the way out. NASCI PENA: anaesthesia had mercifully done something to vitiate that dogmatic assertion. LABOR VITA: not if twentieth-century technological man could help it. NECESSI MORI: ah, there was still the rub. Death. One could ignore it, fear it, even welcome it, but never defeat it. It remained as obtrusive but more durable than these commemorative stones. Death: the same yesterday, today and for ever. Had Wilfred Mancroft Anstey himself chosen and taken comfort from this stark memento mori?

He continued walking along the cliff edge, skirting a small pebbled bay. About twenty yards ahead was a rough path to the beach, steep and probably treacherous in wet weather but obviously partly the result of a felicitous natural arrangement of the rock face and partly the work of man. Immediately beneath him, however, the cliff fell away in an almost vertical face of limestone. He saw with surprise that even at this early hour there were two roped climbers on the rock. The upper and bareheaded figure was instantly recognizable as Julius Court. When the second looked up Dalgliesh glimpsed the face under the red climbing helmet and saw that his companion was Dennis Lerner.

They were climbing slowly but competently, so competently that he felt no temptation to move back in case the unexpected sight of a spectator should break their concentration. They had obviously done this climb before; the route, the techniques were familiar to them. Now they were on the last pitch. Watching Court's smooth unhurrying movements, the splayed limbs leech-like on the rock face, he found himself reliving some of the climbs of his boyhood and making the ascent with them, mentally documenting each stage. Traverse right about fifteen feet with peg protection; step up with difficulty; then on to a small pinnacle block; gain the next ledge by a mantelshelf; climb the groove with the aid of two pegs and one sling to the horizontal crack; follow the groove again to a small ledge in the corner; finally climb with the aid of two pegs to the top.

Ten minutes later Dalgliesh strolled slowly round to where Julius was heaving his shoulders over the edge of the cliff. He drew himself up and stood, slightly panting, beside Dalgliesh. Without speaking he banged a peg into the crack of the rock beside one of the larger boulders, clipped a sling through the peg and into his waistline and started hauling in the rope. There was a cheerful shout from the rock face. Julius settled himself back against the boulder, rope around his waist, shouted 'Climb when you're ready,' and began inching the rope through careful hands. Less than fifteen minutes later, Dennis Lerner stood beside him and began coiling the rope. Blinking rapidly Dennis took off his steel-rimmed spectacles, rubbed away what could have been spray or rain drops from his face and twisted the ends behind his ears with shaking fingers. Julius looked at his watch:

'One hour twelve minutes, our best so far.'

He turned to Dalgliesh.

'There aren't many climbs on this part of the coast because of the shale, so we try to improve our time. Do you climb? I could lend you some gear.'

'I haven't done much since I left school and judging from what I've just seen, I'm not in your class.'

He didn't bother to explain that he was still too convalescent to climb safely. Once he might have found it necessary to justify his reluctance, but it had been some years now since he bothered how other people judged his physical courage. Julius said:

'Wilfred used to climb with me but about three months ago we discovered that someone had deliberately frayed one of his ropes. We were about to tackle this particular climb, incidentally. He refused to try to discover who was responsible. Someone at the Grange expressing a personal grievance, I suppose. Wilfred must expect these occasional contretemps. It's an occupational hazard for playing God. He was never in real danger. I always insist on checking equipment before we start. But it unnerved him, perhaps gave him the excuse he was looking for to give up climbing. He was never much good. Now I depend on Dennis when he has a day off, as today.'

Lerner turned and smiled directly at Dalgliesh. The smile transformed his face, releasing it from strain. He looked suddenly boyish, confiding:

'I'm just as terrified as Wilfred most of the time but I'm learning. It's fascinating; I'm getting to love it. There's a mild climb about half a mile back, guillemot ledge. Julius started me off there. It's really quite gentle. We could tackle that if you'd like to try.'

His naïve eagerness to communicate and share his pleasure was endearing.

Dalgliesh said:

'I hardly think I shall be long enough at Toynton to make it worthwhile.'

He intercepted their quick glance at each other, an almost imperceptible meeting of eyes in what? Relief? Warning? Satisfaction?

The three men stood silently while Dennis finished coiling the rope. Then Julius nodded towards the black tower.

'Ugly, isn't it? Wilfred's great-grandfather built it shortly after he rebuilt the Grange. It replaced – the Grange I mean – a small Elizabethan manor house which originally stood on the site and was destroyed by fire in 1843. A pity. It must have been more agreeable than the present house. Great-grandfather had no eye for form. Neither the house nor the folly have quite come off, have they?'

Dalgliesh asked:

'How did he die here, by design?'

'You could say that. He was one of those unamiable and obstinate eccentrics which the Victorian age seemed to breed. He invented his own religion, based, I understand, on the Book of Revelation. In the early autumn of 1887 he walled himself up inside the tower and starved himself to death. According to the somewhat confused testament he left, he was waiting for the second coming. I hope it arrived for him.'

'And no one stopped him?'

'They didn't know he was here. The old man was crazy but cunning. He made his secret preparations here, stones and mortar and so on, and then pretended to set off to winter in Naples. It was over three months before they found him. Long before that he'd torn his fingers to the bone trying to claw himself out. But he'd done his brick and mortar work too well, poor devil.'

'How horrible!'

'Yes. In the old days before Wilfred closed the headland, the locals tended to avoid the place, and so to be honest do I. Father Baddeley used to come here occasionally. According to Grace Willison, he said some prayers for great-grandfather's soul, sprinkled holy water around and that decontaminated the tower as far as he was concerned. Wilfred uses it for meditation, or so he says. Personally I think it's to get away from the Grange. The sinister family association doesn't seem to worry him. But then, it doesn't really touch him personally. He was adopted. But I expect Millicent Hammitt has told you about that.'

'Not yet. I've hardly spoken to her.'

'She will, she will.'

Dennis Lerner said surprisingly:

'I like the black tower, particularly in summer when the headland is peaceful and golden and the sun glints on the black stone. It's a symbol really, isn't it? It looks magical, unreal, a folly built to amuse a child. And underneath there's horror, pain, madness and death. I said that to Father Baddeley once.'

'And what did he reply?' asked Julius.

'He said, "Oh, no my son. Underneath there's the love of God." '

Julius said roughly:

'I don't need a phallic symbol erected by a Victorian eccentric to remind me of the skull under my skin. Like any reasonable man I prepare my own defences.'

Dalgliesh asked:

'What are they?'

The quiet question, even in his own ears, sounded stark as a command. Julius smiled:

'Money and the solace it can buy. Leisure, friends, beauty, travel. And when they fail, as your friend Father Baddeley would have reminded me they inevitably will, and Dennis's four horses of the apocalypse take over, three bullets in a Luger.' He looked up once more at the tower.

'In the meantime, I can do without reminders. My half-Irish blood makes me superstitious. Let's go down to the beach.'

They slid and clambered cautiously down the cliff path. At the foot of the cliff Dennis Lerner's brown

143

monk's habit lay neatly folded, topped by a rock. He corded it round himself, exchanged his climbing boots for sandals taken from the pocket of the cloak and, thus metamorphosed and with his climbing helmet tucked under his arm, joined his companions as they trudged through the shingle.

All three seemed weary and no one spoke until the cliffs changed and they passed under the shadow of the black shale. The shore was even more remarkable seen close-to, a wide shining platform of boulder-strewn clay, fractured and crevassed as if by an earthquake, a bleak uncompromising shore. The pools were blue-black pits festooned with slimy seaweed; surely no northern sea bred such an exotic green? Even the ubiquitous litter of the shore – tarred splinters of wood, cartons in which the foam bubbled like brown scum, bottles, ends of tarred rope, the fragile bleached bones of sea birds – looked like the sinister debris of catastrophe, the sad sludge of a dead world.

As if by common consent they moved closer together and picked their way cautiously over the viscous rocks and Dennis Lerner had to hitch up his cloak. Suddenly Julius paused and turned towards the rock face. Dalgliesh turned with him, but Dennis still looked steadfastly out to sea.

'The tide was coming in fast. It must have reached about here. I got down to the beach by the path we used. It took some minutes of hard running but it was the nearer, really the only way. I didn't see either him or the chair as I plunged and scrambled through the shingle. When I reached the black cliff I had to force myself to look at him. At first I could see nothing unusual, only the sea boiling between the rocks. Then I caught sight of one of the wheels of his chair. It was lying in the centre of a flat rock, the sun gleaming on the chrome and the metal spokes. It looked so decorative, so precisely placed, it couldn't surely have landed there by chance. I suppose that it bounced off with the shock of impact and finally rolled on to the stone. I remember that I picked it up and hurled it towards the shore, laughing aloud. Shock, I suppose. The sound echoed back from the rock face.'

Lerner, without turning, said in a stifled voice:

'I remember. I heard you. I thought it was Victor laughing; it sounded like Victor.'

Dalgliesh asked:

'You saw the accident, then?'

'From a distance of about fifty yards. I'd got back to the cottage from London after lunch and decided to have a swim. It was an exceptionally warm day for September. I was just coming over the headland when I saw the chair lurch forward. There was nothing I, or anyone, could do. Dennis was lying on the grass about ten yards from Holroyd. He scrambled to his feet and ran after the chair hooting like a banshee. Then he ran backwards and forwards along the cliff edge, flailing his arms like a great brown demented crow.'

Lerner said through tight lips:

'I know that I didn't behave with much courage.'

'It wasn't exactly an occasion for courage, dear boy. No one could expect you to hurl yourself over the cliff after him, although, for a second, I thought you were going to.'

He turned to Dalgliesh.

'I left Dennis lying prone on the grass in what I suppose was a state of shock, paused long enough to yell at him to get help from Toynton Grange, and made for the cliff path. It took Dennis about ten minutes to pull himself together and get moving. It might have been more sensible if I'd paid more attention to him and then got him down here with me to help with the corpse. I nearly lost it.'

Dalgliesh said:

'The chair must have come over the cliff with considerable speed if he landed as far out as here.'

'Yes, odd isn't it? I was looking for him further inshore. Then I saw a tangle of metal about twenty feet to the right already being washed by the tide. And lastly I saw Holroyd. He looked like a great stranded fish rolling in the tide. His face was pale and bloated, even when he was alive poor devil; something to do with the steroids Eric was giving him. Now he looked grotesque. He must have parted from the chair before impact; anyway he was some distance from the wreckage. He was wearing only slacks and a cotton shirt when he died, and now the shirt had been torn away by the rocks and the sea so that all I could see was this great white torso turning and rising as the tide washed over him. He had gashed open his head and cut the neck artery. He must have bled copiously, and the sea had done the rest. By the time I reached him the foam was still stained pink, pretty as a bubble bath. He looked bloodless, as if he had been in the sea for months. A bloodless corpse, half naked, wallowing in the tide.'

A bloodless corpse. A bloodless murder.

The phrase fell unbidden into Dalgliesh's mind. He asked, making his voice unemphatic, hardly interested:

'How did you manage to get hold of him?'

'It wasn't easy. As I've said, the tide was coming in fast. I managed to get my bathing towel under his belt and tried to haul him on to one of the higher rocks, an undignified clumsy business for both of us. He was considerably heavier than I and his waterlogged trousers added to the weight. I was afraid they would come off. I suppose it wouldn't have mattered if they had, but it seemed important at the time to preserve some dignity for him. I took advantage of each onrush of wave to heave him further to shore and managed to get him on to this rock here, as far as I can remember. I was soaking myself and shivering despite the heat. I remember thinking it odd that the sun didn't seem to have the power to dry my clothes.'

Dalgliesh had glanced at Lerner's profile during this recital. A pulse in the thin sun-reddened neck was beating like a pump. He said coolly:

'We must hope that Holroyd's death was less distressing for him than it obviously was for you.'

Julius Court laughed:

'You must remember that not everyone has your professional predilection for these entertainments. When I'd got him this far I just hung on grimly like a fisherman to his catch until the party from Toynton Grange arrived with a stretcher. They came stumbling along the beach, the quicker way, strung out, falling over the stones, overladen like a disorganized picnic party.'

'What about the wheelchair?'

'I only remembered it when we got back to Toynton. It was a write-off, of course. We all knew that. But I thought that the police might want to examine it to see

147

if the brakes were defective. Rather clever of me wasn't it? The idea didn't seem to occur to anyone else. But when a party from the Grange came back to look they could only find the two wheels and the main part of the body. The two side pieces with the ratchet hand-brakes were missing. The police searched more thoroughly next morning but with no better luck.'

Dalgliesh would have liked to have asked who it was from Toynton Grange who had done the searching. But he was determined not to betray real curiosity. He told himself that he had none. Violent death was no longer his concern and, officially, this violent death never would be. But it was odd that the two vital pieces of the wheelchair hadn't been found. And this rocky shore, with its deep crevices, its pools, its numerous hiding places would have been an ideal place in which to conceal them. But the local police would have thought of that. It was, he supposed, one of the questions he would tactfully have to ask them. Father Baddeley had written to ask for his help the day before Holroyd had died, but that didn't mean that the two events were totally unconnected. He asked:

'Was Father Baddeley very distressed about Holroyd's death? I imagine so.'

'Very much, when he knew. But that wasn't until a week later. We'd had the inquest by then and Holroyd had been buried. I thought Grace Willison would have told you. Michael and Victor between them gave us quite a day. When Dennis arrived back at the Grange with his news, the rescue party set out without saying anything to the patients. It was understandable but unfortunate. When we all staggered through the front

148

door about forty minutes later, with what remained of Holroyd half slipping off the stretcher, Grace Willison was wheeling herself through the hall. Just to add to the excitement, she collapsed with shock. Anyway, Wilfred thought that Michael might start earning his money, and sent Eric off to Hope Cottage. Eric found Father Baddeley in the throes of his heart attack. So yet another ambulance was summoned – we thought it might finish Michael off if he had to share his journey to the hospital with what remained of Victor – and the old man went off in happy ignorance. The ward sister broke the news about Victor as soon as the doctors thought he was well enough to take it. According to her, he took it quietly, but was obviously upset. He wrote to Wilfred I believe; a letter of condolence. Father Baddeley had the professional knack of taking other people's death in his stride, and he and Holroyd weren't exactly close. It was the idea of suicide which upset his professional susceptibilities, I imagine.'

Suddenly Lerner said in a low voice:

'I feel guilty because I feel responsible.'

Dalgliesh said:

'Either you pushed Holroyd over the cliff or you didn't. If you didn't, guilt is an indulgence.'

'And if I did?'

'Then it's a dangerous indulgence.'

Julius laughed:

'Victor committed suicide. You know it, I know it, so does everyone who knew Victor. If you're going to start fantasizing about his death, it's lucky for you that I decided to swim that afternoon and came over the brow of the hill when I did.'

The three of them, as if by common consent, began squelching their way along the shingled shore. Looking at Lerner's pale face, the twitch of muscle at the corner of the slack mouth, the perpetually anxious blinking eyes, Dalgliesh felt they'd had enough of Holroyd. He began to ask about the rock. Lerner turned to him eagerly.

'It's fascinating isn't it? I love the variety of this coast. You get the same shale further to the west at Kimmeridge; there it's known as Kimmeridge coal. It's bituminous you know, you can actually burn it. We did try at Toynton Grange; Wilfred liked the idea that we might be self-supporting even for heating. But the stuff smelt so offensive that we had to give it up. It practically stank us out. I believe people have tried to exploit it from the middle of the eighteenth century but no one's managed yet to deodorize it. The blackstone looks a bit dull and uninteresting now, but if it's polished with beeswax it comes up like jet. Well, you saw the effect on the black tower. People used to make ornaments of it as far back as Roman times. I've got a book on the geology of this coast if you're interested and I could show you my collection of fossils. Wilfred thinks that I ought not to take them now that the cliffs are so denuded, so I've given up collecting. But I've got quite an interesting collection. And I've got what I think is part of an Iron Age shale armlet.'

Julius Court was grating through the shingle a few feet ahead. He turned and shouted back at them:

'Don't bore him with your enthusiasm for old rocks, Dennis. Remember what he said. He won't be long enough at Toynton to make it worthwhile.'

He smiled at Dalgliesh. He made it sound like a challenge.

III

Before setting out for Wareham, Dalgliesh wrote to Bill Moriarty at the Yard. He gave such brief information as he had about the staff and patients at Toynton Grange and asked whether anything was officially known. He thought that he could imagine Bill's reaction to the letter, just as he could predict the style of his reply. Moriarty was a first-class detective but, except mercifully in official reports, he affected a facetious, spuriously jovial style when talking or writing about his cases as if nervously anxious to decontaminate violence with humour, or to demonstrate his professional sang-froid in the face of death. But if Moriarty's style was suspect, his information was invariably detailed and accurate. What was more, it would come quickly.

Dalgliesh, when stopping in Toynton village to post his letter, had taken the precaution of telephoning the police before calling in at divisional headquarters. His arrival was, therefore, expected and provided for. The Divisional Superintendent, called away unexpectedly to a meeting with his Chief Constable, had left apologies and instructions for the entertainment of the visitor. His final words to Detective Inspector Daniel, deputed to do the honours, had been:

'I'm sorry to miss the Commander. I met him last year when he lectured at Bramshill. At least he tempers the arrogance of the Met. with good manners and a plausible show of humility. It's refreshing to meet someone from the smoke who doesn't treat provincial forces as if we recruit by lurking outside the hill caves with lumps of raw meat on a pole. He may be the Commissioner's blue-eyed boy but he's a good copper.'

'Doesn't he write verse, Sir?'

'I shouldn't try to ingratiate yourself by mentioning that. I invent crossword puzzles for a hobby, which probably requires much the same level of intellectual skill, but I don't expect people to compliment me on it. I got his last book from the library. *Invisible Scars*. Do you suppose, given the fact that he's a copper, that the title is ironic?'

'I couldn't say, Sir, not having read the book.'

'I only understood one poem in three but I may have been flattering myself. I suppose he didn't say why we're being honoured.'

'No, Sir, but as he's staying at Toynton Grange he may be interested in the Holroyd case.'

'I can't see why; but you'd better arrange for Sergeant Varney to be available.'

'I've asked Varney to join us for lunch, Sir. The usual pub, I thought.'

'Why not? Let the Commander see how the poor live.'

And so Dalgliesh found himself, after the usual polite preliminaries, invited to lunch at the Duke's Arms. It was an unprepossessing pub, not visible from the High Street, but approached down a dark alleyway between a corn merchant and one of those general stores common in country towns where every possible garden implement and an assortment of tin buckets, hip baths, brooms, twine, aluminium teapots and dogs' leads swing from the ceiling above a pervading smell of paraffin and turpentine. Inspector Daniel and Sergeant Varney were greeted with uneffusive but evident satisfaction by the burly, shirt-sleeved landlord, who was obviously a publican who could afford to welcome the local police to his bar without the fear of giving it a bad name. The saloon bar was crowded, smoky and loud with the burr of Dorset voices. Daniel led the way down the narrow passage smelling strongly of beer and faintly of urine and out into an unexpected and sun-filled cobbled yard. There was a cherry tree in the centre, its trunk encircled by a wooden bench, and half a dozen sturdy tables and slatted wooden chairs set out on the paved stones which surrounded the cobbles. The yard was deserted. The regulars probably spent too much of their working lives in the open air to see it as a desirable alternative to the camaraderie of the snug, smoke-filled bar, while tourists who might have valued it were unlikely to penetrate to the Duke's Arms.

Without being summoned the publican brought out two pints of beer, a plate of cheese-filled rolls, a jar of home-made chutney and a large bowl of tomatoes. Dalgliesh said he would have the same. The beer proved excellent, the cheese was English Cheddar, the bread had obviously been baked locally and was not the gutless pap of some mass-produced oven. The butter was unsalted and the tomatoes tasted of the sun. They ate together in companionable silence.

Inspector Daniel was a stolid six-footer, with a jutting comb of strong undisciplined grey hair and a ruddy suntanned face. He looked close to retirement age. His

153

black eyes were restless, perpetually moving from face to face with an amused, indulgent, somewhat self-satisfied expression as if he felt himself personally responsible for the conduct of the world and was, on the whole, satisfied that he wasn't making too bad a job of it. The contrast between these glittering unquiet eyes and his unhurried movements and even more deliberate countryman's voice was disconcerting.

Sergeant Varney was two inches shorter with a round, bland, boyish face on which experience had so far left no trace. He looked very young, the prototype of that officer whose boyish good looks provoke the perennial middle-aged complaint that the policemen get younger each year. His manner to his superiors was easy, respectful, but neither sycophantic nor deferential. Dalgliesh suspected that he enjoyed an immense self-confidence which he was at some pains to conceal. When he talked about his investigation of Holroyd's death, Dalgliesh could understand why. Here was an intelligent and highly competent young officer who knew exactly where he was going and how he proposed to get there.

Dalgliesh carefully understated his business.

'I was ill at the time Father Baddeley wrote and he was dead when I arrived. I don't suppose he wanted to consult me about anything important, but I have something of a conscience about having let him down. It seemed sensible to have a word with you and see whether anything was happening at Toynton Grange which might have worried him. I must say it seems to me highly unlikely. I've been told about Victor Holroyd's death, of course, but that happened the day after Father Baddeley wrote to me. I did wonder, though, whether there was anything leading up to Holroyd's death which might have worried him.'

Sergeant Varney said:

'There was no evidence that Holroyd's death concerned anyone but himself. As I expect you know, the verdict at the inquest was accidental death. Dr Maskell sat with a jury and if you ask me he was relieved at the verdict. Mr Anstey is greatly respected in the district even if they do keep themselves very much to themselves at Toynton Grange, and no one wanted to add to his distress. But in my opinion, Sir, it was a clear case of suicide. It looks as if Holroyd acted pretty much on impulse. It wasn't his usual day to be wheeled to the cliff top and he seemed to make up his mind to it suddenly. We had the evidence of Miss Grace Willison and Mrs Ursula Hollis, who were sitting with Holroyd on the patients' patio, that he called Dennis Lerner over to him and more or less nagged him into wheeling him out. Lerner testified that he was in a particularly difficult mood on the journey and when they got to their usual place on the cliff he became so offensive that Lerner took his book and lay some little distance from the chair. That is where Mr Julius Court saw him when he breasted the hill in time to see the chair jerk forward and hurtle down the slope and over the cliff. When I examined the ground next morning I could see by the broken flowers and pressed grass exactly where Lerner had been lying and his library book, *The Geology of the Dorset Coast*, was still on the grass where he'd dropped it. It looks to me, Sir, as if Holroyd deliberately taunted him into moving some distance away so that he wouldn't be able to get to him in time once he'd slipped the brakes.'

'Did Lerner explain in court exactly what it was that Holroyd said to him?'

'He wasn't specific, Sir, but he more or less admitted to me that Holroyd taunted him with being a homosexual, not pulling his weight at Toynton Grange, looking for an easy life, and being an ungentle and incompetent nurse.'

'I would hardly describe that as unspecific. How much truth is there in any of it?'

'That's difficult to say, Sir. He may be all of those things including the first; which doesn't mean to say that he'd welcome Holroyd telling him so.'

Inspector Daniel broke in:

'He's not an ungentle nurse and that's for certain. My sister Ella is a staff nurse at the Meadowlands Nursing Home outside Swanage. Old Mrs Lerner – over eighty she is now – is a patient over there. Her son visits her regularly and isn't above lending a hand when they're busy. It's odd that he doesn't take a post there, but perhaps it's no bad thing to keep your professional and private life separate. Anyway, they may not have a vacancy for a male nurse. And no doubt he feels some loyalty to Wilfred Anstey. But Ella thinks very highly of Dennis Lerner. A good son, is how she describes him. And it must take the best part of his salary to keep Mum at Meadowlands. Like all the really good places, it's not cheap. No, I'd say that Holroyd was a pretty impossible chap. The Grange will be a good deal happier without him.'

Dalgliesh said:

'It's an uncertain way of committing suicide, I should have thought. What surprises me is that he managed to move that chair.'

Sergeant Varney took a long drink of his beer.

'It surprised me too, Sir. We weren't able to get the chair intact so I couldn't experiment with it. But Holroyd was a heavy chap, about half a stone heavier than I am, I estimate, and I experimented with one of the older chairs at Toynton Grange as close as possible to the model of his. Provided it were on fairly firm ground and the slope was more than one in three, I could get it moving with a sharp jerk. Julius Court testified that he saw Holroyd's body jerk although he couldn't say from that distance whether the chair was being thrust forward or whether it was spontaneous reaction on Holroyd's part to the shock of finding himself moving. And one has to remember, Sir, that other methods of killing himself weren't readily at hand. He was almost entirely helpless. Drugs would have been the easiest way, but those are kept locked in the clinical room on the upper floor; he hadn't a hope of getting to anything really dangerous without help. He might have tried hanging himself with a towel in the bathroom but there are no locks on the bathroom or lavatory doors. That, of course, is a precaution against patients collapsing and being too ill to summon assistance, but it does mean that there's a lack of privacy about the place.'

'What about a possible defect of the chair?'

'I thought about that, Sir, and it was, of course, brought out at the inquest. But we only recovered the seat of the chair and one of the wheels. The two side pieces with the hand-brakes and the cross-bar with the ratchets have never been found.'

'Exactly the parts of the chair where any defects of the brakes, whether natural or deliberately produced, might have been apparent.'

'If we could have found the pieces in time, Sir, and the sea hadn't done too much damage. But we never found them. The body had broken free of the chair in mid-air or on impact and Court naturally concentrated on retrieving the body. It was being tumbled by the surf, the trousers were waterlogged and it was too heavy for him to shift far. But he got his bathing towel into Holroyd's belt and managed to hold on until help, in the persons of Mr Anstey, Dr Hewson, Sister Moxon and the handyman Albert Philby, arrived with a stretcher. Together they managed to get the body on to it and struggled back along the beach to Toynton Grange. It was only then that they rang us. It occurred to Mr Court as soon as they reached the Grange that the chair ought to be retrieved for examination and he sent Philby back to look for it. Sister Moxon volunteered to go with him. The tide had gone out about twenty yards by then and they found the main part of the chair, that is the seat and the back, and one of the wheels.'

'I'm surprised that Dorothy Moxon went to search, I would have expected her to stay with the patients.'

'So should I, Sir. But Anstey refused to leave Toynton Grange and Dr Hewson apparently thought that his place was with the body. Nurse Rainer was off duty for the afternoon, and there was no one else to send unless you count Mrs Millicent Hammitt, and I don't think anyone thought of counting Mrs Hammitt. It did seem important that two pairs of eyes should be looking for the chair before the light faded.'

'And what about Julius Court?'

'Mr Court and Mr Lerner thought they ought to be at Toynton Grange to meet us when we arrived, Sir.'

'A very proper thought. And by the time you did arrive no doubt it was too dark to make an effective search.'

'Yes, Sir, it was seven fourteen when we got to Toynton Grange. Apart from taking statements and arranging for the body to be removed to the mortuary, there was very little we could do until the morning. I don't know whether you've seen that shore at low tide, Sir. It looks like a great sheet of black treacle toffee which some pro-digious giant has amused himself by smashing-up with a gigantic hammer. We searched pretty thoroughly over a wide area but if the metal pieces are lodged in the cre-vasses between any of those rocks it would take a metal detector to find them – and we'd be lucky then – and lift-ing tackle to retrieve them. It's most likely, I think, that they've been dragged down under the shingle. There's a great deal of turbulence there at high tide.'

Dalgliesh said:

'Was there any reason to suppose that Holroyd had suddenly become suicidal, I mean – why choose that particular moment?'

'I asked about that, Sir. A week earlier, that is on 5th September, Mr Court with Dr Hewson and Mrs Hewson had taken him in Court's car up to London to see his solicitors and a consultant at St Saviour's Hospital. That's Dr Hewson's own training hospital. I gather that Holroyd wasn't given much hope that anything more could be done for him. Dr Hewson said that the news didn't seem to depress him unduly. He hadn't expected anything else. Dr Hewson more or less told me that Holroyd had insisted on the consultation just for the trip to London. He was a restless man and liked an

159

excuse to get away from Toynton Grange occasionally. Mr Court was travelling up anyway and offered the use of his car. That matron, Mrs Moxon, and Mr Anstey were both adamant that Holroyd hadn't come back particularly depressed; but then they've got something of a vested interest in discrediting the suicide theory. The patients told me a rather different story. They noticed a change in Holroyd after his return. They didn't describe him as depressed, but he certainly wasn't any easier to live with. They described him as excited. Miss Willison used the word elated. She said that he seemed to be making up his mind to something. I don't think that she has much doubt that Holroyd killed himself. When I questioned her she was obviously shocked by the idea and distressed on Mr Anstey's account. She didn't want to believe it. But I think that she did.'

'What about Holroyd's visit to his solicitor? Did he learn anything there to distress him I wonder?'

'It's an old family firm, Holroyd and Martinson in Bedford Row. Holroyd's elder brother is now the senior partner. I did ring him to ask but I didn't get far. According to him, the visit was almost entirely social and Victor was no more depressed than usual. They were never close but Mr Martin Holroyd did visit his brother occasionally at Toynton Grange, particularly when he wanted to talk to Mr Anstey about his affairs.'

'You mean that Holroyd and Martinson are Anstey's solicitors?'

'They've acted for the family for over 150 years I understand. It's a very old connection. That's how Victor Holroyd came to hear about the Grange. He was Anstey's first patient.'

'What about Holroyd's wheelchair? Could anyone at Toynton Grange have sabotaged that, either on the day Holroyd died or on the evening before?'

'Philby could, of course. He had the best opportunity. But a number of people could have done it. Holroyd's rather heavy chair, the one which was used for these outings, was kept in the workroom at the end of the passage in the southern extension. I don't know whether you know it, Sir, but it's perfectly accessible even to wheelchairs. Basically it's Philby's workshop. He has the usual standard equipment and tools for carpentry and some metal work there. But the patients can use it too and are, in fact, encouraged either to help him or to indulge in their own hobbies. Holroyd used to do some fairly simple carpentry before he got too ill and Mr Carwardine occasionally models in clay. The women patients don't usually use it but there'd be nothing surprising to see one of the men there.'

Dalgliesh said:

'Carwardine told me that he was in the workroom when Philby oiled and checked the brakes at eight forty-five.'

'That's rather more than he told me. He gave me the impression that he hadn't really seen what Philby was up to. Philby was a bit coy about whether he could actually remember testing the brakes. I wasn't surprised. It was pretty obvious that they all wanted it to look like an accident if that could be done without provoking the coroner into too many strictures about carelessness. I had a bit of luck, however, when I questioned them about the actual morning of Holroyd's death. After breakfast Philby went back to the workroom shortly after eight forty-five. He was there for just an hour and when he left he locked the place up. He was glueing some repairs and didn't want them disturbed. I got the impression that Philby thinks of the workroom as his domain and doesn't exactly welcome the patients being allowed to use it. Anyway, he pocketed the key and didn't unlock the room until Lerner came fussing to ask for the key shortly before four o'clock so that he could get Holroyd's wheelchair. Assuming that Philby was telling the truth, the only people at Toynton Grange without alibis for the time when the workroom was unlocked and unoccupied early on the morning of 12th September are Mr Anstey, Holroyd himself, Mr Carwardine, Sister Moxon and Mrs Hewson. Mr Court was in London and didn't arrive back at his cottage until just before Lerner and Holroyd set out. Lerner is clear too. He was busy with the patients at all the relevant times.'

That was all very well, thought Dalgliesh, but it proved very little. The workroom had been unlocked the previous evening after Carwardine and Philby had left and, presumably, also during the night. He said:

'You were very thorough, Sergeant. Did you manage to discover all this without alarming them too much?'

'I think so, Sir. I don't think they thought for a moment that I was checking up on what opportunity Holroyd had to muck about with the chair himself. And if it were deliberately damaged, then my bet is he did it. He was a malicious man, from what I hear. It probably amused him to think that, when the chair was recovered from the sea and the damage discovered, then everyone at Toynton Grange would be under suspicion.

That's the kind of final thought that would give him quite a kick.'

Dalgliesh said:

'I just can't believe that both brakes failed simultaneously and accidentally. I've seen those wheelchairs at the Grange. The brakes system is very simple but it's effective and safe. And it's almost as difficult to imagine that there was deliberate sabotage. How could the murderer possibly rely on the brakes failing at that particular moment? Lerner or Holroyd might easily have tested them before starting out. The defect might be discovered when the chair was braked on the cliff top or even on the journey. Besides, no one apparently knew that Holroyd was going to insist on an outing that afternoon. What did exactly happen on the cliff top, by the way? Who braked the chair?'

'According to Lerner, Holroyd did. Lerner admits that he never looked at the brakes. All he can say is that he noticed nothing wrong with the chair. The brakes weren't used until they reached their usual stopping place.'

For a moment there was silence. They had finished eating and Inspector Daniel felt in the pocket of his tweed jacket and produced a pipe. As he stroked its bowl with his thumb before filling it, he said quietly:

'Nothing was worrying you about the old gentleman's death was it, Sir?'

'He was medically diagnosed as a dying man and somewhat inconveniently for me he died. I worry that I didn't visit him in time to hear what was on his mind; but that's a private worry. Speaking as a policeman, I should rather like to know who saw him last before he died. Officially, it was Grace Willison, but I've a feeling he had a later visitor than she; another patient. When he was found dead next morning he was wearing his stole. His diary was missing, and someone broke into his bureau. As I haven't seen Father Baddeley for over twenty years it's probably unreasonable of me to be so sure that it wasn't he.'

Sergeant Varney turned to his Inspector.

'What would be the theological position, Sir, if someone confessed to a priest, got absolution and then killed him to make sure that he kept his mouth shut. Would the confession take as it were?'

The young face was preternaturally grave, it was impossible to tell whether the inquiry had been serious, whether this was a private joke directed against the Inspector, or made with some more subtle motive. Daniel took his pipe from his mouth:

'God, you young men are an ignorant lot of heathens! When I was a kid in Sunday School I put pennies in the collection plate for black bambinos not half as ignorant as your lot. Take it from me, lad, it would do you no good theologically or otherwise.'

He turned to Dalgliesh.

'Wearing his stole, was he? Now that's interesting.'

'I thought so.'

'And yet, is it so unnatural? He was alone and may have known he was dying. Maybe he just felt more comfortable with the feel of it around his neck. Wouldn't you say that, Sir?'

'I don't know what he'd do, or what he'd feel. I've been content not to know for the past twenty years.'

'And the forced bureau. Maybe he'd decided to make a start with destroying his papers and couldn't remember where he'd put the key.'

'It's perfectly possible.'

'And he was cremated?'

'Cremated, on the insistence of Mrs Hammitt, and his ashes buried with the appropriate rite of the Church of England.'

Inspector Daniel said nothing more. There was, Dalgliesh thought bitterly as they rose to go, nothing else to say.

IV

Father Baddeley's solicitors, the firm of Loder and Wainwright, occupied a simple but harmonious house of red brick facing directly on to South Street and typical, Dalgliesh thought, of the more agreeable houses which were built after the old town was virtually destroyed by fire in 1762. The door was propped open by a brass doorstop shaped like a miniature cannon, its dazzling muzzle pointing intimidatingly towards the street. Apart from this bellicose symbol the house and its furnishings were reassuringly welcoming, producing an atmosphere of solid affluence, tradition and professional rectitude. The white painted hall was hung with prints of eighteenth-century Dorchester and smelt of furniture polish. To the left, an open door led to a large waiting-room with an immense circular table on a carved pedestal, half a dozen carved mahogany chairs heavy enough to accommodate a robust farmer in upright discomfort, and an oil painting of an unnamed Victorian gentleman, presumably the founder of the firm, bewhiskered and beribboned and displaying the seal of his watch chain between a delicate thumb and finger as if anxious that the painter should not overlook it. It was a house in which any of Hardy's more prosperous characters would have felt themselves at home, could with confidence have discussed the effects of the abolition of the corn laws or the perfidy of the French privateers. Opposite the waiting-room was a partitioned office occupied by a young girl, dressed up to the waist in black boots and a long skirt like a Victorian governess and above the waist like a pregnant milkmaid. She was laboriously typing at a speed which could have explained Maggie Hewson's strictures about the firm's dilatoriness. In response to Dalgliesh's inquiry she glanced up at him through a curtain of lank hair and said that Mr Robert was out at present but was expected back in ten minutes. Taking his time over lunch, thought Dalgliesh, and resigned himself to a half-hour wait.

Loder returned some twenty minutes later. Dalgliesh heard him galumphing happily into the reception office; there was the murmur of voices and a second later he appeared in the waiting-room and invited his visitor into his office at the rear of the house. Neither the room – poky, stuffy and untidy – nor its owner were quite what Dalgliesh had expected. Neither suited the house. Bob Loder was a swarthy, heavily built, square-faced man with a blotched skin and unhealthy pallor and small, discouraged eyes. His sleek hair was uniformly dark – too dark to be entirely natural – except for a thin line of silver at the brow and sides. His moustache was dapper and trim above lips so red and moist that they looked about to ooze blood. Noting the lines at the corner of the eyes and the sagging muscles of the neck Dalgliesh suspected that he was neither as young nor as vigorous as he was at pains to suggest.

He greeted Dalgliesh with a heartiness and *bonhomie* which seemed as unsuited to his personality as it was to the occasion. His manner recalled to Dalgliesh something of the desperate heartiness of ex-officers of his acquaintance who hadn't adjusted themselves to civilian life, or perhaps of a car salesman with little confidence that the chassis and engine will hang together long enough to complete the sale.

Dalgliesh briefly explained the ostensible reason for his visit.

'I didn't know that Father Baddeley was dead until I arrived at Toynton and the first I heard about his bequest to me was from Mrs Hewson. That isn't important. You probably haven't had a chance to write yet. But Mr Anstey wants the cottage cleared for the new occupant and I thought that I'd better check with you before removing the books.'

Loder put his head outside the door and yelled for the file. It was produced in a surprisingly quick time. After a perfunctory examination he said:

'That's OK. Perfectly. Sorry about no letter. It wasn't so much the lack of time as no address, don't you know. The dear old chap didn't think of that. Name familiar, of course. Ought I to know you?'

'I don't think so. Perhaps Father Baddeley mentioned my name when he visited you. I believe he did call in a day or so before the start of his last illness.'

'That's right, on Wednesday 11th p.m. That was only the second time we'd met, come to think of it. He first consulted me about three years ago, soon after he arrived at Toynton Grange. That was to make his will. He didn't have much but, then, he hadn't been spending much and it had accumulated into quite a nice little sum.'

'How did he hear of you?'

'He didn't. The dear old chap wanted to make his will, knew that he'd need a solicitor and just took the bus into Wareham, and walked into the first solicitor's office he came to. I happened to be here at the time so I got him. I drew up the will there and then since that was what he wanted and two of the staff here signed it. I'll say this for the old dear, he was the easiest client I've ever had.'

'I wondered whether his visit on 11th was to consult you about anything that was worrying him. From his last letter to me I rather gathered that he had something on his mind. If there's anything I ought to do . . .'

He let his voice trail away in a long interrogation.

Loder said cheerfully:

'The dear old chap came in some perturbation of the spirit. He was thinking of changing his will but hadn't quite made up his mind. He seemed to have got the idea that I could somehow put the money into limbo for him while he came to a decision. I said: "My dear Sir, if you die tonight the money goes to Wilfred Anstey and Toynton Grange. If you don't want that to happen, then you'll have to make up your mind what you do want and I'll draw up a new will. But the money exists. It won't disappear. And if you don't cancel the old will or change it, then it stands."'

'Did he strike you as sensible?'

'Oh, yes, muddled perhaps but more in his imagination than his comprehension if you get me. As soon as I pointed out the facts he understood them. Well, he always had understood them. It's just that he wished for a moment that the problem wasn't there. Don't we all know the feeling?'

'And a day later he went into hospital, and less than a fortnight later the problem was solved for him.'

'Yes, poor old dear. I suppose he would have said that providence decided it for him. Providence certainly made its views known in no uncertain way.'

'Did he give you any idea what was on his mind? I don't want to pry into professional confidences, but I did get a strong impression that he wanted to consult me about something. If he had a commission for me I'd like to try to carry it out. And I suppose I have the policeman's curiosity to find out what he wanted, to clear up unfinished business.'

'A policeman?'

Was the flicker of surprise and polite interest in those tired eyes a little too obvious to be natural?

Loder said:

'Did he invite you as a friend or in a professional capacity?'

'Probably a bit of both.'

'Well, I don't see what you can do about it now. Even if he'd told me his intentions about the will and I knew whom he wanted to benefit it's too late to do anything about it now.'

Dalgliesh wondered whether Loder seriously thought that he had been hoping for the money himself and was inquiring into a possible way of upsetting Father Baddeley's will.

He said:

'I know that. I doubt whether it was anything to do with his will. It's odd, though, that he never wrote to tell me about my legacy, and he left the main beneficiary in the same ignorance apparently.' It was entirely a shot in the dark but it found its mark. Loder spoke carefully, a trifle too carefully.

'Did he? I'd rather thought that that particular embarrassment was part of the old chap's dilemma, the reluctance to disappoint when he'd promised.'

He hesitated, seeming to think that he had said either too much or too little, and added:

'But Wilfred Anstey could confirm that.'

He paused again as if disconcerted by some subtle implication in his words and, obviously irritated at the devious paths into which the conversation was leading him, said more strongly:

'I mean if Wilfred Anstey says he didn't know that he was the principal legatee then he didn't know and I'm wrong. Are you staying long in Dorset?'

'Rather less than a week, I imagine. Just long enough to sort out and pack the books.'

'Oh, yes, the books, of course; perhaps that's what Father Baddeley meant to consult you about. He may have thought that a library of theological tomes would be more of a liability than an acceptable bequest.'

'It's possible.' The conversation seemed to have died. There was a brief, somewhat embarrassed pause before Dalgliesh said, rising from his chair:

'So there was nothing else worrying him as far as you know except this problem of the disposal of his money? He didn't consult you about anything else?'

'No, nothing. If he had, it might have been something I wouldn't have felt able to tell you without breaking a professional confidence. But, as he didn't, I don't see why you shouldn't know that. And what would he have to consult me over, poor old gentleman? No wife, no children, no relatives, as far as I know, no family troubles, no car, a blameless life. What would he need a solicitor for except to draw up his will?'

It was a little late to talk about professional confidence thought Dalgliesh. There was really no need for Loder to have confided that Father Baddeley had been thinking of changing his will. Given the fact that he hadn't in fact done so that was the kind of information which a prudent solicitor would feel was best left undisclosed. As Loder walked with him to the door, Dalgliesh said casually:

'Father Baddeley's will probably gave nothing but satisfaction. One can hardly say as much of Victor Holroyd's.'

The dull eyes were suddenly sharp, almost conspiratorial. Loder said:

'So you've heard about that, have you?'

'Yes. But I'm surprised that you have.'

'Oh, news gets around, don't you know, in a country district. As a matter of fact I have friends at Toynton. The Hewsons. Well, Maggie really. We met at the Conservative dance here last winter. It's a pretty dull life stuck there on the cliff for a lively girl.'

'Yes. It must be.'

'She's quite a lass is our Maggie. She told me about Holroyd's will. I gather that he went up to London to see his brother and it was rather taken for granted that he wanted to discuss his will. But it looks as if big brother didn't much like what Victor proposed and suggested that he thought again. In the event, Holroyd drew up the codicil himself. It wouldn't exactly present any problem for him. All the family have been brought up in the law and Holroyd started reading for the Bar himself before he decided to switch to school-teaching.'

'I understand that Holroyd and Martinson act for the Anstey family.'

'That's right, and have for four generations. It's a pity grandfather Anstey didn't consult them before drawing up his will. That case was quite a lesson in the unwisdom of trying to act as your own lawyer. Well, good afternoon, Commander. I'm sorry I couldn't be of more help.'

As he looked back when turning out of South Street, Dalgliesh could see Loder still watching after him, the brass cannon shining like a toy at his feet. There were a number of things about the solicitor which he found interesting. Not the least was how Loder had learned his rank.

But there was one other task before he turned his mind to his shopping. He called at the early nineteenth-century hospital, Christmas Close. But here he was unlucky. The hospital knew nothing of Father Baddeley; they admitted only chronic cases. If his friend had suffered a heart attack he would almost certainly have been admitted to the acute ward of a district general hospital despite his age. The courteous porter suggested that he should try either Poole General Hospital,

Blandford or the Victoria Hospital at Wimborne, and helpfully directed him to the nearest public telephone.

He tried Poole Hospital first as being the nearest. And here he was luckier than he could have hoped. The clerk who answered the telephone was efficient. Given the date of Father Baddeley's discharge he was able to confirm that the Reverend Baddeley had been a patient and to put Dalgliesh through to the right ward. The staff nurse answered. Yes, she remembered Father Baddeley. No, they hadn't heard that he had died. She spoke the conventional words of regret and was able to make them sound sincere. Then she fetched Nurse Breagan to the telephone. Nurse Breagan usually offered to post the patients' letters. Perhaps she could help Commander Dalgliesh.

His rank, he knew, had something to do with their helpfulness, but not all. They were kindly women who were disposed to take trouble, even with a stranger. He explained his dilemma to Nurse Breagan.

'So you see, I didn't know my friend had died until I arrived yesterday at Toynton Grange. He promised to return the papers we were working on to me, but they're not among his things. I wondered whether he posted them back to me from hospital, either to my London address or to the Yard.'

'Well now, Commander, the Father wasn't a great one for writing. Reading, yes; but not writing. But I did post two letters for him. They were both local as far as I can remember. I have to look at the addresses, you see, so that I post them in the right box. The date? Well, I couldn't remember that. But he did hand them to me together.'

'Would those be the two letters he wrote to Toynton, one to Mr Anstey and one to Miss Willison?'

'Come to think of it, Commander, I do seem to remember those names. But I couldn't be sure, you understand.'

'It's very clever of you to remember so much. And you're quite sure you only posted those two?'

'Oh, quite sure. Mind you, one of the other nurses might have posted a letter for him, but I couldn't find out for you without difficulty. Some of them have changed wards. But I don't think so. It's usually me that takes the letters. And he wasn't one for writing. That's how I remember the two letters he did send.'

It could mean something or nothing. But the information had been worth the trouble. If Father Baddeley had made an appointment for the night of his return home, he must have done so either by telephoning from the hospital once he was well enough, or by letter. And only Toynton Grange itself, the Hewsons and Julius Court were on the telephone. But it might have been more convenient for him to write. The letter to Grace Willison would have been the one arranging her appointment for confession. The one to Anstey might have been the letter of condolence on Holroyd's death to which she had referred. But, on the other hand, it might not.

Before ringing off he asked whether Father Baddeley had made any telephone calls from the hospital.

'Well, he made one, that I do know. That was when he was up and about. He went down to make it from the out-patients' waiting-hall and he asked me if there'd be a London directory there. That's how I remember.'

'At what time was this?'

'The morning. Just before I went off duty at twelve.'

So Father Baddeley had needed to make a London call, to a number he had to look up. And he had made it, not during the evening, but in office hours. There was one obvious inquiry Dalgliesh could make. But not yet. He told himself that as yet he had learned nothing which could justify even his unofficial involvement. And even if he had, where would all the suspicions, all the clues, ultimately lead? Only to a few fistfuls of ground bones in Toynton churchyard.

V

It wasn't until after an early dinner at the inn near Corfe Castle that Dalgliesh drove back to Hope Cottage and settled down to begin sorting Father Baddeley's books. But first there were small but necessary domestic chores to tackle. He replaced the dim bulb in the table lamp with a higher wattage; cleaned and adjusted the pilot light on the gas boiler over the sink; cleared a space in the food cupboard for his provisions and wine; and discovered in the outside shed by the aid of his torch a pile of driftwood for kindling, and a tin bath. There was no bathroom at Hope Cottage. Father Baddeley had probably taken his baths at Toynton Grange. But Dalgliesh had every intention of stripping and sluicing himself in the kitchen. Austerity was a small price to pay to avoid the bathroom at Toynton with its hospital smell of strong disinfectant, its intrusive reminders of sickness and deformity. He put a match to the dried grasses in the grate and watched them flare instantaneously into black needles in one sweet-smelling flame. Then he lit a small experimental fire and found to his relief that the chimney was clear. With a wood fire, a good light, books, food and a stock of wine he saw no reason to wish himself elsewhere.

He estimated that there were between two hundred and three hundred books on the sitting-room shelves and three times as many in the second bedroom; indeed the books had so taken over the room that it was impossible to get to the bed. The books presented very few surprises. Many of the theological tomes might be of interest to one of the London theological libraries; some, he thought, his aunt might be glad to give a home to; some were destined for his own shelves. There was H. B. Swete's *Greek Old Testament* in three volumes, Thomas à Kempis's *Imitation of Christ*; William Law's *Serious Call*; a leather-bound *Life and Letters of Eminent 19th Century Divines* in two volumes; a first edition of Newman's *Parochial and Plain Sermons*. But there was also a representative collection of the major English novelists and poets and since Father Baddeley had indulged himself by buying an occasional novel, there was a small but interesting collection of first editions.

At a quarter to ten he heard approaching footsteps and the squeak of wheels, there was a peremptory knock on the door, and Millicent Hammitt entered bringing with her an agreeable smell of fresh coffee and wheeling after her a laden trolley. There was a sturdy banded blue jug of coffee, a similar jar of hot milk, a bowl of brown sugar, two blue banded mugs, and a plate of digestive biscuits.

Dalgliesh felt that he could hardly object when Mrs Hammitt cast an appreciative glance at the wood fire, poured out two mugs of coffee and made it obvious that she was in no hurry to go.

Dalgliesh had been briefly introduced to her before dinner the previous evening, but there had been time for only half a minute's conversation before Wilfred had taken his stance at the reading desk and the ordained silence fell. She had taken the opportunity to discover, by the expedient of a blunt interrogation with no attempt at finesse, that Dalgliesh was holidaying alone because he was a widower and that his wife had died in childbirth with her baby. Her response to this had been, 'Very tragic. And unusual, surely, for these days?' spoken with an accusatory glance across the table and in a tone which suggested that someone had been inexcusably careless.

She was wearing carpet slippers and a thick tweed skirt, incongruously topped by an open-work jumper in pink wool, liberally festooned with pearls. Dalgliesh suspected that her cottage was a similar unhappy compromise between utility and fussiness, but had no inclination to find out. To his relief she made no attempt to help with the books but sat squatting on the edge of the chair, coffee mug cradled in her lap, her legs planted firmly apart to reveal twin balloons of milky white and varicosed thigh above the bite of the stockings. Dalgliesh continued with his job, coffee mug on the floor at his side. He shook each volume gently before allocating it to its pile in case some message should drop out. If it did, Mrs Hammitt's presence would be embarrassing. But he knew that the precaution was merely his professional habit of leaving nothing to chance. This wouldn't be Father Baddeley's way.

Meanwhile Mrs Hammitt sipped her coffee and talked, encouraged in her volubility and occasional indiscretion by the belief which Dalgliesh had noticed before that a man who is physically working only hears half what is said to him.

'No need to ask you if you had a comfortable night. Those beds of Wilfred's are notorious. A certain amount of hardness is supposed to be good for disabled patients but I like a mattress I can sink into. I'm surprised that Julius didn't invite you to sleep at his cottage, but he never does have visitors. Doesn't want to put Mrs Reynolds out I suppose. She's the village constable's widow from Toynton village and she does for Julius whenever he's here. Grossly overpaid, of course. Well, he can afford it. And you'll be sleeping here tonight, I understand. I saw Helen Rainer coming in with the bed linen. I suppose it won't worry you, sleeping in Michael's bed. No, of course it wouldn't, being a policeman. You aren't sensitive or superstitious about things like that. Quite right too; our death is but a sleep and a forgetting. Or do I mean life? Wordsworth anyway. I used to be very fond of poetry when I was a girl but I can't get along with these modern poets. Still, I should have quite looked forward to your reading.'

Her tone suggested that it would have been a solitary and eccentric pleasure. But Dalgliesh had momentarily stopped listening to her. He had found the first edition of *Diary of a Nobody* with an inscription written in a boyish hand, on the title page.

To Father Baddeley for his Birthday with love from Adam. I bought this from Mr Snelling in Norwich and he let me have it cheap because of the red stain on page twenty. But I've tested it and it isn't blood.

Dalgliesh smiled. So he'd tested it, had he, the arrogant little blighter. What mysterious concoction of acids and crystals from the remembered chemistry set had resulted in that confident scientific pronouncement? The inscription reduced the value of the book rather more than the stain, but he didn't think that Father Baddeley thought so. He placed it on the pile reserved for his own shelves and again let Mrs Hammitt's voice pierce his consciousness.

'And if a poet can't take the trouble to make himself intelligible to the educated reader, then the educated reader had better leave him alone, that's what I always say.'

'I'm sure you do, Mrs Hammitt.'

'Call me Millicent, won't you? We're supposed to be one happy family here. If I have to put up with Dennis Lerner and Maggie Hewson and even that appalling Albert Philby calling me by my Christian name – not that I give him much opportunity, I assure you – I don't see why you shouldn't. And I shall try to call you Adam but I don't think it's going to come easily. You aren't a Christian-name person.'

Dalgliesh carefully dusted the volumes of Maskell's *Monumenta Ritualica Ecclesiae Anglicanae* and said that, from what he had heard, Victor Holroyd hadn't done much towards promoting the concept of one happy family.

'Oh, you've heard about Victor then? Maggie gossiping, I suppose. He really was an extremely difficult man, inconsiderate in life and in death. I managed to get on with him fairly well. I think he respected me. He was a very clever man and full of useful information. But no one at the Grange could stand him. Even Wilfred more or less gave up in the end and left him alone. Maggie Hewson was the exception. Odd woman; she always has to be different. Do you know, I believe she thought Victor had willed his money to her. Of course we all knew that he had money. He took good care to let us know that he wasn't one of those patients paid for by the local authority. And I suppose she thought that if she played her cards right some of it might come to her. She more or less hinted to me once. Well, she was half drunk at the time. Poor Eric! I give that marriage another year at the most. Some men might find her physically attractive, I suppose, if you like that dyed blonde, blowzy, over-sexed type. Of course, her affair, if you can call it an affair, with Victor was just indecent. Sex is for the healthy. I know that the disabled are supposed to have feelings like the rest of us but you'd think that they'd put that sort of thing behind them when they get to the wheelchair stage. That book looks interesting. The binding's good anyway. You might get a shilling or two for that.'

Placing a first edition of *Tracts for the Times* out of reach of Millicent's nudging foot and among the books selected for himself, Dalgliesh recognized with transitory self-disgust that, however much he deplored Mrs Hammitt's uninhibited expression, the sentiment wasn't far from his own thoughts. What, he wondered, must it be like to feel desire, love, lust even, and be imprisoned in an unresponsive body? Or worse, a body only too responsive to some of its urges, but uncoordinated, ugly, grotesque. To be sensitive to beauty, but to live always with deformity. He thought that he could begin to understand Victor Holroyd's bitterness. He asked:

'What happened in the end to Holroyd's money?'

'It all went to his sister in New Zealand, all sixty-five thousand of it. Very right too. Money ought to be kept in the family. But I daresay Maggie had her hopes. Probably Victor more or less promised her. It's the sort of thing he would do. He could be very spiteful at times. But at least he left his fortune where it ought to go. I should be very displeased indeed if I thought that Wilfred had bequeathed Toynton Grange to anyone but me.'

'But would you want it?'

'Oh, the patients would have to go, of course. I can't see myself running Toynton Grange as it is now. I respect what Wilfred's trying to do, but he has a particular need to do it. I expect you've heard about his visit to Lourdes and the miracle. Well, that's all right by me. But I haven't had a miracle, thank God, and I've no intention of putting myself in the way of one. Besides, I've done quite enough for the chronic sick already. Half the house was left to me by father and I sold out to Wilfred so that he could start the Home. We had a proper valuation made at the time, naturally, but it wasn't very high. At the time large country houses were a drag on the market. Now, of course, it's worth a fortune. It's a beautiful house isn't it?'

'It's certainly interesting architecturally.'

'Exactly. Regency houses of character are fetching fantastic prices. Not that I'm set on selling. After all, it was our childhood home and I have an affection for it. But I should probably get rid of the land. As a matter of fact, Victor Holroyd knew someone locally who would be interested in buying, someone who wants to set up another holiday caravan camp.'

Dalgliesh said involuntarily:

'What a horrible thought!'

Mrs Hammitt was unabashed. She said complacently:

'Not at all. A very selfish attitude on your part, if I may say so. The poor need holidays just like the rich. Julius wouldn't like it, but I'm under no obligation to consider Julius. He'd sell his cottage and get out I suppose. He owns that acre and a half of the headland, but I can't see him driving through a caravan park every time he comes here from London. Besides, they'd more or less have to pass his windows to get down to the beach. That's the only spot with a beach at high tide. I can see them, can't you; knobbly-kneed fathers in natty little shorts carrying the picnic bag, mum following with a blaring transistor, squealing kids, yelling babies. No, I can't see Julius staying here.'

'Does everyone here know that you stand to inherit Toynton Grange?'

'Of course; it's no secret. Who else should get it? As a matter of fact, the whole estate should belong to me by right. Perhaps you know that Wilfred isn't really an Anstey, that he was adopted?'

Dalgliesh said cautiously that he thought someone had mentioned as much.

'Then you may as well know the whole of it. It's quite interesting if you're concerned with the law.'

Mrs Hammitt refilled her mug and wriggled back into her chair as if settling herself for a complicated dissertation.

'My father was particularly anxious for a son. Some men are like that, daughters don't really count with them. And I can quite see that I was a disappointment. If a man really wants a son, the only thing that reconciles him to a daughter is her beauty. And that I've never had. Luckily, it didn't seem to worry my husband. We suited very well.'

As the only possible answer to this announcement was a vague, congratulatory murmur, Dalgliesh made the appropriate sound.

'Thank you,' said Mrs Hammitt, as if acknowledging a compliment. She went on happily:

'Anyway, when the doctors told father that my mother couldn't bear another child, he decided to adopt a son. I believe he got Wilfred from a children's home, but I was only six at the time and I don't think I was ever told how and when they found him. Illegitimate, of course. People minded more about that kind of thing in 1920 and you could take your pick of unwanted babies. I remember how excited I was at the time to have a brother. I was a lonely child and with more than my share of natural affection. At the time, I didn't see Wilfred as a rival. I was very fond of Wilfred when we were young. I still am. People forget that sometimes.'

Dalgliesh asked what happened.

'It was my grandfather's will. The old man distrusted lawyers, even Holroyd and Martinson who were the family solicitors, and he drew up his own will. He left a life interest in the estate to my parents and the whole property in equal shares to his grandchildren. The question was, did he intend to include Wilfred? In the end we had to go to law about it. The case made quite a stir at the time and raised the whole question of rights of adopted children. Perhaps you remember the case?'

Dalgliesh did have a vague memory of it. He asked:

'When was your grandfather's will made, I mean in relation to your brother's adoption?'

'That was the vital part of the evidence. Wilfred was legally adopted on 3rd May 1921, and grandfather signed his will exactly ten days later on 13th May. It was witnessed by two servants, but they were dead by the time the case was fought. The will was perfectly clear and in order, except that he didn't put in the names. But Wilfred's lawyers could prove that grandfather knew about the adoption and was happy about it. And the will did say children, in the plural.'

'But he might have had it in mind that your mother would die first and your father remarry.'

'How clever of you! I can see that you've a lawyer's devious mind. That's exactly what my counsel argued. But it was no good. Wilfred won. But you can understand my feelings over the Grange. If grandfather had only signed that will before 3rd May things would be very different, I can tell you.'

'But you did get half the value of the estate?'

'That didn't last long I'm afraid. My dear husband got through money very quickly. It wasn't women, I'm glad to say. It was horses. They're just as expensive and even more unpredictable but a less humiliating rival for a wife. And, unlike another woman, you can at least be glad when they win. Wilfred always said that Herbert became senile when he retired from the army, but I didn't complain. I rather preferred him that way. But he did get through the money.'

Suddenly she glanced around the room, leaned forward and gave Dalgliesh a sly conspiratorial glance.

'I'll tell you something that no one at Toynton Grange knows, except Wilfred. If he does sell out I shall get half the sale price. Not just half the extra profit, fifty per cent of what he gets. I've got an undertaking from Wilfred, properly signed and witnessed by Victor. Actually it was Victor's suggestion. He thought it would stand up in law. And it isn't kept where Wilfred can get his hands on it. It's with Robert Loder, a solicitor in Wareham. I suppose Wilfred was so confident that he'd never need to sell, that he didn't care what he signed or perhaps he was arming himself against temptation. I don't think for one minute that he will sell. He cares too much about the place for that. But if he should change his mind, then I shall do very nicely.'

Dalgliesh said, greatly daring:

'When I arrived, Mrs Hewson said something about the Ridgewell Trust. Hasn't Mr Anstey got it in mind to transfer the Home?'

Mrs Hammitt took the suggestion more calmly than he had expected. She retorted robustly:

'Nonsense! I know Wilfred talks about it from time to time, but he'd never just hand over Toynton Grange. Why should he? Money's tight, of course, but money always is tight. He'll just have to put up the fees or get the local authorities to pay more for the patients they send. There's no reason why he should subsidize the local authorities. And if he still can't make the place pay, then he'd do better to sell out, miracle or no miracle.'

Dalgliesh suggested that, in all the circumstances, it was surprising that Anstey hadn't become a Roman Catholic. Millicent seized on the thought with vehemence.

'It was quite a spiritual struggle for him at the time.' Her voice deepened and throbbed with the echo of cosmic forces linked in mortal struggle. 'But I was glad that he decided to remain in our church. Our father' – her voice boomed out in such a sudden access of hortatory fervour that Dalgliesh, startled, half expected that she was about to launch into the Lord's prayer – 'would have been so very distressed. He was a great churchman, Commander Dalgliesh. Evangelical of course. No, I was glad that Wilfred didn't go over.'

She spoke as if Wilfred, faced with the Jordan river, had neither liked the look of the water nor had confidence in his boat.

Dalgliesh had already asked Julius Court about Anstey's religious allegiance and had received a different and, he suspected, a more accurate explanation. He recalled their conversation on the patio before they had rejoined Henry; Julius's amused voice: 'Father O'Malley, who was supposed to be instructing Wilfred, made it plain that his church would in future proclaim on a number of matters that Wilfred had seen as coming within his personal jurisdiction. It occurred to dear Wilfred that he was on the point of joining a very large organization and one which thought that, as a convert, he was receiving rather than bestowing benefit. In the

end, after what I have no doubt was a gratifying struggle, he decided to remain in a more accommodating
fold.'

'Despite the miracle?' Dalgliesh had asked.

'Despite the miracle. Father O'Malley is a rationalist.
He admits the existence of miracles but prefers the evidence to be submitted to the proper authorities for
thorough examination. After a seemly delay the Church
in her wisdom will then pronounce. To go about pro-
claiming that one has been the recipient of special grace
smacks to him of presumption. Worse, I suspect he
thinks it in poor taste. He's a fastidious man, is Father
O'Malley. He and Wilfred don't really get on. I'm afraid
that Father O'Malley has lost his church a convert.'

'But the pilgrimages to Lourdes still go on?' Dalgliesh
had asked.

'Oh, yes. Twice a year regularly. I don't go. I used to
when I first came here but it isn't, in the contemporary
idiom, exactly my scene. But I usually make it my business to provide a slap-up tea to welcome them all back.'

Dalgliesh, his mind recalled to the present, was aware
that his back was beginning to ache. He straightened up
just as the clock on the mantelshelf struck the three-
quarters. A charred log tumbled from the grate shoot-
ing up a final cascade of sparks. Mrs Hammitt took it as
a signal that it was time to go. Dalgliesh insisted first on
washing up the coffee mugs and she followed him into
the kitchen.

'It has been a pleasant hour, Commander, but I doubt
whether we shall repeat it. I'm not one of those neighbours who keep dropping in. Thank God I can stand
my own company. Unlike poor Maggie, I have resources.

And I'll say one thing for Michael Baddeley, he did keep himself to himself.'

'Nurse Rainer tells me that you persuaded him of the advantages of cremation.'

'Did she say that? Well, I daresay she's right. I may have mentioned it to Michael. I strongly disapprove of wasting good ground to bury putrifying bodies. As far as I remember the old man didn't care what happened to him as long as he ended up in consecrated earth with the proper words said over him. Very sensible. My view entirely. And Wilfred certainly didn't object to the cremation. He and Dot Moxon agreed with me absolutely. Helen protested over the extra trouble, but what she didn't like was having to get a second doctor's signature. Thought it cast some kind of aspersion on dear Eric's clinical judgement, I suppose.'

'But surely no one was suggesting that Dr Hewson's diagnosis was wrong?'

'Of course not! Michael died of a heart attack, and even Eric was competent to recognize that, I should hope. No, don't bother to see me home, I've got my torch. And if there's anything you need at any time, just knock on the wall.'

'But would you hear? You didn't hear Father Baddeley.'

'Naturally not, since he didn't knock. And after about nine-thirty I wasn't really listening for him. You see, I thought someone had already visited to settle him for the night.'

The darkness outside was cool and restless, a black mist, sweet-tasting and smelling of the sea, not the mere absence of light but a positive, mysterious force.

Dalgliesh manoeuvred the trolley over the doorstep. Walking beside Millicent down the short path, and steadying the trolley with one hand, he asked with careful uninterest:

'Did you hear someone, then?'

'Saw, not heard. Or so I thought. I was thinking of making myself a hot drink and I wondered whether Michael would like one. But when I opened my front door to call in and ask, I thought I saw a figure in a cloak disappearing into the darkness. As Michael's light was off – I could see that the cottage was completely dark – naturally I didn't want to disturb him. I know now that I was mistaken. Either that or I'm going potty. It wouldn't be difficult in this place. Apparently no one did visit him and now they've all got a bad conscience about it. I can see how I was deceived. It was a night like this. Just a slight breeze but the darkness seeming to move and form itself into shapes. And I heard nothing, not even a footfall. Just a glimpse of a bent head, hooded, and a cloak swirling into the darkness.'

'And this was at about nine-thirty?'

'Or a little later. Perhaps it was about the time he died. A fanciful person could frighten herself imagining that she'd seen his ghost. That was what Jennie Pegram actually suggested when I told them at Toynton Grange. Ridiculous girl!'

They had almost reached the door of Faith Cottage. She hesitated and then said as if on impulse, and, he thought, with some embarrassment:

'They tell me that you're worried about the broken lock of Michael's bureau. Well, it was all right the night before he came back from hospital. I found I'd run out

189

of envelopes and I had an urgent letter to write. I thought that he wouldn't mind if I took a look in the bureau. It was locked then.'

Dalgliesh said:

'And broken when your brother looked for the will shortly after the body was found.'

'So he says, Commander. So he says.'

'But you have no proof that he broke it?'

'I've no proof that anyone did. The cottage was full of people running in and out. Wilfred, the Hewsons, Helen, Dot, Philby, even Julius when he arrived from London; the place was like a wake. All I know is that the bureau was locked at nine o'clock on the night before Michael died. And I've no doubt that Wilfred was keen to get his eyes on that will and see if Michael really had left Toynton Grange all he possessed. And I do know that Michael didn't break the lock himself.'

'How, Mrs Hammitt?'

'Because I found the key, just after lunch on the day he died. In the place where, presumably, he always kept it – that old tea tin on the second shelf of the food cupboard. I didn't think he'd mind my having any little bits of food he'd left. I slipped it into my pocket in case it got lost when Dot cleared the cottage. After all, that old bureau desk is quite valuable and the lock ought to be repaired. As a matter of fact, if Michael hadn't left it to Grace in his will, I would have moved it into here and looked after it properly.'

'So you still have the key?'

'Of course. No one has ever bothered about it but you. But, as you seem so interested you may as well take it.'

She dug her hand into the pocket of her skirt and he felt the cold metal pressed into his palm. She had opened the door of her cottage now and had reached for the light switch. In the sudden glare he blinked, and then saw it clearly, a small silver key, delicate as filigree, but tied now with thin string to a red plastic clothes peg, the red so bright that, for a dazzled second, it looked as if his palm were stained with blood.

FIVE

Act of Malice

I

When he looked back on his first weekend in Dorset, Dalgliesh saw it as a series of pictures, so different from the later images of violence and death that he could almost believe that his life at Toynton Head had been lived on two levels and at different periods of time. These early and gentle pictures, unlike the later harsh black and white stills from some crude horror film, were suffused with colour and feeling and smell. He saw himself plunging through the sea-washed shingle of Chesil Bank, his ears loud with bird cries and the grating thunder of the tide to where Portland reared its dark rocks against the sky; climbing the great earthworks of Maiden Castle and standing, a solitary windblown figure, where four thousand years of human history were compassed in numerous contours of moulded earth; eating a late tea in Judge Jeffrey's lodgings in Dorchester as the mellow autumn afternoon faded into dusk; driving through the night between a falling tangle of golden bracken and high untrimmed hedgerows to where the stone-walled pub waited with lighted windows on some remote village green.

And then, late at night when there could be small risk of a visitor from Toynton Grange disturbing him, he would drive back to Hope Cottage to the familiar and welcoming smell of books and a wood fire. Somewhat to his surprise, Millicent Hammitt was faithful to her promise not to disturb him after that first visit. He soon guessed why; she was a television addict. As he sat drinking his wine and sorting Father Baddeley's books, he could hear through the chimney breast the faint and not disagreeable sounds of her nightly entertainment; the sudden access of a half-familiar advertising jingle; the antiphonal mutter of voices; the bark of gun shots; feminine screams; the blaring fanfare to the late-night film.

He had a sense of living in a limbo between the old life and the new, excused by convalescence from the responsibility of immediate decision, from any exertion which he found disagreeable. And he found the thought of Toynton Grange and its inmates disagreeable. He had taken what action he could. Now he was waiting on events. Once, looking at Father Baddeley's empty and shabby chair, he was reminded irreverently of the fabled excuse of the distinguished atheist philosopher, ushered after death to his astonishment into the presence of God.

'But Lord, you didn't provide sufficient evidence.'

If Father Baddeley wanted him to act he would have to provide more tangible clues than a missing diary and a broken lock.

He was expecting no letters except Bill Moriarty's reply since he had left instructions that none were to be forwarded. And he intended to collect Bill's letter himself from the postbox. But it arrived on the Monday, at least a day earlier than he had thought possible. He had spent the morning in the cottage and hadn't walked to the postbox until after his lunch at two-thirty when he had taken back his milk bottles for collection.

The postbox contained the one letter, a plain envelope with a W. C postmark; the address was typed but his rank omitted. Moriarty had been careful. But as he slipped his thumb under the flap, Dalgliesh wondered if he himself had been careful enough. There was no obvious sign that the letter had been opened; the flap was intact. But the glue was suspiciously weak, and the flap slid open a little too easily under the pressure of his thumb. And the postbox was otherwise empty. Someone, probably Philby, must already have the Toynton Grange post. It was odd that he hadn't delivered this letter at Hope Cottage. Perhaps he should have used a poste restante in Toynton village or Wareham. The thought that he had been careless irritated him. The truth is, he thought, that I don't know what, if anything, I'm investigating, and I only spasmodically care. I haven't the stomach to do the job properly or the will and courage to leave it alone. He was in the mood to find Bill's prose style more than usually irritating.

'Nice to see your elegant handwriting again. There's general relief here that the reports of your impending decease were exaggerated. We're keeping the wreath contributions for a celebration party. But what are you doing anyway gum-shoeing in Dorset among such a questionable group of weirdies? If you pine for work there's plenty here. However, here's the gen.

'Two of your little lot have records. You know, apparently, something about Philby. Two convictions for G. B. H. in 1967 and 1969, four for theft in 1970 and a miscellany of earlier misdemeanours. The only extraordinary thing about Philby's criminal history is the leniency with which judges have sentenced him. Looking at his C. R. O. I'm not altogether surprised. They probably felt that it was unjust to punish too harshly a man who was following the only career for which physiognomy and talents had fitted him. I did manage to have a word with "the open door" about him. They admit his faults, but say that he is capable, given affection, of a ferocious loyalty. Watch out that he doesn't take a fancy to you.

'Millicent Hammitt was convicted twice for shoplifting by the Cheltenham Magistrates in 1966 and 1968. In the first case there was the usual defence of menopausal difficulties, and she was fined. She was lucky to escape so easily the second time. But that was a couple of months after her husband, a retired army major, had died and the court was sympathetic. They were probably influenced too by Wilfred Anstey's assurances that she was coming to live with him at Toynton Grange and would be under his eye. There's been no trouble since so I assume that Anstey's surveillance has been effective, the local shopkeepers more accommodating, or Mrs Hammitt more skilful in lifting the goods.

'That's all the official gen. The rest of them are clean, at least as far as the C. R. O is concerned. But if you're looking for an interesting villain – and I hardly suppose that Adam Dalgliesh is wasting his talents on Albert Philby – then may I recommend Julius Court? I got a line on him from a man I know who works at the F. C. O. Court is a bright grammar-school boy from Southsea who entered the foreign service after university equipped with all the usual elegant appurtenances but rather short on cash. He was at the Paris Embassy in 1970 when he gave evidence in the notorious murder trial when Alain Michonnet was accused of murdering Poitaud the racing driver. You may remember the case. There was a fair amount of publicity in the English press. It was pretty clear-cut, and the French police were salivating happily at the thought of nailing Michonnet. He's the son of Theo d'Estier Michonnet, who owns a chemical manufacturing plant near Marseilles, and they've had their eyes on père and fils for quite a time. But Court gave his chum an alibi. The odd thing was that they weren't really chums – Michonnet is aggressively heterosexual as the media make only too boringly plain – and the horrid word blackmail was hissed round the Embassy. No one believed Court's story; but no one could shake it. My informant thinks that Court's motive was nothing more sinister than a desire to amuse himself and to get his superiors twisting their knickers. If that was his motive he certainly succeeded. Eight months later his godfather conveniently died leaving him £30,000 and he chucked the service. He's said to have been rather clever with his investments. Anyway, that's all water under the bridge. Nothing is known to his discredit as they say, except, perhaps, a tendency to be a little too accommodating to his friends. But I give you the story for what it's worth.'

Dalgliesh folded the letter and stuffed it into his jacket pocket. He wondered how much, if any, of either story was known at Toynton Grange. Julius Court was unlikely to worry. His past was his own affair; he was independent of Wilfred's suffocating hold. But Millicent Hammitt had a double weight of gratitude. Who else except Wilfred knew, he wondered, about these two discreditable and pathetic incidents? How much would she care if the story became generally known at Toynton Grange? He wished again that he had used a poste restante.

A car was approaching. He looked up. The Mercedes, driven very fast, was coming down the coast road. Julius stepped on the brakes and the car rocked to a stop, its front bumper inches from the gate. He wrenched himself out and began tugging at the gate, calling out to Dalgliesh.

'The black tower's on fire! I saw smoke from the coast road. Have you a rake at Hope Cottage?'

Dalgliesh put his shoulder to the gate.

'I don't think so. There's no garden. But I found a yard broom – a besom – in the shed.'

'Better than nothing. D'you mind coming? It may take the two of us.'

Dalgliesh slipped quickly into the car. They left the gate open. Julius drove to Hope Cottage with little regard for the car springs or his passenger's comfort. He opened the boot while Dalgliesh ran to the yard shed. There among the paraphernalia of past occupants were the remembered besom, two empty sacks and, surprisingly, an old shepherd's crook. He threw them into the capacious boot. Julius had already turned the car and the engine was running. Dalgliesh got in beside him and the Mercedes leapt forward.

As they swung on to the coast road Dalgliesh asked:

'Is anyone there do you know? Anstey?'

'Could be. That's the worry. He's the only one who goes there now. And I can't see otherwise how the fire

197

started. We can get closest to the tower this way, but it means foot slogging it over the headland. I didn't try when I first spotted the smoke. It's no use without something to tackle the fire.'

His voice was tight, the knuckles on the wheel shone white. In the driving mirror Dalgliesh saw that the irises of his eyes were large and bright. The triangular scar above the right eye, normally almost invisible, had deepened and darkened. Above it he could see the insistent beat of the temple pulse. He glanced at the speedometer; they were doing over a hundred but the Mercedes, beautifully handled, held the narrow road easily. Suddenly the road twisted and rose and they caught a glimpse of the tower. The broken panes in the slitted windows below the cupola were belching puffballs of greyish smoke like miniature cannonfire. They tumbled merrily over the headland until the wind shook them into shredded dusters of cloud. The effect was absurd and picturesque, as innocuous as a child's entertainment. And then the road dipped and the tower was lost to view.

The coast road, wide enough only for a single car, was bounded to the seaward by a drystone wall. Julius was sure of his way. He had swung the car to the left even before Dalgliesh noticed the narrow gap, gateless but still bounded by two rotting posts. The car bumped to a standstill in a deep hollow to the right of the entry. Dalgliesh seized the crook and sacks and Julius the broom. Thus ridiculously lumbered, they began running across the headland.

Julius had been right; this was the quickest way. But they had to do it on foot. Even had he been willing to drive over this rough, rock-strewn ground it wouldn't have been possible. The headland was crossed with fragmented stone walls, low enough to leap over and with plenty of gaps, but none wide enough for a vehicle. The ground was deceptive. At one minute the tower seemed to recede, separated from them by interminable barriers of tumbling stone. Then it was upon them.

The smoke, acrid as a damp bonfire, was rolling strongly from the half-open door. Dalgliesh kicked it wide and leapt to one side as the gusts billowed out. There was an immediate roar and the tongue of flame fanged out at him. With the crook he began raking out the burning debris, some still identifiable – long dried grass and hay, rope ends, what looked like the remains of an old chair – the years of accumulated rubbish since the headland had been public land and the black tower, unlocked, used as a shepherd's shelter or a night lodging for tramps. As he raked out the burning malodorous clumps he could hear Julius behind him frantically beating them out. Little fires started and crawled like red tongues among the grasses.

As soon as the doorway was clear Julius rushed in stamping down the smouldering remnants of grass and hay with the two sacks. Dalgliesh could see his smoke-shrouded figure coughing and reeling. He dragged him unceremoniously out and said:

'Keep back until I've cleared it. I don't want the two of you on my hands.'

'But he's there! I know he is. He must be. Oh, God! The bloody fool!'

The last smouldering clump of grass was out now. Julius, pushing Dalgliesh aside, ran up the stone stairway which circled the walls. Dalgliesh followed. A wooden door to a middle chamber was ajar. Here there was no window, but in the smoke-filled darkness they could see the huddled sack-like figure against the far wall. He had drawn the hood of the monk's cloak over his head and had swathed himself into its folds like a human derelict wrapped against the cold. Julius's feverish hands got lost in the folds. Dalgliesh could hear him cursing. It took seconds before Anstey's arms were freed and, together, they dragged him to the door and, with difficulty, supported and manoeuvred the inert body between them down the narrow stairs and into the fresh-smelling air.

They laid him prone on the grass. Dalgliesh had dropped to his knees, ready to turn him and start artificial respiration. Then Anstey slowly stretched out both arms and lay in an attitude both theatrical and vaguely blasphemous. Dalgliesh, relieved that he wouldn't now have to fasten his mouth over Anstey's, got to his feet. Anstey drew up his knees and began to cough convulsively in hoarse whooping gasps. He turned his face to one side, his cheek resting on the headland. The moist mouth, coughing out saliva and bile, seemed to be sucking at the grass as if avid for nourishment. Dalgliesh and Court knelt and raised him between them. He said weakly:

'I'm all right. I'm all right.'

Dalgliesh asked:

'We've got the car on the coast road. Can you walk?'

'Yes. I'm all right, I tell you. I'm all right.'

'There's no hurry. Better rest for a few minutes before we start.'

They lowered him against one of the large boulders and he sat there a little apart from them, still coughing spasmodically, and looking out to sea. Julius paced the cliff edge, restlessly as if fretting at the delay. The stench of the fire was blown gently from the blackened headland like the last waves of a fading pestilence.

After five minutes Dalgliesh called:

'Shall we start now?'

Together and without speaking, they raised Anstey and supported him between them across the headland and to the car.

II

No one spoke on the drive back to Toynton Grange. As usual, the front of the house seemed deserted, the tessellated hall was empty, unnaturally silent. But Dorothy Moxon's sharp ears must have heard the car, perhaps from the clinical room at the front of the house. Almost immediately she appeared at the top of the stairs.

'What is it? What happened?'

'It's all right. Wilfred managed to set fire to the black tower with himself inside. He isn't hurt, just shocked. And the smoke hasn't done his lungs any good.'

She glanced accusingly from Dalgliesh to Julius as if it were their fault, then put both her arms round Anstey in a gesture fiercely maternal and protective and began to urge him gently up the stairs, muttering encouragement and remonstration into his ear in a soft grumbling monotone which, to Dalgliesh, sounded like an endearment. Anstey, he noticed, seemed less capable of supporting himself now than he had been on the headland and they made slow progress. But when Julius came forward to help, a glance from Dorothy Moxon made him draw back. With difficulty she got Anstey into his small white-painted bedroom at the back of the house and helped him on to the narrow bed. Dalgliesh made a swift mental inventory. The room was much as he had expected. One small table and chair set under the window giving a view of the patients' rear courtyard; a well-stocked bookcase; one rug; a crucifix over the bed; a bedside table with a simple lamp and a carafe of water. But the thick mattress bounced gently as Wilfred rolled on to it. The towel hanging beside the wash basin looked luxuriantly soft. The bedside rug, plain in design, was no strip of worn, discarded carpet. The hooded dressing-gown in white towelling hanging behind the door had a look of simplicity, almost austerity; but Dalgliesh did not doubt that it was agreeably soft to the skin. This might be a cell, but it lacked none of the essential comforts.

Wilfred opened his eyes and fixed his blue gaze on Dorothy Moxon. It was interesting, Dalgliesh thought, how he managed to combine humility with authority in one look. He held out a suppliant hand.

'I want to talk to Julius and Adam, Dot dear. Just for a moment. Will you?'

She opened her mouth, clamped it shut again, and stomped out without a word, closing the door firmly behind her. Wilfred closed his eyes again and appeared mentally to withdraw himself from the scene. Julius looked down at his hands. His right palm was red and swollen and a blister had already formed over the bowl of the thumb. He said with a note of surprise:

'Funny! My hand's burnt. I never felt it at the time. Now it's beginning to hurt like hell.'

Dalgliesh said:

'You should get Miss Moxon to dress it. And it might be as well to let Hewson have a look at it.'

Julius took a folded handkerchief from his pocket, soaked it in cold water at the wash basin and wrapped it inexpertly round his hand.

He said:

'It can wait.'

The realization that he was in pain appeared to have soured his temper. He stood over Wilfred and said crossly:

'Now that a definite attack has been made on your life and damn nearly succeeded, I suppose you'll act sensibly for once and send for the police.'

Wilfred did not open his eyes, he said weakly:

'I have a policeman here.'

Dalgliesh said:

'It isn't for me. I can't undertake an official investigation for you. Court is right, this is a matter for the local police.'

Wilfred shook his head.

'There's nothing to tell them. I went to the black tower because there were things I needed to think over in peace. It's the only place where I can be absolutely alone. I was smoking; you know how you all complain about my smelly old pipe. I remember knocking it out against the wall as I went up. It must have been still alight. All that dried grass and straw would have gone up at once.'

Julius said grimly:

203

'It did. And the outside door? I suppose you forgot to lock it after you, despite all the fuss you make about never leaving the black tower open. You're a careless lot at Toynton Grange aren't you? Lerner forgets to check the wheelchair brakes and Holroyd goes over the cliff. You knock out your pipe above a floor strewn with highly combustible dry straw, leave the door open to provide a draught, and bloody nearly immolate yourself.'

Anstey said:

'That's how I prefer to believe it happened.'

Dalgliesh said quickly:

'Presumably there's a second key to the tower. Where is it kept?'

Wilfred opened his eyes and stared into space as if patiently dissociating himself from this dual interrogation.

'Hanging on a nail on the keyboard in the business room. It was Michael's key, the one I brought back here after his death.'

'And everyone knows where it's hung?'

'I imagine so. All the keys are kept there and the one to the tower is distinctive.'

'How many people at Toynton Grange knew that you planned to be in the tower this afternoon?'

'All of them. I told them my plans after prayers. I always do. People have to know where to find me in an emergency. Everyone was there except Maggie and Millicent. But what you're suggesting is ridiculous.'

'Is it?' asked Dalgliesh.

Before he could move, Julius, who was nearer the door had slipped out. They waited in silence. It was another two minutes before he returned. He said with grim satisfaction:

'The business room is empty and the key isn't there. That means whoever took it hasn't yet had the chance to put it back. Incidentally, I called Dot on my way back. She's lurking in her surgical hell sterilizing enough equipment for a major operation. It's like confronting a harpy through a hiss of steam. Anyway, she claims with bad grace that she was in the business room continually from 2 p.m. until about five minutes before we got back. She can't remember whether the tower key was on the keyboard. She didn't notice it. I'm afraid I've made her suspicious, Wilfred, but it seemed important to establish some facts.'

Dalgliesh thought that the facts could have been established without direct questioning. But it was too late now to initiate inquiries and in any case he had neither the heart nor stomach to undertake them. Certainly he had no wish to pit the claims of orthodox detection against Julius's enthusiastic amateurism. But he asked:

'Did Miss Moxon say whether anyone had come into the business room while she was there? They may have made an attempt to replace the key.'

'According to her, the place was – untypically – like a railway station. Henry wheeled himself in shortly after two, and then went out again. No explanation. Millicent dropped in about half an hour ago looking, so she said, for you, Wilfred. Dennis arrived a few minutes later to look up an unspecified telephone number. Maggie arrived just before we did. Again, no explanation. She didn't stay, but she did ask Dot whether she'd seen Eric. The only safe deduction from all this is that Henry couldn't have been on the headland at the material time.

But then, we know he wasn't. Whoever started that fire had the use of a pair of very sound legs.'

His own, or someone else's, thought Dalgliesh.

He spoke again directly to the quiet figure on the bed.

'Did you see anyone when you were in the tower, either before or after the fire started?'

Wilfred paused before replying.

'I think so.'

Seeing Julius's face, he went on quickly:

'I'm sure I did, but only very briefly. When the fire started I was sitting at the southern window, the one overlooking the sea. I smelt smoke and went down into the middle chamber. I opened the door to the base of the tower and saw the hay smouldering and a sudden tongue of flame. I could have got out then, but I panicked. I'm terrified of fire. It isn't a rational fear. It goes well beyond that. I suppose you'd call it a phobia. Anyway, I scrambled ignominiously back into the top room and began running from window to window looking hopelessly for help. It was then I saw – unless it was an hallucination – a figure in a brown habit slipping between that clump of boulders to the south-west.'

Julius said:

'From which he could escape unrecognized by you either to the road or down the cliffs to the beach. That's if he were agile enough for the cliff path. What sort of figure, a man or a woman?'

'Just a figure. I only had a glimpse. I shouted but the wind was against me and he obviously didn't hear. I never thought of it being a woman.'

'Well, think now. The hood was up, I suppose?'

'Yes. Yes it was.'

206

'And on a warm afternoon! Think it out for yourself, Wilfred. Incidentally, there are three brown habits hanging in the business room. I felt in the pockets for the key. That's why I noticed. Three habits. How many do you have altogether?'

'Eight of the lightweight summer ones. They're always kept hanging in the business room. Mine has rather different buttons, but otherwise we have them in common. We're not really particular which one we take.'

'You're wearing yours; presumably Dennis and Philby are wearing theirs. That means two are missing.'

'Eric may be wearing one, he does occasionally. And Helen sometimes slips into one if the day is chilly. I seem to remember that one is in the sewing room being mended. And I think one was missing just before Michael died, but I can't be sure. It may have turned up again. We don't really keep a check on them.'

Julius said:

'So it's practically impossible to know whether one is missing. I suppose what we ought to be doing, Dalgliesh, is to check up on them now. If she hasn't had a chance to replace the key, presumably she's still got the habit.'

Dalgliesh said:

'We've no proof that it was a woman. And why hang on to the habit? It could be discarded anywhere in Toynton Grange without suspicion.'

Anstey propped himself up and said with sudden strength:

'No, Julius, I forbid it! I won't have people questioned and cross-examined. It was an accident.'

Julius, who seemed to be relishing his role of chief inquisitor, said:

'All right. It was an accident. You forgot to lock the door. You knocked out your pipe before it was dead and started the fire smouldering. The figure you saw was just someone from Toynton Grange taking an innocent stroll on the headland, somewhat overclad for the time of year and so immersed in the beauty of nature that he, or she, neither heard your shout, smelt the fire nor noticed the smoke. What happened then?'

'You mean, after I saw the figure? Nothing. I realized of course that I couldn't get out of the windows and I climbed down to the middle room. I opened the door to the bottom of the tower. The last thing I remember was a great billow of choking smoke and a sheet of flame. The smoke was suffocating me. The flames seemed to be searing my eyes. I hadn't even time to shut the door again before I was overcome. I suppose I should have kept both doors shut and sat tight. But it isn't easy to make sensible decisions in a state of panic.'

Dalgliesh asked:

'How many people here knew that you are abnormally afraid of fire?'

'Most of them suspect, I think. They may not know just how obsessive and personal a fear it is, but they do know that fire worries me. I insist on all the patients sleeping on the ground floor. I've always worried about the sickroom, and I was reluctant to let Henry have an upper room. But someone had to sleep in the main part of the house, and we must have a sickroom close to the clinical room and the nurses' bedrooms in case there's an emergency at night. It's sensible and prudent to fear fire in a place like this. But prudence has nothing to do with the terror I feel at the sight of smoke and flame.'

He put one hand up to his eyes and they saw that he had begun to tremble. Julius looked down at the shaking figure with almost clinical interest.

Dalgliesh said:

'I'll get Miss Moxon.'

He had hardly turned to the door when Anstey shot out a protesting hand. They saw that the trembling had stopped. He said, looking at Julius:

'You do believe that the work I'm doing here is worthwhile?'

Dalgliesh wondered if only he had noticed a fraction of a second's pause before Julius replied evenly:

'Of course.'

'You're not just saying that to comfort me, you believe it?'

'I wouldn't say it otherwise.'

'Of course not, forgive me. And you agree that the work is more important than the man?'

'That's more difficult. I could argue that the work is the man.'

'Not here. This place is established now. It could go on without me if it had to.'

'Of course it could, if it's adequately endowed, and if the local authorities continue to send contractual patients. But it won't have to go on without you if you act sensibly instead of like the reluctant hero of a third-rate TV drama. It doesn't suit you, Wilfred.'

'I'm trying to be sensible and I'm not being brave. I haven't much physical courage you know. It's the virtue I most regret. You two have it – no, don't argue. I know, and I envy you for it. But I don't really need courage for this situation. You see, I can't believe that someone is really trying to kill me.' He turned to Dalgliesh.

'You explain, Adam. You must see what I'm getting at.'

Dalgliesh said carefully:

'It could be argued that neither of the two attempts were serious. The frayed climbing rope? It's hardly a very certain method, and most people here must know that you wouldn't start a climb without checking your equipment and that you certainly wouldn't climb alone. This afternoon's little charade? You would probably have been safe enough if you'd closed both the doors and stayed in the top room; uncomfortably hot probably, but in no real danger. The fire would have burnt itself out in time. It was opening the middle door and gasping in a lungful of smoke which nearly did for you.'

Julius said:

'But suppose the grass had burnt fiercely and the flames had caught the wooden floor of the first storey? The whole of the middle tower would have gone up in a matter of seconds; the fire must have reached the top room. If it had, nothing could have saved you.' He turned to Dalgliesh:

'Isn't that true?'

'Probably. That's why you ought to tell the police. A practical joker who takes risks like that has to be taken seriously. And the next time there mightn't be someone handy to rescue you.'

'I don't think there will be a next time. I think I know who's responsible. I'm not really quite as foolish as I seem. I'll take care, I promise. I have a feeling that the person responsible won't be here with us much longer.'

Julius said:

'You're not immortal, Wilfred.'

'I know that, too, and I could be wrong. So I think it's time I spoke to the Ridgewell Trust. The Colonel is overseas, visiting his homes in India, but he's due back on the 18th. The trustees would like my answer by the end of October. It's a question of tying up capital for future developments. I wouldn't hand it over to them without a majority agreement from the family. I propose to hold a family council. But, if someone is really trying to frighten me into breaking my vow, then I'll see that my work here is made indestructible, whether I'm alive or dead.'

Julius said:

'If you hand the whole property over to the Ridgewell Trust, it isn't going to please Millicent.'

Wilfred's face set into a mask of obstinacy. Dalgliesh was interested to see how the features changed. The gentle eyes became stern and glazed as if unwilling to see, the mouth set into an uncompromising line. And yet the whole expression was one of petulant weakness.

'Millicent sold out to me perfectly willingly and at a fair valuation. She can't reasonably complain. If I'm driven out of here, the work goes on. What happens to me isn't important.'

He smiled at Julius.

'You aren't a believer, I know, so I'll find another authority for you. How about Shakespeare? "Be absolute for death; either death or life shall thereby be the sweeter." '

Julius Court's eyes briefly met Dalgliesh's over Wilfred's head. The message simultaneously passed was simultaneously understood. Julius had some difficulty in controlling his mouth. At last he said dryly:

211

'Dalgliesh is supposed to be convalescent. He's already practically passed out with the exertion of saving you. I may look healthy enough but I need my strength for the pursuit of my own personal pleasures. So if you are determined to hand over to the Ridgewell Trust by the end of the month, try being absolute for life, at least for the next three weeks, there's a good chap.'

III

When they were outside the room Dalgliesh asked:

'Do you believe he's in real danger?'

'I don't know. It was probably a closer thing this afternoon than someone intended.' He added with affectionate scorn:

'Silly old pseud! Absolute for death! I thought we were about to move on to *Hamlet* and be reminded that the readiness is all. One thing is certain though, isn't it? He isn't putting on a show of courage. Either he doesn't believe that someone at Toynton Grange has it in for him, or he thinks he knows his enemy and is confident that he can deal with him, or her. Or, of course, he started the fire himself. Wait until I've had this hand bandaged and then come in for a drink. You look as if you need it.'

But there were things Dalgliesh had to do. He left Julius, volubly apprehensive, to the mercies of Dorothy Moxon and walked back to Hope Cottage to collect his torch. He was thirsty, but there was no time for anything but cold water from the kitchen tap. He had left the cottage windows open but the little sitting-room, insulated by thick stone walls, was as warm and stuffy as on the day he arrived. As he closed the door, Father Baddeley's cassock swung against it and he caught again the musty, faintly ecclesiastical smell. The crochet chair back and arm covers were sleekly in place uncrumpled by Father Baddeley's head and hands. Something of his personality still lingered here, although already Dalgliesh felt its presence less strongly. But there was no communication. If he wanted Father Baddeley's counsel he would have to seek it in paths familiar but unaccustomed and to which he no longer felt that he had any right of way.

He was ridiculously tired. The cool, rather harsh-tasting water only brought him to a clearer realization of just how tired. The thought of the narrow bed upstairs, of throwing himself down upon its hardness, was almost irresistible. It was ridiculous that so comparatively little exertion could so exhaust him. And it seemed to have become insufferably hot. He drew a hand over his brow and felt the sweat, clammy and cold on his fingers. Obviously he had a temperature. He had, after all, been warned by the hospital that the fever might recur. He felt a surge of anger against his doctors, against Wilfred Anstey, against himself.

It would be easy now to pack his things and get back to the London flat. It would be cool and unencumbered there high above the Thames at Queenhythe. People would leave him alone supposing him to be still in Dorset. Or he could leave a note for Anstey and drive away now; the whole of the West Country was open to him. There were a hundred better places for convalescence than this claustrophobic, self-regarding community dedicated to love and self-fulfilment through suffering, where people sent each other poison pen letters, played at childish and malicious pranks or got tired of waiting for death and hurled themselves into annihilation. And there was nothing to keep him at Toynton; he told himself so with stubborn insistence, resting his head against the coolness of the small square of glass over the sink which had obviously served Father Baddeley as a shaving mirror. It was probably some freak aftermath of illness that made him at once so indecisive and so stubbornly reluctant to leave. For someone who had made up his mind never to go back to detection, he was giving a good imitation of a man committed to his job.

He saw no one as he left the cottage and began the long trudge up the cliff. It was still a bright day on the headland with that sudden almost momentary intensification of light which comes before the setting of the autumn sun. The cushions of moss on the fragmented walls were an intense green, dazzling the eye. Each individual flower was bright as a gem, its image shimmering in the gently moving air. The tower, when at last he came up to it, glistened like ebony and seemed to shiver in the sun. He felt that if he touched it it would reel and dissolve. Its long shadow lay like a monitory finger across the headland.

Taking advantage of the light, since the torch would be more use inside the tower, he began his search. The burnt straw and blackened debris lay in untidy heaps close to the porch, but the light breeze, never absent from this peak of the headland, had already begun to shift the humps and had strewn odd strands almost to the edge of the cliff. He began by scrutinizing the ground close to the walls, then moved out in widening circles. He found nothing until he reached the clump of boulders about fifty yards to the south-west. They were a curious formation, less a natural outcrop of the headland than an artefact, as if the builder of the tower had transported to the site double the weight of stone needed and had amused himself by arranging the surplus in the form of a miniature mountain range. The stones formed a long semi-circle about forty yards long, the peaks, from six to eight feet high, linked by smaller, more rounded uplands. There was adequate cover here for a man to escape undetected either to the cliff path or by way of the rapidly falling ground to the north-west to within a couple of hundred yards of the road.

It was here, behind one of the larger boulders, that Dalgliesh found what he had expected to find, a lightweight brown monk's habit. It was tightly rolled into a bolster and wedged into the crevice between two smaller stones. There was nothing else to be seen, no discernible footprints in the firm dry turf, no tin smelling of paraffin. Somewhere he expected to find a tin. Although the straw and dry grass in the base of the tower would have burned quickly enough once a fire was well established, he doubted whether a thrown match could have been relied upon to start a blaze.

He tucked the habit under his arm. If this were a murder hunt the forensic scientists would examine it for traces of fibre, for dust, for paraffin, for any biological or chemical link with someone at Toynton Grange. But it wasn't a murder hunt; it wasn't even an official investigation. And even if fibres were identified on the habit which matched those from a shirt, a pair of slacks, a jacket, a dress even, of someone at Toynton Grange, what did that prove? Apparently any of the helpers had a right to array themselves in Wilfred's curious idea of a working uniform. The fact that the habit had been abandoned, and at that point, suggested that the wearer had chosen to escape down the cliff rather than by way of the road; otherwise why not continue to rely on its camouflage? Unless, of course, the wearer were a woman and one who didn't normally thus array herself. In that case, to be seen by chance on the headland shortly after the fire would be damning. But no one, man or woman, would choose to wear it on the cliff path. It was the quicker but the more difficult route and the habit would be a dangerously entangling garment. Certainly it would bear tell-tale traces of sandy earth or green stains from the seaweed-covered rocks on that difficult scramble to the beach. But perhaps that was what he was meant to believe. Had the habit, like Father Baddeley's letter, been planted for him to discover, so neatly, so precisely placed exactly where he might have expected to find it? Why abandon it at all? Thus rolled, it was hardly an impossible burden to manage on that slippery path to the shore.

The door of the tower was still ajar. Inside the smell of the fire still lingered but half pleasantly now in the first cool of the early evening, an evocative autumnal smell of burnt grass. The lower part of the rope banister had burnt away and hung from the iron rings in scorched and tattered fragments.

He switched on his torch and began systematically to search among the blackened threads of burnt straw. He found it within minutes, a battered, soot-covered and lidless tin which could once have held cocoa. He smelt it. It could have been his imagination that a trace of paraffin still lingered.

He made his way up the stone steps carefully hugging the fire-blackened wall. He found nothing in the middle chamber and was glad to climb out of this dark, windowless and claustrophobic cell into the upper room. The contrast with the chamber below was immediate and striking. The little room was filled with light. It was only six feet wide and the domed and ribbed ceiling gave it a charming, feminine and slightly formal air. Four of the eight compass point windows were without their glass and the air streamed in, cool and scented with the sea. Because the room was so small the height of the tower was accentuated. Dalgliesh had the sensation of being suspended in a decorative pepper pot between sky and sea. The quiet was absolute, a positive peace. He could hear nothing but the ticking of his watch and the ceaseless anodyne surge of the sea. Why, he wondered, hadn't that self-tormented Victorian Wilfred Anstey signalled his distress from one of these windows? Perhaps, by the time his will to endure had been broken by the tortures of hunger and thirst, the old man had been too weak to mount the stairs. Certainly nothing of his final terror and despair had penetrated to this miniature light-filled eyrie. Looking out of the southern window Dalgliesh could see the crinkled sea layered in azure and purple with one red triangle of sail stationary on the horizon. The other windows gave a panoramic view of the whole sunlit headland; Toynton Grange and its clutter of cottages could be identified only by the chimney of the house itself since they lay in the valley. Dalgliesh noticed too that the square of mossy turf, where Holroyd's wheelchair had rested before that final convulsive heave towards destruction, and the narrow sunken lane were also invisible. Whatever had happened on that fateful afternoon, no one could have seen it from the black tower.

The room was simply furnished. There was a wooden table and a chair set against the seaward window, a small oak cupboard, a rush mat on the floor, a slatted old-fashioned easy chair with cushions set in the middle of the room, a wooden cross nailed to the wall. He saw that the door of the cupboard was ajar and the key in the lock. Inside he found a small and unedifying collection of paperback pornography. Even allowing for the natural tendency – to which Dalgliesh admitted himself not immune – to be disdainful of the sexual tastes of others, this was not the pornography that he would have chosen. It was a paltry and pathetic little library of flagellation, titillation and salacity, incapable, he thought, of stimulating any emotion beyond ennui and vague disgust. True it contained *Lady Chatterley's Lover* – a novel which Dalgliesh considered overrated as literature and not qualifying as pornography – but the rest was hardly respectable by any standard. Even after a gap of over twenty years, it was difficult to believe that the gentle, aesthetic and fastidious Father Baddeley had developed a taste for this pathetic trivia. And if he had, why leave the cupboard unlocked or the key where Wilfred could find it? The obvious conclusion was that the books were Anstey's and that he had only just had time to unlock the cupboard before he smelt the fire. In the subsequent panic he had forgotten to lock away the evidence of his secret indulgence. He would probably return in some haste and confusion as soon as he was fit enough and got the opportunity. And, if this were true, it proved one thing: Anstey could not have started the fire.

Leaving the cupboard door ajar precisely as he had found it, Dalgliesh then carefully searched the floor. The rough mat of what looked like plaited hemp was torn in places and overlaid with dust. From the drag on its surface and the lie of the torn and minute filaments of fibre he deduced that Anstey had moved the table from the eastern to the southern window. He found, too, what looked like traces of two different kinds of tobacco ash, but they were too small to be collected without his magnifying glass and tweezers. But, a little to the right of the eastern window and resting between the interstices of the mat, he found something which could be identified easily with the naked eye. It was a single used yellow match identical with those in the booklet by Father Baddeley's bed, and it had been peeled down in five separate pieces to its blackened head.

IV

The front door of Toynton Grange was, as usual, open. Dalgliesh walked swiftly and silently up the main staircase to Wilfred's room. As he approached he could hear talking, Dot Moxon's expostulatory and belligerent voice dominating the broken murmur of male voices.

Dalgliesh went in without knocking. Three pairs of eyes regarded him with wariness and, he thought, with some resentment. Wilfred was still lying propped up in his bed. Dennis Lerner quickly turned away to look fixedly out of the window, but not before Dalgliesh had seen that his face was blotched as if he had been crying. Dot was sitting by the side of the bed, stolid and immovable as a mother watching a sick child. Dennis muttered, as if Dalgliesh had asked for an explanation:

'Wilfred has told me what happened. It's unbelievable.'

Wilfred spoke with a mulish obstinacy which only emphasized his satisfaction at not being believed.

'It happened, and it was an accident.'

Dennis was beginning 'How could . . .' when Dalgliesh interrupted by laying the rolled habit on the foot of the bed. He said:

'I found this among the boulders by the black tower. If you hand it over to the police it may tell them something.'

'I'm not going to the police and I forbid anyone here – anyone – to go on my behalf.'

Dalgliesh said calmly:

'Don't worry; I've no intention of wasting their time. Given your determination to keep them out of it, they'd probably suspect that you lit the fire yourself. Did you?'

Wilfred cut swiftly into Dennis's gasp of incredulity and Dot's outraged protest.

'No, Dot, it's perfectly reasonable that Adam Dalgliesh should think as he does. He has been professionally trained in suspicion and scepticism. As it happens, I didn't attempt to burn myself to death. One family suicide in the black tower is enough. But I think

I know who did light the fire and I shall deal with that person in my own time and in my own way. In the meantime nothing is to be said to the family, nothing. Thank God I can be sure of one thing, none of them can have had a hand in this. Now that I'm assured of that I shall know what to do. And now if you would all be kind enough to leave . . .'

Dalgliesh didn't wait to see if the others proposed to obey. He contented himself with one final word from the door.

'If you're thinking of private vengeance, then forget it. If you can't, or daren't, act within the law, then don't act at all.'

Anstey smiled his sweet infuriating smile.

'Vengeance, Commander? Vengeance? That word has no place in our philosophy at Toynton Grange.'

Dalgliesh saw and heard no one as he passed again through the main hall. The house might have been an empty shell. After a second's thought he walked briskly over the headland to Charity Cottage. The headland was deserted except for a solitary figure making its way down the slope from the cliff; Julius carrying what looked like a bottle in either hand. He held them aloft in a half-pugilistic, half-celebratory gesture. Dalgliesh lifted his hand in a brief salute and, turning, made his way up the stone path to the Hewsons' cottage.

The door was open and at first he heard no sign of life. He knocked, and getting no reply, stepped inside. Charity Cottage, standing on its own, was larger than the other two and the stone sitting-room, bathed now in sunshine from its two windows, was agreeably proportioned. But it looked dirty and unkempt, reflecting in its untidiness Maggie's dissatisfied and restless nature. His first impression was that she had proclaimed her intention that their stay would be brief by not bothering to unpack. The few items of furniture looked as if they still stood where the whim of the removal men had first deposited them. A grubby sofa faced the large television screen which dominated the room. Eric's meagre medical library was stacked flat on the shelves of the bookcase, which held also a miscellany of crockery, ornaments, records and crushed shoes. A standard lamp of repellent design was without its shade. Two pictures were propped with their faces against the wall, their cords hanging knotted and broken. There was a square table set in the middle of the room bearing what looked like the remains of a late lunch; a torn packet of water biscuits spilling crumbs; a lump of cheese on a chipped plate; butter oozing from its greasy wrapping; a topless bottle of tomato ketchup with the sauce congealed round the lip. Two bloated flies buzzed their intricate convolutions above the debris.

From the kitchen came the rush of water and the roar of a gas boiler. Eric and Maggie were washing up. Suddenly the boiler was turned off and he heard Maggie's voice:

'You're so bloody weak! You let them all use you. If you are poking that supercilious bitch – and don't think I care a damn either way – it's only because you can't say no to her. You don't really want her any more than you want me.'

Eric's reply was a low mutter. There was a crash of crockery. Then Maggie's voice rose again:

'For Christ's sake, you can't hide away here for ever! That trip to St Saviour's, it wasn't as bad as you feared. No one said anything.'

This time Eric's reply was perfectly intelligible:

'They didn't need to. Anyway, who did we see? Just the consultant in physical medicine and that medical records officer. She knew all right and let me see it. That's how it'd be in general practice, if I ever got a job. They'd never let me forget it. The practice delinquent. Every female patient under sixteen tactfully diverted to one of the partners, just in case. At least Wilfred treats me like a human being. I can make a contribution. I can do my job.'

Maggie almost yelled at him: 'What kind of a job, for God's sake?' And then both their voices were lost in the roar from the boiler and the rush of water. Then it stopped and Dalgliesh heard Maggie's voice again, high, emphatic.

'All right! All right! All right! I've said I won't tell, and I won't. But if you keep on nagging about it, I may change my mind.'

Eric's reply was lost but it sounded like a long expostulatory murmur. Then Maggie spoke again:

'Well, what if I did? He wasn't a fool, you know. He could tell that something was up. And where's the harm? He's dead, isn't he? Dead. Dead. Dead.'

Dalgliesh suddenly realized that he was standing stock still, straining his ears to hear as if this were an official case, his case, and every surreptitiously stolen word was a vital clue. Irritated, he almost shook himself into action. He had taken a few steps back to the doorway and had raised his fist to knock again and more loudly when Maggie, carrying a small tin tray, emerged from the kitchen with Eric at her back. She recovered quickly from her surprise and gave a shout of almost genuine laughter.

'Oh God, don't say Wilfred has called in the Yard itself to grill me. The poor little man has got himself into a tizzy. What are you going to do, darling, warn me that anything I say will be taken down and may be given in evidence?'

The door darkened and Julius came in. He must, thought Dalgliesh, have run down the headland to arrive so quickly. Why the hurry, he wondered. Breathing heavily, Julius swung two bottles of whisky on to the table.

'A peace offering.'

'So I should think!' Maggie had become flirtatious. Her eyes brightened under the heavy lids and she slewed them from Dalgliesh to Julius as if uncertain where to bestow her favours. She spoke to Dalgliesh:

'Julius has been accusing me of attempting to roast Wilfred alive in the black tower. I know: I realize that it isn't funny. But Julius is, when he's trying to be pompous. And honestly, it's a nonsense. If I wanted to get my own back on St Wilfred I could do it without pussyfooting about the black tower in drag, couldn't I, darling?'

She checked her laughter and her glance at Julius was at once minatory and conspiratorial. It provoked no response. Julius said quickly:

'I didn't accuse you. I simply inquired with the utmost tact where you'd been since one o'clock.'

'On the beach, darling. I do go there occasionally. I know I can't prove it, but neither can you prove that I wasn't there.'

'That's rather a coincidence isn't it, your happening to walk on the beach?'

'No more a coincidence than your happening to drive along the coast road.'

'And you didn't see anyone?'

'I told you, darling, not a soul. Was I expected to? And now, Adam, it's your turn. Are you going to charm the truth out of me in the best Metropolitan tradition?'

'Not I. This is Court's case. That's one of the first principles of detection, never interfere with another man's conduct of his case.'

Julius said:

'Besides, Maggie dear, the Commander isn't interested in our paltry concerns. Strange as it may seem, he just doesn't care. He can't even pretend an interest in whether Dennis hurled Victor over the cliff and I'm covering up for him. Humiliating, isn't it?'

Maggie's laugh was uneasy. She glanced at her husband like an inexperienced hostess who fears that the party is getting out of control.

'Don't be silly, Julius. We know that you aren't covering up. Why should you? What would there be in it for you?'

'How well you know me, Maggie! Nothing. But then, I might have done it out of sheer good nature.' He looked at Dalgliesh with a sly smile and added:

'I believe in being accommodating to my friends.'

Eric said suddenly and with surprising authority:

'What was it you wanted, Mr Dalgliesh?'

'Just information. When I arrived at the cottage I found a booklet of matches by Father Baddeley's bed advertising the Olde Tudor Barn near Wareham. I thought I might try it for dinner tonight. Did he go there often, do you know?'

Maggie laughed:

'God, no! Never I should think. It's hardly Michael's scene. I gave him the matches. He liked trifles like that. But the Barn's not bad. Bob Loder took me there for lunch on my birthday and they did us quite well.'

Julius said:

'I'll describe it. Ambience: a chain of coloured fairy lights strung round an otherwise genuine and agreeable seventeenth-century barn. First course: tinned tomato soup with a slice of tomato to add verisimilitude and colour contrast; frozen prawns in bottled sauce on a bed of limp lettuce; half a melon – ripe if you're lucky; or the chef's own home-made pâté fresh from the local supermarket. The rest of the menu you may imagine. It's usually a variety of steak served with frozen vegetables and what they describe as french fried. If you must drink, stick to the red. I don't know whether the owner makes it or merely sticks the labels on the bottles but at least it's wine of a kind. The white is cat's pee.'

Maggie laughed indulgently.

'Oh, don't be such a snob, darling, it's not as bad as that. Bob and I had quite a decent meal. And whoever bottled the wine, it had the right effect as far as I was concerned.'

Dalgliesh said:

'But it may have deteriorated. You know how it is. The chef leaves and a restaurant changes almost overnight.'

Julius laughed:

'That's the advantage of the Olde Barn menu. The chef can and does change fortnightly but the tinned soup is guaranteed to taste the same.'

Maggie said:

'It won't have changed since my birthday. That was only 11th September. I'm Virgo, darlings. Appropriate, isn't it?'

Julius said:

'There are one or two decent places within driving distance. I can let you have a few names.'

He did so and Dalgliesh dutifully noted them at the back of his diary. But as he walked back to Hope Cottage his mind had already registered more important information.

So Maggie was on lunching terms with Bob Loder; the obliging Loder, equally ready to alter Father Baddeley's will – or to dissuade him from altering it? – and to help Millicent cheat her brother out of half his capital from the sale of Toynton Grange. But that little ploy had, of course, been Holroyd's idea. Had Holroyd and Loder cooked it up between them? Maggie had told them about her luncheon date with sly satisfaction. If her husband neglected her on her birthday she wasn't without consolation. But what of Loder? Was his interest no more than a readiness to avail himself of a complaisant and dissatisfied woman, or had he a more sinister motive for keeping in touch with what happened at Toynton Grange? And the shredded match? Dalgliesh hadn't yet compared it with the stubs in the booklet still by Father Baddeley's bed, but he had no doubt that one of the stubs would match. He couldn't question Maggie further without rousing suspicion, but he didn't need to. She couldn't have given the booklet of matches to Father Baddeley before the afternoon of 11th September, the day before Holroyd's death. And on the afternoon of the eleventh, Father Baddeley had visited his solicitor. He couldn't, then, have received the booklet of matches until that evening at the earliest. And that meant that he must have been in the black tower on either the following morning or afternoon. It would be useful, when opportunity offered, to have a word with Miss Willison and ask whether Father Baddeley had been at the Grange on the Wednesday morning. According to the entries in his diary it had certainly been his invariable routine to visit the Grange every morning. And that meant that he had almost certainly been in the black tower on the afternoon of the twelfth, and, possibly, sitting at the eastern window. Those drag marks on the fibre matting had looked very recent. But even from that window, he couldn't have seen Holroyd's chair go over the cliff; couldn't even have watched the distant figures of Lerner and Holroyd making their way along the sunken lane to that patch of green turf. And, even if he could, what would his evidence be worth, an old man sitting alone, reading and probably dozing in the afternoon sun? It was surely ludicrous to search here for a motive for murder. But suppose Father Baddeley had known beyond doubt that he had neither dozed nor read? Then it wasn't a question of what he had seen, but of what he had singularly failed to see.

SIX

A Bloodless Murder

I

The next afternoon, on the last day of her life, Grace Willison sat in the courtyard in the afternoon sun. Its rays were still warm on her face but now they touched her parched skin with a gentler valedictory warmth. From time to time a cloud moved across the face of the sun and she found herself shivering with the first intimation of winter. The air smelt keener, the afternoons were darkening fast. There wouldn't be many more days warm enough for her to sit outside. Even today she was the only patient in the courtyard and she was grateful for the warmth of the rug across her knees.

She found herself thinking about Commander Dalgliesh. She wished that he had come more often to Toynton Grange. He was still at Hope Cottage apparently. Yesterday he had helped Julius rescue Wilfred from the fire in the black tower. Wilfred had bravely made light of his ordeal as one would expect. It had only been a small fire caused entirely by his own carelessness; he had never been in real danger. But, all the same, she thought, it was fortunate that the Commander had been on hand to help.

Would he leave Toynton, she wondered, without coming to say goodbye to her? She hoped not. She had liked him so much in their brief time together. How pleasant it would be if he could be sitting here with her now, talking about Father Baddeley. No one at Toynton Grange now ever mentioned his name. But, of course, the Commander couldn't be expected to give up his time.

The thought was entirely without bitterness or resentment. There really wasn't anything to interest him at Toynton Grange. And it wasn't as if she could issue a personal invitation. She allowed herself for one minute to indulge in regret for the retirement which she had hoped for and planned. Her small pension from the Society, a little cottage, sun-filled and bright with chintz and geraniums; her dear mother's possessions, the ones she had sold before she came to Toynton – the rose-patterned tea service; the rosewood writing table; the series of water-colours of English cathedrals. How lovely to be able to invite anyone she liked to her own home to take tea with her. Not a communal institutional tea at a bleak refectory table, but proper afternoon tea. Her table; her tea service; her food; her guest.

She became aware of the weight of the book on her lap. It was a paperback edition of Trollope's *Last Chronicle of Barset*. It had lain there all the afternoon. Why, she wondered, was she so strangely reluctant to read it? And then she remembered. This had been the book she was re-reading on that dreadful afternoon when Victor's body had been brought home. She hadn't opened it since. But that was ridiculous. She must put the thought out of her mind. It was stupid, no, it was wrong, to spoil a book she so loved – its leisurely world of cathedral intrigue, its sanity, its delicate moral sensibility – by contaminating it with images of violence, hatred and blood.

She curved her deformed left hand around the book and parted the pages with her right. There was a bookmark between the last pages she had read, a single pink antirrhinum pressed between a sheet of tissue. And then she remembered it. It was a flower from the small posy Father Baddeley had brought her on the afternoon of Victor's death. Normally he never picked wild flowers except for her. They hadn't lasted long, less than a day. But this single flower she had pressed at once between the leaves of her book. She gazed at it, motionless.

A shadow fell across the page. A voice said:

'Anything wrong?'

She looked up and smiled.

'Nothing. It's just that I've remembered something. Isn't it extraordinary how the mind rejects anything which it associates with horror or great distress? Commander Dalgliesh asked me if I knew what Father Baddeley did on the few days before he went into hospital. And, of course, I do know. I know what he did on the Wednesday afternoon. I don't suppose it's the least important, but it would be nice to tell him. I know that everyone here is terribly busy but do you think that . . .?'

'Don't worry. I'll find time to drop in at Hope Cottage. It's time he showed his face here if he proposes to stay on much longer. And now, don't you think it would be wise for you to come in? It's getting chilly.'

Miss Willison smiled her thanks. She would have preferred to have stayed out a little longer. But she didn't like to insist. It was meant kindly. She closed her book again and her murderer grasped the chair with strong hands and wheeled her to her death.

II

Ursula Hollis always asked her nurses to leave her curtains undrawn and tonight in the faint haze of light from her luminous bedside clock, she could still just discern the oblong frame which separated darkness outside from the darkness within. It was nearly midnight. The night was starless and very still. She lay in blackness so thick that it was almost a weight on her chest, a dense curtain descending to stifle breath. Outside, the headland was asleep, except, she supposed, for the small animals of the night scurrying among the rigid grasses. Inside Toynton Grange she could still hear distant sounds; brisk footsteps passing down a passage; the quiet closing of a door; the squeak of unoiled wheels as someone moved a hoist or a wheelchair; the mouse-like scrabbling sounds from next door as Grace Willison moved restlessly in her bed; a sudden blare of music, instantly muted, as someone opened and shut the sitting-room door. Her bedside clock snatched at the seconds and ticked them into oblivion. She lay rigid, the warm tears flowing in a constant stream over her face to seep, suddenly cold and sticky, into her pillow. Under the pillow was Steve's letter. From time to time she folded her right arm painfully across her chest and insinuated her fingers under the pillow to feel the envelope's knife-sharp edge.

Mogg had moved into the flat; they were living together. Steve had written the news almost casually as if it were merely a temporary and mutually convenient arrangement for sharing the rent and the chores. Mogg was doing the cooking; Mogg had redecorated the sitting-room and put up more shelves; Mogg had found him a clerical job with his publishers which might lead to a permanent and better post. Mogg's new book of poems was due out in the spring. There was only a perfunctory inquiry after Ursula's health. He hadn't even made the usual vague and insincere promises to visit. He had written no word about her return home, the planned new flat, his negotiations with the local authority. There was no need. She never would return. They both knew it. Mogg knew it.

She hadn't received the letter until teatime. Albert Philby had been unaccountably late in fetching the post and it was after four o'clock before it was placed in her hand. She was grateful that she had been alone in the sitting-room, that Grace Willison hadn't yet come in from the courtyard to get ready for tea. There had been no one to watch her face as she read it, no one to make tactful inquiries, or, more tactfully, to refrain. And anger and shock had carried her through until now. She had held on to anger, feeding it with memory and imagination, willing herself to eat her usual two slices of bread, to drink her tea, to contribute her sentences of platitude and small talk to the party. Only now, when Grace Willison's heavy breathing had settled into a gentle snoring, when there was no longer a risk that Helen or Dot might pay a last visit, when Toynton Grange was finally wrapping itself in silence for the night, could she

233

give way to desolation and loss and indulge in what she knew was self-pity. And the tears, when once they started, would not stop. The grief once indulged was unassuageable. She had no control over her crying. It no longer even distressed her; it had nothing to do with grief or longing. It was a physical manifestation, involuntary as a hiccup, but silent and almost consoling; an interminable stream.

She knew what she had to do. She listened through the rhythm of her tears. There was no sound from next door except Grace Willison's snoring, which was now regular. She put out her hand and switched on the light. The bulb had the lowest wattage which Wilfred could buy but the brightness was still blinding. She imagined it, a dazzling oblong of light shining out to signal her intention to all the world. She knew that there was no one to see it, but in imagination the headland was suddenly full of running feet and loud with calling voices. She had stopped crying now but her swollen eyes saw the room as if it were a half-developed photograph, an image of bleared and distorted shapes, shifting and dissolving and seen through a stinging curtain pierced with needles of light.

She waited. Nothing happened. There was still no sound from next door but Grace's harsh and regular breathing. The next step was easy; she had done it twice before. She dropped both her pillows on the floor and, manoeuvring her body to the edge of the bed, let herself drop gently on top of their soft cushion. Even with the pillows to break her weight it seemed that the room shook. Again she waited. But there were no quick footsteps hurrying down the passage. She raised herself

234

upwards on the pillows against the bed and began propelling herself towards its foot. It was an easy matter to stretch out her hand and withdraw the cord from her dressing-gown. Then she began her painful progress towards the door.

Her legs were powerless; what strength she had was in her arms. Her dead feet lay white and flabby as fish on the cold floor, the toes splayed like obscene excrescences vainly scrabbling for a grip. The linoleum was unpolished but smooth and she slid along with surprising speed. She remembered with what joy she had discovered that she could do this; that, ridiculous and humiliating as the trick might be, she could actually move around her room without the use of her chair.

But now she was going farther afield. It was lucky that the modern insubstantial doors of the annexe rooms were opened by depressing a handle and not turning a knob. She made the dressing-gown cord into a loop and, at the second attempt, managed to throw it over the handle. She tugged and the door quietly opened. Discarding one of the pillows, she edged her way into the silent passage. Her heart was thudding with such power it must surely betray her. Again she slipped the cord over the handle and, manoeuvring herself a few feet down the passage, heard the door click shut.

One single light bulb, heavily shaded, was always kept burning at the far end of the corridor and she could see without difficulty where the short staircase led to the upper floor. This was her objective. Reaching it proved astonishingly easy. The linoleum in the passage, although never polished, seemed smoother than that in her room;

or perhaps she had gained the knack of progress. She slid forward with almost exhilarating ease.

But the staircase was more difficult. She was relying on pulling herself up by the banisters, step by step. But it was necessary to take the pillow with her. She would need it on the floor above. And the pillow seemed to have swollen into a gigantic, soft, white encumbrance. The stairs were narrow and it was difficult to prop it safely. Twice it tumbled down and she had to slide after it to retrieve it. But after four steps had been painfully negotiated she worked out the best method of progress. She tied one end of the dressing-gown cord around her waist and the other tightly round the middle of the pillow. She wished she had put on the dressing-gown. It would have hampered her progress, but she was already shivering.

And so, step by step, grasping and sweating despite the cold, she pulled herself up, grasping the banisters with both hands. The stairs creaked alarmingly. She expected any minute to hear the faint summons of a bedside bell and hear from the distance Dot or Helen's hurrying footsteps.

She had no idea how long it took to reach the top of the stairs. But at last she was sitting crouched and shivering on the final step, grasping the banisters with both hands so convulsively that the wood shook, and peering down at the hall below. It was then that the cloaked figure appeared. There were no warning footsteps, no cough, no sound of human breath. One second the passage was empty. In the next a brown cloaked figure – head bent, hood drawn well over the face – had moved silently and swiftly beneath her, and disappeared down the passage. She waited terrified, hardly daring to breathe, huddling herself as far as possible out of view. It would come back. She knew that it would come back. Like the dreadful figure of death which she had seen in old books, carved on monumental tombs, it would pause beneath her and throw back the concealing hood to reveal the grinning skull, the eyeless sockets, would poke at her through the banisters its fleshless fingers. Her heart, beating in icy terror against the rib cage, seemed to have grown too large for her body. Surely its frantic thudding must betray her! It seemed an eternity, but she realized that it could only have been less than a minute before the figure reappeared and passed, beneath her terrified eyes, silently and swiftly into the main house.

Ursula realized then that she wasn't going to kill herself. It had only been Dot, or Helen, or Wilfred. Who else could it have been? But the shock of that silent figure, passing like a shadow, had restored in her the will to live. If she had really wanted to die, what was she doing here crouched in cold discomfort at the top of the stairs? She had her dressing-gown cord. Even now she could tie it round her neck and let herself slip unresisting down the stairs. But she wouldn't. The very thought of that last fall, the strangling cord biting into her neck, made her moan in agonized protest. No, she had never meant to kill herself. No one, not even Steve, was worth an eternity of damnation. Steve might not believe in Hell, but what did Steve really know about anything that mattered? But she had to complete her journey now. She had to get hold of that bottle of aspirin which she knew must be somewhere in the clinical room. She wouldn't use it, but she would keep it always within reach. She would know that, if life became intolerable, the means to end it was at hand. And perhaps, if she just took a handful and left the bottle by the bed, they would realize at least that she was unhappy. That was all she intended; all she had ever intended. They would send for Steve. They would take some notice of her misery. Perhaps they might even force Steve to take her back to London. Having come so far at such cost, she had to get to the clinical room.

The door presented no problem. But when she had sidled through, she realized that this was the end. She couldn't switch on the light. The low bulb in the corridor gave a faint diffused glow but, even with the door of the clinical room ajar, it was inadequate to show her the position of the light. And if she were to succeed in switching it on with the dressing-gown cord, she had to know accurately at what spot to aim. She stretched out her hand and felt along the wall. Nothing. She held the cord in a loop and flung it softly and repeatedly where she thought the switch might be. But it fell away uselessly. She began to cry again, defeated, desperately cold, suddenly realizing that she had the whole painful journey to do again in reverse, and that dragging herself back into bed would be the most difficult and painful of all.

And then, suddenly, a hand stretched out of the darkness and the light was switched on. Ursula gave a little scream of fright. She looked up. Framed in the doorway, wearing a brown habit open down the front and with the hood flung back was Helen Rainer. The two women, petrified, stared at each other speechlessly. And

Ursula saw that the eyes bent on hers were as full of terror as her own.

III

Grace Willison's body jerked into wakefulness and immediately began to tremble uncontrollably as if a strong hand were shaking her into full consciousness. She listened in the darkness, raising her head with difficulty from the pillow; but she could hear nothing. Whatever noise, real or imagined, had woken her was now stilled. She switched on her bedside lamp; nearly midnight. She reached for her book. It was a pity that the paperback Trollope was so heavy. It meant that it had to be propped up on the coverlet and since, once stretched into her conventional attitude for sleep she couldn't easily bend her knees, the effort of slightly raising her head and peering down at the small print was tiring both to her eyes and to the muscles of her neck. The discomfort sometimes made her wonder whether reading in bed was the pleasant indulgence she had always believed it to be since those childhood days, when her father's parsimony over the electricity bill and her mother's anxiety about eye strain and eight hours' good sleep each night had denied her a bedside lamp.

Her left leg was jerking uncontrollably and she watched, detached and interested, the erratic jump of the coverlet as if an animal were loose among the bed clothes. To wake suddenly like this once she had first fallen asleep was always a bad sign. She was in for a restless night. She dreaded sleeplessness and for a moment was tempted to pray that she might be spared it just for tonight. But she had finished her prayers and it seemed pointless to pray again for a mercy which experience had taught her she wasn't going to receive. Pleading to God for something which he had already made it perfectly plain he wasn't disposed to give you was to behave like a peevish, importunate child. She watched her limb's antics with interest, vaguely comforted by the sensation which was now almost self-induced of being detached from her unruly body.

She lay down her book and decided instead to think about the pilgrimage to Lourdes in fourteen days' time. She pictured the happy bustle of departure – she had a new coat saved for the occasion – the drive across France with the party gay as a picnic; the first glimpse of the mists swirling around the foothills of the Pyrenees; the snowcapped peaks; Lourdes itself with its concentrated business, its air of being always *en fête*. The Toynton Grange party, except for the two Roman Catholics, Ursula Hollis and Georgie Allan, were not part of an official English pilgrimage, did not take Mass, grouped themselves with becoming humility at the back of the crowd when the bishops in their crimson robes made their slow way round Rosary Square, the golden monstrance held high before them. But how inspiring, how colourful, how splendid it all was! The candles weaving their patterns of light, the colours, the singing, the sense of belonging again to the outside world but a world in which sickness was honoured, no longer regarded as an alienation, a deformity of the spirit as well as of the body. Only thirteen more days now. She wondered what her father, implacably Protestant, would have said about this keenly awaited pleasure. But she had consulted Father Baddeley about the propriety of going on pilgrimage and his advice had been very clear. 'My dear child, you enjoy the change and the journey, and why not? And surely no one could believe themselves harmed by a visit to Lourdes. By all means help Wilfred to celebrate his bargain with the Almighty.'

She thought about Father Baddeley. It was still difficult to accept that she wouldn't ever again be talking with him in the patients' courtyard or praying with him in the quiet room. Dead; an inert, neutral, unattractive word. Short, uncompromising, a lump of a word. The same word, come to think of it, for a plant, an animal or a man. That was an interesting thought. One would have expected a distinctive, more impressive or momentous word for the death of a man. But why? He was only part of the same creation, sharing its universal life, dependent on the same air. Dead. She had hoped to be able to feel that Father Baddeley was close to her; but it hadn't happened, it just wasn't true. They are all gone into the world of light. Well, gone away; not interested any more in the living.

She ought to put out her light; electricity was expensive; if she didn't intend to read it was her duty to lie in the darkness. Lighten our darkness; her mother had always liked that Collect; and by Thy great mercy defend us from all the perils and dangers of this night. Only there was no peril here, only sleeplessness and pain; the familiar pain to be tolerated, almost welcomed as an old acquaintance because she knew that she could cope with the worst it could do; and this new frightening pain which, sometime soon, she would have to worry someone about.

The curtain trembled in the breeze. She heard a sudden click, unnaturally loud, so that for a second her heart thudded. There was a rasp of metal on wood. Maggie hadn't checked the window fastening before bedding her down for the night. It was too late now. Her chair was at the side of the bed but she couldn't get into it without help. But all would be well unless it were a stormy night. And she was perfectly safe, no one would climb in. There was nothing at Toynton Grange to steal. And beyond that fluttering curtain of white, nothing; nothing but a black void, dark cliffs stretching to the unsleeping sea.

The curtain billowed, bursting into a white sail, a curve of light. She exclaimed at the beauty of it. Cool air streamed across her face. She turned her eyes to the door and smiled a welcome. She began to say:

'The window – would you be good enough . . .?'

But she didn't finish. There were three seconds only left to her of earthly time. She saw the cloaked figure, hood well down obscuring the face, moving swiftly towards her on silent feet like an apparition, familiar but horribly different, ministering hands that held death, blackness bearing down on her. Unresisting, since that was her nature and how could she resist, she did not die ungently, feeling at the last through the thin veil of plastic only the strong, warm, oddly comforting lineaments of a human hand. Then the hand reached out and delicately, without touching the wooden stand, switched off the bedside lamp. Two seconds later the light was switched on again, and, as if by afterthought, the cloaked figure stretched out a hand for the Trollope, gently rustled the pages, found the pressed flower between the fold of tissue, and crumpled them both with strong fingers. Then the hand reached out for the lamp again and the light went out for the last time.

IV

At last they were back in Ursula's room. Helen Rainer closed the door with quiet firmness and leaned back momentarily against it as if exhausted. Then she went quickly over to the window and swept the curtains across in two swift gestures. Her heavy breathing filled the little room. It had been a difficult journey. Helen had left her in the clinical room briefly while she positioned Ursula's wheelchair at the foot of the stairs. Once they reached it all would be well. Even if they were seen together on the ground-floor corridor it would be assumed that Ursula had rung her night bell and was being helped to the bathroom. The stairs were the problem and the descent, with Helen half-supporting, half-carrying her, had been exhausting and noisy, five long minutes of laboured breathing, creaking banisters, hissed instructions, of Ursula's half-stifled moans of pain. It seemed now like a miracle that no one had appeared in the hall. It would have been quicker and easier to have moved into the main part of the Grange and used the lift, but the clanging metal grille and the noisy engine would have woken half the house.

But at last they were safely back and Helen, white faced but calm, pulled herself together and moved away from the door and began with professional competence to put Ursula to bed. Neither spoke until the task was completed and Ursula lay in rigid half-fearful silence.

Helen bent her face close to Ursula's, unpleasantly close. In the glare of the bedside lamp she could see the features magnified, coarsened, pores like miniature craters, two unplucked hairs standing like bristles at the corner of her mouth. Her breath smelt slightly sour. Odd, thought Ursula, that she hadn't noticed it before. The green eyes seemed to grow and protrude as she hissed her instructions, her dreadful warning.

'When the next patient goes, he'll have to start admitting from the waiting list or give in. He can't run this place on less than six patients. I've taken a look at the books when he's left them about in the business room and I know. He'll either sell out completely or hand over to the Ridgewell Trust. If you want to get out of here there are better ways than killing yourself. Help me to ensure that he sells out, and get back to London.'

'But how?'

Ursula found herself whispering back like a conspirator.

'He'll hold what he calls a family council. He always does when there's something important affecting all the household to decide. We all give our views. Then we go away to meditate in silence for one hour. Then we all vote. Don't let anyone persuade you to vote for the Ridgewell Trust. That way you'll be trapped here for life. It's hard enough for local authorities to find a place for the young chronic sick. Once they know you're being looked after, they'll never transfer you.'

'But if the Grange does close down, will they really send me home?'

'They'll have to, back to London anyway. That's still your permanent address. You're the responsibility of your own local authority, not of Dorset. And once back, at least you'll see him. He could visit you, take you out, you could go home for weekend leaves. Besides, the disease isn't really advanced yet. I don't see why you shouldn't manage together in one of those flats for disabled couples. After all he is married to you. He's got responsibilities, duties.'

Ursula tried to explain:

'I don't mind about responsibilities and duties. I want him to love me.'

Helen had laughed, a coarse, uncomfortable sound.

'Love. Is that all? Isn't that what we all want? Well he can't stay in love with someone he never sees, can he? It doesn't work like that with men. You've got to get back to him.'

'And you won't tell?'

'Not if you promise.'

'To vote your way?'

'And to keep your mouth shut about trying to kill yourself, about everything that's happened here tonight. If anyone mentions hearing a noise in the night, you rang for me and I was taking you to the lavatory. If Wilfred discovers the truth he'll send you to a mental hospital. You wouldn't want that, would you?'

No, she wouldn't want that. Helen was right. She had to get home. How simple it all was. She felt suddenly filled with gratitude, and struggled to hold out her arms towards Helen. But Helen had moved away. Firm hands were tucking in the bed clothes, rocking the mattress. The sheets were drawn taut. She felt imprisoned, but secure, a baby swaddled for the night. Helen stretched out her hand to the light. In the darkness a white blur moved towards the door. Ursula heard the soft click of the latch.

Lying there alone exhausted but strangely comforted she remembered that she hadn't told Helen about the cloaked figured. But it could be of no importance. It was probably Helen herself answering Grace's bell. Was that what Helen had meant when she warned, say nothing about anything that happened here tonight? Surely not. But she would say nothing. How could she speak without betraying that she had been crouching there on the stairs. And everything was going to be all right. She could sleep now. How lucky that Helen had gone to the clinical room to get a couple of aspirin for a headache and had found her! The house was blessedly unnaturally quiet. There was something strange, something different, about the silence. And then, smiling into the darkness, she remembered. It was Grace. No sound, no rasp of snoring breath came through the thin partition to disturb her. Tonight even Grace Willison was sleeping in peace.

V

Usually Julius Court fell asleep within minutes of turning out his bedside light. But tonight he turned in restless wakefulness, mind and nerves fidgety, his legs as cold and heavy as if it were winter. He rubbed them together, considering whether to dig out his electric blanket. But the bother of re-making the bed discouraged him. Alcohol seemed a better and quicker remedy both for sleeplessness and the cold.

He walked over to the window and looked out over the headland. The waning moon was obscured by scudding clouds; the darkness inland pierced only by a single oblong of yellow light. But as he watched, blackness was drawn like a shutter over the far window. Instantaneously the oblong became a square; then that, too, was extinguished. Toynton Grange lay, a faintly discerned shape etched in the darkness on the silent headland. Curious, he looked at his watch. The time was eighteen minutes past midnight.

VI

Dalgliesh awoke at first light, to the cold, quiet morning, and dragging on his dressing-gown, went downstairs to make tea. He wondered if Millicent was still at the Grange. Her television had been silent all the previous evening and now, although she was neither an early nor a noisy riser, Hope Cottage was wrapped in the slightly clandestine and unmistakable calm of complete isolation. He lit the lamp in the sitting-room, carried his cup to the table, and spread out his map. Today he would explore the north-east of the county aiming to arrive at Sherborne for lunch. But first it would be courteous to call at Toynton Grange and inquire after Wilfred. He felt no real concern; it was difficult to think of yesterday's charade without irritation. But it might be worth making one more attempt to persuade Wilfred to call in the police, or at least to take the attack on himself more seriously. And it was time that he paid some rent for the use of Hope Cottage. Toynton Grange could hardly be so prosperous that a tactful contribution wouldn't be welcome. Neither chore need keep him at the Grange for longer than ten minutes.

There was a knock on the door and Julius came in. He was fully dressed and, even at this early hour, gave his usual impression of slightly elegant informality. He said, calmly, and as if the news were hardly worth the trouble of telling:

'I'm glad you're up. I'm on my way to Toynton Grange. Wilfred has just rung. Apparently Grace Willison has died in her sleep and Eric is in a tizzy about the death certificate. I don't know what Wilfred thinks I can do about it. Restoring Eric to the medical register seems to have restored him also to the customary arrogance of his profession. Grace Willison wasn't due, in his opinion, to die for at least another eighteen months, possibly two years. That being so he's at a loss to put a name to this insubordination. As usual, they're all extracting the maximum drama from the situation. I shouldn't miss it if I were you.'

Dalgliesh glanced towards the adjacent cottage without speaking. Julius said cheerfully:

'Oh, you needn't worry about disturbing Millicent; I'm afraid she's there already. Apparently her television broke down last night so she went up to Toynton Grange to see a late programme and decided, for some unaccountable reason, to stay the night. Probably saw an opportunity of saving her own bed linen and bath water.'

Dalgliesh said:

'You go on, I'll follow you later.'

He drank his tea without haste and spent three minutes shaving. He wondered why he had been so reluctant to accompany Julius, why, if he had to go to Toynton Grange, he preferred to walk there on his own. He wondered, too, why he felt so keen a regret. He had no wish to involve himself in the controversy at Toynton. He had no particular curiosity about Grace Willison's death. He was aware of feeling nothing except an inexplicable unease amounting almost to grief for a woman he had barely known and a vague distaste that the start of a beautiful day should have been spoilt by the intimations of decay. And there was something else; a sense of guilt. It seemed to him both unreasonable and unfair. By dying she seemed to have allied herself with Father Baddeley. There were two accusing ghosts, not one. This was to be a double failure. It was by an effort of will that he set out for Toynton Grange.

He could be in no doubt which room was Grace Willison's, he could hear the raised voices even as he entered the annexe. When he opened the door he saw that Wilfred, Eric, Millicent, Dot and Julius were grouped around the bed with the desultory, uneasy air of strangers meeting fortuitously at the scene of an accident with which they would much prefer not to become involved but which they hardly like to leave.

Dorothy Moxon stood at the end of the bed, her heavy hands, red as hams, clasped to the rail. She was wearing her matron's cap. The effect, so far from providing a touch of professional reassurance, was grotesque. The high frilled pie crust of muslin looked like a morbid and bizarre celebration of death. Millicent was still in her dressing-gown, an enveloping plaid in heavy wool frogged like a ceremonial uniform which must once have belonged to her husband. In contrast, her slippers were insubstantial fripperies in pink fur. Wilfred and Eric were wearing their brown habits. They glanced briefly at their door when he entered, then immediately turned their attention back to the bed. Julius was saying:

'There was a light in one of the annexe rooms shortly after midnight. Isn't that when you say she died, Eric?'

'It could have been about then. I'm only going by the cooling of the body and the beginning of rigor mortis. I'm not an expert in these things.'

'How odd! I thought that death was the one thing you were expert at.'

Wilfred said quietly:

'The light was from Ursula's room. She rang shortly after midnight to be taken to the lavatory. Helen looked after her, but she didn't go in to Grace. There was no need. She didn't ring. No one saw her after Dot put her to bed. She made no complaint then.'

Julius turned to Eric Hewson:

'You haven't any option, have you? If you can't say what she died of, you can't write a certificate. Anyway, I should play for safety if I were you. After all, you've only recently been permitted to sign a death certificate. Better not take any chances of getting it wrong.'

Eric Hewson said:

'You keep out of it, Julius, I don't need your advice. I don't know why Wilfred rang you.'

But he spoke without conviction, like an insecure and frightened child, his eyes flicking to the door as if hoping for the arrival of an ally. Julius was unabashed:

'It seems to me that you need any advice that's going. What's worrying you anyway? Do you suspect foul play? What a ridiculous phrase that is, come to think of it, so delightfully British, compounded of the public school ethos and the boxing ring.'

Eric exerted himself to make a show of authority.

'Don't be ridiculous! Obviously it's a natural death. The difficulty is that I'm puzzled why it should have happened now. I know D. S. patients can go off quickly like that, but in her case I didn't expect it. And Dot says that she seemed just as usual when she put her to bed at ten o'clock. I'm wondering whether there was some other organic disease present which I missed.'

Julius went on happily:

'The police do not suspect foul play. Well, you've got a representative of them here if you want professional advice. Ask the Commander if he suspects foul play.'

They turned and looked at Dalgliesh as if fully aware of his presence for the first time. The window latch was rattling with irritating insistence. He went across to the window and glanced out. The ground close to the stone wall had been dug for a width of about four feet as if someone had intended to plant a border. The sandy earth was smooth and undisturbed. But of course it was! If a secret visitor had wanted to get into Grace's room unseen, why climb in at the window when the door of Toynton Grange was never locked?

He fastened the catch and, moving back to the bed, looked down at the body. The dead face looked not exactly peaceful, but slightly disapproving, the mouth a little open, the front teeth, more rabbity than in life, pressing against the lower lip. The eyelids had contracted showing a glimpse of the irises of the eye so that she seemed to be peering at her own two hands disposed so neatly over the taut coverlet. The strong right hand, blotched with the brown stigmata of age, was curved over the withered left as if instinctively protecting it from his pitying gaze. She was shrouded for her last sleep in an old-fashioned white nightdress of creased cotton with a child's bow in narrow blue ribbon tied incongruously under her chin. The long sleeves were gathered into frilled wrists. There was a fine darn about two inches from her elbow. His eyes fixed obsessively on it. Who today, he wondered, would take such trouble? Certainly her diseased tormented hands couldn't have woven that intricate pattern of repair. Why should he find that darn more pathetic, more heart-shaking, than the concentrated calm of the dead face?

He was aware that the company had stopped arguing, that they were looking at him in a half-wary silence. He picked up the two books on Miss Willison's bedside table, her prayer book and a paperback copy of *The Last Chronicle of Barset*. There was a bookmark in the prayer book. She had, he saw, been reading the Collect and Gospel for the day. The place was marked by one of those sentimental cards favoured by the pious, a coloured picture of a haloed St Francis surrounded by birds and apparently preaching to a motley and incongruous congregation of animals remote from their habitat and drawn with finicky precision. He wondered, irrelevantly, why there was no bookmark in the Trollope. She was not a woman to turn down the pages, and surely of the two volumes this was the one in which she would more easily lose her place. The omission vaguely worried him.

'Is there a next of kin?' he asked, and Anstey answered:

'No. She told me that her parents were only children. They were both over forty when she was born and they died within months of each other about fifteen years ago. She had an older brother but he was killed in the war in North Africa. El Alamein, I believe.'

'What about her estate?'

'Oh, nothing, nothing at all. After her parents' death she worked for several years for The Open Door, the discharged prisoners' charity, and had a small disability pension from them, a pittance merely. That, of course, dies with her. Her fees here were paid by the local authority.'

Julius Court said with sudden interest:

'The Open Door. Did she know Philby before you took him on?'

Anstey looked as if he found this irrelevant question in poor taste.

'She may have done; she certainly never said so. It was Grace who suggested that The Open Door might find us a handyman, that this was a way in which Toynton Grange could help the work of the charity. We have been very glad of Albert Philby. He's one of the family. I haven't repented my decision to take him on.'

Millicent broke in:

'And you got him cheap, of course. Besides it was Philby or no one wasn't it? You didn't have much luck with the labour exchange when the applicants found that you were offering £5 a week and all found. I sometimes wonder why Philby stays.'

Discussion of this point was prevented by the entrance of Philby himself. He must have been told of Miss

Willison's death for he showed no surprise to find her room full of people and gave no explanation of his presence. Instead he stationed himself beside the door like an embarrassing and unpredictable guard dog. The company behaved as if they had decided that it would be prudent not to notice him. Wilfred turned to Eric Hewson:

'Can't you reach a diagnosis, without a post-mortem? I hate the idea of her being cut up, the indignity, the impersonality. She was so sensitive about her body, so modest in a way we don't understand nowadays. An autopsy is the last thing she herself would have wanted.'

Julius said coarsely:

'Well, it's the last thing she's going to get, isn't it?'

Dot Moxon spoke for the first time. She swung round on him in sudden anger, her heavy face blotched, hands clenched.

'How dare you! What has it to do with you? You didn't care about her dead or alive, her or any of the patients. You only use this place for your own purpose.'

'Use?' The grey eyes flickered and then widened; Dalgliesh could almost see the irises growing. Julius stared at Dot with incredulous anger.

'Yes, use! Exploit, if you like. It gives you a kick, doesn't it, to come visiting Toynton Grange when London begins to bore you, patronizing Wilfred, pretending to advise him, handing out treats to the inmates like Father Christmas? It makes you feel good, reinforces your ego to contrast your health with their deformity. But you take damned good care not to put yourself out. The kindness doesn't really cost you anything. No one but Henry gets invited to your cottage.

But then Henry was quite important in his time wasn't he? He and you have things to gossip about. You're the only one here with a view of the sea, but we don't find you inviting us to wheel the chairs on to your patio. No bloody fear! That's one thing you could have done for Grace, take her to your place occasionally, let her sit quietly and look at the sea. She wasn't stupid, you know. You might even have enjoyed her conversation. But that would have spoilt the appearance of your elegant patio wouldn't it, an ugly middle-aged woman in a wheelchair? And now she's dead you come here pretending to advise Eric. Well, for God's sake, cut it out!'

Julius laughed uneasily. He seemed to have himself in hand but his voice was high and brittle.

'I don't know what I've done to deserve that outburst. I didn't realize that by buying a cottage from Wilfred I'd made myself responsible for Grace Willison or for anyone else at Toynton Grange for that matter. I've no doubt it's a shock for you, Dot, losing another patient so soon after Victor, but why take it out on me? We all know that you're in love with Wilfred and I've no doubt that's pretty unrewarding for you, but it's hardly my fault. I may be a little ambivalent in my sexual tastes but I'm not competing for him, I assure you.'

Suddenly she blundered up to him and threw back her arm to slap his face in a gesture at once theatrical and absurd. But before she could strike, Julius had caught her wrist. Dalgliesh was surprised at the quickness and effectiveness of his reaction. The taut hand, white and trembling with effort, held hers high in a muscled vice so that they looked like two ill-matched contestants locked in a tableau of conflict. Suddenly he laughed and dropped her hand. He lowered his hand more slowly, his eyes still on her face, and began massaging and twisting his wrist. Then he laughed again, a dangerous sound, and said softly:

'Careful! Careful I'm not a helpless geriatric patient, you know.'

She gave a gasp and, bursting into tears, blundered sobbing from the room, an ungainly and pathetic but not a ridiculous figure. Philby slipped out after her. His departure caused as little interest as his arrival. Wilfred said softly:

'You shouldn't have said that, Julius, any of it.'

'I know. It was unforgivable. I'm sorry. I'll tell Dot so when we are feeling calmer.'

The brevity, the absence of self-justification and the apparent sincerity of the apology silenced them. Dalgliesh said quietly:

'I imagine that Miss Willison would have found this quarrelling over her body a great deal more shocking than anything that could happen to her on the mortuary slab.'

His words recalled Wilfred to the matter in hand; he turned to Eric Hewson:

'But we didn't have all this trouble with Michael, you gave a certificate without difficulty then.'

Dalgliesh could detect the first trace of peevishness in his voice.

Eric explained:

'I knew why Michael had died, I had seen him only that morning. It was only a matter of time for Michael after the last heart attack. He was a dying man.'

'As we all are,' said Wilfred. 'As we all are.'

The pious platitudes seemed to irritate his sister. She spoke for the first time.

'Don't be ridiculous, Wilfred. I'm certainly not dying and you would be very disconcerted to be told that you were. And as for Grace, she always looked to me a great deal sicker than anyone here seemed to understand. Now perhaps you will realize that it isn't always the ones who make the most fuss who need the most attention.'

She turned to Dalgliesh:

'What exactly will happen if Eric doesn't give a certificate? Does it mean that we'll have the police here again?'

'A policeman will probably come, yes; just an ordinary policeman. He'll be the coroner's officer and he will take charge of the body.'

'And then?'

'The coroner will arrange for a post-mortem. According to the result he will either issue a certificate for the registrar or he'll conduct an inquest.'

Wilfred said:

'It's all so horrible, so unnecessary.'

'It's the law and Dr Hewson knows that it is the law.'

'But what do you mean, it's the law? Grace died of D. S., we all know that. What if there was some other disease present? Eric can't treat her or do anything to help her now. What law are you talking about?'

Dalgliesh patiently explained:

'The doctor who attends a dead person during his last illness is required to sign and deliver to the registrar a certificate in a prescribed form stating the cause of death to the best of his knowledge and belief. At the same time he is required to deliver to a qualified informant, and that could be the occupant of the house where the death occurred, a notice to the effect that he has signed such a certificate. There is no statutory duty on a doctor to report any death to the coroner, but it's usual to do so where there is any doubt. When the doctor reports a death to a coroner he's not relieved of his duty to issue a certificate of the cause of death but there is provision for him to state on the form that he has reported the death so that the registrar will know that he must defer registration until he hears from the coroner. Under Section 3 of the Coroners Act 1887 a coroner has a duty to make inquiries whenever he is informed that there is lying within his jurisdiction the body of a person who there is reason to believe may have died a violent or unnatural death or a sudden death, the cause of which is unknown, or who has died in prison or in any place or circumstances which under another Act require an inquest to be held. That, since you have inquired – and in somewhat tedious detail – is the law. Grace Willison has died suddenly and in Dr Hewson's opinion the cause is at present unknown. His best course is to report the death to the coroner. It will mean a post-mortem, but not necessarily an inquest.'

'But I hate the thought of her lying mangled on an autopsy slab.' Wilfred was beginning to sound like an obstinate child. Dalgliesh said coolly:

'Mangled isn't exactly the word. A post-mortem is an organized and perfectly tidy procedure. And now if you will excuse me I'll get back to my breakfast.'

Suddenly Wilfred made an almost physical effort to pull himself together. He straightened up, and crossed his hands into the wide sleeves of his habit and stood for a moment in silent meditation. Eric Hewson looked at him, puzzled, then glanced from Dalgliesh to Julius as if seeking guidance. Then Wilfred spoke:

'Eric, you had better ring the coroner's office now. Normally Dot would lay out the body but that had better wait until we get instructions. After you have telephoned, please let everyone know that I want to talk to all the family immediately after breakfast. Helen and Dennis are with them at present. Millicent, perhaps you could find Dot and see that she is all right. And now I should like to speak to you Julius, and to Adam Dalgliesh.'

He stood for a moment, eyes closed, at the foot of Grace's bed. Dalgliesh wondered whether he were praying. Then he led the way out. As they followed, Julius whispered with hardly a movement of his lips:

'Unpleasantly reminiscent of those summonses to the headmaster's study. We should have fortified ourselves with breakfast.'

In the business room Wilfred wasted no time.

'Grace's death means that I have to make my decision sooner than I'd hoped. We can't carry on with only four patients. On the other hand, I can hardly start admitting from the waiting list if the Grange isn't going to continue. I shall hold a family council on the afternoon Grace is buried. I think it would be right to wait until then. If there are no complications, that should be in less than a week's time. I should like you both to take part and help us to our decision.'

Julius said quickly:

'That's impossible, Wilfred. I've absolutely no interest; interest, I mean, in the legal or insurance sense. It just isn't my business.'

'You live here. I've always thought of you as one of the family.'

'Sweet of you, and I'm honoured. But it isn't true. I'm not one of the family and I have absolutely no right to vote on a decision that can't really affect me one way or the other. If you decide to sell out, and I wouldn't blame you, I probably shall too. I don't fancy living on Toynton Head once it's a caravan site. But it won't matter to me. I'll get a good price from some bright young executive from the Midlands who won't give a damn about peace and quiet but who will build a natty cocktail bar in the sitting-room and run up a flagpole on the patio. I shall probably look for my next cottage in the Dordogne after careful inquiries about any bargains which the owner may have made with God or the devil. Sorry, but it's a definite no.'

'And you, Adam?'

'I've even less right to an opinion than Court. This place is home to the patients. Why on earth should their future be decided, at least in part, by the vote of a casual visitor?'

'Because I greatly trust your judgement.'

'There's no reason why you should. In this matter, better trust your accountant.'

Julius asked:

'Are you inviting Millicent to the family council?'

'Of course. She may not have always given me the support I hoped for from her, but she is one of the family.'

'And Maggie Hewson?'

Wilfred said curtly:

'No.'

'She's not going to like that. And isn't it a little hurtful to Eric?'

Wilfred said magisterially:

'As you have just made it plain that you don't consider yourself in any way concerned, why not leave me to decide what's hurtful to Eric. And now, if you will both excuse me, I shall join the family for breakfast.'

VII

As they left Wilfred's room, Julius said roughly and as if on impulse:

'Come up to the cottage and have breakfast. Have a drink anyway. Or if it's too early for alcohol, have coffee. Anyway, please come. I've started the day in a mood of self-disgust and I'm bad company for myself.'

It was too close to an appeal to be easily disregarded. Dalgliesh said:

'If you can give me about five minutes. There's someone I want to see. I'll meet you in the hall.'

He remembered from his first conducted tour of the Grange which was Jennie Pegram's room. There might, he thought, be a better time for this encounter but he couldn't wait for it. He knocked and heard the note of surprise in her answering 'come in'. She was sitting in her wheelchair in front of her dressing-table, her yellow hair flowing over her shoulders. Taking the poison pen letter from his wallet he walked up behind her and laid it in front of her. In the mirror their eyes met.

'Did you type that?'

She let her glance travel over it without picking it up. Her eyes flickered; a red stain began to travel like a wave over her neck. He heard the hiss of in-drawn breath, but her voice was calm.

'Why should I?'

'I can suggest reasons. But did you?'

'Of course not! I've never seen it before.'

She glanced at it again dismissively, contemptuously.

'It's . . . it's stupid, childish.'

'Yes, a poor effort. Done in a hurry, I imagine. I thought you might take rather a poor view of it. Not quite as exciting or imaginative as the others.'

'What others?'

'Come now, let's start with the one to Grace Willison. That did you credit. An imaginative effort, cleverly composed to spoil her pleasure in the only real friend she had made here, and nasty enough to ensure that she would be ashamed to show it to anyone. Except, of course, to a policeman. Even Miss Willison didn't mind showing it to a policeman. Where obscenity is concerned, we enjoy an almost medical dispensation.'

'She wouldn't dare! And I don't know what you're talking about.'

'Wouldn't she? It's a pity you can't ask her. You know that she's dead?'

'That's nothing to do with me.'

'Luckily for you, I don't think it is. She wasn't the suicidal type. I wonder if you were as lucky – or unlucky – with your other victims, with Victor Holroyd for example.'

There was no mistaking her terror now. The thin hands were twisting the handle of her hairbrush in a desperate pantomime.

'That wasn't my fault! I never wrote to Victor! I never wrote to anyone.'

'You aren't as clever as you think you are. You forget about fingerprints. Perhaps you didn't realize that forensic laboratories can detect them on writing paper. And then there's the timing. All the letters have been received since you arrived at Toynton Grange. The first was received before Ursula Hollis was admitted and I think we can rule out Henry Carwardine. I know that they've stopped since Mr Holroyd's death. Was that because you realized just how far you'd gone? Or did you hope that Mr Holroyd would be held responsible? But the police will know that those letters weren't written by a man. And then there's the saliva test. All except fifteen per cent of the population excrete their blood group in their saliva. It's a pity you didn't know that before you licked the envelope flaps.'

'The envelopes . . . but they weren't . . .'

She gasped at Dalgliesh. Her eyes widened with terror. The flush receded leaving her very pale.

'No, there weren't any envelopes. The notes were folded and placed in the victim's library book. But no one knows that except the recipients and you.'

She said, not looking at him:

'What are you going to do?'

'I don't know yet.'

And he didn't know. He felt a mixture, strange to him, of embarrassment, anger and some shame. It had been so easy to trick her, so easy and so contemptible. He saw himself as clearly as if he were on onlooker, healthy and able, sitting magisterially in judgement on her weakness, delivering the customary admonition from the bench, deferring sentence. The picture was distasteful. She had caused Grace Willison pain. But at least she could claim some psychological excuse. How much of his own anger and disgust had its roots in guilt? What had he done to make Grace Willison's last days happier? Yet something would have to be done about her. She was unlikely at present to make more mischief at Toynton Grange, but what of the future? And Henry Carwardine presumably had a right to know. So, one could argue, had Wilfred and the Ridgewell Trustees if they took over. Some people, too, would argue that she needed help. They would produce the orthodox contemporary solution, referral to a psychiatrist. He just didn't know. It wasn't a remedy in which he had much confidence. It would gratify her vanity, perhaps, and minister to her urge for self-importance to be taken seriously. But if the victims had resolved to keep silent, if only to protect Wilfred from worry, what right had he to deride their motive or break their confidence? He had been used in his job to working to rules. Even when he had taken an unorthodox decision, which wasn't seldom, the moral issues – if one could use that word and he never had – had been clear and unambiguous. His illness must have sapped his will and judgement as well as his physical strength for his paltry problem to defeat him. Ought he to leave a sealed note for Anstey or his successor to open in case of further trouble? Really it was ridiculous to be driven to such a weak and histrionic expedient. For God's sake, why couldn't he make a straight decision? He wished that Father Baddeley were alive, knowing on whose frail shoulders he could safely have lain this particular burden.

He said:

'I shall leave it to you to tell the victims, all of them, that you were responsible and that it won't happen again. You had better see that it doesn't. I leave it to your ingenuity to think out an excuse. I know that you must miss all the fuss and attention you had at your last hospital. But why compensate by making other people unhappy?'

'They hate me.'

'Of course they don't. You hate yourself. Did you write these notes to anyone else except Miss Willison and Mr Carwardine?'

She looked up at him slyly from under her eyelids.

'No. Only those two.'

It was probably a lie, he thought wearily. Ursula Hollis had probably had a letter. Would it do more harm or less if he asked her?

He heard Jennie Pegram's voice, stronger now, more confident. She lifted her left hand and began stroking her hair, drawing the strands across her face. She said:

'No one here cares about me. They all despise me. They never wanted me to come here. I didn't want it either. You could help me but you don't really care. You don't even want to listen.'

'Get Dr Hewson to refer you to a psychiatrist and confide in him. He's paid to listen to neurotics talking about themselves. I'm not.'

He regretted the unkindness as soon as the door was closed. He knew what had prompted it; the sudden remembrance of Grace Willison's shrunken, ugly body in its cheap nightdress. It was well, he thought, in a mood of self-disgust, that he was giving up his job if pity and anger could so destroy his detachment. Or was

265

it Toynton Grange? This place, he thought, is getting on my nerves.

As he walked quickly down the passage the door next to Grace Willison's room opened and he saw Ursula Hollis. She beckoned him in, swivelling her wheelchair to clear the doorway.

'They've told us to wait in our rooms. Grace is dead.'

'Yes, I know.'

'What is it? What happened?'

'No one really knows yet. Dr Hewson is arranging for a post-mortem.'

'She didn't kill herself – or anything.'

'I'm not sure. It looked as if she died quietly in her sleep.'

'You mean like Father Baddeley?'

'Yes, just like Father Baddeley.'

They paused, staring at each other. Dalgliesh asked:

'You didn't hear anything last night?'

'Oh, no! Nothing! I slept very well, that is, after Helen had been in to me.'

'Would you have heard if she called out or if anyone went in to her?'

'Oh yes, if I wasn't asleep. Sometimes she kept me awake with her snoring. But I didn't hear her call out, and she went to sleep before I did. My light was out before twelve-thirty and I thought then how quiet she was.'

He moved towards the door and then paused, feeling that she was reluctant to see him go. He asked:

'Is anything worrying you?'

'Oh, no! Nothing. It was just the uncertainty about Grace, not knowing, everyone being so mysterious. But if they're going to do a post-mortem . . . I mean the post-mortem will tell us how she died.'

'Yes,' he said without conviction, as if reassuring himself as well as her, 'the post-mortem will tell us.'

VIII

Julius was waiting alone in the front hall and they left the Grange together walking through the bright morning air, abstracted, a little apart, their eyes fixed on the path. Neither spoke. As if yoked by an invisible cord, they paced, carefully distanced, towards the sea. Dalgliesh was glad of his companion's silence. He was thinking about Grace Willison, trying to understand and analyse the root of his concern and unrest, emotions which seemed to him illogical to the point of perversity. There had been no visible marks on the body; no lividity; no petechiae on the face or forehead; no sign of disturbance in her room; nothing unusual except an unlatched window. She had lain there stiffening in the quietus of natural death. Why then this irrational suspicion? He was a professional policeman, not a clairvoyant. He worked by evidence not by intuition. How many post-mortems were carried out in a year? Over 170,000 wasn't it? 170,000 deaths which required at least some preliminary investigation. Most of them could provide an obvious motive, at least for one person. Only the pathetic derelicts of society had nothing to leave, however meagre, however uncoveted to sophisticated eyes. Every death benefited someone, enfranchised someone, lifted a burden from someone's shoulders, whether of responsibility, the pain of vicarious suffering or the tyranny of love. Every death was a suspicious death if one looked only at motive, just as every death, at the last, was a natural death. Old Dr Blessington, one of the first and greatest of the forensic pathologists, had taught him that. It had, he remembered, been Blessington's last post-mortem, the young Detective Constable Dalgliesh's first. The hands of both had been shaking, but for very different reasons, although the old man had been as steady as a surgeon once the first incision was made. The body of a forty-two-year-old, red-haired prostitute was on the slab. The post-mortem assistant had with two strokes of his gloved hand wiped from her face the blood, the dirt, the pancake of paint and matted powder, leaving it pale, vulnerable, anonymous. His strong living hand, not death, had erased from it all personality. Old Blessington had demonstrated the cunning of his craft:

'You see, lad, the first blow, warded off by her hand, slipped down the neck and throat towards the right shoulder. A lot of blood, a lot of mess, but no great harm done. With the second, directed upwards and across, he severed the trachea. She died of shock, blood loss and asphyxia, probably in that order from the look of the thymus. When we get them on the slab, lad, there's no such thing as unnatural death.'

Natural or unnatural, he was through with it now. It was irritating that with a will so strong, his mind apparently needed this constant reassurance, that it was so obstinately reluctant to leave the problems alone. What possible justification, anyway, had he for going to the local police with a complaint that death was becoming a little too common at Toynton? An old priest dying of heart disease, without enemies, without possessions, except a modest fortune unexceptionally willed for charitable purposes to the man who had befriended him, a notable philanthropist whose character and reputation were beyond reproach. And Victor Holroyd? What could the police do about that death other than what they had already most competently done. The facts had been investigated, the inquest jury had pronounced their finding. Holroyd had been buried, Father Baddeley cremated. All that remained was a coffin of broken bones and decaying flesh and a fistful of grey, gritty dust in Toynton churchyard; two more secrets added to the store of secrets buried in that consecrated earth. All of them were beyond human solving now.

And now this third death, the one for which everyone at Toynton Grange had probably been superstitiously waiting, in thrall to the theurgy that death comes in threes. They could all relax now. He could relax. The coroner would order a post-mortem, and Dalgliesh had little doubt of the result. If Michael and Grace Willison had both been murdered, their killer was too clever to leave signs. And why should he? With a frail, sick, disease-ridden woman, it would have been only too easy, as simple and quick as a firm hand placed over nose and mouth. And there would be nothing to justify his interference. He couldn't say: I, Adam Dalgliesh, have had one of my famous hunches – I disagree with the coroner, with the pathologist, with the local police, with all the facts. I demand in the light of this new death that Father Baddeley's incinerated bones be resurrected and forced to yield up their secret.

They had reached Toynton Cottage. Dalgliesh followed Julius round to the seaward porch which led
directly from the stone patio into the sitting-room. Julius
had left the door unlocked. He pushed it open and stood
a little aside so that Dalgliesh could go in first. Then they
both stood stock still, stricken into immobility. Someone
had been there before them. The marble bust of the smiling child had been smashed to pieces.

Still without speaking they moved together warily
over the carpet. The head, hacked into anonymity, lay
among a holocaust of marble fragments. The dark grey
carpet was bejewelled with gleaming grits of stone.
Broad ribbons of light from the windows and open
door lay across the room and, in their rays, the jabbed
slivers twinkled like a myriad infinitesimal stars. It
looked as if the destruction had at first been systematic.
Both ears had been cleanly severed, and lay together,
obscene objects oozing invisible blood, while the bouquet of flowers, so delicately carved that the lilies of the
valley had seemed to tremble with life, lay a little distance from the hand as if tossed lightly aside. A miniature dagger of marble had lodged upright in the sofa, a
microcosm of violence.

The room was very still; its ordered comfort, the measured ticking of the carriage clock on the mantelshelf, the
insistent thudding of the sea, all heightened the sense of
outrage, the crudity of destruction and hate.

Julius dropped to his knees and picked up a shapeless
lump which had once been the child's head. After a second he let it drop from his loosened grasp. It rolled
clumsily, obliquely, across the floor and came to rest
against the foot of the sofa. Still without speaking, he

reached over and picked up the posy of flowers cradling it gently in his hands. Dalgliesh saw that his body was shaking; he was very pale and his forehead, bent over the carving, glistened with sweat. He looked like a man in shock.

Dalgliesh went over to the side table which held a decanter and poured out a generous measure of whisky. Silently he handed the glass to Julius. The man's silence and the dreadful shaking worried him. Anything, he thought, violence, a storm of rage, a spate of obscenity, would be better than this unnatural silence. But when Julius did speak his voice was perfectly steady. He shook his head at the offered glass.

'No, thank you. I don't need a drink. I want to know what I'm feeling, know it here in my belly not just in my head. I don't want my anger dulled, and by God, I don't need it stimulated! Think of it, Dalgliesh. He died three hundred years ago, this gentle boy. The marble must have been carved very shortly afterwards. It was of absolutely no practical use to anyone for three hundred years except to give comfort and pleasure and remind us that we are dust. Three hundred years. Three hundred years of war, revolution, violence, greed. But it survived. It survived until this year of grace. Drink that whisky yourself, Dalgliesh. Raise the glass and toast the age of the despoiler. He didn't know that this was here, unless he peers and pries when I am away. Anything of mine would have served. He could have destroyed anything. But when he saw this, he couldn't resist it. Nothing else could have given him quite such an exaltation of destruction. This isn't just hatred of me you know. Whoever did it, hated this too. Because it gave pleasure, was made with

271

an intention, not just a lump of clay thrown against a wall, paint stamped into a canvas, a piece of stone smoothed into innocuous curves. It had gravity and integrity. It grew out of privilege and tradition, and contributed to it. God, I should have known better than to bring it here among these barbarians!'

Dalgliesh knelt beside him. He picked up two portions of a smashed forearm and fitted them together like a puzzle. He said:

'We know probably to within a few minutes when it was done. We know that it needed strength and that he – or she – probably used a hammer. There ought to be marks on that. And he couldn't have walked here and back in the time. Either he escaped down your path here to the shore, or he came by van and then went on to collect the post. It shouldn't be difficult to find out who is responsible.'

'My God, Dalgliesh, you have a policeman's soul haven't you? Is that thought supposed to comfort me?'

'It would me; but then, as you say, it's probably a matter of soul.'

'I'm not calling in the police if that's what you're suggesting. I don't need the local fuzz to tell me who did this. I know, and so do you, don't you?'

'No. I could give you a short list of suspects in order of probability, but that's not the same thing.'

'Spare yourself the trouble. I know and I'll deal with him in my own way.'

'And give him the added satisfaction of seeing you brought up on a charge of assault or G.B.H. I suppose.'

'I wouldn't get much sympathy from you would I, or from the local bench? Vengeance is mine saith Her

Majesty's Commission of the Peace. Naughty, destructive boy, under-privileged lad! Five pounds fine and put him on probation. Oh! don't worry! I shan't do anything rash. I'll take my time, but I'll deal with it. You can keep your local pals out of it. They weren't exactly a flaming success when they investigated Holroyd's death were they? They can keep their clumsy fingers out of my mess.'

Getting to his feet he added with sulky obstinacy, almost as an afterthought:

'Besides, I don't want any more fuss here at present, not just after Grace Willison's death. Wilfred's got enough on his plate. I'll clear this mess away and tell Henry that I have taken the marble back to London. No one else from the Grange comes here, thank God, so I shall be spared the usual insincere condolences.'

Dalgliesh said:

'I find it interesting, this concern for Wilfred's peace of mind.'

'I thought you might. In your book I am a selfish bastard. You've got an identikit to selfish bastards, and I don't precisely fit. Ergo, find a reason. There has to be a first cause.'

'There's always a cause.'

'Well, what is it? Am I somehow in Wilfred's pay? Am I fiddling the books? Has he some hold over me? Is there perhaps some truth in Moxon's suspicions? Or perhaps I'm Wilfred's illegitimate son.'

'Even a legitimate son might reasonably feel that it was worth causing Wilfred some distress to discover who did this. Aren't you being too scrupulous? Wilfred must know that someone at Toynton Grange, probably one of his disciples, nearly killed him, intentionally or otherwise. My guess is that he'd take the loss of your marble fairly philosophically.'

'He doesn't have to take it. He's not going to know. I can't explain to you what I don't understand myself. But I am committed to Wilfred. He is so vulnerable and pathetic. And it is all so hopeless! If you must know, he reminds me in some way of my parents. They had a small general store in Southsea. Then when I was about fourteen, a large chain store opened next door. That was the end of them. They tried everything; they wouldn't give in. Extended credit when they weren't getting their money anyway; special offers when their profit margins were practically nil; hours spent after closing time rearranging the window; balloons given free to the local kids. It didn't matter, you see. It was all utterly pointless and futile. They couldn't succeed. I thought I could have borne their failure. What I couldn't bear was their hope.'

Dalgliesh thought that, in part, he did see. He knew what Julius was saying. Here am I, young, rich, healthy. I know how to be happy, if only the world were really as I want it to be. If only other people wouldn't persist in being sick, deformed, in pain, helpless, defeated, deluded. Or if only I could be just that bit more selfish so that I didn't care. If only there weren't the black tower. He heard Julius speaking:

'Don't worry about me. Remember I am bereaved. Don't they say that the bereaved always have to work through their grief? The appropriate treatment is a detached sympathy and plenty of good plain nourishment. We'd better get some breakfast.'

Dalgliesh said quietly:

'If you're not going to ring the police, then we might as well clear up this mess.'

'I'll get a dustpan. I can't bear the noise of the vacuum cleaner.'

He disappeared into his immaculate, fashionable over-equipped kitchen, and came back with a dustpan and two brushes. In an odd companionship they knelt together to their task. But the brushes were too soft to dislodge the slivers of marble, and in the end they had to pick them up laboriously one by one.

IX

The forensic pathologist was a locum tenens senior registrar, and if he had expected this three-week stint of duty in the agreeable West Country to be less arduous than his London job, he was disappointed. When the telephone rang for the tenth time that morning he peeled off his gloves, tried not to think about the fifteen naked cadavers still waiting on their refrigerated shelves and lifted the receiver philosophically. The confident masculine voice, except for its pleasant country burr, could have been the voice of any Metropolitan police officer, and the words, too, he had heard before.

'That you, Doc? We've got a body in a field three miles north of Blandford which we don't like the look of. Could you come to the scene?'

The summons seldom differed. They always had a body they didn't like the look of, in a ditch, a field, a gutter, in the tangled steel of a smashed car. He took up his message pad and asked the usual questions, heard the expected replies. He said to the mortuary assistant:

'OK, Bert, you can sew her up now. She's no twelve-guinea special. Tell the Coroner's office that he can issue the disposal order. I'm off to a scene. Get the next two ready for me, will you?'

He glanced for the last time at the emaciated body on the table. There had been nothing difficult about Grace Miriam Willison, spinster, aged 57. No external signs of violence, no internal evidence to justify sending the viscera for analysis. He had muttered to his assistant with some bitterness that if the local GPs were going to look to an over-stretched forensic pathology service to settle their differential diagnoses the service might as well pack up. But her doctor's hunch had been right. There was something he'd missed, the advanced neoplasm in the upper stomach. And much good that knowledge now would do him or her. That, or the D. S. or the heart condition had killed her. He wasn't God and he'd taken his choice. Or maybe she'd just decided that she had had enough and turned her face to the wall. In her state it was the mystery of continuing life not the fact of death that needed explaining. He was beginning to think that most patients died when they decided that it was their time to die. But you couldn't put that on a certificate.

He scribbled a final note on Grace Willison's record, called out a final instruction to his assistant, then pushed his way through the swing doors towards another death, another body, towards, he thought, with something like relief, his proper job.

SEVEN

Mist on the Headland

I

The church of All Saints at Toynton was an uninteresting Victorian reconstruction of an earlier building, the
churchyard a triangular patch of swathed grass between
the west wall, the road and a row of rather dull cottages. Victor Holroyd's grave, pointed out by Julius,
was an oblong mound crudely patched with squares of
weedy turf. Beside it, a simple wooden cross marked the
spot where Father Baddeley's ashes had been buried.
Grace Willison was to lie next to him. Everyone at
Toynton Grange was at the funeral except Helen Rainer,
who had been left to nurse Georgie Allan, and Maggie
Hewson, whose absence, unremarked, was apparently
taken for granted. But Dalgliesh, when he arrived alone,
had been surprised to see Julius's Mercedes parked
opposite the lych-gate beside the Toynton Grange bus.

The churchyard was encumbered and the path
between the headstones narrow and overgrown so that
it took some time to manoeuvre the three wheelchairs
round the open grave.

The local vicar was taking a belated holiday and his
substitute, who apparently knew nothing of Toynton
Grange, was obviously surprised to see four mourners

garbed in brown monk's habits. He asked if they were Anglican Franciscans, an inquiry which provoked a fit of nervous giggling from Jennie Pegram, Anstey's answer, unheard by Dalgliesh, apparently failed to reassure and the priest, puzzled and disapproving, took the service with carefully controlled speed as if anxious to free the churchyard as soon as possible from the risk of contamination by the imposters. The little party sang, at Wilfred's suggestion, Grace's favourite hymn, 'Ye Holy Angels Bright'. It was, thought Dalgliesh, a hymn peculiarly unsuited for amateur unaccompanied singing and their uncertain and discordant voices rose reed thin in the crisp autumnal air.

There were no flowers. Their absence, the rich smell of newly turned earth, the mellow autumn sunlight, the ubiquitous scent of burning wood, even the sense of unseen but inquisitive eyes peering morbidly from behind the hedges, brought back with stabbing pain the memory of another funeral.

He had been a fourteen-year-old schoolboy, at home for his half-term. His parents were in Italy and Father Baddeley was in charge of the parish. A local farmer's son, a shy, gentle, over-conscientious eighteen-year-old, home for the weekend from his first term at university, had taken his father's gun and shot dead both parents, his fifteen-year-old sister and, finally, himself. They were a devoted family, he a loving son. For the young Dalgliesh, who was beginning to imagine himself in love with the girl, it had been a horror eclipsing all subsequent horrors. The tragedy unexplained, appalling, had at first stunned the village. But grief had quickly given way to a wave of superstitious anger, terror and repulsion. It was unthinkable that the boy should be buried in consecrated ground and Father Baddeley's gentle but inexorable insistence that all the family should lie together in one grave had made him temporarily an outcast. The funeral, boycotted by the village, had been held on such a day as this. The family had no close relatives. Only Father Baddeley, the sexton and Adam Dalgliesh had been there. The fourteen-year-old boy, rigid with uncomprehending grief, had concentrated on the responses willing himself to divorce the unbearably poignant words from their sense, to see them merely as black unmeaning symbols on the prayer book page, and to speak them with firmness, even with nonchalance, across the open grave. Now, when this unknown priest raised his hand to speak the final blessing over Grace Willison's body Dalgliesh saw instead the frail upright figure of Father Baddeley, the wind ruffling his hair. As the first sods fell on the coffin and he turned away he felt like a traitor. The memory of one occasion on which Father Baddeley had not relied on him in vain only reinforced his present nagging sense of failure.

It was probably this which made him reply tartly to Wilfred when he walked up to him and said:

'We are going back for luncheon now. We shall start the family council at half past two and the second session at about four. Are you quite sure you won't help us?'

Dalgliesh opened the door of his car.

'Can you give me one reason why it would be right that I should?' Wilfred turned away; for once he looked almost disconcerted. Dalgliesh heard Julius's low laugh.

'Silly old dear! Does he really think that we don't know that he wouldn't be holding a family council if he

279

weren't confident that the decision would go his way. What are your plans for the day?'

Dalgliesh said that they were still uncertain. In fact he had decided to exercise away his self-disgust by walking along the cliff path as far as Weymouth and back. But he wasn't anxious to invite Julius's company.

He stopped at a nearby pub for a luncheon of cheese and beer, drove quickly back to Hope Cottage, changed into slacks and windcheater and set off eastwards along the cliff path. It was very different from that first early morning walk the day after his arrival when all his newly awakened senses had been alive to sound and colour and smell. Now he strode strongly forward deep in thought, eyes on the path, hardly aware even of the laboured, sibilant breath of the sea. He would soon have to make a decision about his job; but that could wait for another couple of weeks. There were more immediate if less onerous decisions. How much longer should he stay at Toynton? He had little excuse to linger. The books had been sorted, the boxes were almost ready for cording. And he was making no progress with the problem which had kept him in Hope Cottage. There was small hope now of solving the mystery of Father Baddeley's summons. It was as if, living in Father Baddeley's cottage, sleeping in his bed, Dalgliesh had absorbed something of his personality. He could almost believe that he smelt the presence of evil. It was an alien faculty which he half resented and almost wholly distrusted. And yet it was increasingly strong. He was sure now that Father Baddeley had been murdered. And yet, when as a policeman he looked hard at the evidence, the case dissolved like smoke in his hand.

Perhaps because he was deep in unproductive thought the mist took him by surprise. It rode in from the sea, a sudden physical invasion of white obliterating clamminess. At one moment he was striding in the mellow afternoon sunlight with the breeze prickling the hairs on his neck and arms. The next, sun, colour and smell were blotted out and he stood stock still pushing at the mist as if it were an alien force. It hung on his hair, caught at his throat and swirled in grotesque patterns over the headland. He watched it, a writhing transparent veil passing over and through the brambles and bracken, magnifying and altering form, obscuring the path. With the mist came a sudden silence. He was only aware that the headland had been alive with birds now that their cries were mute. The silence was uncanny. In contrast, the sound of the sea swelled and became all-pervasive, disorganized, menacing, seeming to advance on him from all sides. It was like a chained animal, now moaning in sullen captivity, now breaking free to hurl itself with roars of impotent rage against the high shingles.

He turned back towards Toynton, uncertain of how far he had walked. The return journey was going to be difficult. He had no sense of direction except for the thread of trodden earth under his feet. But he thought that the danger would be slight if he went slowly. The path was barely visible but for most of the route it was fringed with brambles, a welcome if prickly barrier when, momentarily disorientated, he lost his way. Once the mist lifted slightly and he strode forward more confidently. But it was a mistake. Only just in time he realized that he was teetering on the edge of a wide crevice splitting the path and that what he had thought was a rising bank of moving mist was foam dying on the cliff face fifty feet below.

The black tower reared out of the mist so suddenly that his first realization of its presence was to scrape his palms – instinctively flung forward – against its cold infrangible scales. Then, suddenly, the mist rose and thinned and he saw the top of the tower. The base was still shrouded in swirls of white clamminess but the octagonal cupola with its three visible slits seemed to float gently from behind the last sinuous threads of mist to hang motionless in space, dramatic, menacingly solid, and yet unsubstantial as a dream. It moved with the mist, a fugitive vision, now descending so low that he could almost believe it within his reach, now rising, numinous and unobtainable, high over the thudding sea. It could surely have no contact with the cold stones on which his palms rested or the firm earth beneath his feet. To steady his balance he rested his head against the tower and felt reality hard and sharp against his forehead. Here at least was a landmark. From here he thought he could remember the main twists and turns of the path.

It was then that he heard it; the spine-chilling scrape, unmistakable, of bone ends clawing against the stone. It came from inside the tower. Reason asserted itself over superstition so quickly that his mind hardly had time to recognize its terror. Only the painful thudding of his heart against the rib cage, the sudden ice in the blood, told him that for one second he had crossed the border into the unknowable world. For one second, perhaps less, childish nightmares long suppressed rose to confront him. And then the terror passed. He listened more carefully, and then explored. The sound was quickly identified. To the seaward side of the tower and hidden in the corner between the porch and the round wall was a sturdy bramble. The wind had snapped one of the branches and two sharp unleashed ends were scraping against the stone. Through some trick of acoustics the sound, distorted, seemed to come from within the tower. From such coincidences, he thought, smiling grimly, were ghosts and legends born.

Less than twenty minutes later he stood above the valley and looked down on Toynton Grange. The mist was thinning now and he could just discern the Grange itself – a substantial, dark shadow marked by blurs of lights from the windows. His watch showed that it was eight minutes past three. So they would all be closeted now in solitary meditation waiting for the four o'clock summons to announce their final votes. He wondered how, in fact, they were passing their time. But the result was hardly in doubt. Like Julius he thought it unlikely that Wilfred would have called a council unless he were sure of getting his way. And that, presumably, would mean handing over to the Ridgewell Trust. Dalgliesh assessed how the votes might go. Wilfred would no doubt have received an undertaking that all jobs would be safe. Given that assurance Dot Moxon, Eric Hewson and Dennis Lerner would probably vote for the take-over. Poor Georgie Allan would have little choice. The views of the other patients were less certain but he had the feeling that Carwardine would be content enough to stay, particularly with the increased comfort and professional skill which the Trust would bring. Millicent, of course, would want to sell out and she would have had an ally in Maggie Hewson, if Maggie had been allowed to participate.

Looking down on the valley he saw the twin squares of light from the windows of Charity Cottage where, excluded, Maggie waited alone for the return of Eric. There was a stronger and brighter haze from the edge of the cliff. Julius, when at home, was extravagant with electricity.

The lights, although temporarily obscured as the mist shifted and re-formed, were a useful beacon. He found himself almost running down the slope of the headland. And then, curiously, the light in the Hewson cottage windows went off and on again three times, deliberate as a signal.

He had such a strong impression of an individual call for help that he had to remind himself of reality. She couldn't know that he, or anyone, was on the headland. It could only be by chance if the signal were seen by anyone at Toynton Grange, preoccupied as they were with meditation and decision. Besides, most of the patients' rooms were at the back of the house. It had probably been no more than a fortuitous flickering of the lights; she had been uncertain, perhaps, whether to watch television in the dark.

But the twin smudges of yellow light, now shining more strongly as the mist thinned, drew him towards the Hewson cottage. It was only about three hundred yards out of his way. She was there alone. He might as well look in, even at the risk of becoming involved in an alcoholic recital of grievances and resentment.

The front door was unlocked. When no voice responded to his knock he pushed it open and went in. The sitting-room, dirty, untidy, with its grubby air of temporary occupation, was empty. All three bars of the portable electric fire were glowing red and the room struck very warm. The television screen was a blank. The single unshaded light bulb in the middle of the ceiling shone down garishly on the square table, the opened and almost empty bottle of whisky, the upturned glass, the sheet of writing paper with its scrawl of black Biro, at first relatively firm, then erratic as an insect trail across the white surface. The telephone had been moved from its usual place on the top of the bookcase and stood now, cord taut, on the table, the receiver hanging loosely over the edge.

He didn't wait to read the message. The door into the back hall was ajar and he pushed it open. He knew, with the sick and certain premonition of disaster, what he would find. The hall was very narrow and the door swung against her legs. The body twisted so that the flushed face slowly turned and looked down at him with what seemed a deprecating, half-melancholy, half-rueful surprise at finding herself at such a disadvantage. The light in the hall, from a single bulb, was garish, and she hung elongated like a bizarre and gaudily painted doll strung up for sale. The scarlet tight-fitting slacks, the white satin overblouse, the painted toe and finger nails and the matching gash of mouth looked horrible but unreal. One thrust of a knife and the sawdust would surely spill out from the stuffed veins to pyramid at his feet.

The climber's rope, a smooth twist of red and fawn, gay as a bell rope, was made to take the weight of a man. It hadn't failed Maggie. She had used it simply. The rope had been doubled and the two ends passed through the loop to form a noose, before being fastened, clumsily but effectively, to the top banister. The surplus yards lay tangled on the upper landing.

A high kitchen stool fitted with two steps had fallen on its side obstructing the hallway as if she had kicked it from under her. Dalgliesh placed it beneath the body and, resting her knees on its cushioned plastic, mounted the steps and slipped the noose over her head. The whole weight of her inert body sagged against him. He let it slip through his arms to the floor and half carried it into the sitting-room. Laying her on the mat in front of the fireplace he forced his mouth over hers and began artificial respiration.

Her mouth was fumed with whisky. He could taste her lipstick, a sickly ointment on his tongue. His shirt, wet with sweat, stuck to her blouse, gumming together his thudding chest and her soft, still warm but silent body. He pumped his breath into her, fighting an atavistic repugnance. It was too like raping the dead. He felt the absence of her heartbeat as keenly as an ache in his chest.

He was aware that the door had opened only by the sudden chill of flowing air. A pair of feet stood beside the body. He heard Julius's voice.

'Oh, my God! Is she dead? What happened?'

The note of terror surprised Dalgliesh. He glanced up for one second into Court's stricken face. It hung over him like a disembodied mask, the features bleached and distorted with fear. The man was fighting for control. His whole body was shaking. Dalgliesh, intent on the desperate rhythm of resuscitation, jerked out his commands in a series of harsh disjointed phrases.

'Get Hewson. Hurry.'

Julius's voice was a high, monotonous mutter.

'I can't! Don't ask me. I'm no good at that sort of thing. He doesn't even like me. We're never been close. You go. I'd rather stay here with her than face Eric.'

'Then ring him. Then the police. Wrap the receiver in your handkerchief. May be prints.'

'But they won't answer! They never do when they are meditating.'

'Then for God's sake fetch him!'

'But her face! It's covered with blood!'

'Lipstick. Smudged. Phone Hewson.'

Julius stood unmoving. Then he said:

'I'll try. They will have finished meditating by now. It's just four. They may answer.'

He turned to the telephone. From the corner of his eye Dalgliesh glimpsed the lifted receiver shaking in his hands, and the flash of white handkerchief which Julius had wrapped around the instrument as awkwardly as if trying to bandage a self-inflicted wound. After two long minutes the telephone was answered. He couldn't guess by whom. Nor did he afterwards remember what Julius had said.

'I've told them. They're coming.'

'Now the police.'

'What shall I tell them?'

'The facts. They'll know what to do.'

'But oughtn't we to wait? Suppose she comes round?'

Dalgliesh straightened himself up. He knew that for the last five minutes he had been working on a dead body. He said:

'I don't think she's going to come round.'

Immediately he bent again to his task, his mouth clamped over hers, feeling with his right palm for the first pulse of life in the silent heart. The pendant light bulb swung gently in the movement of air from the open door so that a shadow moved like a drawn curtain over the dead face. He was aware of the contrast between the inert flesh, the cool unresponsive lips bruised by his own, and her look of flushed intentness, a woman preoccupied in the act of love. The crimson stigmata of the rope was like a double-corded bracelet clasping the heavy throat. Remnants of cold mist stole in the door to twine themselves round the dust-encrusted legs of table and chairs. The mist stung his nostrils like an anaesthetic; his mouth tasted sour with the whisky-tainted breath.

Suddenly there was a rush of feet; the room was full of people and voices. Eric Hewson was edging him aside to kneel beside his wife; behind him Helen Rainer flicked open a medical bag. She handed him a stethoscope. He tore open his wife's blouse. Delicately, unemotionally, she lifted Maggie's left breast so that he could listen to the heart. He pulled off the stethoscope and threw it aside holding out his hand. This time, still without speaking, she handed him a syringe.

'What are you going to do?' It was Julius Court's hysterical voice.

Hewson looked up at Dalgliesh. His face was deathly white. The irises of his eyes were huge. He said:

'It's only digitalis.'

His voice, very low, was a plea for reassurance, for hope. But it sounded, too, like a plea for permission, a small abdication of responsibility. Dalgliesh nodded. If the stuff were digitalis it might work. And surely the man wouldn't be fool enough to inject anything lethal? To stop him now might be to kill her. Would it have been better to carry on with the artificial respiration? Probably not; in any case that was a decision for a doctor. And a doctor was here. But in his heart Dalgliesh knew that the argument was academic. She was as beyond harm as she was beyond help.

Helen Rainer now had a torch in her hand and was shining it on Maggie's breast. The pores of the skin between the pendulous breasts looked huge, miniature craters clogged with powder and sweat. Hewson's hand began to shake. Suddenly she said:

'Here, let me do it.'

He handed over the syringe. Dalgliesh heard Julius Court's incredulous 'Oh, no! No!' and then watched the needle go in as cleanly and surely as a *coup de grâce*.

The slim hands didn't tremble as she withdrew the syringe, held a pad of cotton wool over the puncture mark and, without speaking, handed the syringe to Dalgliesh.

Suddenly Julius Court stumbled out of the room. He came back almost immediately holding a glass. Before anyone could stop him he had grasped the whisky bottle by the top of its neck and had poured out the last half inch. Jerking one of the chairs out from the table he sat down and slumped forward, his arms half circling the bottle.

Wilfred said:

'But Julius . . . nothing should be touched until the police arrive!'

Julius took out his handkerchief and wiped it over his face.

'I needed that. And what the hell! I haven't interfered with her prints. And she's had a rope round her neck, or

289

haven't you noticed? What d'you think she died of – alcoholism?'

The rest of them stood in a tableau round the body. Hewson still knelt at his wife's side; Helen cradled her head. Wilfred and Dennis stood one on each side, the folds of their habits hanging motionless in the still air. They looked, thought Dalgliesh, like a motley collection of actors posing for a contemporary diptych, their eyes fixed with wary anticipation on the bright body of the martyred saint.

Five minutes later Hewson stood up. He said dully:

'No response. Move her to the sofa. We can't leave her there on the floor.'

Julius Court rose from his chair and he and Dalgliesh together lifted the sagging body and placed it on the sofa. It was too short, and the scarlet-tipped feet, looking at once grotesque and pathetically vulnerable, stuck out stiffly over the end. Dalgliesh heard the company sigh gently, as if they had satisfied some obscure need to make the body comfortable. Julius looked round, apparently at a loss, searching for something with which to cover the corpse. It was Dennis Lerner who, surprisingly, produced a large white handkerchief, shook it free of its folds and placed it with ritual precision over Maggie's face. They all looked at it intently as if watching for the linen to stir with the first tentative breath.

Wilfred said:

'I find it a strange tradition that we cover the faces of the dead. Is it because we feel that they are at a disadvantage, exposed defenceless to our critical gaze? Or is it because we fear them? I think the latter.'

Ignoring him, Eric Hewson turned to Dalgliesh.

'Where . . .'

'Out there in the hall.'

Hewson went to the door and stood silently survey-ing the dangling rope, the bright chrome and yellow kitchen stool. He turned towards the circle of watchful, compassionate faces.

'How did she get the rope?'

'It may be mine.' Wilfred's voice sounded interested, confident. He turned to Dalgliesh.

'It's newer-looking than Julius's rope. I bought it shortly after the old one was found frayed. I kept it on a hook in the business room. You may have noticed it. It was certainly hanging there when we left for Grace's funeral this morning. You remember, Dot?'

Dorothy Moxon moved forward from her shadowed refuge against the far wall. She spoke for the first time. They looked round as if surprised to find her in the company. Her voice sounded unnatural, high, trucu-lent, uncertain.

'Yes, I noticed. I mean, I'm sure I would have noticed if it hadn't been there. Yes, I remember. The rope was there.'

'And when you got back from the funeral?' asked Dalgliesh.

'I went alone into the business room to hang up my cloak. I don't think it was there then. I'm almost sure not.'

'Didn't that worry you?' asked Julius.

'No, why should it? I'm not sure that I consciously noticed that the rope was missing at the time. It's only now, looking back, that I am fairly confident that it wasn't there. Its absence wouldn't have particularly concerned me even had I registered it. I should have assumed that Albert had borrowed it for some purpose.

He couldn't have done so, of course. He came with us to the funeral, and got into the bus before me.'

Lerner said suddenly:

'The police have been telephoned?'

'Of course,' said Julius, 'I rang them.'

'What were you doing here?' Dorothy Moxon's didactic question sounded like an accusation, but Julius who seemed to have taken control of himself, answered calmly enough:

'She switched the light off and on three times before she died. I happened to see it through the mist from my bathroom window. I didn't come at once. I didn't think it was important or that she was really in trouble. Then I felt uneasy and decided to walk over. Dalgliesh was already here.'

Dalgliesh said:

'I saw the signal from the headland. Like Julius, I didn't feel more than slightly uneasy, but it seemed right to look in.'

Lerner had moved over to the table. He said:

'She's left a note.'

Dalgliesh said sharply:

'Don't touch it!'

Lerner withdrew his hand as if it had been stung. They moved round the table. The note was written in black Biro on the top sheet of a quarto-size pad of white writing paper. They read silently:

> *Dear Eric, I've told you often enough that*
> *I couldn't stick it out in this lousy hole any*
> *longer. You thought it was just talk. You've*
> *been so busy fussing over your precious*

patients I could die of boredom and you
wouldn't notice. Sorry if I've mucked
up your little plans. I don't kid myself you'll
miss me. You can have her now and by
God you're welcome to each other. We had
some good times. Remember them. Try to
miss me. Better dead. Sorry Wilfred.
The black tower.

The first eight lines were plainly and strongly written, the last five were an almost illegible scrawl.

'Her handwriting?' asked Anstey.

Eric Hewson replied in a voice so low that they could barely hear him.

'Oh, yes. Her handwriting.'

Julius turned to Eric and said with sudden energy:

'Look, it's perfectly plain how it happened. Maggie never intended to kill herself. She wouldn't. She's not the type. For God's sake why should she? She's young enough, healthy, if she didn't like it here she could walk out. She's an SRN. She's not unemployable. This was all meant to frighten you. She tried to telephone Toynton Grange and get you over here – just in time, of course. When no one replied, she signalled with the lights. But by that time she was too drunk to know exactly what she was doing and the whole thing became horribly real. Take that note, does it read like a suicide note?'

'It does to me,' said Anstey. 'And I suspect it will to the coroner.'

'Well, it doesn't to me. It could just as well be the note of a woman planning to go away.'

Helen Rainer said calmly:

'Only she wasn't. She wouldn't be leaving Toynton wearing just a shirt and slacks. And where is her case? No woman plans to leave home without taking her make-up and nightwear.'

There was a capacious black shoulder bag beside a leg of the table. Julius picked it up and began rummaging in it. He said:

'There's nothing here. No nightdress or toilet bag.'

He continued his inspection. Then he glanced suddenly from Eric to Dalgliesh. An extraordinary succession of emotions crossed his face: surprise, embarrassment, interest. He closed the bag and placed it on the table.

'Wilfred's right. Nothing should be touched until the police arrive.'

They stood in silence. Then Anstey said:

'The police will want to know where we all were this afternoon, no doubt. Even in an obvious case of suicide these questions have to be asked. She must have died when we were nearly at the end of our meditation hour. That means, of course, that none of us has an alibi. Given the circumstances it is perhaps fortunate that Maggie chose to leave a suicide note.'

Helen Rainer said calmly:

'Eric and I were together in my room for the whole of the hour.'

Wilfred stared at her, disconcerted. For the first time since he had entered the cottage he seemed at a loss. He said:

'But we were holding a family council! The rules are that we meditate in silence and alone.'

'We didn't meditate and we weren't precisely silent.

294

But we were alone–alone together.' She stared past him, defiant, almost triumphant, into the eyes of Eric Hewson. He gazed at her appalled.

Dennis Lerner, as if to dissociate himself from controversy, had moved over to stand by Dot Moxon by the door. Now he said quietly:

'I think I can hear cars. It must be the police.'

The mist had muffled the sound of their approach. Even as Lerner spoke Dalgliesh heard the dual slam of car doors. Eric's first reaction was to kneel by the sofa, shielding Maggie's body from the door. Then he scrambled clumsily to his feet as if afraid to be discovered in a compromising position. Dot, without looking round, moved her solid body away from the door.

The little room was suddenly as overcrowded as a bus shelter on a wet night, smelling of mist and damp raincoats. But there was no confusion. The new arrivals moved solidly and calmly in, bringing with them their equipment, moving as purposefully as encumbered members of an orchestra taking their appointed places. The group from Toynton Grange fell back and regarded them warily. No one spoke. Then Inspector Daniel's slow voice broke the silence.

'Well, now, and who found the poor lady?'

'I did,' said Dalgliesh. 'Court arrived about twelve minutes later.'

'Then I'll just have Mr Dalgliesh, Mr Court and Dr Hewson. That'll do to start with.'

Wilfred said:

'I should prefer to stay, if you please.'

'Well, Sir, I daresay. Mr Anstey isn't it? But we can't

always have what we'd prefer. Now if you'll all go back to the Grange, Detective Constable Burroughs will accompany you and anything that's on your minds you can say to him. I'll be with you later.'

Without a further word, Wilfred led the way.

Inspector Daniel looked at Dalgliesh:

'Well, Sir, seemingly for you there's no convalescence from death at Toynton Head.'

II

When he had handed over the syringe and given his account of the finding of the body Dalgliesh didn't wait to watch the investigation. He had no wish to give the impression that he was keeping a critical eye on Inspector Daniel's handling of the case; he disliked the role of spectator, and he felt uncomfortably that he was getting in their way. None of the men present were getting in each other's. They moved confidently in the cramped space, each a specialist, yet giving the impression of a team. The photographer manoeuvred his portable lights into the narrow hall; the plain-clothes fingerprint expert, his case open to display the neatly arranged tools of his craft, settled down at the table, brush poised, to begin his methodical dusting of the whisky bottle; the police surgeon knelt, absorbed and judicial, beside the body and plucked at Maggie's mottled skin as if hoping to stimulate it into life. Inspector Daniel leaned over him and they conferred together. They looked, thought Dalgliesh, like two poulterers expertly assessing the qualities of a dead chicken. He was interested that Daniel had brought the police surgeon and not a forensic pathologist. But why not? A Home Office pathologist, given the huge areas which most of them had to cover, could seldom arrive promptly on the scene. And the initial medical examination here presented no obvious problems. There was no sense in committing more resources than were needed for the job. He wondered whether Daniel would have come himself if it hadn't been for the presence at Toynton Grange of a Metropolitan Police Commander.

Dalgliesh formally asked Daniel's permission to return to Hope Cottage. Eric Hewson had already left. Daniel had asked him only a few necessary brief and gentle questions before suggesting that he should join the others at Toynton Grange. Dalgliesh sensed the relief at his departure. Even these imperturbable experts moved more freely released from the inhibiting restraints of public grief. Now the Inspector exerted himself to do more than nod a curt dismissal. He said:

'Thank you, Sir. I'll call in for a word with you before I leave if I may,' and bent again to his contemplation of the body.

Whatever Dalgliesh had expected to find at Toynton Head it wasn't this; the old familiar routine commemoration of unnatural death. For a moment he saw it with Julius Court's eyes, an esoteric necromantic rite, carried out by its drab practitioners in silence or between grunts and muttered words as brief as incantations, a secret ministration to the dead. Certainly Julius seemed engrossed by the procedure. He made no move to leave but stood to one side of the door and, without taking his fascinated eyes from Inspector Daniel, held it open for Dalgliesh. Daniel didn't suggest that he, too, might now leave but Dalgliesh thought it unlikely that this was because the Inspector had forgotten his presence.

It was nearly three hours later before Inspector Daniel's car drove up to Hope Cottage. The Inspector was alone; Sergeant Varney and the others, he explained, had already left. He came in bringing with him remnants of mist like ectoplasm and a rush of cold damp air. His hair was jewelled with moisture and his long ruddy face glowed as if he had come in from a walk in the sun. At Dalgliesh's invitation he took off his trench coat and settled himself in the wheel-backed chair in front of the wood fire. His black lively eyes roamed over the cottage, taking in the scruffed rug, the meagre grate, the shabbiness of the wallpaper. He said:

'So this is where the old gentleman lived.'

'And died. You'll take whisky? Or there's coffee if you prefer it.'

'Whisky, thank you, Mr Dalgliesh. Mr Anstey didn't exactly make him comfortable, did he? But I daresay all the money goes on the patients, and very rightly no doubt.'

Some went on Anstey himself, thought Dalgliesh, remembering the sybaritic cell which was Wilfred's bedroom. He said:

'It's better than it looks. My packing cases don't exactly add to the cosiness. But I doubt whether Father Baddeley noticed the shabbiness or if he did, that he cared.'

'Well, it's warm enough anyway. This sea mist seems to seep into your bones. It's clearer inland, though, once you get beyond Toynton village. That's why we made good time.'

He sipped his whisky gratefully. After a minute's silence he said:

'This business tonight, Mr Dalgliesh. It looks straight-forward enough. Her prints and Court's on the whisky bottle, and hers and Hewson's on the telephone. There's no hope of getting any dabs from the electric light switch, of course, and those on the Biro don't amount to anything. We found a couple of samples of her hand-writing. The document chappies at the lab can take a look at them but it's clear enough to me – and Dr Hewson incidentally – that she wrote that suicide note. It's a strong distinctive scrawl for a woman.'

'Except for the last three lines.'

'The reference to the black tower? She was pretty far gone when she added that. Incidentally, Mr Anstey takes it as an admission that it was she who started the fire which nearly killed him. And that wasn't the first attempt according to him. You've heard, no doubt, about the frayed climbing rope? He gave me a full account of the incident in the black tower including your finding the brown habit.'

'Did he? He was anxious enough at the time to keep it from the police. So now it's to be laid very neatly at Maggie Hewson's door.'

'It always surprises me – although it shouldn't by now – how violent death unlooses tongues. He says that she was the one he suspected from the start; that she made no secret of her hatred of Toynton Grange or her resentment of him in particular.'

Dalgliesh said:

'Nor did she. I would be surprised if a woman who expressed her feelings with such uninhibited relish should feel the need for any other release. The fire; the frayed climbing rope; they strike me as being either part of a deliberate stratagem or the manifestations of frustrated hatred. Maggie Hewson was nothing if not candid about her dislike of Anstey.'

'Mr Anstey sees the fire as part of a deliberate stratagem. According to him she was trying to frighten him into selling out. She was desperate to get her husband away from Toynton Grange.'

'Then she'd misjudged her man. My guess is that Anstey isn't selling out. By tomorrow he'll have made up his mind to pass Toynton Grange to the Ridgewell Trust.'

'He's making up his mind now, Mr Dalgliesh. Apparently Mrs Hewson's death interrupted their final decision. He was anxious for me to interview all the inmates as quickly as possible so that they could get down to it. Not that it took much time, to get the basic facts, anyway. No one was seen leaving Toynton Grange after the party arrived back after the funeral. Apart from Dr Hewson and Nurse Rainer, who admit to having spent the meditation hour together in her room, all the others claim that they were alone. The patients' quarters, as you no doubt know, are at the back. Anyone, anyone not disabled that is, could have left the house. But there's no evidence that anyone did.'

Dalgliesh said:

'And even if someone did, this mist would have been an effective shield. Anyone could have walked about the headland unseen. Were you convinced, by the way, that Maggie Hewson did start the fire?'

'I'm not investigating arson or attempted murder, Mr Dalgliesh. Mr Anstey told me what he did in confidence and said that he wanted the whole subject dropped. She could have done it, but there is no real evidence. He could have done it himself.'

'I doubt that. But I did wonder if Henry Carwardine might have had a hand in it. He couldn't have started the fire himself, of course, but he might have paid an accomplice. I don't think he likes Anstey. But that's hardly a motive. He doesn't have to stay at Toynton Grange. But he's highly intelligent and, I should have thought, fastidious. It's difficult to imagine him embroiling himself with such childish mischief.'

'Ah, but he isn't using his intelligence is he, Mr Dalgliesh? That's his trouble. He gave up too easily and too early, that one. And who can know the truth about motive? Sometimes I think not even the villain himself. I daresay it isn't easy for a man like that, living in such a restricted community, dependent always on others, having always to be grateful to Mr Anstey. Well, no doubt he is grateful to Mr Anstey; they all are. But gratitude can be the very devil sometimes, particularly if you have to be grateful for services you'd rather be without.'

'You're probably right. I know little of Carwardine's feelings, or of anyone else's at Toynton Grange. I've taken very good care not to know. Did the proximity of violent death induce any of the others to reveal their little secrets?'

'Mrs Hollis had a contribution. I don't know what she thought it proved, or why she thought it worth telling for that matter. But she may have wanted her little moment of importance. That blonde patient was the same – Miss Pegram isn't it? Kept hinting that she knew Dr Hewson and Nurse Rainer were lovers. No real evidence, of course, just spite and self-importance. I may have my ideas about those two, but I'd want more evidence than I heard tonight before I started thinking about conspiracy to murder. Mrs Hollis's story wasn't even particularly relevant to Maggie Hewson's death. She said that the night Grace Willison died she glimpsed Mrs Hewson passing along the dormitory corridor wearing a brown habit and with the hood drawn over her face. Apparently Mrs Hollis is in the habit of slipping out of bed at night and propelling herself round the room on her pillow. She says that it's a form of exercise, that she's trying to be more mobile and independent. Anyway on the night in question, she managed to get her door ajar – no doubt with the idea of taking a skid down the passage – and saw this cloaked figure. She thought afterwards that it must have been Maggie Hewson. Anyone with proper business – any of the staff – would have worn the hood down.'

'If they were about their proper business. When exactly was this?'

'A little after midnight she says. She closed the door again and got back into bed with some difficulty. She heard and saw nothing more.'

Dalgliesh said consideringly:

'I'm surprised from the little I've seen of her that she could manage to get back to bed unaided. Getting out is one thing, pulling herself back would be a great deal more difficult. Hardly worth the exercise, I should have thought.'

There was a short silence. Then Inspector Daniel asked, his black eyes full on Dalgliesh's face:

'Why did Dr Hewson refer that death to the coroner, Sir? If he had doubts about his medical diagnosis, why not ask the hospital pathologist, or one of his local chums to open her up for him?'

'Because I forced his hand and gave him no choice. He couldn't refuse to refer it without looking suspicious. And I don't think he has any local chums. He's not on those terms with his medical colleagues. How did you hear about it?'

'From Hewson. After hearing the girl's story I had another word with him. But Miss Willison's death was apparently straightforward.'

'Oh, yes. Just like this suicide. Just like Father Baddeley's death. All apparently straightforward. She died of cancer of the stomach. But this business tonight. Did you find out anything about the rope?'

'I forgot to mention that, Mr Dalgliesh. It's the rope which has clinched it. Nurse Rainer saw Mrs Hewson taking it from the business room at about half past eleven this morning. Nurse Rainer had been left behind to look after that bed-bound patient – Georgie Allan isn't it? – but everyone else was at Miss Willison's funeral. She was writing up the patient's medical record and needed a fresh sheet. All the stationery is kept in a filing cabinet in the business room. It's expensive and Mr Anstey doesn't like to issue it wholesale. He's afraid that people will use it as scribbling pads. When she reached the hall Nurse Rainer saw Mrs Hewson slipping out of the business room with the rope over her arm.'

'What explanation did Maggie give?'

'According to Nurse Rainer all she said was: "Don't worry, I'm not going to fray it. Quite the reverse. You'll get it back practically as good as new, if not from me."'

Dalgliesh said:

'Helen Rainer wasn't in any particular hurry to provide that information when we first found the body. But, assuming she isn't lying, it certainly completes your case.'

'I don't think she is lying, Mr Dalgliesh. But I did look at the boy's medical record. Nurse Rainer began a fresh sheet this afternoon. And there seems little doubt that the rope was hanging in the business room when Mr Anstey and Sister Moxon left for the funeral. Who else could have taken it? They were all at the funeral except Nurse Rainer, that very sick boy and Mrs Hammit.'

Dalgliesh said:

'I'd forgotten about Mrs Hammitt. I noticed that almost everyone from Toynton Grange was at the cemetery. It didn't occur to me that she wasn't.'

'She says she disapproves of funerals. People ought to be cremated in what she calls decent privacy. She says that she spent the morning cleaning her gas stove. For what it's worth, the stove has certainly been cleaned.'

'And this evening?'

'Meditating at Toynton Grange with the others. They were all supposed to be separate and alone. Mr Anstey placed the small interviewing room at her disposal. According to Mrs Hammitt, she never left it until her brother rang the bell to summon them together just before four o'clock. Mr Court telephoned shortly afterwards. Mrs Hewson died sometime during the meditation hour, no doubt about that. And the police surgeon reckons nearer four than three.'

Was Millicent strong enough, Dalgliesh wondered, to have strung up Maggie's heavy body? Probably, with the help of the kitchen stool. And the strangling itself would have been easy enough once Maggie was drunk. A silent movement behind her chair, the noose dropped by gloved hands over the drooping head, the sudden upward jerk as the rope bit into the flesh. Any one of them could have done it, could have crept out unnoticed into the concealing mist towards the smudge of light marking the Hewson cottage. Helen Rainer was the slightest; but Helen was a nurse, skilful in lifting heavy bodies. And Helen Rainer might not have been alone. He heard Daniel speaking:

'We'll get that stuff in the syringe analysed and we had better ask the lab to take a look at the whisky. But those two little jobs shouldn't hold up the inquest. Mr Anstey is anxious to get that over as soon as possible so that it doesn't interfere with the pilgrimage to Lourdes on the twenty-third. None of them seems worried about the funeral. That can wait until they get back. I don't see why they shouldn't get away, if the lab can do the analysis quickly. And we know that the whisky's all right; Court still seems healthy enough. I was wondering, Mr Dalgliesh, just why he took that swig. Incidentally, he'd given her the whisky; half a dozen bottles for her birthday on 11th September. A generous gentleman.'

Dalgliesh said:

'I thought he might have been feeding her whisky. But I don't think Court took that drink to save the forensic boys trouble. He needed it.'

Daniel gazed consideringly into his half-empty glass:

'Court's been pressing his theory that she never intended killing herself, that the whole set-up was play-acting, a desperate plea for attention. She might well have chosen that moment. They were all at the Grange making an important decision which affected her future, and yet she'd been excluded. He could be right; the jury may buy it. But it won't provide much consolation for the husband.'

Hewson, thought Dalgliesh, might be looking elsewhere for consolation. He said:

'It seems out of character. I can see her making some dramatic *démarche* if only to relieve the monotony. What I can't see is her wanting to stay on at Toynton as a failed suicide, attracting the slightly pitying contempt that people feel for someone who can't even succeed in killing herself. My problem is that I find a genuine suicide attempt even less in character.'

Daniel said:

'Maybe she didn't expect to have to stay at Toynton. Maybe that was the idea, to convince her husband that she'd kill herself unless he found another job. I can't see many men taking that risk. But she did kill herself, Mr Dalgliesh, whether she intended to or not. This case rests on two bits of evidence: Nurse Rainer's story about the rope, and the suicide note. If Rainer convinces the jury, and the document examiner confirms that Mrs Hewson wrote that note, then I'll be taking no bets on the verdict. In character or not, you can't get away from the evidence.'

But there was other evidence, thought Dalgliesh, less strong but not uninteresting. He said:

'She looked as if she were going somewhere, or perhaps expecting a visitor. She'd recently had a bath, her pores were clogged with powder. Her face was made up and she'd painted her nails. And she wasn't dressed for a solitary evening at home.'

'So her husband said. I thought myself that it looked as if she'd dolled herself up. That could support the theory of a faked suicide attempt. If you're planning to be the centre of attraction you may as well dress for the show. There's no evidence that she did have a visitor, although it's true enough that no one would have seen him in the mist. I doubt whether he could have found his way once he'd left the road. And if she was planning to leave Toynton, then someone would have had to fetch her. The Hewsons have no car, Mr Anstey doesn't allow private transport; there's no bus today; and we've checked the car hire firms.'

'You've wasted no time.'

'A matter of a few telephone calls, Mr Dalgliesh. I like to get these details out of the way while they're in my mind.'

'I can't see Maggie sitting quietly at home while the rest of them settled her future. She was friendly with a solicitor in Wareham, Robert Loder. I suppose he wasn't calling for her?'

Daniel shifted his heavy weight forward and threw another plank of driftwood on the fire. The fire was burning sluggishly as if the chimney were blocked with mist. He said:

'The local boyfriend. You aren't the only one to suggest that, Mr Dalgliesh. I thought it as well to ring the gentleman's home and have a word. Mr Loder's in Poole

General Hospital having his piles operated on. He was admitted yesterday and they gave him a week's notice. A nasty painful complaint. Hardly a comfortable time, you might say, to plan to run away with another man's wife.'

Dalgliesh asked:

'What about the one person at Toynton who did have his own car? Court?'

'It was an idea I had put to him, Mr Dalgliesh. I got a definite reply if not a very gentleman-like one. What it amounted to was that he'd do a great deal for dear Maggie but that self-preservation was the first law of nature and it just happens that his tastes don't run in that direction. Not that he was against the idea that she planned to leave Toynton. As a matter of fact, he suggested it, although I don't know how he thought it tied up with his previous view that Mrs Hewson faked a suicide attempt. Both theories can't be true.'

Dalgliesh asked:

'What was it that he found in her bag, a contraceptive?'

'Ah, you noticed that, did you? Yes, her Dutch cap. She wasn't on the pill seemingly. Court tried to be tactful about it, but as I told him, you can't be tactful about violent death. That's the one social catastrophe that the etiquette books can't help with. It's the strongest indication that she might have been planning to leave, that and her passport. They were both in the bag. You could say she was equipped for any eventuality.'

Dalgliesh said:

'She was equipped with the two items which she couldn't replace by a brief visit to the nearest chemist. I suppose you could argue that it's reasonable to keep the passport in her handbag. But the other?'

'Who's to know how long it was there. And women do keep things in odd places. No point in getting fanciful. And there's no reason to suppose that the two of them were set for a flit, she and Hewson. If you ask me he's as tied to Anstey and the Grange as any of the patients, poor devil. You know his story, I suppose?'

'Not really. I told you. I've taken good care not to become involved.'

'I had a sergeant like him once. The women couldn't leave him alone. It's that vulnerable, lost small boy look they have, I suppose. Name of Purkiss. Poor devil. He couldn't cope with the women and he couldn't cope without them. It did for his career. He runs a garage now, somewhere near Market Harborough, they tell me. And it's worse for Hewson. He doesn't even like his job. Forced into it, I gather, by one of those strong-minded mothers, a widow, determined to make her ewe lamb into a doctor. Appropriate enough, I suppose. It's the modern equivalent of the priesthood isn't it? He told me that the training wasn't so bad. He's got a phenomenal memory and can learn almost any facts. It's the responsibility he can't take. Well, there's not much of that at Toynton Grange. The patients are incurable and there's not much that they or anyone else expect him to do about it. Mr Anstey wrote to him and took him on, I gather, after he'd had his name removed from the Register by the G.M.C. He'd been having an affair with a patient, a girl of sixteen. There was a suggestion that it had started a year or so earlier, but he was lucky. The girl stuck to her story. He couldn't write prescriptions for dangerous drugs at Toynton Grange or sign death certificates, of course. Not until they restored his name to the Register six months ago. But they couldn't take away his medical knowledge and I've no doubt that Mr Anstey found him useful.'

'And cheap.'

'Well, there's that, of course. And now he doesn't want to leave. I suppose he might have killed his wife to stop her nagging him to go, but personally I don't believe it and neither will a jury. He's the sort of man who gets a woman to do his dirty work.'

'Helen Rainer?'

'That'd be daft, wouldn't it, Mr Dalgliesh? And where's the evidence?'

Dalgliesh wondered briefly whether to tell Daniel about the conversation between Maggie and her husband which he had overheard after the fire. But he put the thought from him. Hewson would either deny it or be able to explain it. There were probably a dozen petty secrets in a place like Toynton Grange. Daniel would feel bound to question him, of course. But he would see it as an irritating duty forced on him by an over-suspicious and officious intruder from the Met. determined to twist plain facts into a tangle of complicated conjecture. And what possible difference could it make? Daniel was right. If Helen stuck to her story about seeing Maggie collect the rope; if the document examiner confirmed that Maggie had written the suicide note; then the case was closed. He knew now what the inquest verdict would be, just as he had known that the post-mortem on Grace Willison would reveal nothing suspicious. Once again he saw himself, as if in a nightmare, watching impotently as the bizarre chara-banc of facts and conjecture hurtled on its predestined course. He couldn't stop it because he had forgotten how. His illness seemed to have sapped his intelligence as well as his will.

The spar of driftwood, charred now into a blackened spear, jewelled with sparks, slowly toppled and died. Dalgliesh was aware that the room was very cold and that he was hungry. Perhaps because of the occluding mist smudging the twilight hour between day and night, the evening seemed to have lasted for ever. He wondered whether he ought to offer Daniel a meal. Presumably the man could eat an omelette. But even the effort of cooking seemed beyond him.

Suddenly the problem solved itself. Daniel got slowly to his feet and reached for his coat. He said:

'Thank you for the whisky, Mr Dalgliesh. And now I'd best be on my way. I'll see you at the inquest, of course. It'll mean your staying on here. But we'll get on with the case as quickly as we can.'

They shook hands. Dalgliesh almost winced at the grip. At the doorway Daniel paused, tugging on his coat.

'I saw Dr Hewson alone in that small interviewing room which they tell me Father Baddeley used to use. And if you ask me, he'd have been better off with a priest. No difficulty in getting him to talk. Trouble was to stop him. And then he began crying and it all came out. How could he go on living without her? He'd never stopped loving her, longing for her. Funny, the more they're feeling, the less sincere they sound. But you'll have noticed that, of course. And then he looked up at me, his face blubbered with tears and said:

' "She didn't lie for me because she cared. It was only a game to her. She never pretended to love me. It was just that she thought the G.M.C. committee were a set of pompous old bores who despised her and she wasn't going to give them the satisfaction of seeing me go to prison. And so she lied."

'Do you know, Mr Dalgliesh, it was only then that I realized that he wasn't speaking about his wife. He wasn't even thinking of her. Or of Nurse Rainer for that matter. Poor devil! Ah, well, it's an odd job we have, you and I.'

He shook hands again as if he had already forgotten that last crushing grip, and with a final keen-eyed survey of the sitting-room as if to reassure himself that everything was still in place, slipped out into the mist.

III

In the business room Dot Moxon stood with Anstey at the window and looked out of the curtain of misty darkness. She said bitterly:

'The Trust won't want either of us, you realize that? They may name the home after you, but they won't let you stay on as Warden, and they'll get rid of me.'

He laid his hand on her shoulder. She wondered how she could ever have longed for that touch or been comforted by it. He said with the controlled patience of a parent comforting a wilfully obtuse child:

'They've given me an undertaking. No one's job will be lost. And everyone will get a rise. From now on you'll all be paid National Health Service rates. And they have a contributory pension scheme, that's a big advantage. I've never been able to provide that.'

'And what about Albert Philby? You're not telling me that they've promised to keep Albert on, an established, respectable national charity like the Ridgewell Trust.'

'Philby does present a problem. But he'll be dealt with sympathetically.'

'Dealt with sympathetically! We all know what that means. That's what they said to me in my last job, before they forced me out! And this is his home! He trusts us. We've taught him to trust us! And we have a responsibility for him.'

'Not any longer, Dot.'

'So we betray Albert and exchange what you've tried to build up here for Health Service rates of pay and a pension scheme! And my position? Oh, they won't sack me, I know that. But it won't be the same. They'll make Helen matron. She knows that too. Why else did she vote for the take-over?'

He said quietly:

'Because she knew that Maggie was dead.'

Dot laughed bitterly: 'It's worked out very nicely for her hasn't it? For both of them.'

He said: 'Dot dear, you and I have to accept that we cannot always choose the way in which we are called to serve.'

She wondered how she had never noticed it before, that irritating note of unctuous reproof in his voice. She turned abruptly away. The hand, thus rejected, slipped heavily from her shoulders. She remembered suddenly what he reminded her of: the sugar Father Christmas on her first Christmas tree, so desirable, so passionately desired. And you bit into nothingness; a trace of sweetness on the tongue and then an empty cavity grained with white sand.

IV

Ursula Hollis and Jennie Pegram sat together in Jennie's room, the two wheelchairs side by side in front of the dressing table. Ursula was leaning across and brushing Jennie's hair. She wasn't sure how she came to be here, so oddly employed. Jennie had never asked her before. But tonight, waiting for Helen to put them to bed, Helen, who had never before been so late, it was comforting not to be alone with her thoughts, comforting even to watch the corn-gold hair rise with each brush stroke, to fall slowly, a delicate shining mist, over the hunched shoulders. The two women found themselves whispering, cosily, like conspiring schoolgirls. Ursula said:

'What do you think will happen now?'

'To Toynton Grange? The Trust will take over and Wilfred will go, I expect. I don't mind. At least there'll be more patients. It's boring here now with so few of us. And Wilfred told me that they plan to build a sun-lounge out on the cliff. I'll like that. And we're bound to get more treats, trips and so on. We haven't had many recently. As a matter of fact, I was thinking of leaving. They keep writing from my old hospital wanting me back.'

Ursula knew that they hadn't written. But it didn't matter. She contributed her own morsel of fantasy.

314

'So was I. Steve is keen for me to move nearer London so that he can visit. Just until he's found us a more suitable flat of course.'

'Well, the Ridgewell Trust have a home in London haven't they? You could be transferred there.'

How strange that Helen hadn't told her that! Ursula whispered:

'It's odd that Helen voted for the take-over. I thought she wanted Wilfred to sell out.'

'Probably she did until she knew that Maggie was dead. Now that she's got rid of Maggie, I suppose she feels she may as well stay on. I mean the field's clear now, isn't it?'

Got rid of Maggie. But surely no one had got rid of Maggie but Maggie herself? And Helen couldn't have known that Maggie was going to die. Only six days ago she had been urging Ursula to vote for the sell-out. She couldn't have known then. Even at the preliminary family council, before they all parted for their meditation hour, she made it plain where her interests lay. And then during that meditation hour, she had changed her mind. No, Helen couldn't have known that Maggie was going to die. Ursula found the thought comforting. Everything was going to be all right. She had told Inspector Daniel about the hooded figure she had seen on the night of Grace's death, not the whole truth, of course, but enough to lift a weight of nagging and irrational worry from her mind. He hadn't thought it important. She had sensed that from the way he had listened, his few brief questions. And he was right, of course. It wasn't important. She wondered now how she could ever have lain awake fretted by inexplicable anxieties, haunted by images of evil and death, cloaked and hooded, stalking the silent corridors. And it must have been Maggie. With the news of Maggie's death she had suddenly become sure of it. It was difficult to know why, except that the figure had looked at once theatrical and surreptitious, so much a stranger, wearing the monk's robe with none of the slovenly familiarity of the Toynton Grange staff. But she had told the Inspector about it. There was no need to worry any more. Everything was going to be all right. Toynton Grange wouldn't close down after all. But it didn't matter. She would get a transfer to the London home, perhaps on exchange. Someone there was sure to want to come to the seaside. She heard Jennie's high childish voice.

'I'll let you into a secret about Maggie if you swear not to tell. Swear.'

'I swear.'

'She wrote poison pen letters. She sent one to me.'

Ursula's heart seemed to lurch. She said quickly:

'How do you know?'

'Because mine was typed on Grace Willison's typewriter and I actually saw Maggie typing it the evening before. The office door was ajar. She didn't know that I was watching.'

'What did she say?'

'It was all about a man who is in love with me. One of the television producers actually. He wanted to divorce his wife and take me away with him. It made a great deal of fuss and jealousy at the hospital at the time. That's partly why I had to leave. As a matter of fact I could still go to him if I chose.'

'But how did Maggie know?'

'She was a nurse, wasn't she? I think she knew one of the staff nurses at my old hospital. Maggie was clever at finding out things. I think she knew something about Victor Holroyd, too, but she didn't say what. I'm glad that she's dead. And if you had one of the letters, then you won't have any more now. Maggie's dead and the letters will stop. Brush a little harder and to the right, Ursula. That's lovely, lovely. We ought to be friends, you and me. When the new patients start arriving we must stick together. That's if I decide to stay, of course.'

Brush poised in mid-air, Ursula saw in the mirror the reflection of Jennie's sly, self-satisfied smile.

V

Shortly after ten o'clock, his supper eaten, Dalgliesh walked out into the night. The mist had lifted as mysteriously as it had appeared and the cool air, smelling of rain-washed grass, moved gently against his hot face. Standing in the absolute silence he could just hear the sibilant whisper of the sea.

A torch light, erratic as a will-o'-the-wisp, was weaving towards him from the direction of the Grange. Out of the darkness a bulky shadow emerged and took form. Millicent Hammitt had returned home. At the door of Faith Cottage she paused and called out to him.

'Goodnight, Commander. Your friends have left, then?'

Her voice was high, almost belligerent.

'The inspector has gone, yes.'

'You may have noticed that I didn't join the rush to participate in Maggie's ill-considered charade. I have no taste for these excitements. Eric has decided to sleep tonight at Toynton Grange. Much the best thing for him, no doubt. But, as I understand that the police have taken away the body, he needn't pretend to over-sensitivity. Incidentally, we've voted for the Ridgewell Trust takeover. What with one thing and another, quite an eventful evening.'

She turned to open the door. Then paused and called out again. 'They tell me that her nails were painted red.'

'Yes, Mrs Hammitt.'

'Her toe nails, too.'

He didn't reply. She said with sudden anger:

'Extraordinary woman!'

He heard the door close. A second later her light shone through the curtains. He went inside. Almost too weary to climb the stairs to bed, he stretched himself in Father Baddeley's chair staring into the dead fire. As he watched, the white ash shifted gently, a blackened spar of driftwood glowed momentarily into life, and he heard for the first time that night the familiar and comforting moan of the wind in the chimney. And then there followed another familiar sound. Faintly through the wall came a merry syncopated jingle. Millicent Hammitt had turned on the television.

EIGHT

The Black Tower

I

Next day Dalgliesh walked up to the Grange to explain to Wilfred that he must now stay on at Hope Cottage until after the inquest, and to pay his token rent. He found Wilfred alone in the business room. Surprisingly, there was no sign of Dot Moxon. Wilfred was studying a map of France spread out on the desk. A bundle of passports in a rubber band weighed down one corner. He seemed hardly to hear what his guest said. He replied, 'The inquest. Yes, of course,' as if it were a forgotten luncheon engagement, then bent again over the map. He made no mention of Maggie's death and Dalgliesh's formal condolences were coldly received as if they were in poor taste. It was as if by divesting himself of Toynton Grange, he had detached himself from further responsibility, even from concern. Now nothing remained but his twin obsessions, his miracle and the pilgrimage to Lourdes.

Inspector Daniel and the forensic laboratory worked quickly. The inquest was held exactly one week after Maggie's death, a week in which the inhabitants of Toynton Grange seemed as resolutely determined to keep out of Dalgliesh's way as he was to avoid them.

No one, not even Julius, showed any inclination to chat over Maggie's death. It was as if they saw him now merely as a police officer, an unwelcome intruder of uncertain allegiance, a potential spy. He drove away from Toynton Head early every morning and returned late each night to darkness and silence. Neither the police activities nor the life at Toynton Grange touched him. He continued his daily, compulsive exploration of Dorset like a prisoner on licence and looked forward to the inquest as the final day of release.

It came at last. None of the patients from Toynton Grange attended except Henry Carwardine, surprisingly since he was not required to give evidence. As the company stood in whispering reverential groups outside the courthouse in the usual disorganized hiatus which follows attendance at the more sombre public rituals, he wheeled his chair with vigorous thrusts of the arms to where Dalgliesh stood. He looked and sounded euphoric.

'I realize that these ceremonial tidyings-up of legal loose ends aren't exactly a novelty to you as they are to me. But this one wasn't without interest, I thought. Less fascinating technically and forensically than Holroyd's, but with more human interest.'

'You sound like a connoisseur of inquests.'

'If we go on like this at Toynton Grange I soon shall be. Helen Rainer was the star turn today, I thought. That extraordinary suit and hat in which she chose to appear were, I take it, the dress uniform of a state registered nurse. A very wise choice. Hair up; the merest trace of make-up; a general air of dedicated professionalism. "Mrs Hewson may have believed that there was a relationship between me and her husband. She had too much free time to brood. Naturally Dr Hewson and I have to work closely together. I have a high opinion of his kindness and competence but there has never been anything improper between us. Dr Hewson was devoted to his wife." Nothing improper! I never believed that people actually used that expression.'

Dalgliesh said:

'At inquests they do. Did the jury believe her, do you suppose?'

'Oh, I think so, don't you? Difficult to imagine our lady with the lamp garbed as she was this afternoon in grey samite – gaberdine anyway – mystic, wonderful, romping between the sheets. She was wise, I think, to admit that she and Hewson had spent the meditation hour together in her room. But that, as she explained, was because both had already come to their decision and couldn't afford to waste sixty minutes mulling it over when they had so much to discuss professionally together.'

'They had to choose between their alibi, for what it was worth, and the risk to reputation. On the whole they chose wisely.'

Henry swung round his wheelchair with aggressive exuberance.

'It rather foxed the honest jurymen of Dorset, though. You could see the way their minds were working. If they aren't lovers why were they closeted together? But if they were together, then Hewson couldn't have killed his wife. But unless they were lovers he wouldn't have had a motive for murdering his wife. But if he had such a motive, why admit that they were together? Obviously to give him an alibi. But he wouldn't need an alibi if he hadn't the usual motive. And if he had such a motive, then he and the girl would have been together. Very puzzling.'

Mildly amused, Dalgliesh asked:

'What did you think about Hewson's performance?'

'He did well too. Not quite the professional competence and detachment of yourself, my dear Commander, but quiet, sincere, some natural grief bravely under control. Sensible of him to admit that Maggie desperately wanted him to leave Toynton Grange but that he felt an obligation to Wilfred, "who took me on when I wasn't finding it easy to get a job". No mention, of course, of being struck off the Medical Register and no one tactless enough to bring it up.'

Dalgliesh said:

'And no one tactless enough to suggest that he and Helen may have been lying about their relationship.'

'What else do you expect? What people know and what they can legally prove – or care to state in a court of law – are two very different things. Besides, we must at all costs protect dear Wilfred from the contamination of truth. No, I thought it went very well. Suicide while the balance of mind, etc., etc. Poor Maggie! Stigmatized as a selfish, pleasure-seeking slut addicted to the bottle, out of sympathy with her husband's dedication to his noble profession and not even competent to make a comfortable home for him. Court's suggestion that it might have been an accidental death, play-acting which got out of hand, received no credence from the jury, did it? They took the view that a woman who drank the best part of a bottle of whisky, borrowed a rope and wrote a farewell letter was carrying play-acting a little far and did Maggie

322

the compliment of believing that she intended what she did. I thought that the forensic scientist was extraordinarily definite in his opinion, given the basically subjective nature of document examination. There seems no doubt that Maggie did write the suicide note.'

'The first four lines of it, which were all he felt competent to pronounce on. What did you think of the verdict?'

'Oh, I agree with Julius. She was planning to be cut down just in time amidst general hullabaloo. But with the best part of a bottle of whisky inside her she wasn't even competent to stage-manage her own resurrection. Incidentally, Julius gave me a graphic description of the drama in Charity Cottage, including Helen's impressive debut in the role of Lady Macbeth;

> Give me the syringe. The sleeping and the dead,
> Are but as pictures; 'tis the eye of childhood
> That fears a painted devil.'

There was no expression on Dalgliesh's face or in his voice. He said:

'How entertaining for you both. It's a pity Court wasn't as detached at the time. He might have made himself useful instead of behaving like a hysterical queer.'

Henry smiled, gratified to have provoked the response he wanted. He said:

'So you don't like him? Neither, I suspect, did your friend in holy orders.'

Dalgliesh spoke on impulse:

'I know that this is nothing to do with me, but isn't it time that you got away from Toynton Grange?'

'Got away? To where do you suggest?'

'There must be other places.'

'The world is full of places. But what do you suppose I could do, or be, or hope for in any of them? As a matter of fact, I did once plan to leave. It was a particularly foolish dream. No, I shall stay on at the Grange. The Ridgewell Trust have the professionalism and experience which Anstey lacks. I could do worse. Besides, Wilfred himself is to stay; and I still have a debt to pay Wilfred. In the meantime, this formality over, we can all relax and set off tomorrow to Lourdes in peace. You ought to come with us, Dalgliesh. You've hung around here so long that I suspect you rather enjoy our company. Besides, I don't think your convalescence has really done you a great deal of good. Why not come to Lourdes and see what the odour of incense and a change of scene can do for you?'

The Toynton Grange bus, driven by Philby, had drawn level with them now and the back ramp was being lowered. Dalgliesh watched in silence as Eric and Helen detached themselves from Wilfred, laid their hands simultaneously on the handlebars and wheeled Henry briskly into the bus. The ramp was raised, Wilfred took his seat in the front beside Philby, and the Toynton Grange bus disappeared from view.

Colonel Ridgewell and the trustees arrived after lunch. Dalgliesh watched as the car drew up and the sombre-suited party disappeared into the house. Later they emerged and walked with Wilfred over the headland towards the sea. Dalgliesh was a little surprised to see that Eric and Helen were with them but not Dorothy Moxon. He could see the Colonel's grey hair lifting in the breeze as he paused to swing his walking stick in wide explanatory sweeps or stood suddenly still conferring with the little group who quickly closed round him. No doubt, thought Dalgliesh, they would want to inspect the cottages. Well, Hope Cottage was ready for them. The bookshelves were empty and dusted, the packing cases corded and labelled for the carrier, his suitcase packed except for the few things he needed on this his last night. But he had no wish to get involved in introductions or to stand making small talk.

When the party finally turned back and made their way towards Charity Cottage, he got into his car and drove off, with no clear direction in mind, no particular aim, no intention except to keep driving long into the night.

II

The next morning was airless and sultry, inducing headache, the sky a tent of stained calico ponderous with unspilt rain. The pilgrimage party was due to set out at nine o'clock and at half past eight Millicent Hammitt barged in, without a preliminary knock, to say goodbye. She was wearing a blue-grey tweed suit badly seated, with a short double-breasted jacket; a blouse in a harsher and discordant blue adorned with a garish brooch at the neck; brogues; and a grey felt hat pulled down to cover the ears. She dumped a bulging airline bag and her shoulder bag at her feet, drew on a pair of fawn cotton gloves and held out her hand. Dalgliesh put down his coffee cup. His right hand was grasped in a crushing grip.

'Goodbye then, Commander. Odd, but I've never really got used to using your Christian name. You'll be gone, I understand, by the time we return?'

'I plan to drive back to London later this morning.'

'I hope you've enjoyed your stay. At least it has been eventful. One suicide, one natural death and the end of Toynton Grange as an independent institution. You can't have been bored.'

'And one attempted murder.'

'Wilfred in the burning tower? It sounds like the title of an *avant-garde* play. I've always had my doubts about that particular excitement. If you ask me, Wilfred set it up himself to justify handing over his responsibilities. No doubt that explanation occurred to you.'

'Several explanations occurred to me but none of them made much sense.'

'Little at Toynton Grange ever does. Well, the old order changeth yielding place to new and God fulfils Himself in many ways. We must hope that He will.'

Dalgliesh asked if Millicent had any plans.

'I shall stay on in the cottage. Wilfred's agreement with the Trust stipulates that I may live there for life, and I assure you, I've every intention of dying at my own convenience. It won't be the same, of course, knowing that the place belongs to strangers.'

Dalgliesh asked:

'How does your brother feel about the hand-over?'

'Relieved. Well, it's what he schemed for isn't it? He doesn't know what he's let himself in for, of course. Incidentally, he hasn't given this cottage to the Trust. This will continue to belong to him and he plans to move in after the place has been converted into something more civilized and comfortable. He's also offered to help at Toynton Grange in any capacity in which the Trust feel he can be of use. If he imagines that they'll let him stay on as Warden he's in for a shock. They've got their own plans for the Grange and I doubt whether they include Wilfred, even if they have agreed to pander to his vanity by naming the home after him. I suppose Wilfred imagines that everyone will defer to him as their benefactor and the original owner. I can assure you they won't. Now that the deed of gift – or whatever it is – is signed and the Trust are the legal owners, Wilfred counts for as little as Philby, less probably. It's his own fault. He should have sold out completely.'

'Wouldn't that have broken faith?'

'Superstitious nonsense! If Wilfred wanted to dress up in monk's garb and behave like a medieval abbot he should have applied for entry to a monastery. An Anglican one would have been perfectly respectable. The twice-yearly pilgrimage will go on, of course. That's one of Wilfred's stipulations. It's a pity you aren't coming with us, Commander. We stay at an agreeable little pension, really quite cheap and the food is excellent; and Lourdes is a cheerful little place. Quite an atmosphere. I don't say I wouldn't have preferred Wilfred to have had his miracle in Cannes, but it might have been worse. He could have got cured at Blackpool.'

She paused at the door to turn and say:

'I expect the bus will stop here so that the others can take leave of you.' She made it sound as if they would be conferring a privilege. Dalgliesh said that he would walk up with her and say goodbye at Toynton Grange. He had discovered one of Henry Carwardine's books on Father Baddeley's shelf and wanted to return it. There was also his bed linen to take back and some leftover tins of food which Toynton Grange could probably use.

'I'll take the tins later. Just leave them here. And you can return the linen any time. The Grange is never locked. Philby will be back later anyway. He only drives us to the port and sees us on the boat and then comes back to caretake and feed Jeoffrey and, of course, the hens. They're rather missing Grace's help with the hens although no one thought that she did anything very useful when she was alive. And it's not only the hens. They can't lay their hands on her list of the Friends. Actually, Wilfred wanted Dennis to stay at home this time. He's got one of his migraines and looks like death. But no one can make Dennis miss a pilgrimage.'

Dalgliesh walked up to the Grange with her. The bus was drawn up outside the front door and the patients were already loaded. The pathetically depleted party had a bizarre air of slightly spurious joviality. Dalgliesh's first impression from their varied garb was that they proposed to pursue quite different and unrelated activities. Henry Carwardine, in a belted tweed coat and deerstalker hat, looked like an Edwardian gentleman on his way to the grouse moors. Philby, incongruously formal in a dark suit with high collar and black tie, was an undertaker's man loading a hearse. Ursula Hollis had dressed like a Pakistani immigrant in full fig whose only concession to the English climate was an ill-cut jacket in mock fur. Jennie Pegram, wearing a long blue headscarf, had apparently made an attempt to impersonate Saint Bernadette. Helen Rainer, dressed as she had been at the inquest, was a prison matron in charge of a group of unpredictable delinquents. She had already taken her seat at the head of Georgie Allan's stretcher. The boy's eyes were feverishly bright and Dalgliesh could hear his high frenetic chatter. He was wearing a blue and white striped woollen scarf and clutching an immense teddy bear, its neck adorned with pale-blue ribbon and what, to Dalgliesh's astounded eyes, looked like a pilgrimage medal. The party could have been an oddly assorted party of team supporters on their way to a football match, but one, Dalgliesh thought, that hardly expected the home side to win.

Wilfred was gently fussing over the remainder of the luggage. He, Eric Hewson and Dennis Lerner were wearing their monk's habits. Dennis looked desperately ill, his face was taut with pain and his eyes half closed as if even the dull morning light were intolerable. Dalgliesh heard Eric whisper to him:

'For God's sake, Dennis, give up and stay at home! With two wheelchairs less we can perfectly well manage.'

Lerner's high voice held a tinge of hysteria.

'I'll be all right. You know it never lasts more than twenty-four hours. For God's sake leave me alone!'

At last the medical paraphernalia, decently shrouded, was loaded, the ramp was raised, the rear door finally slammed and they were off. Dalgliesh waved in response to the frantically signalling hands and watched as the brightly painted bus lurched slowly over the headland looking, as it receded, as vulnerable and insubstantial as a child's toy. He was surprised, and a little saddened, that he could feel such pity and regret for people with whom he had taken such care not to become involved.

He remained watching until the bus bumped slowly up the slope of the valley and finally tipped over the headland out of sight.

Now the headland was deserted, Toynton Grange and its cottages stood unlit and unpeopled under the heavy sky. It had grown darker in the last half-hour. There would be a storm before midday. Already his head ached with the premonition of thunder. The headland lay in the sinister anticipatory calm of a chosen battlefield. He could just hear the thudding of the sea, less a noise than a vibration on the dense air like the sullen menace of distant guns.

Restless and perversely reluctant to leave now that he was at last free to go, he walked up to the gate to collect his paper and any letters. The bus had obviously stopped for the Toynton Grange post and there was nothing in the box but the day's copy of *The Times*, an official-looking buff envelope for Julius Court and a square white one addressed to Father Baddeley. Tucking the newspaper under his arm he split open the stout linen-backed envelope and began to walk back, reading on his way. The letter was written in a firm, strong masculine hand; the printed address was a Midlands deanery. The writer was sorry not to have replied earlier to Father Baddeley's letter but it had been posted on to him in Italy, where he had taken a locum post for the summer. At the end of the conventional inquiries, the methodical recording of family and diocesan concerns, the perfunctory and predictable comments on public affairs, came the answer to the mystery of Father Baddeley's summons:

'I went at once to visit your young friend, Peter Bonnington, but he had, of course, been dead for some

330

months. I am so very sorry. In the circumstances there seemed little point in inquiring whether he had been happy at the new home or had really wanted to move from Dorset. I hope that his friend at Toynton Grange managed to visit before he died. On your other problem, I don't think I can offer much guidance. Our experience in the diocese where, as you know, we are particularly interested in young offenders, is that providing residential care for ex-prisoners whether in a home or in the kind of self-supporting hostel you envisage requires a great deal more capital than you have available. You could probably buy a small house even at today's prices, but at least two experienced staff would be needed initially and you would have to support the venture until it became established. But there are a number of existing hostels and organizations who would very much welcome your help. There certainly couldn't be a better use for your money, if you have decided, as you obviously have, that it ought not now to go to Toynton Grange. I think that you were wise to call in your policeman friend. I'm sure that he will be best able to advise you.'

Dalgliesh almost laughed aloud. Here was an ironical and fitting end to failure. So that was how it had begun! There had been nothing sinister behind Father Baddeley's letter, no suspected crime, no conspiracy, no hidden homicide. He had simply wanted, poor, innocent, unworldly old man, some professional advice on how to buy, equip, staff and endow a hostel for young ex-offenders for the sum of £19,000. Given the present state of the property market and the level of inflation, what he had needed was a financial genius. But he had written to a policeman, probably the only one he knew. He had written to an expert in violent death. And why not? To Father Baddeley all policemen were fundamentally alike, experienced in crime and familiar with criminals, dedicated to prevention as well as detection. And I, thought Dalgliesh bitterly, have done neither. Father Baddeley had wanted professional advice, not advice on how to deal with evil. There he had his own infallible guidelines, there he was at home. For some reason, almost certainly connected with the transfer of that young, unknown patient, Peter Bonnington, he had become disenchanted with Toynton Grange. He had wanted advice on how else to use his money. How typical of my arrogance, thought Dalgliesh, to suppose that he wanted me for anything more.

He stuffed the letter into his jacket pocket and strolled on, letting his eyes glance over the folded newspaper. An advertisement stood out as clearly as if it had been marked, familiar words leaping to the eye.

'Toynton Grange. All our friends will wish to know that from the day of our return from the October Pilgrimage we shall be part of the larger family of the Ridgewell Trust. Please continue to remember us in your prayers at this time of change. As our list of Friends has unfortunately been mislaid will all those who wish to keep in touch please write to me urgently.
                              Wilfred Anstey, Warden.'

Of course! The list of Toynton Grange Friends, unaccountably mislaid since Grace Willison's death, those sixty-eight names which Grace had known by heart. He stood stock still under the menacing sky and read the notice again. Excitement gripped him, as violently physical as a twist of the stomach, a surge of the blood. He knew with immediate, with heart-lifting certainty that here at last was the end of the tangled skein. Pull gently on this one fact and the thread would begin, miraculously, to run free.

If Grace Willison had been murdered, as he obstinately believed, post-mortem result notwithstanding, it had been because of something she knew. But it must have been vital information, knowledge which she alone possessed. One did not kill merely to silence intriguing but evidentially useless suspicions about where Father Baddeley had been on the afternoon of Holroyd's death. He had been in the black tower. Dalgliesh knew it and could prove it; Grace Willison might have known it too. But the shredded match and Grace's testimony taken together could prove nothing. With Father Baddeley dead, the worst anyone could do would be to point out that it was strange that the old priest hadn't mentioned seeing Julius Court walking over the headland. And Dalgliesh could imagine Julius's contemptuous, sardonic smile. A sick, tired old man, sitting with his book at the eastern window. Who could say now that he hadn't slept the hours away before making his way back to Toynton Grange across the headland, while, on the beach unseen below, the rescue party toiled with their burden? With Baddeley dead, his testimony silenced, no police force in the world would re-open the case on that second-hand evidence. The worst harm Grace could have done to herself might have been to betray that Dalgliesh wasn't just convalescing at Toynton, that he too was suspicious.

That betrayal might just have tipped the scales for her from life to death. Then she might have become too dangerous to let live. Not because she knew that Father Baddeley had been in the black tower on the afternoon of 12th September, but because she possessed more specific, more valuable information. There was only one distribution list of the Friends of Toynton Grange and she could type it by heart. Julius had been present when she made that claim. The list could be torn up, burnt, utterly destroyed. But there was only one way in which those sixty-eight names could be erased from one frail woman's consciousness.

Dalgliesh quickened his pace. He found himself almost running down the headland. His headache seemed surprisingly to have lifted despite the lowering sky, the dense, storm-laden air. Change the metaphor, still trite but well proved. In this job it wasn't the last piece of jigsaw, the easiest of all, that was important. No, it was the neglected, uninteresting small segment which, slotted into place, suddenly made sense of so many other discarded pieces. Delusive colours, amorphous and ambiguous shapes came together as now to reveal the first recognizable outline of the finished picture.

And now, that piece in place, it was time to move the others speculatively over the board. For the present, forget proof, forget autopsy reports and the formal legal certainty of inquest verdicts; forget pride, the fear of ridicule, the reluctance to become involved. Get back to the first principle applied by any divisional detective constable when he smelt villainy on his patch. *Cui bono?* Who was living above his means? Who was in possession of more money than could reasonably be explained? There were two such people at Toynton Grange, and they were linked by Holroyd's death. Julius Court and Dennis Lerner. Julius, who had said that his answer to the black tower was money and the solace it could buy: beauty, leisure, friends, travel. How could a legacy of £30,000, however cleverly invested, enable him to live as he lived now? Julius, who helped Wilfred with the accounts and knew better than anyone how precarious were the finances of Toynton Grange. Julius, who never went to Lourdes because it wasn't his scene, but who took care to be at his cottage to give a welcome home party for the pilgrims. Julius, who had been so untypically helpful when the pilgrimage bus had an accident, driving immediately to the scene, taking charge, buying a new and specially adapted bus so that the pilgrimages could be independent. Julius, who had provided the evidence to clear Dennis Lerner from any suspicion of Holroyd's murder.

Dot had accused Julius of using Toynton Grange. Dalgliesh recalled the scene at Grace's death bed; Dot's outburst, the man's first incredulous look, the quick reactive spite. But what if he were using the place for a more specific purpose than to gratify the insidious pleasure of patronage and easy generosity. Using Toynton Grange. Using the pilgrimage. Scheming to preserve them both because both were essential to him.

And what of Dennis Lerner? Dennis, who stayed on at Toynton Grange being paid less than the normal wages and who could yet support his mother in an expensive nursing home. Dennis, who resolutely overcame his fear so that he could go climbing with Julius.

What better opportunity to meet and talk in absolute privacy without exciting suspicion? And how convenient that Wilfred had been frightened by the frayed rope into giving up rock climbing. Dennis, who could never bear to miss a pilgrimage even when, as today, he could hardly stand with migraine. Dennis, who was in charge of distributing the handcream and bath powder, who did most of the packing himself.

And it explained Father Baddeley's death. Dalgliesh had never been able to believe that his friend had been killed to prevent him disclosing that he hadn't glimpsed Julius walking over the headland on the afternoon of Holroyd's death. In the absence of clear proof that the old man hadn't, even momentarily, slumbered at his window, an allegation that Julius had lied, based on that evidence, would have been embarrassing perhaps but hardly dangerous. But what if Holroyd's death had been part of a larger and more sinister conspiracy? Then it might well have seemed necessary to snuff out – and how simply! – an obstinate, intelligent and ever-present watcher who could have been silenced in no other way once he smelt out the presence of evil. Father Baddeley had been taken to hospital before he learnt of Holroyd's death. But when he did learn, the significance of what he had so singularly failed to see must have struck him. He would have taken some action. And he had taken action. He made a telephone call to London, to a number he had needed to look up. He had made an appointment with his murderer.

Dalgliesh walked quickly on, past Hope Cottage and, almost without conscious decision, to Toynton Grange. The heavy front door opened to his touch. He smelt again the slightly intimidating spicy smell, masking more sinister, less agreeable odours. It was so dark that he had at once to switch on the light. The hall blazed like an empty film set. The black and white chequered floor was dazzling to the eye, a gigantic chess board, waiting for the pieces to move into place.

He paced through the empty rooms switching on the lights as he went. Room after room burst into brilliance. He found himself touching tables and chairs as he passed as if the wood were a talisman, looking intently around with the wary eye of a traveller returning, unwelcomed to a deserted home. And his mind continued to shuffle the pieces of jigsaw. The attack on Anstey, the final and most dangerous attempt in the black tower. Anstey himself assumed that it was a final attempt to frighten him into selling out. But suppose it had had another purpose, not to close Toynton Grange but to make its future secure? And there was no other way, given Anstey's dwindling resources, than to pass it over to an organization financially sound and already well established. And Anstey hadn't sold out. Satisfied by the last, the most dangerous attack on him, that it couldn't have been the work of a patient and that his dream was still intact, he had given his inheritance away. Toynton Grange would go on. The pilgrimages would continue. Was that what someone – someone who knew only too well how financially precarious the home was – had always schemed for and intended?

Holroyd's visit to London. It was obvious that he had learnt something on that visit, had somehow acquired knowledge which had sent him back to Toynton Grange restless and elated. Was it also knowledge which had made him too dangerous to live? Dalgliesh had assumed that he had been told something by his solicitor, something perhaps about his own financial concerns or those of the Anstey family. But the visit to the solicitor hadn't been the main purpose of the trip. Holroyd and the Hewsons had also been to St Saviour's Hospital, the hospital where Anstey had been treated. And there, in addition to seeing the consultant in physical medicine with Holroyd, they had visited the medical records department. Hadn't Maggie said when she and Dalgliesh first met: 'He never went back to St Saviour's Hospital so that they could record the miraculous cure on his medical record. It would have been rather a joke if he had'? Suppose Holroyd had gained some knowledge in London but gained it, not directly, but through a confidence from Maggie Hewson given, perhaps, during one of their lonely periods together on the cliff edge. He remembered Maggie Hewson's words:

'I've said I won't tell. But if you keep on nagging about it I may change my mind.' And then: 'What if I did? He wasn't a fool you know. He could tell that something was up. And he's dead, dead, dead!' Father Baddeley was dead. But so was Holroyd. And so was Maggie. Was there any reason why Maggie had to die, and at that particular time?

But this was to go too fast. It was still all conjecture, all speculation. True, it was the only theory which fitted all the facts. But that wasn't evidence. He had still no proof that any of the deaths at Toynton Head had been murder. One fact was certain. If Maggie had been killed, then somehow she had been persuaded unwittingly to connive in her own death.

He became aware of a faint bubbling sound and detected the pungent smell of grease and hot soap from the direction of the kitchen. The kitchen itself stank like a Victorian workhouse laundry. A pail of teacloths was simmering on the old-fashioned gas stove. In the bustle of departure Dot Moxon must have forgotten to turn off the gas. The grey linen was billowing above the dark evil-smelling scum, the gas plate was splattered with sponges of dried foam. He turned off the gas and the teacloths subsided into their murky bath. With the extinguishing plop of the flame the silence was suddenly intensified; it was as if he had turned off the last evidence of human life.

He moved on into the activity room. The work tops were shrouded with dust sheets. He could see the outline of the row of polythene bottles and the tins of bath powder waiting to be sieved and packed. Henry Carwardine's bust of Anstey still stood on its wooden plinth. It had been covered by a white plastic bag tied at the throat with what looked like one of Carwardine's old ties. The effect was peculiarly sinister; the nebulous features under the transparent shroud, the empty eye sockets, the sharp nose pointing the thin plastic made it as potent an image as a severed head.

In the office at the end of the annexe Grace Willison's desk still stood squarely under the north window, the typewriter under its grey cover. He pulled open the desk drawers. They were as he expected, immaculately tidy and ordered, banks of writing paper with Toynton Grange heading; envelopes carefully graded by size; typewriter ribbons; pencils; erasers; carbon paper still in its box; the sheets of perforated sticky labels on which she had typed the names and addresses of the Friends. Only the bound list of names was missing, the list of sixty-eight addresses; one of them in Marseilles. And here typed in that book and imprinted on Miss Willison's mind had been the vital link in the chain of greed and death.

The heroin had travelled far before it was finally packed at the bottom of a tin of bath powder in Toynton Grange. Dalgliesh could picture each stage of that journey as clearly as if he had travelled it himself. The fields of opium poppies on the high Anatolian plateau, the bulging pods oozing their milky sap. The secret rendering down of the raw opium into base morphine even before it left the hills. The long journey by mule train, rail, road or air towards Marseilles, one of the main distribution ports of the world. The refinement into pure heroin in one of a dozen clandestine laboratories. And then, the arranged rendezvous among the crowds at Lourdes, perhaps at Mass, the package slipped quickly into the waiting hand. He remembered wheeling Henry Carwardine across the headland on his first evening at Toynton, the thick rubber handgrips twisting beneath his hand. How simple to wrench one off, to insert a small plastic bag into the hollow strut, its drawstring taped to the metal. The whole operation would take less than a minute. And there would be plenty of opportunity. Philby didn't go on the pilgrimages. It would be Dennis Lerner who would have charge of the wheelchairs. What safer way for a drug smuggler to pass through customs than as the member of a recognized and respected pilgrimage. And the subsequent arrangements had been equally foolproof. The suppliers would need to know in advance the date of each pilgrimage, just as the customers and distributors would need to be told when the next consignment would come in. How more easily than by means of an innocuous newsletter from a respectable charity, a newsletter despatched so conscientiously and so innocently each quarter by Grace Willison.

And Julius's testimony in a French court, the alibi for a murderer. Had that been, not a reluctant yielding to blackmail, not a payment for services rendered, but payment in advance for services to come? Or had Julius, as Bill Moriarty's informant suggested, given Michonnet his alibi with no other motive than a perverse pleasure in thwarting the French police, gratuitously obliging a powerful family and causing his superiors the maximum of embarrassment? Possibly. He might neither have expected nor wanted any other reward. But if one were offered? If it were tactfully made known to him that a certain commodity could be supplied in strictly limited quantities if he could find a way to smuggle it into England? Would he later have been able to resist the temptation of Toynton Grange and its six-monthly pilgrimage?

And it was so easy, so simple, so foolproof. And so incredibly profitable. What was illegal heroin fetching now? Something like £4,000 an ounce. Julius had no need to deal in bulk or complicate his distribution arrangements beyond the one or two trusted agents to make himself secure for life. Ten ounces brought in each time would buy all the leisure and beauty that any man could desire. And with the Ridgewell Trust take-over the future was secure. Dennis Lerner would keep his job.

The pilgrimages would continue. There would be other homes open to his exploitation, other pilgrimages. And Lerner was completely in his power. Even if the newsletter was discontinued and the home no longer needed to pack and sell its handcream and powder, the heroin would still come in. The arrangements for notification and distribution were a minor matter of logistics compared with the fundamental problem of getting the drug safely, reliably and regularly through the port.

There was as yet no proof. But with luck, and if he were right, there would be in three days' time. He could telephone the local police now and safely leave it to them to contact the central drug control branch. Better still, he could telephone Inspector Daniel and arrange to call in to see him on his way back to London. Secrecy was essential. There must be no risk of suspicion. It would take only one telephone call to Lourdes to cancel this consignment and leave him again with nothing but a hotchpotch of half-formulated suspicions, coincidences, unsubstantiated allegations.

The nearest telephone, he remembered, was in the dining-room. It had an external line, and he saw that this had been switched through to the exchange. But when he lifted the receiver, the line was dead. He felt the usual momentary irritation that an instrument, taken for granted, should be reduced to a ridiculous and useless lump of plastic and metal, and reflected that a house with a dead telephone seemed always so much more isolated than one with no telephone at all. It was interesting, perhaps even significant, that the line was silent. But it didn't matter. He would get on his way and hope to find Inspector Daniel at police headquarters. At this stage when his theory was still little more than conjecture he was reluctant to talk to anyone else. He replaced the receiver. A voice from the doorway said:

'Having difficulty, Commander?'

Julius Court must have stepped through the house as delicately as a cat. He stood now, one shoulder resting lightly against the door post, both hands deep in his jacket pockets. The assumption of ease was deceptive. His body, poised on the balls of his feet as if to spring, was rigid with tension. The face above the high rolled collar of his sweater was as skeletal and defined as a carving, the muscles taut under the flushed skin. His eyes unblinking, unnaturally bright, were fixed on Dalgliesh with the speculative intentness of a gambler watching the spinning balls.

Dalgliesh said calmly:

'It's out of order apparently. It doesn't matter. My housekeeper will expect me when she sees me.'

'Do you usually roam about other people's houses to make your private calls? The main telephone is in the business room. Didn't you know?'

'I doubt whether I should have been any luckier.'

They looked at each other, silent in the greater silence. Across the length of the room Dalgliesh could recognize and follow the process of his adversary's thought as plainly as if it were registering visibly on a graph, the black needle tracing the pattern of decision. There was no struggle. It was the simple weighing of probabilities.

When Julius at last drew his hand slowly out of his pocket it was almost with relief that Dalgliesh saw the muzzle of the Luger. The die was cast. Now there was no going back, no more pretence, no more uncertainty.

Julius said quietly:

'Don't move, I'm an excellent shot. Sit down at the table. Hands on the top. Now, tell me how you found me out. I'm assuming that you have found me out. If not, then I've miscalculated. You will die and I shall be put to a great deal of trouble and inconvenience and we'll both be aggrieved to know that it wasn't after all necessary.'

With his left hand Dalgliesh took Father Baddeley's letter from his jacket pocket and slid it across the table.

'This will interest you. It came this morning addressed to Father Baddeley.'

The grey eyes did not move from his.

'Sorry. I'm sure it's fascinating but I have my mind on other matters. You read it to me.'

'It explains why he wanted to see me. You needn't have worried to concoct the poison pen letter or destroy his diary. His problem had nothing to do with you. Why kill him anyway? He was in the tower when Holroyd died; he knew perfectly well that he hadn't slept, that you hadn't come over the headland. But was that knowledge dangerous enough to snuff him out?'

'It was, in Baddeley's hands. The old man had a deep-rooted instinct for what he would describe as evil. That meant he had a deep-rooted suspicion of me, particularly of what he saw as my influence over Dennis. We were playing out our private comedy on a level which I don't think the procedures of the Metropolitan Police would recognize. It could only have one end. He telephoned me at my London flat from the hospital three days before he was discharged and asked me to come to see him on 26th September after nine o'clock. I went prepared. I drove down from London and left the Mercedes in that hollow behind the stone wall off the coast road. I took one of the habits from the business room while they were all at dinner. Then I walked to Hope Cottage. If anyone had seen me, then I should have had to change my plan. But no one did. He was sitting alone by the dying fire waiting for me. I think he knew about two minutes after I entered that I would kill him. There wasn't even a flicker of surprise when I pressed the plastic against his face. Plastic, you note. It wouldn't leave any tell-tale threads in the nostrils or windpipe. Not that Hewson would have noticed, poor fool. Baddeley's diary was on the table and I took it away with me just in case he'd made any incriminating entries. Just as well. He had, I discovered, a tedious habit of recording precisely where he'd been and when. But I didn't break into the bureau. I didn't need to. You can put that little peccadillo down to Wilfred. He must have been frantic to get his eyes on the old man's will. Incidentally, I never found your postcard and I suspect Wilfred looked no further once he'd found the will. Probably the old man tore it up. He disliked keeping trifles. Afterwards I went back and slept in some discomfort in the car. Next morning I rejoined the London road and arrived here when all the excitement was over. I saw in the diary that he had invited an A. D. to stay and that the visitor was expected on the first of October. It struck me as a bit odd. The old man didn't have visitors. So I planted the poison pen letter the evening before, just in case Baddeley had confided that something was on his mind. I must say, it was a bit disconcerting to discover that the mysterious A.D. was you, my dear Commander. Had I known, I might have tried for a little more subtlety.'

'And the stole? He was wearing his stole.'

'I should have removed it, but one can't remember everything. You see, he didn't believe I was protecting Dennis to save Wilfred grief or out of kindness to Dennis. He knew me too well. When he accused me of corrupting Dennis, of using Toynton for some purpose of my own, I said that I would tell him the truth, that I wanted to make my confession. He must have known in his heart that this was death, that I was only amusing myself. But he couldn't take the risk. If he refused to take me seriously, then all his life would have been a lie. He hesitated for just two seconds, then he put the stole round his neck.'

'Didn't he even give you the gratification of a flicker of fear?'

'Oh, no! Why should he? We were alike in one thing. Neither of us feared death. I don't know where Baddeley thought he was going as he just had time to make that last archaic sign of his allegiance, but wherever it was he apparently saw nothing to fear. Neither do I. I know just as certainly as he did what will follow my death. Annihilation. It would be unreasonable to fear that. I'm not so unreasonable. Once you have lost the fear of death – absolutely lost it – then all other fears are meaningless. Nothing can touch you. All that is necessary is to keep the means of death to hand. Then one is invulnerable. I apologize for the fact that, in my case, it has to be a gun. I do realize that at the moment I look melodramatic, ridiculous. But I can't fancy killing myself any other way. Drowning? That onrush of suffocating water? Drugs? Some interfering fool might drag me back. Besides, I do fear that shadow land between life and death. A knife? Messy and uncertain. There are three bullets here, Dalgliesh. One for you, and two, in case they should be needed, for me.'

'If you trade in death as you do, it's as well no doubt to come to terms with it.'

'Everyone who takes hard drugs wants to die. You know that as well as I do. There is no other way they can do it with so little inconvenience and so much profit to others, and with such pleasure to themselves, at least initially.'

'And Lerner? I suppose you paid his mother's nursing home fees. What are they, about £200 a month? You got him cheap. Even so, he must have known what he was bringing in.'

'Will be bringing in, three days from now. Will go on bringing in. I told him that it was cannabis, a perfectly harmless drug; one which an over-sensitive government have chosen to make illegal but which my London friends happen to fancy and are prepared to pay highly for. He chooses to believe me. He knows the truth, but he won't admit to himself that he knows. That's reasonable, sensible, a necessary self-deception. It's how we all manage to go on living. You must know that your job is a dirty job, crooks catching crooks, and that you waste your intelligence by doing it. But it wouldn't exactly add to your peace of mind to admit the fact. And if you ever chuck it, you won't give that as your reason. Are you going to chuck it, by the way? Somehow I've gained the impression that you might be.'

'That shows some discernment. I did have it in mind. But not now.'

The decision to go on, arrived at when and why Dalgliesh didn't know, seemed to him as irrational as the decision to give up. It wasn't a victory. A kind of defeat even. But there would be time enough, if he lived, to analyse the vicissitudes of that personal conflict. Like Father Baddeley, a man lived and died as he had to. He heard Julius's amused voice.

'A pity. But as this seems likely to be your last job, why not tell me how you found me out.'

'Is there time? I don't relish spending my last five minutes in a recital of professional incompetence. It won't give me any satisfaction and I don't see why I should gratify your curiosity.'

'No. But it's more in your interests than mine. Oughtn't you to be playing for time? Besides, if it's fascinating enough I might relax my guard, might give you a chance to pounce or fling a chair at me or whatever they train you to do in this kind of situation. Or somebody may come, or I may even change my mind.'

'Will you?'

'No.'

'Then gratify my curiosity. I can guess about Grace Willison. You killed her in the same way you killed Father Baddeley once you decided that I was getting dangerously suspicious, because she could type by heart the list of Friends, the list which included your distributors. But Maggie Hewson, why did she have to die?'

'Because of something she knew. Haven't you guessed that? I've over-estimated you. She knew that Wilfred's miracle was a delusion. I drove the Hewsons and Victor to London for his appointment at St Saviour's Hospital. Eric and Maggie went to the medical records department to have a look at Wilfred's folder. I suppose they wanted to gratify a natural professional curiosity while they were there. They discovered that he'd never had disseminated sclerosis, that his latest tests had shown that it was a wrong diagnosis. All he'd suffered from was hysterical paralysis. But I must be shocking you, my dear Commander. You're a pseudo-scientist, aren't you? It must be hard for you to accept that medical technology can err.'

'No. I believe in the possibility of a wrong diagnosis.'

'Wilfred, apparently, doesn't share your healthy scepticism. He never returned to the hospital for his next check-up, so no one bothered to write to him about their little mistake. Why should they? But it was knowledge that the two Hewsons couldn't keep to themselves. They told me, and subsequently Maggie must have told Holroyd. He probably guessed on the drive back to Toynton that something was up. I tried to bribe her with whisky to keep the knowledge to herself – she actually believed in my solicitude for dear Wilfred – and it worked until Wilfred excluded her from the decision on the future of the home. She was furious. She told me that she planned to burst into the last session at the end of the meditation and publicly proclaim the truth. I couldn't risk that. It was the one fact, the only fact, that could have made him sell out. It would have stopped the hand-over to the Ridgewell Trust. Toynton Grange and the pilgrimage had to go on.

'She wasn't really looking forward to the fracas that would follow breaking the news and it was easy enough to persuade her to leave the party at Toynton Grange to indulge their various reactions to her news and escape up to town with me immediately afterwards. I suggested that she should leave a deliberately ambiguous note, one which could be read as a threat of suicide. Then she could return to Toynton if and when she felt like it and see how Eric was reacting as a presumptive widower. It was the kind of histrionic gesture which appealed to dear Maggie. It got her out of an awkward situation here, provided the maximum of worry and inconvenience to Wilfred and Eric, and provided her with a free holiday in my London flat and the prospect of plenty of excitement if and when she chose to return. She even volunteered to fetch the rope herself. We sat there drinking together until she was too fuddled to suspect me but still sober enough to write the note. The last scrawled lines, the reference to the black tower, were, of course, added by me.'

'So that was why she was bathed and dressed.'

'Of course. Tarted up to make an effective entrance at Toynton Grange, and also, I flatter myself, to impress me. I was gratified that I ranked clean underclothes and painted toe nails. I don't know what precisely she thought I had in mind for us when we reached London. Dear Maggie was never quite in touch with reality. To pack her contraceptive was perhaps more optimistic than discreet. But she may have had her plans. The dear girl was certainly delirious at the thought of leaving Toynton. She died happy I assure you.'

'And, before leaving the cottage, you gave the signal with the light.'

'I had to have some excuse for turning up and finding the body. It seemed prudent to add verisimilitude. Someone might have looked out of a window and been able to confirm my story. I didn't bargain for it being you. Finding you here busily doing your boy scout turn gave me a bad moment. And you were remarkably obstinate about not leaving the body.'

It must have been almost as bad a moment, thought Dalgliesh, as finding Wilfred so nearly choked to death. There had been nothing faked about Julius's terror either then or after Maggie's death. He asked:

'And was Holroyd pushed over the cliff for the same reason, to stop him talking?'

Julius laughed:

'Now this will amuse you; a delicious irony. I didn't even know that Maggie had confided in Holroyd until I challenged her with it after his death. And Dennis Lerner never knew. Holroyd began taunting Dennis as he usually did. Dennis was more or less inured to it and merely moved with his book a little way apart. Then Holroyd began on a more sinister line of torment. He began shouting at Dennis. He wondered what Wilfred would say when he learned that his precious pilgrimages were a fraud, that Toynton Grange itself was founded on a lie. He told Dennis to make the most of the next pilgrimage; it would certainly be the last. Dennis panicked; he thought that Holroyd had discovered about the drug smuggling. He didn't pause to ask himself how in the hell Holroyd could have found out. He told me afterwards that he couldn't even remember scrambling to his feet, releasing the brakes and hurling the chair forward. But he did, of course. There was no one else to do it. It couldn't have landed where it did if it hadn't gone over the cliff with considerable force. I was on the beach beneath them when Holroyd came over. One of the irritating things about that murder was that I've never received any sympathy for the traumatic experience of having Holroyd smashed to death only twenty yards from me. I hope you will give it to me now.'

Dalgliesh reflected that the murder must have been doubly convenient for Julius. It removed Holroyd and his dangerous knowledge; it put Dennis Lerner finally in his power. He said:

'And you disposed of the two side pieces of the wheel-chair while Lerner was fetching help.'

'About fifty yards away, down a deep cleft between two rocks. It seemed, at the time, a sensible way of complicating the case. Without the brakes no one could be sure that it wasn't an accident. On reflection I should have left well alone and let it be assumed that Holroyd killed himself. Essentially he did. That's what I've persuaded Dennis.'

Dalgliesh asked:

'What are you going to do now?'

'Put a bullet in your head, conceal your body in your own car and get rid of both together. It's a trite method of murder I know, but I understand that it works.'

Dalgliesh laughed. He was surprised that the sound could be so spontaneous.

'You propose to drive about sixty miles, I take it, in an easily identifiable car with the murdered body of a Commander of the Metropolitan Police in the boot – his own boot incidentally. A number of men of my acquaintance in the maximum security wings of Parkhurst and Durham would admire your nerve even while not exactly relishing the prospect of welcoming you to their company. They're a quarrelsome, uncivilized bunch. I don't think you're going to have a lot in common.'

'I shall be at risk. But you'll be dead.'

'Of course. So in effect will you from the moment the bullet enters my body, unless you count a life sentence as living. Even if you try to fake fingerprints on the trigger, they'll know that I was murdered. I'm not the type to kill myself or to drive my car into remote woods and quarries to put a bullet in my brain. And the forensic evidence will give the lab a field day.'

'If they find your body. How long before they even begin looking? Three weeks?'

'They'll be looking hard. If you can think of a suitable spot to dump me and the car, so can they. Don't assume that the police can't read an ordnance survey. And how do you propose to get back here? By picking up a train at Bournemouth or Winchester? By hitch-hiking, hiring a bicycle, walking through the night? You can hardly travel on to London by train, and pretend that you joined the train at Wareham. It's a small station and you're known there. Going or returning, you'll be remembered.'

Julius said consideringly:

'You're right, of course. Then it means the cliffs. They must fish you out of the sea.'

'With a bullet in my head? Or are you expecting me to walk over the cliff edge to suit your convenience? You could try physical force, of course, but then you'll have to come dangerously close, close enough for a fight. We're fairly evenly matched. I take it you don't intend to be dragged over with me? Once they find my body and that bullet, then you're finished. The trail begins here remember. I was last seen alive when the Toynton Grange bus left, and there's no one here but we two.'

It was then that, simultaneously, they heard the distant slam of the front door. The sound, sharp as a gun shot, was followed by the thud of footsteps, heavy and firm, crossing the front hall.

III

Julius said quickly:

'Call out, and I kill you both. Stand to the left of the door.'

The footsteps were crossing the central hall now unnaturally loud in the eerie silence. Both men held their breath. Philby stood in the doorway.

He saw the gun immediately. His eyes widened and then blinked rapidly. He looked from one man to the other. When he spoke he sounded hoarse, apologetic. He spoke directly to Dalgliesh like a child explaining a misdemeanour:

'Wilfred sent me back early. Dot thought she'd left the gas on.'

His eyes turned again to Julius. This time the terror was unmistakable. He said 'Oh, no!' Almost instantaneously, Julius fired. The crack of the revolver, although expected, was still shattering, still unbelievable. Philby's body stiffened, rocked, then fell backward like an axed tree with a crash which shook the room. The bullet had gone in precisely between the eyes. Dalgliesh knew that this was where Julius had intended it to go; that he had used this necessary killing to demonstrate that he knew how to use his gun. This had been target practice. He said calmly, his gun now turned on Dalgliesh again:

'Go over to him.'

Dalgliesh bent by the dead man. The eyes still seemed to hold their last look of wild surprise. The wound was a neat grumous slit in the low heavy forehead, so unremarkable that it could have been used for a forensic ballistics demonstration of the effect of discharge at six feet. There were no powder marks, as yet little blood, only the soiling of the skin by the spin of the bullet. It was a precise, almost decorative stigma giving no clue to the destructive tumult within.

Julius said:

'That settles the score for my smashed marble. Is there an exist wound?'

Gently Dalgliesh turned the heavy head.

'No. You must have hit a bone.'

'That's what I intended. Two bullets left. But this is a bonus, Commander. You were wrong about my being the last person to see you alive. I shall drive away to establish my alibi and, in the eyes of the police, the last person to see you alive will have been Philby, a criminal with a propensity to violence. Two bodies in the sea with bullet wounds. A pistol, licensed, I may say, stolen from my bedside drawer. Let the police concoct a theory to explain that. It shouldn't be difficult. Is there any blood?'

'Not yet. There will be. But not much.'

'I'll remember that. It will be easy enough to wipe it from this linoleum. Get that plastic hood from Carwardine's bust of Wilfred and tie it over his head. Use his own tie. And hurry. I shall be just six paces behind you. And if I get impatient I might feel it worthwhile doing my own work.'

Hooded with white plastic, his wound a third eye, Philby was transformed into an inert guy, its bulging body grotesquely stuffed into a dapper undersized suit, its tie askew under the clownish features. Julius said:

'Now get one of the lighter wheelchairs.'

He motioned Dalgliesh once again towards the work-room and followed, always a careful six feet behind. Three folded chairs were standing against the wall. Dalgliesh prised one open and wheeled it in beside the body. There would be fingerprints to find here. But what did they prove? This might even be the chair in which he had wheeled Grace Willison.

'Now get him into it.'

As Dalgliesh hesitated he said, allowing his voice a trace of controlled impatience:

'I don't want to have to manage two bodies alone. But I can if I need to. There's a hoist in the bathroom. If you can't lift him unaided, then get it. But I thought they taught policemen useful little knacks like this.'

Dalgliesh managed without the hoist. But it wasn't easy. The wheel brakes slid on the linoleum and it took more than two minutes before the heavy, unresponsive body slumped back against the canvas. Dalgliesh had succeeded in gaining some time but at a cost; he had lost strength. He knew that he would stay alive just as long as his mind, with its store of dreadfully appropri-ate experience, and his physical strength could be used by Julius. It would be inconvenient for Julius to have to carry two bodies to the cliff edge, but it could be done. Toynton Grange had facilities for moving inert bodies. At present Dalgliesh was less of an encumbrance alive than dead, but the margin was dangerously narrow;

there was no sense in reducing it further. The optimum moment for action would come, and it would come for both of them. Both of them were waiting for it, Dalgliesh to attack, Julius to shoot. Both knew the cost of a mistake in recognizing that moment. Two bullets left and he had to ensure that neither of them ended in his body. And as long as Julius kept his distance and held the gun he was inviolable. Somehow Dalgliesh had to draw him close enough for physical contact. Somehow he had to divert that concentration if only for a fraction of a second.

Julius said: 'And now we'll take a walk together to Toynton Cottage.'

He still kept his careful distance behind as Dalgliesh wheeled the chair with its grotesque burden down the ramp of the front door and across the headland. The sky was a grey suffocating blanket pressing down on them. The close air was harsh and metallic on the tongue and smelt as strong as rotting seaweed. In the half-light the pebbles on the path glittered like semi-precious stones. Half-way across the headland Dalgliesh heard a high querulous wail and, looking back, saw that Jeoffrey was following them, tail erect. The cat padded behind Julius for another fifty yards and then, as unpredictably as he had appeared, turned tail and made off for home. Julius, his unblinking eyes on Dalgliesh's back, seemed to notice neither his arrival nor his departure. They walked on in silence. Philby's head had fallen back, his neck collared by the canvas of the chair. His cyclops wound, gummed to the plastic, stared into Dalgliesh's face in what seemed mute reproach. The path was dry. Looking down Dalgliesh

357

saw that the wheels made only an imperceptible thread on the patches of dry turf and the dusty, gritty path. And behind him he could hear Julius's shoes scuffing the marks into oblivion. There would be no useful evidence left here.

And now they stood on the stone patio. It seemed to shake under their feet with the thunder of the waves as if earth and sea anticipated the coming storm. But the tide was ebbing. No curtain of spray rose between them and the cliff edge. Dalgliesh knew that it was the moment of great danger. He made himself laugh aloud, and wondered whether the sound rang as false to Julius's ears as it did to his own.

'Why so amused?'

'It's easy to see that your killing is normally done at a distance, a commercial transaction merely. You propose to hurl us into the sea at your own back door, a broad enough hint for even the stupidest detective constable. And they won't be putting stupid officers on this crime. Your cleaning woman is expected this morning isn't she? And this is one part of the coast with a beach, even at high tide. I thought you wanted to delay discovery of the bodies.'

'She won't come out here. She never does.'

'How do you know what she does when you aren't here? She may shake the dusters over the cliff. It may even be her habit to paddle. But have it your own way. I'm merely pointing out that your only hope of success – and I don't rate it high – is to delay discovery of our bodies. No one will start looking for Philby until the pilgrimage returns in three days' time. If you get rid of my car it will be even longer before they start looking for me. That gives you the opportunity to dispose of this consignment of heroin before the hunt is up, assuming you still intend to let Lerner bring it in. But don't let me interfere.'

Julius's hand on the gun did not waver. As if considering a proposition for a picnic site, he said:

'You're right, of course. You ought to go into deep water and further along the coast. The best place is the black tower. The sea will be still washing the cliffs there. We've got to get him to the tower.'

'How? He must weigh over twelve stone. I can't push him unaided up the cliff edge. You'll hardly be much help if you walk behind with a gun in my back. And what about the wheel marks?'

'The rain will finish those. And we shan't go up the headland. We'll drive along the coast road and approach the tower over the cliff as we did when we rescued Anstey. Once the couple of you are in the boot of the car I'll watch for Mrs Reynolds through my glasses. She cycles in from Toynton village, and she's always exactly on time. We ought to plan to meet her just outside the boundary gate. I'll stop and let her know that I shan't be back for dinner. That pleasant minute of ordinary conversation should impress the coroner if they ever get your bodies to an inquest. And eventually, the tedious business over, I'll drive off to Dorchester for an early luncheon.'

'With the wheelchair and the plastic hood in the boot?'

'With the chair and the hood locked in the boot. I shall establish an alibi for the whole of today and return to Toynton Grange this evening. And I shan't forget to wash the plastic hood before replacing it, dust the chair to remove your prints and examine the floor for blood-stains. And, of course, retrieve the cartridge case. Were you hoping I would overlook that? Don't worry, Commander. I do realize that, by then, I'll be planning without your valuable assistance, but thanks to you, I shall have a day or two to work out the details. One of two sophistications attract me. I'm wondering if I could make use of the smashed marble. Couldn't that be worked in to provide the motive for Philby's murderous attack on you?'

'I should keep it simple.'

'Perhaps you're right. My first two murders were models of simplicity and none the worse for it. Now get him into the boot of the Mercedes. It's parked at the back. But first through into the scullery. You'll find two sheets in the washing machine. Take the one from the top. I don't want fibres and shoe dust in the car.'

'Won't Mrs Reynolds notice that one is missing?'

'She washes and irons tomorrow. A woman of strict routine. By this evening I shall have replaced it. Don't waste time.'

Julius's mind must be registering every second, thought Dalgliesh, yet his voice betrayed no anxiety. Not once did he glance at his watch, or even at the clock on the kitchen wall. He kept his eyes and the muzzle of the Luger on his victim. Somehow that concentration had to be broken. And the time was running out.

The Mercedes was parked outside the stone garage. Under Julius's direction Dalgliesh raised the unlocked lid of the boot and spread the creased sheet over the floor. It was an easy matter to tumble Philby's body from the wheelchair. Dalgliesh folded the chair and placed it on top of the body. Julius said:

'Now get in beside him.'

Could this be the best opportunity, the last opportunity even, to act; here outside Julius's own cottage with the murdered man in his car and the evidence plain? But plain to whom? Dalgliesh knew that if he sprang on Julius now he would gain nothing but a second's release from frustration and anger before the bullet hit him. Two bodies instead of one would be driven to the black tower and tumbled into deep water. In his mind's eye he could see Julius poised in solitary triumph on the edge of the cliff, the gun curving through the air like a falling bird to cleave the tumbling waves, beneath which two bodies were being torn and tugged by the ebbing tide. The plan would go ahead. A little more tedious, taking longer since there would be two bodies to wheel unaided across the headland. But who was there to prevent it? Certainly not Mrs Reynolds even now cycling along the road from Toynton village. And if she suspected, if she even mentioned casually when she dismounted to greet Julius on the road that she had heard what sounded like a shot? Then there were still two bullets left in the gun. And he was no longer sure that Julius was sane.

But there was at least something he could do at this moment, something he had planned to do. But it wasn't going to be easy. He had hoped that, for a couple of seconds at least, the raised lid of the boot would have partly screened him from Julius's view. But Julius was standing immediately behind the car; Dalgliesh was in full view. But there was one advantage. The grey eyes never flickered, dared not flicker from his face. If he were quick and cunning, if he were lucky, he might bring it off. He placed his hands as if casually on his hips. He could feel the slight weight of his thin leather wallet in his back trouser pocket lying curved against his buttock. Julius said with dangerous quietness:

'I said get in on top of him. I'm not risking driving with you any closer.'

Dalgliesh's right thumb and forefinger twisted at the pocket button. Thank God the button hole was reasonably loose. He said:

'Then you'd better drive fast unless you want to have a corpse dead of suffocation to explain.'

'A night or two in the sea and your lungs will be too waterlogged for that kind of diagnosis.'

The button was undone now. He insinuated his right forefinger and thumb gently into the top pocket and grasped the wallet. Everything now depended on its sliding out easily, on his being able to drop it unseen behind the wheel of the car. He said:

'They won't, you know. The P.M. will show perfectly clearly that I was dead before I hit the water.'

'And so you will be, with a bullet in your head. Given that, I doubt whether they'll look for signs of suffocation. But thank you for the warning. I'll drive fast. Now get in.'

Dalgliesh shrugged his shoulders and bent with sudden energy to get into the boot as if momentarily relinquishing hope. He rested his left hand on the bumper. Here, at least, there would be a palm mark which would be difficult to explain. But then he remembered. He had rested his palm on the bumper when loading the shepherd's crook, the sacks and the besom into the boot. It was only a small discouragement but it depressed him. He let his right hand dangle and the leather slipped from his finger and thumb to fall under the right wheel. No dangerously quiet word of command followed. Julius neither spoke nor moved, and he was still alive. With luck he would stay alive now until they reached the black tower. He smiled at the irony that his heart should now rejoice at a gift which a short month ago he had so grudgingly welcomed.

The boot lid slammed down. He was cramped in total blackness, total silence. He felt a second of claustrophobic panic, the irresistible urge to stretch his curled body and batter his clenched hands against the metal. The car did not move. Julius would be free now to check his timing. Philby's body lay heavily against him. He could smell the dead man as if he still breathed, an amalgam of grease, mothballs and sweat, the air of the boot was hot with his presence. He felt a moment of guilt that Philby was dead; he alive. Could he have saved him by calling out a warning? It could only have resulted, he knew, in both their deaths. Philby would have come on; must have come on. And even if he had turned and run, Julius would have followed and disposed of him. But now the feel of the cold moist flesh pressing against him, the hairs on the limp wrist sharp as bristles, pricked him like a reproach. The car rocked gently and began to move.

He had no means of knowing if Julius had seen the wallet and removed it; he thought it unlikely. But would Mrs Reynolds find it? It was lying in her path. She would almost certainly dismount from her bicycle outside the garage. If she did find it, then he guessed she would have no rest until it was returned. He thought of his own Mrs Mack, a Metropolitan police constable's widow who cleaned and occasionally cooked for him; of her almost obsessive honesty, her meticulous concern for her employer's belongings, the perpetual explanatory notes about missing laundry, the increased cost of shopping, a mislaid cufflink. No, Mrs Reynolds wouldn't rest with the wallet in her possession. He had cashed a cheque on his last visit to Dorchester; the three ten pound notes, the bundle of credit cards, his police warrant, all would particularly worry her. She would probably waste some time going to Hope Cottage. Not finding him there, what then? His guess was that she would ring the local police, terrified that he might discover his loss before she had reported it. And the police? If he were lucky they would see the incongruity of a wallet dropped so conveniently in her path. Suspicious or not, they would be courteous enough to get in touch with him at once. They might find it worthwhile ringing Toynton Grange since the cottage was not on the telephone. They would discover that the telephone was inexplicably out of order. It was at least an even chance that they would think it worthwhile sending a patrol car, and if one were reasonably close it could come quickly. Logically, one action must follow another. And he had one piece of luck. Mrs Reynolds, he remembered, was the village constable's widow. At least she wouldn't be afraid of using the telephone, would know whom to ring. His life depended on her seeing the wallet. A few square inches of brown leather on the paved courtyard. And the light was darkening under the storm-laden sky.

Julius was driving very fast even over the bumpy ground of the headland. The car stopped. Now he would be opening the boundary gate. Another few seconds of driving and the car stopped again. Now he must have met Mrs Reynolds and was exchanging that half-minute of conversation. Now they were off again, this time with smooth road under their wheels.

There was something else he could do. He moved his hand under his cheek and bit into his left thumb. The blood tasted warm and sweet. He smeared it across the roof of the boot and, scuffing aside the sheet, pressed his thumb into the carpet. Group AB rhesus negative. It was a rare enough group. And with any luck Julius would miss these minute tell-tale smears. He hoped the police searcher would be more perspicacious.

He began to feel stifled, his head thudded. He told himself that there was plenty of air, that this pressure on his chest was no more than psychological trauma. And then the car rocked gently and he knew that Julius was driving off the road and into the hollow behind the stone wall which divided the headland from the road. It was a convenient stopping place. Even if another car passed, and this was unlikely, the Mercedes wouldn't be visible. They had arrived. The final part of the journey was about to begin.

There were only about one hundred and fifty yards of rock-strewn and lumpy turf to where the black tower stood squat and malignant under the menacing sky. Dalgliesh knew that Julius would prefer to make a single journey. He would want to get as quickly as possible out of all sight of the road. He would want the business over so that he could get on his way. More important, he needed to make no physical contact with either victim. Their clothes would yield nothing when their bloated bodies were finally fished from the sea; but Julius would know how difficult to eradicate, without tell-tale cleaning, would be the infinitesimally small traces of hair, fibre or blood on his own clothes. So far he was absolutely clean. It would be one of his strongest cards. Dalgliesh would be allowed to live at least until they reached the shelter of the tower. He felt confident enough of this to take his time in getting Philby's body strapped into the chair. Afterwards he leaned for a moment over the handlebars breathing heavily, simulating more exhaustion than he felt. Somehow, despite the hard pushing ahead, he must conserve his strength. Julius slammed down the boot lid and said:

'Get a move on. The storm is almost on us.'

But he didn't shift his fixed gaze to glance at the sky, nor had he need. They could almost smell the rain in the freshening breeze.

Although the wheels of the chair were well oiled the going was hard. Dalgliesh's hands slid on the rubber handgrips. Philby's body, strapped like a recalcitrant child, jerked and rolled as the wheels struck stones or clumps of grass. Dalgliesh felt the sweat rolling into his eyes. It gave him the opportunity he needed to get rid of his jacket. When it came to the last physical struggle the man least encumbered would have an advantage. He stopped pushing and stood gasping. The feet behind him stopped too.

It might happen now. There was nothing he could do if it did. He comforted himself with the thought that he would know nothing. One press of Julius's finger on the

366

trigger and his busy fearful mind would be stilled. He remembered Julius's words. 'I know what will happen to me when I die; annihilation. It would be unreasonable to fear that.' If only it were that simple! But Julius did not press. The dangerously quiet voice behind him said:

'Well?'

'I'm hot. May I take off my jacket?'

'Why not? Drape it over Philby's knees. I'll chuck it in the sea after you. It would be torn off your body by the tide anyway.'

Dalgliesh slid his arms from his jacket and placed it folded over Philby's knees. Without looking round he said:

'You'd be unwise to shoot me in the back. Philby was killed instantly. It has to look as if he shot me first but only to wound, before I wrenched the gun from him and finished him off. No fight with only one gun could reasonably result in two instantaneous killings, and one in the small of the back.'

'I know. Unlike you, I may be inexperienced in the cruder manifestations of violence but I'm not a fool and I do understand about firearms. Get on.'

They moved forward, carefully distanced, Dalgliesh pushing his macabre passenger and hearing behind him the soft rustle of the following feet. He found himself thinking about Peter Bonnington. It was because an unknown boy, now dead, had been moved from Toynton Grange that he, Adam Dalgliesh, was now walking across Toynton Head with a gun at his back. Father Baddeley had believed that there was a great underlying pattern. Given that assurance, all human perplexities were no more than exercises in spiritual geometry. Suddenly Julius began speaking. Dalgliesh could almost imagine that he felt the need to entertain his victim on this last tedious walk, that he was making some attempt at justification.

'I can't be poor again. I need money as I need oxygen. Not just enough; more than enough. Much more. Poverty kills. I don't fear death but I fear that particular slow and corrosive process of dying. You didn't believe me, did you – that story about my parents?'

'Not altogether. Was I expected to?'

'Yet that at least was true. I could take you to pubs in Westminister – Christ, you probably know them – and bring you face to face with what I fear; the pathetic elderly queens managing on their pensions. Or not managing. And they, poor sods, haven't even been used to having money. I have. I'm not ashamed of my nature. But if I'm to live at all, I have to be rich. Did you really expect me to let one sick old fool and a dying woman stand in my way?'

Dalgliesh didn't reply. Instead he asked:

'I suppose you came this way when you set fire to the tower.'

'Of course. I did as we've done now, drove to the hollow and came on foot. I knew when Wilfred, a creature of habit, was likely to be in the tower and I watched him walk over the headland through my binoculars. If it wasn't that day, it would be another. There was no difficulty in helping myself to the key and a habit. I saw to that a day in advance. Anyone who knows Toynton Grange can move about it undetected. Even if I were seen, I don't have to explain my presence there. As

Wilfred says, I'm one of the family. That's why killing Grace Willison was so easy. I was home and in bed soon after midnight and with no worse effects than cold legs and a little difficulty in getting to sleep. By the way, I ought to say, in case you harbour any doubts, that Wilfred knows nothing of the smuggling. If I were about to die and you to live instead of the other way round you could look forward to the pleasure of breaking the news. Both pieces of news. His miracle a delusion and his abode of love a staging post for death. I should give a great deal to see his face.'

They were within feet now of the black tower. Without overtly changing direction Dalgliesh steered the wheelchair as close as he dared to the porch. The wind was gently rising in short moaning crescendos. But then, there would always be a breeze on this wind-scoured promontory of grass and rock. Suddenly he stopped. He held the chair, with his left hand and half turned towards Julius, carefully balancing his weight. It was now. It had to be now.

Julius said sharply:

'Well, what is it?'

Time stopped. A second was stilled into infinity. In that brief, timeless lacuna, Dalgliesh's mind was drained free of tension and fear. It was as if he were detached from the past and the future, aware simultaneously of himself, of his adversary, of the sound, scent and colour of sky, cliff and sea. The pent-up anger at Father Baddeley's death, the frustration and indecision of the last few weeks, the controlled suspense of the past hour: all were calmed in this moment before their final release. He spoke, his voice, high and cracked, simulating terror.

But, even to his own ears, the terror sounded horribly real.

'The tower! There's someone inside!'

It came again as he prayed it would, the bone ends, piercing the torn flesh, scrabbling frantically against unyielding stone. He sensed rather than heard the sharp hiss of Julius's intake of breath. Then time moved on, and in that second, Dalgliesh sprang.

As they fell, Julius's body beneath him, Dalgliesh felt the hammer blow on his right shoulder, the sudden numbness, the sticky warmth, soothing as a balm, flowing into his shirt. The shot echoed back from the black tower, and the headland came alive. A cloud of gulls rose screaming from the rock face. Sky and cliff were a tumult of wildly beating wings. And then as if the laden clouds had waited for this signal, the sky was ripped open with the sound of tearing canvas, and the rain fell.

They fought like famished animals clawing at their prey, without skill, eyes stung and blinded by rain, locked in a rigor of hate.

Dalgliesh, even with the weight of Julius's body beneath him, felt his strength ebbing. It had to be now, now while he was on top. And he still had the use of his good left shoulder. He twisted Julius's wrist into the clammy earth and pressed with all his strength on the beat of the pulse. He could feel Julius's breath like a hot blast on his face. They lay cheek to cheek in a horrible parody of exhausted love. And still the gun did not drop from those rigid fingers. Slowly, in painful spasms, Julius bent his right arm towards Dalgliesh's head. And then the gun went off. Dalgliesh felt the bullet pass over his hair to spend itself harmlessly in the sheeting rain.

And now they were rolling towards the cliff edge. Dalgliesh, weakening, felt himself clutching Julius as if for support. The rain was a stinging lance on his eyeballs. His nose was pressed suffocatingly into the sodden earth. Humus. A comforting and familiar last smell. His fingers clawed impotently at the turf as he rolled. It came apart in moist clumps in his hands. And suddenly Julius was kneeling over him, hands at his throat, forcing his head back over the cliff edge. The sky, the sea and the sheeting rain were one turbulent whiteness, one immense roaring in his ears. Julius's streaming face was out of his reach, the rigid arms pressing down the cruel encircling hands. He had to bring that face closer. Deliberately he slackened his muscles and loosened his already weakening hold on Julius's shoulders. It worked. Julius relaxed his grasp and instinctively bent his head forward to look into Dalgliesh's face. Then he screamed as Dalgliesh's thumbs gouged into his eyes. Their bodies fell apart. And Dalgliesh was on his feet and scrambling up the headland to fling himself behind the wheelchair.

He crouched behind it, heaving against the sagging canvas for support, watching Julius advance, hair streaming, eyes wild, the strong arms stretched forward, eager for that final clutch. Behind him the tower streamed black blood. The rain slashed like hail against the boulders, sending up a fine mist to mingle with his hoarse breath. Its painful rhythm tore at his chest and filled his ears like the death throes of some great animal. Suddenly he released the brakes and with his last strength hurled the chair forward. He saw his murderer's astonished and desperate eyes. For one second he thought that Julius would fling himself against the chair.

But at the last moment he leapt aside, and the chair and its dreadful burden sailed over the cliff.

'Explain that when they fish it out!' Dalgliesh never knew whether he spoke to himself or shouted the words aloud. And then Julius was on him.

This was the end. He wasn't fighting now, only letting himself be rolled downwards towards death. He could hope for nothing except to carry Julius over with him. Hoarse, discordant cries were hurting his ears. The crowd were shouting for Julius. All the world was shouting. The headland was full of voices, of shapes. Suddenly the weight on his chest lifted. He was free. He heard Julius whisper 'Oh, no!' Dalgliesh heard the sad despairing protest as clearly as if the voice had been his own. It wasn't the last horrified cry of a desperate man. The words were quiet, rueful, almost amused. Then the air was darkened by a shape, black as a great bird, passing spread-eagled over his head in what seemed slow motion. Earth and sky turned slowly together. A solitary seagull screamed. The earth thudded. A white ring of amorphous blobs was bending over him. But the ground was soft, irresistibly soft. He let his consciousness bleed away into it.

IV

The surgical registrar came out of Dalgliesh's room to where a group of large men were obstructing the corridor. He said: 'He'll be OK for questioning in about half an hour or so. We've extracted the bullet. I've handed it over to your chap. We've put up a drip but don't let that

372

worry you. He's lost a fair amount of blood but there's no real damage. There's no harm now in your going in.'

Daniel asked:

'Is he conscious?'

'Barely. Your chap in there says he's been quoting King Lear. Something about Cordelia anyway. And he's fretting because he hasn't said thank you for the flowers.'

Daniel said:

'He won't be needing flowers this time, thank God. He can thank Mrs Reynold's sharp eyes and common sense for that. And the storm helped. But it was a close thing. Court would have carried him over the cliff if we hadn't come up on them before he noticed us. Well, we may as well go in if you think it's OK.'

A uniformed constable appeared, helmet under his arm.

'Well?'

'The Chief Constable's on his way, Sir. And they've pulled out Philby's body half-strapped to a wheelchair.'

'And Court's?'

'Not yet, Sir. They reckon he'll be washed in further down the coast.'

Dalgliesh opened his eyes. His bed was ringed with black and white figures advancing and receding in a ritual dance. Nurses' caps floating like disembodied wings above the smudged faces as if uncertain where to settle. Then the picture cleared and he saw the circle of half-familiar faces. Sister was here, of course. And the consultant had got back early from his wedding. He wasn't wearing his rose any more. The faces broke simultaneously into wary smiles. He made himself smile back. So it wasn't acute leukaemia; it wasn't any kind of leukaemia. He was going to get better. And once they'd removed this heavy contraption which for some reason they'd fixed to his right arm he could get out of here and back to his job. Wrong diagnosis or not, it was nice of them, he thought sleepily, looking up into the ring of smiling eyes, to look so pleased that he wasn't going to die after all.

ff

Faber and Faber – a home for writers

Faber and Faber is one of the great independent publishing houses in London. We were established in 1929 by Geoffrey Faber and our first editor was T. S. Eliot. We are proud to publish prize-winning fiction and non-fiction, as well as an unrivalled list of modern poets and playwrights. Among our list of writers we have five Booker Prize winners and eleven Nobel Laureates, and we continue to seek out the most exciting and innovative writers at work today.

www.faber.co.uk – a home for readers

The Faber website is a place where you will find all the latest news on our writers and events. You can listen to podcasts, preview new books, read specially commissioned articles and access reading guides, as well as entering competitions and enjoying a whole range of offers and exclusives. You can also browse the list of Faber Finds, an exciting new project where reader recommendations are helping to bring a wealth of lost classics back into print using the latest on-demand technology.